Beauty

Other Books by Lexi Blake

ROMANTIC SUSPENSE

Masters and Mercenaries
The Dom Who Loved Me
The Men With The Golden Cuffs
A Dom is Forever
On Her Master's Secret Service
Sanctum: A Masters and Mercenaries Novella
Love and Let Die
Unconditional: A Masters and Mercenaries Novella
Dungeon Royale
Dungeon Games: A Masters and Mercenaries Novella
A View to a Thrill
Cherished: A Masters and Mercenaries Novella
You Only Love Twice
Luscious: Masters and Mercenaries~Topped
Adored: A Masters and Mercenaries Novella
Master No
Just One Taste: Masters and Mercenaries~Topped 2
From Sanctum with Love
Devoted: A Masters and Mercenaries Novella
Dominance Never Dies
Submission is Not Enough
Master Bits and Mercenary Bites~The Secret Recipes of Topped
Perfectly Paired: Masters and Mercenaries~Topped 3
For His Eyes Only
Arranged: A Masters and Mercenaries Novella
Love Another Day
At Your Service: Masters and Mercenaries~Topped 4
Master Bits and Mercenary Bites~Girls Night
Nobody Does It Better
Close Cover
Protected: A Masters and Mercenaries Novella
Enchanted: A Masters and Mercenaries Novella
Charmed: A Masters and Mercenaries Novella
Treasured: A Masters and Mercenaries Novella, Coming June 29, 2021

URBAN FANTASY
Thieves
Steal the Light
Steal the Day
Steal the Moon
Steal the Sun
Steal the Night
Ripper
Addict
Sleeper
Outcast
Stealing Summer

LEXI BLAKE WRITING AS SOPHIE OAK

Texas Sirens
Small Town Siren
Siren in the City
Siren Enslaved
Siren Beloved
Siren in Waiting
Siren in Bloom
Siren Unleashed
Siren Reborn

Nights in Bliss, Colorado
Three to Ride
Two to Love
One to Keep
Lost in Bliss
Found in Bliss
Pure Bliss
Chasing Bliss
Once Upon a Time in Bliss
Back in Bliss
Sirens in Bliss
Happily Ever After in Bliss
Far From Bliss, Coming 2021

A Faery Story
Bound
Beast
Beauty

Standalone
Away From Me
Snowed In

Beauty

A Faery Story, Book 3

**Lexi Blake
writing as
Sophie Oak**

Beauty
A Faery Story, Book 3

Published by DLZ Entertainment LLC

Copyright 2019 DLZ Entertainment LLC
Edited by Chloe Vale
ISBN: 978-1-942297-30-7

Sign up for Lexi Blake's newsletter
and be entered to win a $25 gift certificate
to the bookseller of your choice.

Join us for news, fun, and exclusive content
including free short stories.

There's a new contest every month!

Go to www.LexiBlake.net to subscribe.

Dedication 2012

This one is for the fans. May you all find your happily ever after.

Dedication 2019

Again, for everyone who took this journey with me, thank you. And special thanks to Margarita Coale who made it possible to unite this series with Thieves where it always belonged. You are a knight in high heels and pretty, chunky jewelry, fighting for every writers' happily ever after.

Prologue

The Seelie plane
Thirteen years before

Bronwyn Finn looked down at the hole in her stomach and wondered how long it would take to die. She stumbled into her mother's room, pushing back the ornate double doors. She held her hand to her gut, trying desperately to stem the tide. Smoke and tears seemed to be all she could see now, obliterating her home. She'd grown up in the White Palace, the marbled floors always beneath her feet. Her father's room had been off-limits to all but Beck, but her mother's room had been a sanctuary.

It was why she'd run here when the world had exploded around her.

But her mother was nowhere to be found.

Her hands shook. She was losing control. *Of course you are, Bron. You took a knife to the gut. Not much coming back from that.*

Her uncle's men. Torin had turned on them all. She made it to her mother's big bed, pushing past the filmy curtains and collapsing on the mattress. As a child, she would pull them closed and pretend she was in a whole other world. A world where the friends from her dreams were real. Tears blurred her eyes. Her Dark Ones. They'd been with her for as long as she could remember, but she'd stopped speaking of them years ago. Her father had called her crazy when she told him of their nightly visitations. Her mother had called in healers. Only Cian had listened without prejudice. Beck couldn't listen. He didn't have time, and he was almost never allowed out of their father's sight. Still, he would catch her eyes and wink or ruffle her hair as he walked past. He was going to be a king.

Bronwyn cried out. Was Beckett even alive? Had Torin killed them all?

When she died, would she see them? Her Dark Ones?

"You ain't dead yet, girl." A menacing voice pulled her from her misery.

She looked up and saw the soldier who had attacked her. He was dressed in her uncle's colors, black and gold, with the Finn family crest upon his breast. Her crest. Her kingdom. But it didn't matter. It was her Uncle Torin's world now.

Bron tried to move, to force herself to run. There was a nasty gleam in the soldier's eye that told her he was happy she hadn't died yet. He wanted to play. She shook her head. She was dying and yet, in the moment, the thought of his bloodied hands on her body was more repugnant than death itself.

But she had no choice. None. So much of her life had been thus. *Do your hair just so, Bronwyn. Stand up straight. A princess shouldn't be friends with her servants. Don't speak so freely to the brownies. Put that book down. A princess doesn't need to know such things.*

A princess hadn't needed to know how to protect herself. A princess hadn't needed to understand politics.

A princess died as easily as her sweet brownie friend had.

His hand snaked out, grabbing her ankle and pulling her down the bed. She could see she'd soaked her mother's pristine white sheets with bright red blood. Her blood.

Her mother had given birth to her in this bed. Bronwyn would die here.

"Don't," she begged. She wanted to close her eyes. Goddess, she wanted to see them one last time. She was shocked to find that in her last moments, all she wanted to do was sleep and be with them again. Her Dark Ones. Her friends. The shadow men who held her heart. She wanted their arms around her, their voices whispering. The dreams had changed recently, become more physical. She'd kissed them the night before, a soft touch of the lips, moving from one to the other because she couldn't favor either. She loved them both.

No more phantom kisses. Only pain and humiliation and death.

She tried to kick out, but she was weak, so weak. Her legs wouldn't move. It didn't matter. The soldier could move them. He spread them wide, shoving her skirt up. Stupid skirt. She'd tripped over it. It was how he'd caught her in the first place, but a princess didn't wear anything practical.

"I never had me a lady before." His hands worked at the ties of his pants.

She closed her eyes. She didn't want to see him. She tried to bring her hands up but it hurt. And then it didn't. Not quite as much. And the voice in her head became different. Not her own.

Get me close, love. Get me close. Can you feel me? I am with you always. Always, love.

She knew that voice. The softer of the two. Why hadn't she found out their names? In her dreams, they didn't need names. Now she wanted to call out for him. She laughed a bit. She was going insane.

"Ain't nothing going to save you, girl." The soldier put his hands on her thighs, spreading her further.

Her hands tingled, heat spreading where before there had been only cold. Her whole body felt warm again as though a fire had started somewhere deep inside her. She felt a boost of energy charge through her veins, and she reached for him, ignoring her instinct to try to run. She knew in her head she should be trying to get away, but she grabbed him and felt the heat flare. Smoke began, and she would have sworn she felt fire lick from her hands. It was right there. All she had to do was focus it. She had the power.

"What?" The soldier looked down at the place where she gripped him. He screamed and tried to move.

She had to hold on. She could start the fire. She could envelop them all. Torin would get nothing. If the blaze she began didn't kill him, at least the palace would go. Char and ruin would be all that Torin enjoyed of his bloody inheritance.

There was a grunt and the tip of a sword pierced the soldier's torso from behind.

And then the soldier's eyes went blank, unseeing. He slumped over, and the fire left her hands. She wanted to scream, to wail that he'd been her kill, but the energy she'd felt had fled as though a wall had come down, cutting her off from that strange power.

And from that sweetly familiar voice in her head.

She sagged back on the bed even as she felt the soldier's body being dragged away. Had another come to take his place? Her mind was so misty, filled with odd, disjointed memories. Her brother chasing her. Cousin Dante's fangs popping out for the first time at the most inopportune moment. She laughed, remembering the vampire's embarrassment. Dante. She would miss him. And her mother and Beck and Cian and Nola, the brownie who had been her constant companion, her servant, her friend.

She would miss them all.

She heard someone cry and felt herself being pulled into strong arms. She was so weak, but she still recognized her brother's face. Cian. Cian was weeping, his handsome face covered with soot and dirt. Cian had killed the soldier. Beck was the warrior half, but Cian, her sweet, intellectual brother, had slain the man who would have raped her and taken her final dignity.

"Mama?" Bron asked. She didn't know where her mother had gone. She'd lost her when the battle had begun. Battle? It had been a slaughter.

Cian's head shook. Loss marked his face, aging him. His gray eyes were dulled by pain. "She's gone, Bron. Father's gone, too."

Cian, her sweet playmate. He was older than her by several years, but he'd always made time for her. She didn't know Beck as well, but Beck and Cian were halves of a whole, symbiotic twins who shared a soul. She knew that what one felt, the other did as well, no matter how cool he appeared. Beck loved her, too.

"Love you, brother." Her lips felt dry. She wanted to say more but darkness was coming.

"I love you, too." Cian seemed to force the words out. He held her so tight, but it didn't matter. She could feel herself slipping away. Darkness took her, and she heard a mighty roar. It seemed to take over her mind. That single shout filled the world, pushing everything else away. The sound had mass and motion, enveloping her, surrounding her. Goddess, she was only fourteen. She wanted to live. She wanted to

16

wake up and find this had been a terrible dream. She didn't want to lie here knowing her brothers were gone, her future dead. She didn't want to die until she knew where her dreams would lead her. Just one more dream. Just one more moment with them.

But still the darkness came.

* * * *

Pain wracked her world as she came to consciousness. A hand moved across her mouth.

"Hush, child. If they discover us, they'll take us to Torin, and then we'll both wish we were dead."

Bron opened her eyes. What had happened? Where was she? The room was dark, and there was a hard, cold floor beneath her body.

Her body. She reached for her stomach. She could still feel the knife sliding in. It hadn't hurt at first, as though her body wasn't sure what to make of such evil, but then her whole being had lit with agony as her death had become real. Now she felt only smooth skin where there should be a hole.

A single candle illuminated the small space she was in. She shivered.

"You feel the cold. That's a good thing."

Gillian. Bron tried to get her brain working. The Unseelie princess had arrived a mere two days before. She was an envoy for the Unseelie king, come to discuss some sort of treaty between the two tribes. Bron hadn't been surprised her father had taken the meeting, but she doubted there could be lasting peace between the Seelie and the Unseelie. Too much bad blood. Why was she here? Why hadn't Gillian McIver run?

"Can you move? Don't try to sit up. Just flex your hands at first to get the circulation going. The magic I used was strong."

Magic? Bron flexed both of her hands and was surprised at how strong she felt. She took a moment, stretching and moving each muscle.

Gillian nodded down at her. "You're strong, Your Highness. Stronger than I would have given you credit for."

She felt stronger. Something had taken root in her gut, some deep sense that she was changed forever.

"My parents are dead." She knew it, but she needed to say it. The words would make it real. Her parents were gone, her home taken from her by that vile traitor. Torin. She would call him uncle no more.

Gillian's dark hair brushed the floor, and she gazed down at her. "Yes, Your Highness."

"No. I'm not a princess now. I'm a...what is the word? Fugitive. I'm a fugitive."

Gillian's eyes went hard. "You are the princess of the Seelie Fae. They can take your crown. They can take your palace. But you never let them take your name, Bronwyn Finn."

There it was again—that odd strength surged in her. She sat up. "Are my brothers alive?"

"I think so. Beckett Finn had a chance to kill the pretender, but he chose to save his other half. I believe they ran. It's why I was able to move your body. Torin sent most of his army after your brothers. He believes you're dead."

"He won't once he can't find my body." She needed to run. They both needed to get out of here.

Gillian's nose wrinkled. She was a lovely woman, but now she looked full of mischief. "Oh, he'll find your body. I switched it with one of the servant girls. I didn't kill her. She was already dead. I figured she wouldn't mind. It rather was her duty to protect you. It seems everyone was a bit derelict today."

She was starting to feel a bit stronger. "You can't blame the servants. They're supposed to serve dinner not fight off a coup."

Gillian snorted, an oddly regal sound. "Unseelie servants know a coup can come at any moment."

"Well, I don't see your guards here." Bron felt an inexplicable need to defend her house. She sat up.

"My guards are dead," Gillian said in a flat tone. "They did their duty but we were overrun once the battle began. As far as I can tell, your father was killed almost instantly. Torin seems to have bribed some of your father's guards to his side. Or perhaps he's been playing a long game and he had them placed here. It doesn't matter now. The only thing that matters is getting you away from here."

"How am I alive?" She took a deep breath, her lungs filling, the very act pleasurable in that she'd never expected to do it again. Her feet felt steady beneath her. She'd died. She knew she had. "Magic isn't strong enough to bring back the dead."

Gillian smiled, but even Bron could see the ruthless will behind it. Her father had warned her that the Unseelie princess might look like them, but she was and would always be Unseelie. The blood of goblins and trolls and all the dark creatures of the world ran through her veins. "Perhaps Seelie magic isn't strong enough, but mine is. Well, mine combined with my brothers'. Somehow they managed to help me even across the planes. You owe them your life."

"Are they really symbiotic, like Beck and Cian?" She'd heard the rumor that the Unseelie king's vampire wife had given birth to a set of symbiotic twins, as her own mother had. Symbiotic twins were born with one soul and two bodies. They were extremely powerful when they found the right bondmate, a woman who could bridge their split soul. At least that was what legend said.

"You're going to find out for yourself." Gillian stood and pulled a small pack from the table in the corner. Bron noticed the Unseelie princess was dressed in soft leather pants and a man's shirt. It made her curvy body look a bit round, but with her hair tucked into a cap, she might pass as a peasant man if no one looked too closely.

"What do you mean?"

"I mean we have to find a way off this plane and back to the Unseelie plane before that jackass Torin seals the exits. My father will take care of you, youngling." Her eyes took on a serious air. "And so will my brothers."

"What about Beck and Ci?" She had to find them.

Gillian shook her head. "We have to make sure you're safe before we go looking for your brothers. I assure you they would want it that way. Now get changed. We need to leave while the troops are preoccupied. It's chaotic out there, Your Highness. We have to be careful to not stand out."

Bron looked down at the clothes Gillian had laid out for her. They were very much like Gillian's, though she didn't have Gillian's womanly form. No one would question she was a peasant boy once her hair was dealt with. She dressed quickly, her hand skimming over her now perfectly smooth stomach.

They were quiet as they stole from the palace. They reached a hill, hiding themselves among the fleeing peasants, but Bron turned to look at the White Palace one more time. In the moonlight it looked like a ruin, a place that once had stood but now crumbled, leaving only memories of the world it once represented.

"I can't go back." She wouldn't go home again. She wouldn't run through the palace or swim in the river. She would never again sneak into her mother's bed when the thunder frightened her. She wouldn't play with her friends.

She had no home.

Gillian took her by the shoulders, spinning her around. "Don't you talk like that. You will go back." She pressed an object into Bron's hand. It was small and cold. "That's yours. I found it next to your body. It's the weapon that they tried to kill you with. Never let it go. When the time comes for vengeance, this knife will be in your hand. The world has changed. That does not mean your life is at an end. Dark times are only the end when true leaders refuse to fight. Your brothers are fighting now, and your time will come. Decide, Your Highness. What kind of a princess will you be? A Seelie princess who weeps and hopes someone will save her, or will you choose to avenge your people? This is not just about you. This is about your people and all who will fall to Torin's sword. If you cannot find the strength to be more than a pretty face, then I have no use for you."

Bron turned and looked again with new eyes. She saw what had been taken from her. And one day she would take it back.

When Gillian moved, Bron followed. She'd been born in the White Palace, and she'd died there. She was a new version of herself. She was more than she'd been before, stronger, older, harder.

And alone.

When the darkness had come, she'd been alone. Her Dark Ones had not come for her. It was time to put that dream away.

She walked away from her home with only vengeance in her heart.

Chapter One

The dead things of the world loved Lachlan McIver. It was the shame of his life that he couldn't return the affection.

One half of the heir to the Unseelie throne looked down at the small dog barking and jumping at his feet. He took a deep breath of the forest air and prayed to the gods for patience. He'd walked into the woods behind the palace because he'd looked in all of Shim's other haunts. His brother wasn't at the tavern in the village. He wasn't in the kitchens. He wasn't sitting in their room staring out the window toward the west, the direction of the door to the Seelie plane. It was where he often found Shim these days, a vacant look in his dark eyes.

He needed to talk to his brother about the morning's news, but he found himself alone with a dead dog. He wasn't sure where Shim had gotten off to, but he would more than likely laugh and pet the damn thing. Shim wouldn't even notice that something had taken half the yipping dog's side out. Likely it had been a bear or maybe a troll who had been lucky enough to catch it, but not lucky enough to finish its meal.

"Go away." Lachlan tried to put some distance between him and the now-reanimated corpse of the former terrier. It simply yipped and followed him.

Lach attempted to ignore the creature. It wasn't the first dead thing to imprint on him. He was coming into his power, and without his bondmate near, it tended to go a bit wild.

Bondmate. He closed his eyes as the thought of her coated his senses. He didn't need to be near her to feel her. Gods, he'd never been close to her, but she was in his heart. He felt her every minute of every day. But what would he do if he had to stand in front of her? When he and Shim invaded her dreams at night, he was whole, his face as perfect as his brother's. Would she turn away from him when she saw the real Lachlan McIver? He rather thought she would. She was a beauty, a pure Seelie princess, who would probably run from her beast of an Unseelie prince.

It was, perhaps, better to see her only in dreams, but like many things in his life, he had no choice. He had to find her. His powers were flaring, going wild.

And Shim...

Lach sighed as he realized where his brother was. He turned and jogged toward the beach, praying his idiot brother hadn't fallen asleep where selkies would take him.

He jogged across the grounds, reaching the highest point. From here he could turn back and see the Dark Palace shining like a jewel in the distance. To the east he could see the road. A small party was approaching. His father's advance guard had already confirmed that it was his cousin Julian leading the rebel Seelie kings.

Her brothers.

Gods, he was going to meet Bron's brothers, and he hadn't figured out if he planned to tell them a damn thing. They would scoff and tell him he was bloody insane. His father would shake his head. Only Gillian and Duffy in all the plane believed their secret—that they had already bonded to the Seelie princess. Without permission or even her real knowledge. It had been instinctive, a cry that had crossed two planes, saved her life, and inadvertently ruined Lach's face.

He shook off thoughts of that terrible day and turned back to the sea. He couldn't see his brother, but there was a small figure awkwardly moving on the rocks that made up the beach.

Little gnome. Big axe. That was Duffy. And where Duffy was, his brother couldn't be far behind. The gnome hefted the axe Shim had given him months before on the date they had mutually decided on for the celebration of Duffy's birthday. Duffy had wanted an axe. The damn thing was nearly bigger than the gnome, and more than once he'd fallen on his ass from trying to swing it. The year before, Lach and Shim had bought their lifelong friend a set of custom-made armor. The blacksmith had laughed the whole time he'd made it.

It wasn't that no one had told Duffy that gnomes weren't warriors. It was that Duffy was terribly hard of hearing when he wanted to be.

The dog at Lach's feet yipped and panted as though waiting for the fun to begin.

"Go away." Lach started down the trail that led to the beach, the dog at his heels. He tried to give the dog the command to stay, but it wasn't a well-trained thing. More than likely his lack of discipline was what had led to his untimely death. "Duff!"

Lach yelled at the gnome the minute he hit the beach. Now he could see Shim, lounging with his back against a boulder, one hand over his heart. His legs and feet had sunken in the pebbles beneath, telling Lach that he'd been there for a while. No sandy beaches here in the Unseelie plane. Everything here was hard and deadly. He'd been to the Vampire plane with its tropical beaches. He'd stood looking over the peaceful sea in someplace his cousin had called Hawaii, and he'd wanted to bring Bronwyn there. He'd imagined sinking into the soft sand and reveling in her body. Bonding time, the vampires called it. First bite. Oh, that first bite would be amazing. First blood.

His fangs descended. The damn things did it at the worst times, but he'd gotten used to it. And he'd gotten used to ignoring the hunger. When he wanted real blood in his mouth, he would go hunting and gorge himself on predatory creatures. The hunt fed him as much as the blood did.

His brother had another coping mechanism.

Shim lay with his eyes on the ocean, but Lach knew damn well that wasn't what his brother was seeing.

The dead dog barked, warning Duffy of their approach. The gnome shrieked, and his axe came down on the pebbled sand, barely missing his feet.

"Lachlan. You scared ten years off me life." Duffy leaned over, resting his hands on his knees and dragging cool air into his lungs.

Lach narrowed his eyes, standing over the gnome. At six feet five inches, Lach knew he was intimidating to the four-foot gnome. "And what do you think you're doing to me, Duff?"

Wide blue eyes looked back up. "Ain't doing nothing but protecting Shim."

Lachlan pointed out at the sea. Not forty feet off the shore was a telltale froth of water. That white churning proved how reckless his brother had become.

"Were you going to use that axe on the mermaids?"

Duffy turned quickly, his hat falling off his head. "Mermaids? Bloody hell."

"Yes, bloody is the key point. It's going to be your blood and then Shim's that's going to be all over this beach and all because my brother here can't deal with reality." Lach nearly growled when he turned back to his brother and rolled his eyes. Shim had a smile on his face, his eyes blank. He didn't even notice that half a dog was licking at his chin.

"What the bloody hell is that?" Duffy asked, staring at the dog.

"A straggler." Lach wasn't sure what Duffy was so squeamish about. It wasn't the first time some dead thing had followed him around. "Try to wake Shim up. We have trouble coming." He walked to the edge of the water. The icy tide lapped at his feet as he faced the creatures who would one day be his subjects. If they didn't manage to eat his other half... "I don't need this shit!"

A shimmering presence rose from the foam. Gorgeous and deadly, the mermaid smiled, shrugged, and then dove back down to the depths.

Everything, it seemed, was coming after them. There wasn't a creature on the plane who couldn't sense their weakness, and every single one of them was ready and waiting to pounce.

He turned back and saw his main problem. They were weak because Shim had stopped fighting.

"Where is he?" Lach asked, staring at his brother, the other half of his soul.

"He was mumbling something about fields and wheat." Duffy came to Lach's side, his mouth turned down in a flat line. "I think he feels her more clearly here."

Shim chuckled, but Lach knew damn well he wasn't laughing at anything he heard on this plane. He got to his knees and put both hands on his brother's shirt, hauling him up.

"Wake the fuck up, Shim."

Dark hair covered half of Shim's face as he shook his head. "No. Don't want to."

Lach groaned. It had been so much worse in the last year. Shim had started to sink into a world where he could see her, feel her emotions. Lach could only do that in his dreams, when an invisible thread tethered him to his bondmate. Sometimes he envied his brother the deeper connection, but this wasn't one of those times. Shim had begun to seek the connection to her instead of living his damn life. Their life. His brother was slipping away, and Lach couldn't allow it.

He wasn't ready to give up yet. He wanted a real life with her, not some half life where he only held her in dreams. She was his, damn it. He would prove it to her when he found her. Ruined face or no.

"Do I have to punch you again?" Lach asked.

Shim's eyes focused. "Bloody hell, no. Why would you do such a thing?"

Finally, a wee bit of sense. "Because you're acting like a drunk. I can't wake you anymore. It's harder and harder when you give in during the day. Hell, it can be hard enough to wake you at night. You can't go looking for her in the day."

A smile crossed Shim's face. He'd seen that smile on the face of many a man who had too much whiskey. "She's here, Lach."

"No, she's not." That was the problem. She wasn't here, and they hadn't been able to find her. "But her brothers are."

Shim sat up on his own. "What are you talking about?"

Duffy leaned in. "Is it true, Lach? Are the Seelies coming?"

Lach nodded. "Julian's bringing them in. The Vampire plane has declared for Torin. Beckett and Cian Finn are on the run."

"A sad day when the Seelie kings come looking for a place to hide here," Duffy said with a frown.

Lach lightly smacked the side of his head. "Don't be talking like that. It's talk like that got us in trouble in the first place."

Duffy rubbed his head. "Well, it's not normal. They hate us."

"Not more than we hate them," Lach shot back.

"I don't hate them." Shim seemed to be coming out of his fog. "I don't hate anyone."

Duffy leaned in. "Gods, Shim, don't let your da hear you saying crazy shit like that. He'll beat you for sure."

Lach rolled his eyes. Despite his father's rather intimidating presence, he'd never once beaten them. Not that they didn't know how to take or give a sound thrashing, but it had been part of their training, not at their da's hand. King Fergus of the Unseelie was a ruthless bastard. He wouldn't have remained king if he wasn't, but he cared for his sons.

"Da was the one who sent Gilly in there in the first place, Duff. He wanted a treaty with the Seelie. And given what we've seen is going on there in the Seelie plane, it's no surprise he'll support Beck and Cian Finn in taking back the throne." It went unsaid that, after all, they were family. Beck and Ci Finn didn't know it, but the future queen of the Unseelie was still on the Seelie plane, trapped and in constant danger. Only her death had saved her from, well, death.

"Do you think they know, Lach?" Shim asked, struggling to his feet.

"No." Lach straightened his tunic. He should change, but there wasn't time. "Julian would have warned us if they had any suspicions." He put a hand out to steady his brother. "Even if someone told them and they brought the rumor forward, our father would let it be known that we're crazy. They won't believe us. They won't believe until the full and true bond is in place, and we can't do that until we're in her presence."

"It feels full and true to me." Shim stretched and looked down at the dog at his feet. "Lach, why is that dog's guts on his outside?"

The dog sat and panted, his tail thumping.

"Don't worry about the dog. Worry about the kings. They've brought the queen along."

"Is it time then?" Shim asked, his voice getting serious.

Every muscle in Lachlan's body clenched. It was almost time. They would find their bondmate or they would die trying. And their plane would fall… "It's time."

It had to be.

Shim smiled, his whole face lighting up. "We're going to find her. I know it deep down. I have all the clues we need. Surely the kings will know the place I keep seeing."

Shim slapped Duffy on the back and handed him his axe.

"I bet the queen is going to be crying by now," Duffy said, his chest puffing out. "I can't imagine a sweet Seelie queen having to deal with us rough Unseelie. If she lasts the night, I'll be shocked."

"We have to be on our best behavior, Duff," Shim said seriously. "And we might want to clear the goblins out. They could scare the queen. And the trolls. You know, we might want to clear the whole palace."

Duffy and Shim started up the road, talking about all the things that might frighten the gentle Seelie queen.

Lach stopped. The dog was dead again, his body lay across the rocks, a symbol of all that was wrong with Lach's life.

He should be as thrilled as his brother, but what would their own sweet Seelie wife think of him? What would happen when she saw his decimated face? What would she think when she learned of his power, the power she would make stronger by bonding the two parts of his soul together? Would she be able to live with herself knowing she would be responsible for unleashing a powerful necromancer?

Lach stared down at the dog who had briefly flared back to existence. Shim could offer her life and fire and a perfect face. All Lach could offer was death.

And still he turned and followed his brother. He knew it would be disastrous, but he couldn't resist. After a lifetime of longing, he would see her.

Perhaps then and only then he could be free.

* * * *

Shim stared at the sweet Seelie queen and had to admit that he was slightly afraid of her.

"Look, you little shit, I know you have coffee. I can smell it." She was small but she showed no fear of the goblin. Shim had heard the rumor that she was from some backwater plane called the Earth plane, but she looked *sidhe* to him. Short, though she was curved in all the right places.

"I don't know what you're talking about, Your Highness. I have no idea what this thing called coffee is." The goblin flashed a mouthful of sharp teeth before trying to hide a silvery flask behind his back.

A young woman dressed in simple but expensive clothes walked up behind the queen. She was pretty, a slender, innocent-looking thing. Then she started sniffing the air. There was something almost feral about her when she scented the world around her. "He is lying. He has the coffee."

Queen Meg threw her an affectionate look. "Yes, I believe so, Kaja, since he's drinking it right in front of me."

She drank goblin whiskey? Most *sidhe* avoided it, but Shim rather liked the stuff. He preferred it the way the goblins prepared it. Hot and sweet. Someone, a gnome if he remembered correctly, had cooled the liquor, but Shim had thought it vile in that form.

A Seelie queen who drank goblin liquor? And whose handmaiden appeared to be a bit feral? The slender woman was again scenting the air.

"The food here smells good. And the small ones look easy to catch."

The queen sent her a pointed look. "Dante told you not to eat the brownies."

Kaja wrinkled her nose. "Dante tells me not to eat anything. It's sad. *Don't eat the brownies. Don't eat the pixies. Don't eat the trolls.* He would not even allow me to eat our enemies."

Queen Meg shrugged. "Well, he was definitely right about the troll. It smelled bad. You would have had a tummy ache for days." Her eyes narrowed, and she leaned forward. "What did Dante say about eating selfish goblins who won't even share a drop of their coffee?"

The goblin took another drink. "I ain't scared of no Seelie women. Seelie women are trophies, nothing more."

Kaja growled, a low, menacing sound that seemed to come from the back of her throat, and Shim could have sworn she suddenly had a mouth full of sharp teeth. "I am not Seelie."

Damn, he was going to lose a few goblins if he didn't start to fix this.

"Is that the queen?" Lach asked, walking up behind him.

At least he had an answer for this particular question. So often he didn't. So often he drifted away, his mind seeking Bronwyn's and melding in an odd way. He was the plane's worst peeper. He shook it off. It was always there, that slight invisible tie that bound him to his wife. Well, the woman who didn't even know she was his wife. Years had passed since the single act that had bound them together, and as far as he could tell, Bronwyn hadn't gotten the message that she was a married woman. Not that she was playing around. Shim always managed to fix those problems. A nice fire bolt tended to make would-be suitors think twice about fucking around with his bride.

"Are you still with me?" Lach asked.

Shim groaned. "Sorry. I was thinking about her. Yes, I think that's the queen, and she's not what we thought she would be. And the one named Kaja mentioned Dante. Gods, did Julian really bring Dante Dellacourt here? Shouldn't he be in a strip club on the Vampire plane?"

"I think she heard you." Lach nodded toward the women.

The slim one was watching him with narrowed eyes. "Explain this stripping club to me. I do not like the sound of it. It sounds like a place my husband should stay far from."

Queen Meg smiled. "It sounds like a place Dante more than likely used to frequent before he got married."

"Bloody hell, Dante Dellacourt is married?" Duffy walked up, two big mugs of goblin whiskey steaming in his hands. The gnome belched a bit. "Is it one of the crazy women from the DL we all watched? That was fun. We made it into a drinking game. Every time that idiot would say 'hey, baby,' we would all drink. I never been so drunk in all me life."

Shim was about to apologize when the queen's laughter rang through the hall. The goblin she'd been accosting ran like a demon was on his heels. Queen Meg laughed it off. "We drank every time he took off his shirt or got into a hot tub. I got pretty drunk myself. And yes, Dante Dellacourt took a consort. This is Kaja Dellacourt. I would tread carefully, Your Highnesses. She's a little bitter. We passed many an interesting creature on the road here, and her husband would let her feast on nothing." She got down on one knee. The Seelie queen was dressed in informal clothes, but there was no doubt she was a queen. There was an air of authority to the woman. But there was also a pleasant smile on her face. "Hello, wee one. What's your name? I can make a guess as to who those two are, but I was unaware there were gnomes on this plane."

Duffy stepped forward. She'd gotten down to his level. It was an unexpected sign of respect. Shim was starting to like the Seelie queen. "Me name is Duffy, Your Highness. I was a foundling. Me mum left me on the road, and the Unseelie queen, rest her soul, took pity on me. She brought me to the palace, and I was raised here."

"A third brother." Queen Meg nodded his way. "It is good to meet you. I was wondering, Duffy, if you might have a bit more of that delicious brew?"

Duffy shoved that mug in the queen's hand quicker than Shim had ever seen him move before. He looked back at Shim, apologies on his small face. "Sorry, Shim. I meant that for you, but she's prettier."

Queen Meg winked at the gnome and then took a shockingly long drink of the goblin brew. "Thank god. We've been on the run. I haven't been able to find any. Don't worry, I'll trade for it. Anyone here ever heard of cupcakes?"

The doors to the king's room opened, and a silence fell across the hall. King Fergus entered, followed by their cousin, Julian Lodge, a royal vampire named Taggart who served as Julian's bodyguard, the Seelie kings, his father's chief advisor, a vampire Shim didn't recognize, and the infamous Dante Dellacourt.

None of them looked happy, and it gave Shim a damn good idea of what his place was. He'd been left outside of the meeting. He'd been left with the women.

Queen Meg gave him a wisp of a smile. "If it helps at all, we were a bit earlier than we expected. I don't think your father intended to leave you out."

But his father was overly protective. His father still thought they were children, not thirty years old. He understood why. His father was still waiting for them to fade, to die because they refused to take a bondmate. King Fergus of the Unseelie didn't believe it was possible that his sons had bonded with a woman on another plane. No one believed they had bonded with Bronwyn Finn as she lay dying.

They certainly wouldn't believe that Shim and Lach had been the ones to bring her back to life, giving a piece of their soul and half of Lach's face in return.

"Father isn't interested in our counsel." Shim was well aware of the bitter flavor to his words.

Lach stared down at him. "Well, it doesn't help when half of us goes down to the beach and no one can find us."

He knew he hadn't helped things, but he hadn't been able to resist. He'd woken this morning and he'd felt sunshine on his face. He'd smiled because it was a cloudy day here. But Bron could feel the sun, and he could feel her delight in it. He was suffused with her unique energy as she'd run through the fields.

He never got words, only images and feelings. But if he concentrated, if he went deep into himself and caught hold of the invisible thread that was always there in his brain, he could see through her eyes. It was how he'd known his sister was still alive.

His father didn't believe that either.

"I'll tell you about the men you don't recognize if you'll give me the lowdown on your party," the queen offered.

Kaja had joined her queen, their closeness obvious. "I would like to know their names as well."

Lach reached down and grabbed the mug from Duffy's hand, taking a drink before handing it back. Again, if the queen was shocked that his brother would share with a gnome, she didn't show it. What had she called Duffy? A third brother. The queen, it appeared, might make an interesting ally. Lach caught his eye and gave him an almost imperceptible nod. He was fine with sharing information.

"The man on my father's right is named Maon. He's been Da's advisor since long before we were born. He's been arguing that we should go to war with Torin the Pretender since we got the news of the coup."

"Torin the Pretender?" Lach chuckled gruffly. "More like Torin the Fucking Asshole."

Meg turned to Lach. "I rather like you."

Lach shrugged. "Give it some time. I can probably change your mind."

"Well, at least I know which one is which. It's nice to meet you, Prince Lachlan." She turned to Shim. "Prince Shim. Julian explained to us how the two of you split. I was told you're the sweet one, and he's the big ball of insecurity."

Lach's jaw dropped. "What?"

Kaja laughed. "He did not use such words, Meg. He spoke of

31

Prince Shim's gentle soul and Prince Lach's gruffness."

The queen sighed. "Yeah, well, I've been here and do this on a daily basis. Trust me, Kaj. The gruff one is always hiding his own insecurities. I bet that one there thinks his scars make him unattractive."

Lach went a brutal shade of red. "I don't talk about that. It's rude for you to mention it."

Queen Meg studied Lach for a moment, not a hint of distaste on her face. "See, I told you. And they don't. They're actually quite interesting. They give you character. What do you think, Kaj?"

A sly smile came over the brunette's face. "I think he looks like a warrior. I find him very attractive. He is the First in this group. He simply hasn't taken his place."

But Shim needed to get back to something else that had been said. "I'm not gentle. For the gods' sake, woman. Don't be calling me such names. Do you want to insult me?"

"You are gentle, Shim." Lach had a smile back on his face.

"I bloody well am not."

"I got to agree," Duffy added. "The last time you killed an ogre, you didn't even eat the heart. Soft."

"Ogre gives me indigestion." He wasn't soft. He fucking wasn't. He just had trouble with his gut at times.

Kaja's eyes went wide. "See, Meg, he got to eat the ogre."

"No one's eating ogres." Dante Dellacourt slid an arm around his wife's waist. "Put it out of your mind. And if I see you chasing the brownies, you'll be over my lap."

Dante Dellacourt was a celebrity in his world. Shim and Lach had spent some time on the Vampire plane. They had spent time being educated in more ways than one. They had gone to what the vampires called University, and they had been trained by their cousin, Julian, in the dark arts of Dominance and submission.

A vision of beautiful Bronwyn tied up and trussed for their pleasure crept over him.

"Don't." Lach leaned in, his harsh whisper pulling him out of his thoughts.

Sometimes having a twin who could practically read his mind was irritating.

"Come along, Kaj. We need to settle into our rooms. We're going to have dinner in a bit. Your Highnesses, I look forward to meeting with you." Dante led his wife away, but Kaja turned, giving them both a smile.

Meg waved to her friend and then turned back to Shim and Lach. She pointed at the men left standing in the foyer. "All right, I'll tell you about our party. Obviously, those two are my husbands. I think it's safe to say Cian is the gentler of the two. He would never ever eat an ogre heart, but you could talk Beck into it. You know your cousin. I assume you know Mr. Taggart."

"He's the head of Julian's security, though I heard he's planning on starting his own company." Shim had briefly met the big blond man. "I don't know the other."

"The vampire with them is named William Roan," the queen explained. "He leads a group of mercenaries."

"Cash-poor royal?" Shim asked. It was a good bet. Vampires weren't the most compassionate people. When a vampire family lost its fortune, they tended to lose everything. Many committed suicide rather than move to the lower levels of their great cities, but some, like William Roan, found another way to replace their lost honor. They took up the sword, or in this case, most likely a whole bunch of high-tech sonic weapons. Taggart had started the same way. Julian had a soft spot for those who fought their way back up the ladder.

The queen nodded. "Yes. He's also hungry for a consort, so it's a testament to his loyalty to your cousin that he's not fighting for the other side. The same with Taggart and his group. I know many of the military-style groups on the Vampire plane have thrown in with the government. Torin's promised the royals one hundred consorts. After a thirteen-year drought, I guess I shouldn't be surprised."

Vampires, the royal ones, required a consort to suspend the aging process. They did this through the act of feeding from consort blood. Gods, he wanted to taste his wife. Just like that his damn fangs came out.

Meg giggled a bit, taking another sip of her drink. "It looks like you have that trouble here, too. Why haven't you taken a consort?"

"Because we already have a bondmate." The words came out of Lach's mouth sounding dismissive, but Shim knew why. He was sure the queen wouldn't believe them either. Perhaps the queen had been right. Lach was the one with all the insecurities. But then again, he was also the half who didn't mind a little ogre heart when the occasion called for it.

"The princess in the tower?" Queen Meg asked.

It was what they called her now. They knew her name. Had always known her name, but there were too many ears who could hear the secret. Bronwyn Finn was safer dead. Shim might be softer than his brother, but he wasn't a fool. Even Torin the Wretched Asshole had spies.

"Julian told you. He doesn't believe us." Shim looked at his cousin, who was laughing at something one of the others said. Julian was ridiculously wealthy, ruthless, and intensely perverse. He fit right in with the Unseelie. And Julian had been smart enough to figure out a way to get his own consort off the closed Seelie plane. He'd been set to wed a young bondmate named Daniella when the war had occurred. Nothing so simple as a bloody civil war had ever stopped Julian Lodge. He had his bondmate, and he hadn't blinked an eye when she'd come to him with an extra. Her servant, a young man named Finn, had stowed away and fought to remain by her side. In true Julian Lodge fashion, he'd simply taken them both, and now everyone was happy.

Shim couldn't find his bondmate because he couldn't convince his father that she was still alive.

What if her brothers proved to be more reasonable?

"How old are you?" Meg asked.

"Thirty," Shim replied.

Shrewd eyes studied them. "Well past the age of bonding. Shouldn't you be all crazy and stuff? Beck and Ci were. Beck hid it, but I understand now how close to the edge he was. I don't sense that from either of you."

Lach tensed beside him. "Because we bonded thirteen years ago."

Shim watched as Meg's eyes registered shock, but not quite disbelief.

"You bonded but you lost her?" she asked.

"We were never physically with her. We bonded only in our minds," Shim explained.

He was about to continue when a shout went through the hall. One of the guards ran in, his sword on his hand.

"Your Majesty, the sluagh…" The guard had to take a deep breath. It was obvious he'd run long and hard from his post. "They're coming."

Shim had to take a deep breath because a couple of sluagh coming to the palace wasn't a good sign. The sluagh normally kept to their caves, feasting on the rotten things of the world.

His father sighed. "How many?"

The guard's eyes tightened. "All of them, Your Majesty."

Shim took the cup out of Duffy's hand. He was going to need the courage because it looked like they were all fucked.

Chapter Two

Bron let the sunshine warm her face and the soft sound of the wheat swaying in the breeze calm her. It was nearly time for the threshing, but she had a few days of peace left. When the time came, she would work from morning 'til after the sun went down, and then she would barely manage to eat before she passed out from exhaustion.

She would sleep too deeply to dream. She would miss them.

How could she miss two men she'd never met?

"Issy! Issy!" A high voice pierced her solitude.

Bron smiled. Even after all these years, she still was somewhat shocked to hear herself called by another name. Isolde. She'd selected it when Gillian had finally given up on finding a way off the plane. She could still see Gilly's face, the tears streaking down as she'd told her she had to give up her name.

This plane had been hard on her foster mother.

"Issy!"

"I'm here, Ove!" There was nothing for it. The brownie would call out for her until she found her quarry. Ove was a tenacious thing.

The shafts of wheat moved and shuffled as the brownie ran toward her. Bron braced herself for impact.

"Found you." Ove launched herself into Bron's arms.

"Yes, you did." Bron held her, enjoying the feel of her frail body. She loved the brownies. Their rough faces and scraggly hair evoked a tenderness that called her childhood back. The nannies and housemaids had almost all been brownies, working diligently for their cups of cream.

Ove was a youngling, barely past two, but brownies aged differently. She was a child but well on her way to her own work. Still, the light of youth was in her wide black eyes. She clung to Bron for a moment. Brownies were affectionate creatures when they were allowed to be. Her own nanny had carried her until she'd gotten too big, and then Flanna had stroked her hair and held her hand whenever possible. Her mother had loved the affection between them, and her father had tolerated it.

Where was sweet Flanna now? Probably buried in the wide mass graves she'd seen Torin's men digging as she'd fled the palace.

She shook off the thought and looked down at Ove. "So tell me, little one, why were you looking for me?"

"The mayor's coming."

Three words and her whole day was wrecked. Micha O'Sullivan was a pompous ass who eyed her with far too much familiarity for a man twice her age. Unfortunately, he was a pompous ass with power in this backwater part of the world. This village might be the ass end of the plane, but Torin still had some measure of control through the officials even here.

Bron set the brownie on her feet. "Did your mum know why he's coming?"

Of all the people left on the plane, only Mags had figured out who she and Gillian were. The brownie, who sometimes helped with the house and the fields, had slipped up once a few years back and called Gillian by her title. It seemed she'd been born on the Unseelie plane. Bron had despaired in leaving her tower since it had become her home, but Mags had taken to one fragile knee and pledged to defend the Unseelie princess with her life. It had satisfied Gillian, and then they'd had an ally.

"Mum said she overheard there was talk of new restrictions." Ove's eyes grew round, a wealth of fear.

Bron took a deep breath. New restrictions meant new laws against magic and non-*sidhe* creatures. She took Ove's hand and began to wind her way out of the field. She needed to change clothes if the mayor was coming. He tended to call her to task when she was seen in public in the soft leather pants she'd come to favor.

She regretted leaving the field. She could think out there among the wheat she'd planted. She could close her eyes and almost feel her Dark Ones. What would the mayor think if he knew she dreamed at night of two lovers, one with dark powers and the other who could light up the night?

He would be horrified and possibly accuse her of witchcraft. It was what they accused everyone of these days. Witchcraft, once a valued skill, was now a way to punish anyone who didn't agree with authority.

When she traveled to sell her wheat, they were everywhere— bodies strung up on the side of the road. Witchcraft. Collusion. Improper contact with non-*sidhe* creatures. Whispering the names Beck and Cian. All offenses punishable by hanging.

There were rumors that the ones who had been hanged were the lucky ones.

Gillian stood at the edge of the field, a stern look on her face. She'd dressed for the occasion in a sturdy but respectable gown that would prove completely impractical for work. "Where have you been?"

Bron looked back at the crops pointedly.

"None of your sass, girl." Gillian sighed and shook her head. "If your da could see you now."

He would be perfectly horrified, but the thought brought a bit of a smile to Bron's face. "He would demand to know where his daughter was. Well, if he noticed at all. Now Mama, on the other hand, would have a fit of vapors, and my brothers would laugh."

"Go on then, I see the little ones have already brought the news." She winked down at Ove. "Go back to your mum." She passed her a small container. "Morning milk, to thank her. Stay out of sight. The less they remember you exist, the safer you will be."

Ove nodded her scraggly head and took off, the shafts marking her progress.

Bron was halfway up the stairs when Gillian caught her.

"You have to be more careful. If the guards caught you holding hands with Ove, they would have every right to arrest you."

Anger curled in Bron's stomach. "Then perhaps we should do something about the guards."

Like gather together and show them what a mob could do.

She marched to her room and flung her clothes off with a reckless hand. She slammed open the door to her dresser and pulled out her work dress.

Gillian sat down on the edge of the bed. "Could I talk you into the blue cotton?"

The blue cotton was her best dress, the one she wore to weddings and festivals. "I won't waste it on him."

She hated the mayor with his covetous eyes. She'd selected her work dress because it covered her chest and masked her curves. The mayor was looking for a wife, and he'd already proposed an alliance between them. She'd been trying to put him off.

"Will you please remember what your main job is?" Gillian asked.

This was a lecture she'd heard almost every day of her life on the run. "I don't know. Remind me."

Gillian huffed. "One day you are going to make a couple of men insane. I simply know it. Your job is to stay alive. Your job is to be a living, breathing woman when your brothers return."

If they returned. "I will endeavor to not become a corpse in the next few hours."

Gillian came up behind her, working the buttons up her back. When she was done, she turned Bron around and looked at her, smoothing down the small bit of scalloped edges of the neckline. "I am sometimes glad that Torin planned his coup when you were a youngling since I could never make you pass for a boy now."

Bron smiled, but it was a sarcastic thing. "I prayed for bosoms all my life. Now I rather wish I was slender."

Gillian shook her head. "No, you don't. You're beautiful exactly the way you are. Don't let the current palace fashions make you think otherwise."

There was a knock on the door. Even his knock sounded short and officious, like the man himself.

Gillian took a deep breath. "I know you're angry, love, but hold on for a bit longer. Things are happening. I can't see them clearly yet, but something changed a few months back. I felt it. I still feel it.

Something's coming."

"That might not be a good thing, Gilly."

"Please."

How in all the planes could she deny this woman? Bron nodded, giving her a silent promise to behave. Gillian called out the window to let the mayor know they were coming, and Bron followed her down the stairs.

Gillian had been a princess. She could have gotten out. She more than likely could have negotiated with Torin for her release. Torin had been looking for allies, desperate for them. He would have loved having the Unseelie king in his debt, yet Gillian hadn't abandoned her. She'd sought a way out for them both, and when that failed, Gillian McIver had made a home for them here.

No matter how much Bron wanted to take her weapons and practice on the mayor, she would hold her tongue.

The door was opened, and there stood Micha and his ever-present guard.

"Ladies," he said, bowing slightly.

She could hear him. *Even in a backwater province, courtesy is required.* She wondered if he would be so courteous when she gutted him.

Bron did what was expected and curtsied, though not as deeply as he would have wanted.

"May I come in for tea?" Micha asked with the smile of a man who knew the question was mere formality. "The palace has set forth some exciting new plans. I thought I would talk to my favorite citizens before they're posted in the square for all to see."

Gillian managed a bright smile. Bron's stomach churned. He acted like it was exciting news when it more than likely was a new and inventive way to kill those Torin despised. Fae were starving across the plane, but Torin seemed more interested in coming up with ways to dispose of his enemies.

"Of course, Mayor, please make yourself welcome." Gillian invited him in, her hand sweeping gracefully across the room, as though she were welcoming him into a palace, not the sad tower that was their home. "And your guards?"

Micha's nose wrinkled as though it was common to even

acknowledge they were there. "My guards will do their duties. Two will remain outside and one in the hallway. They have no need for anything so delicate as tea."

The tightness of the guard's mouth told Bron that perhaps he had been looking forward to some food. Even the guards were on rations, it seemed. When he noticed her watching, he gave a tight smile and a nod. Bron thought he was almost giving her permission to ignore him.

"I'll get the tea," Bron said as Gillian showed the mayor into what passed for the parlor.

Bron started the tea and gathered the bread and cheese they had left. It seemed a shame to waste it all on the mayor, who didn't look like a man who had missed many meals.

"How is the crop looking this year?" Micha was asking Gillian.

"Better than even last year. Danu has blessed us."

"The king will be happy to hear it. He's requesting an extra twenty percent this year."

Bron nearly dropped the teapot. An extra twenty percent after he already took half? It was outrageous.

Gillian's response was measured. "An extra twenty percent, did you say? I fear sending so much to the palace will mean our own people will starve."

The mayor laughed. "Don't you worry your pretty head now. We'll be fine. The king has declared rations for all citizens. And he's redefined citizenship. The king and queen will always take care of the *sidhe*."

Bron forced herself to pour the hot water into the pot. So he'd done it. Torin had finally declared that only *sidhe* were true Seelie. The brownies and the trolls, the dryads and leprechauns, would be declared Unseelie and therefore undesirable. They would receive no rations. Any land they possessed would be confiscated. They had no protections.

She passed the guard in the hall. He didn't see her or he surely would have tempered his expression. When the mayor mentioned getting rid of the riffraff, the guard's face became fierce, a dark, vengeful look passing over his handsome countenance.

An ally?

She couldn't be sure, and she certainly couldn't walk up to him and say, hey, I'm the supposedly dead princess of the Seelie Fae.

41

Wanna start a revolution? *Nope.* That would fall under the heading of "stupid things to do." But if the mayor's guard could be swayed to her side, there was no time like the present to begin the process.

She gave him what she hoped was her kindest smile and passed him a sandwich of soft bread and tangy cheese.

The guard's eyes lit, and then he frowned. "Best not, Miss."

He really was hungry. It no longer mattered what damn side he was on. Bron couldn't help but feel for the man. She'd been hungry. She'd felt it gnaw at her stomach and prayed for anything to end the slow torture of starvation.

"Please. We have more than enough, and the mayor won't notice." She pressed the sandwich into his hand. "I won't be able to enjoy a thing if I know you're out here with your stomach rumbling."

The guard smiled, the look softening his face. "My thanks to you, Miss. It's said around town that you and your sister are kind ones." He leaned over and whispered. "Tell the brownies to hide. Leave their homes. They need to go underground. He's going to come for them."

He stood back up, his face red as a beet as though he knew he'd committed treason.

Bron nodded and put a hand on his. "I thank you, sir."

Her heart pounding, she walked into the parlor. She prayed her rage didn't show on her face.

"There she is." The mayor looked up, satisfaction written on every line of his face. "Beautiful Isolde."

Bron was glad the man didn't know her real name. She would hate to hear it on his lips. She set the tray on the table, grateful that unwed women were supposed to be shy. He would think the fact that she wasn't looking at him was charming.

"Come and sit with me, dear."

Panic threatened to overtake her. Gillian shifted uncomfortably, her eyes going to the window where the silhouettes of the two guards Micha had left outside stood, their pikes held high. Bron had dreams at night of Gillian on the end of one of those hated pikes.

She sat down, trying to keep plenty of distance between them.

"Gillian, dear, might I have a word alone with your sister?" The request practically slithered out of his mouth.

Gillian sat straight up, and Bron could see she'd reached the end of her patience. She had to stop her.

"Please, Gilly. I'll be fine. I can handle it. After all, being a good hostess is all a part of my job, right?" She placed careful emphasis on the word "job" since Gillian had recently given her a lecture on what her true job was. Staying alive.

Her jaw tightened, but Bron breathed easier as Gillian got up. "I suppose I can go and find something a bit stronger than tea if Your Honor would prefer it."

The mayor winked. "I think we might be needing that. Find something for a celebration, dear."

Her stomach turned since she knew what was coming.

The minute Gillian was out the door, he scooted over, placing himself so close to her she could smell the rank heat of his body under his layers of proper clothing. No true country Fae would wear such fancy clothes, but the mayor liked to pretend he was going to the palace instead of running a small agricultural province.

"Now, my dear, have you given any thought to my proposal?"

Bron had to force herself to smile. She decided to go for simpering and brainless. "I have thought of little else."

Since the moment the man who could have been her grandfather had blandly proposed marriage to her, she'd tried to think of anything but that old goat getting his hands on her.

A sly smile crossed his face. "Well, then, shall we announce it tomorrow at the festival?"

"Oh, I don't know about that, sir. I don't think I would make a good mayor's wife. I'm a simple country girl." She'd hoped for more time. She'd rather hoped that the man would find a wife at court who suited him more. He'd spent the last two months there.

He shook his head, reaching for her hand. His were clammy and soft, the hands of a man who'd never done an honest day's work. "Not at all, my dear. You're actually quite well educated. As is your sister. Your manners are far beyond a mere country girl. You have everything required to be an excellent wife for me. Once you've been cleaned up and are in proper attire, you'll be quite pretty. You'll fit right in. And I'm going places, Isolde. I spoke to King Torin himself. Our kingdom is changing. He's bringing us back to our rightful place. The Vampire Government is going to acknowledge Torin as the rightful king."

She was sure she'd turned a bit green. If the Vampire plane acknowledged Torin, the others would follow.

If Micha noticed, he didn't show it, merely continued talking in his most pretentious tone. "King Torin was interested in our province, I tell you. Once he sees how well I enact his new laws, he's going to understand that I should be given a much bigger place in the ruling class. But before I can request a new assignment, I truly must have a wife and family in place."

"I don't think it's a good idea, Mayor." She stammered out the words, not sure how to extricate herself.

His face turned cold, his thin lips nearly disappearing. "Well, you're not supposed to think, are you, dear? Do you know what I think? I think it's odd that a girl your age hasn't married and had children. You're what? Five and twenty?"

She nodded, not wanting to explain that she was actually twenty-seven.

"And your sister is at least ten years older. Odd then that she's avoided marriage." He leaned in, his words a cold chill running down her spine. "Some people around here whisper that your sister hasn't married because she's too busy practicing magic. I don't like that rumor, do you?"

Tears threatened, angry, frightened, utterly impotent tears. "No. I don't like it."

That rumor would get Gillian strung up, and no amount of magic would stop it. Gillian could try, and she might take out a few, but Gillian's magic tended to be more about helping than defending. And no matter how often Bronwyn trained with sword and knife and bow, she couldn't stop the troops by herself.

"Can you think of any way to quell such a rumor?"

Bastard. "I think no one would believe it if her sister married someone as important as the mayor."

He had her in a corner, and he knew it. They would be forced to flee, but not before the harvest. Everything they had was invested in that wheat, and until they had the coins in their pockets, there was nothing to do but agree and pray that planning a wedding took lots of time.

"Excellent." He sat back, completely satisfied. "Pass me one of those lovely sandwiches, dear. And pour me some tea."

Feeling like one of the clockwork dolls her cousin, Dante, had loved to bring her from the Vampire plane, she moved as though wound up and set to a task. Pass sandwich. Pour tea. Don't thrust the knife in his neck.

"See, you do that with such grace. An excellent wife indeed. And I was describing you to the queen. What a beauty. She's eager to meet you, dear. I believe she's planning a visit in the next few months."

She passed him the tea and prayed Gillian found something stronger. She was going to need it. And she was going to need to run. The last thing she could do was meet the queen. Bronwyn had already met her—on the day the she had pledged herself to be Beck and Cian's bondmate. Queen Maris had eagerly entered their uncle's bed.

The mayor chatted on, but Bron prayed for darkness. Sleep was the only place she felt safe.

* * * *

Lach took his seat at the far end of the table, bitterness spreading through his veins.

"Don't." Shim sat down beside him, smoothing over the clean tunic he'd donned for this meeting. "You know why he does it."

King Fergus sat on an ornate throne placed at the middle of the long table. It was the position of honor. This was the room he used to receive his guests. It was a large hall that could hold a banquet or play host to a series of negotiations. Long ago, the twin smaller thrones that should have been set for the princes of the realm had been moved out, leaving room only for the king.

The seats closest to the king were reserved for people in the highest positions. Naturally he and Shim were at the end of the table.

"Father is an idiot. He makes us look weak."

"Because he thinks we are weak." Shim sighed and looked up the table at the host of Fae their father considered more important. Including the Seelie twins. "He thinks we're dying."

For a long time, Lach had thought Shim would die, too. It was unspoken between them, but Shim had never fully regained his previous strength after that fateful night and the long period of a fugue-like sleep that followed.

Maon, the king's seneschal, walked up behind them. He looked down his patrician nose, his voice the tiniest bit shrill. "Because you two *are* bloody dying and you know it. This is a power play. If you give in and take a bondmate, your father will restore your rightful place." He softened a bit. "No one wants to see you here. You should be at his side. Your cousin Julian can bring you a mate within days. Say the word and it will be done."

A bit of Lach's rage quelled. Maon, for all his snobbishness, really was loyal. It would have been easy for a truly ruthless man to let them fade. Maon would likely be king since as far as everyone believed, Gillian was dead and he and Shim would fade. Still Maon pushed them, ever devising new manipulations to force them to take a mate and live. There was only one problem with the scenario.

"We already have a mate." It was the only reply Lach could give.

Maon stood, and his mouth flattened in a derisive frown. "The princess in the tower. Yes, I've heard the tale. And you two wonder why you're relegated to the end of the table. You're lucky he allows you to be here at all. Your minds are going. And tell that damn gnome to keep quiet." He tapped on the table. "Yes, we all know you're here."

Duffy's squeak could be heard through the room.

Maon walked away, taking his place among the important men of the kingdom.

Duffy's head came up. "I tried to sneak in quietly."

Shim scooted over. "It doesn't matter. Come on up. They know you're here."

The gnome huffed as he pulled his body up and into the chair beside Shim. "Don't know as I like the way everyone talks about you."

Lach shrugged. "I do know how I feel, but no one seems to care." He stared at the Seelie twins. They were everything legend would have them be. Perfect in form and function. They looked like twins. Neither of them had a ruined face and everyone took them seriously.

His hand slid over the left side of his face, touching the scarred flesh there. He stole a glance at Shim, who'd gone pale, his eyes sliding away, guilt evident every time Lach reminded him of that terrible day.

"So we're meeting the Host, eh?" Duffy sat forward, watching the door with a fierce look on his face. He'd used the formal name for a group of sluagh. The Host. No one wanted to deal with the damn Host. Duffy's tiny hands clenched into fists. "I think I can handle them. After all, they're nothing but shade, right? Warriors of the Fae should be able to take them down no trouble."

"They're non-corporeal dead, Duffy. I doubt your axe is going to work on them," Shim pointed out.

If Duffy could hoist his axe at all. Lach worried for the gnome. Not because he thought Duffy would flee in a real battle, but rather because he knew he wouldn't. "Let Father handle the sluagh."

Three faces turned, shock alighting on them. The guests around Lach gasped.

"Please, Your Highness," one of them begged. The other two glanced back at the door as though the very fact that Lach had said the name might conjure them up.

Lach shook his head. "I can't bring them down on our heads by saying their name. They're already here, so why don't we act like we're not scared of the buggers." He leaned over to one of the men, a *sidhe* from the village outside the palace. Madden was the king's liaison to the villagers. "Do you know if they came from the caves?"

There had been a nest of sluagh living in the caves by the beach for as long as anyone could remember. They, along with the Planeswalker demons, could slip on and off the planes as they pleased, though none had figured out how. It was a closely held secret. To discover it, one had to become a sluagh, and no one came back from that. Lach glanced down at the box at his feet. It was filled with crap. Trinkets from his travels. A cheap broach he'd picked up, several combs, a set of cards from the Vampire plane. It was a load of junk he'd bought and didn't need, but it would be enticing to the sluagh, who lived for such oddities. He'd meant to offer it to his father, but he'd been told to take his seat.

He supposed no one had need for his negotiation skills.

"I hear they're from the Seelie plane," Madden explained. He threaded his fingers together, glancing back at the door. "They have news."

Shim leaned in. "Why would they help? Sluagh don't take sides."

No. Sluagh took people. They took lives and slaves. They took rotted corpses when they wanted a meal. They did not take sides.

A sudden chill fell across the room like a wave slowly crashing on the shore.

The Host was close. Lach could feel it. A spark of power shimmered through him. Yes, the dead were coming. It was an odd thing, but he felt more comfortable, his body relaxing as though he'd finally found his place. He leaned back, his eyes focused on the door.

Madden shivered. "I don't like this. Perhaps the king should bar the door."

Lach felt a smile on his face. Oh, but he was suddenly hungry. "It wouldn't work. They have no need of doors."

They entered from every wall, their forms gliding through rock and wood as though neither existed. They found the in between spaces and worked their way through. A hundred sluagh it seemed formed from near nothingness. Pale and wraithlike, their bodies showed the way each had died. Wounds on a sluagh were like jewels to a highborn lady, an expression of beauty. Even to the Unseelie, who understood the horrors of the planes, sluagh were monstrous.

And yet, Lach saw an odd beauty to them.

"We seek the king." They spoke as one, their voices sending a fresh wave of chilled air through the hall.

His father stood, along with Beck and Cian Finn. They each nodded to the group of sluagh, not an ounce of fear showing.

"The kings of the Seelie Fae welcome you."

His father nodded as well. "As does the king of the Unseelie."

A single sluagh floated to the front of the crowd that had now moved, coalescing into a single mob. This sluagh had obviously been a *sidhe* at one time, the long lines of his body a dead giveaway. The flesh at his throat was mottled and gnarled, signs of the rope that he had been hanged from.

"The sluagh are grateful that such highborn men would stoop to speak with us. King Beckett and King Cian, you might be the rightful owners of the Seelie throne, but you do not sit upon it. King Fergus, you rule the Unseelie, but we have no use for you." His head whipped around, eyes locking firmly on Lachlan. Every one of the sluagh turned in one motion, a great flock of wicked birds of prey. "We seek the King of the Dead."

Duffy tugged at his tunic. "Damn me, Lach. I think they're talking about you. Should I get me axe?"

"Hush, Duffy." For once Shim sounded serious.

"What are you talking about?" His father's voice boomed through the hall. "Leave my son alone. He isn't well. Guards, take the princes out."

Lach stood. He wasn't about to be hauled out like an idiot child who didn't know his place. He did know where he belonged. He hated it, but the dead called to him. He turned his eyes on the guard coming in. "Touch me and I'll kill you. Once you're dead, I'll take control of your corpse and turn you on everyone you love. Do you understand?"

The head of the guard stopped, his eyes widening. "Prince Lachlan, we must do as your father requests. He is king."

The sluagh leader was suddenly right in Lach's space, a cold whisper across his flesh. "He is not the king of us, Your Highness, and you know this to be true. Your power is not whole yet without your bondmate at your side. Take power from us. We give it willingly. Show them. Show them all."

He looked down at Shim, seeking sound counsel, but his brother's face had turned cold and hard. "I feel it, too, brother, though it is not my power to take. Take it. Show them. 'Tis the only way to prove it."

Ice edged through him, the sluagh pushing death power his way. He could command this. This was no flare of uncontrolled talent. This was raw power, and he was the master. He reached out to call the dead to him.

A loud wail went up. A grunting and then a scream as the boar that had been roasted and laid out on the table for feasting struggled to its legs. A headless fowl, plucked and covered in sauce, unfurled grotesque wings and tried to fly. The group of sluagh shimmered, their bodies humming with power.

"Enough!" His father roared through the hall. "Enough, son."

Lach shut the power off with a wink and a great deal of regret. He could have gone further. He'd felt them all in that moment. He'd felt all the dead things of the palace rising again. He'd felt the animals lying dead in the fields and around the palace courtyard, small and large. He sensed the goblins who had died in a recent sickness. He'd felt the ogre they'd killed but days ago stir. He'd felt them all and realized he could have an army.

And then he'd felt a softer stirring and a gentle whisper.

No, Lachlan. Let the dead rest, son.

His mother. He'd reached out and caught his mother asleep forever in her tomb.

Lach fell back into his seat, his hands shaking with fear. Fear of what he could become.

The sluagh smiled, a ghastly thing. "You begin to see, Your Highness."

His father was suddenly at his side. "What have you done to my son?"

Beck Finn was there, too, studying him. "How has your power manifested without the bond? We were told you refused to bond."

"We bonded long ago, but our mate is trapped on the Seelie plane." Shim stared at the Seelie king, waiting to be laughed at.

"Fuck me, they're powerful," Cian Finn said, his eyes wide. "They couldn't have taken on the full bond, yet they're able to do all of this." He frowned. "Could you leave supper alone next time? I don't think I can eat that thing now."

Lach had to smile a bit. "I'll try."

Beck got to one knee. "They want to deal with you, Prince Lachlan. Can you handle them?"

"Yes. I can handle them. I know them well." He'd always been fascinated by the sluagh. "Duffy, grab the box, please."

The gnome hopped down and retrieved the box filled with trinkets. Gifts for the unshriven dead.

"Go on then." Lach nodded to the sluagh leader.

Duffy flushed, standing there with the box in his small hands. "You want me to give it to him?"

"If you're scared, I'll do it." It was said with a harsh edge. Duffy wanted to be a warrior. A warrior should be able to handle the simple passing of a gift.

The gnome's face firmed into a stubborn pout. "I ain't scared of nothing." He marched to the sluagh and held up his box. "Gifts from the princes."

A wicked smile crossed the sluagh's face as he opened the box. "Treasures. Come and take your part."

The group descended like a pack feasting on a kill. There was shuffling and the pressing of shade to shade, but finally they broke up, each holding some small piece in their hands. And one by one they faded away until only the leader remained.

"You are wise, King of the Dead."

Lach shrugged. It had been a good bet he could thin the herd with a simple gift. "I listen to my people."

"And they will listen to you." The sluagh cocked his head, taking in Cian Finn. "I don't like that one. Send him away."

Cian. The Green Man. Light to his darkness.

"No." Lach wouldn't let a sluagh control this. If he was the King of the Dead, then he was king. He could feel his brother's support. "The Green Man stays. Now, sluagh, I've given you your gifts. I've allowed you to feel my power. Tell me your secrets. It's why you've come."

If there was one thing the sluagh loved more than small trinkets, it was secrets. They listened in, hiding always, to hear the great secrets of the planes, hoarding them like diamonds until the time was right to trade. And then they would whisper, a touch here or there, sending one country into war and suggesting another go down a path that led to famine. Both would benefit the sluagh.

Lach knew he was walking along the razor's edge.

"Torin is gathering power." The sluagh waited.

"Tell me something I don't know." Lach stood again, Shim at his side, moving as one. "Only today the Seelie kings have come with this news. This is nothing I can use. Be gone."

He could feel the sluagh's shock. "I have more, Your Highness."

"Then you should tell me more or I will cast you from my kingdom."

The sluagh frowned. "Fine. We have heard the plans of Torin and his hags. They mean to kill all the non-*sidhe* on their plane and then they will move on to this one. They will attempt to control the Vampire Government with fresh consorts, but each one will be spelled to turn on his or her master when the time is right."

Beck Finn went white. "He's promised a hundred consorts to the royals. He'll bring down the whole plane."

Dante Dellacourt stepped in. "The economic ramifications alone would destabilize us. You're talking about the most powerful vampires on the plane. They control everything. And I doubt they'll believe a damn thing I say. I became an outlaw the minute I chose to leave with Beck and Cian. Perhaps Julian could persuade them."

His cousin looked thoughtful. "I can try, but my influence is small compared to how hungry the royals are for proper consorts. We age without consort blood. Look at Lach and Shim. Look at me. I'm fifteen years older and yet I look younger than they do. This is a royal's birthright, and for thirteen years, Torin has held us hostage. They won't want to listen to reason."

Lach turned back to the sluagh. "There's more, isn't there?"

The sluagh sighed, his whole form moving in a lazy wave. "There's always more, Your Highness."

A long pause. Bloody sluagh. "We'll fill your bellies for a month."

The ogre alone would keep the carrion eaters happy for weeks. Another could be found.

"More, Your Highness."

There would always be more if he didn't take a stand. The sluagh would be greedy.

Shim whispered, his hand cupping his mouth. "There's a reason they're here, Lach. And it's not for corpses. They wouldn't pick a side if it didn't benefit them. Think on it. Devastating the Vampire plane would be good for the sluagh. The Unseelie falling would bring more than enough corpses to feed their armies. Why are they here, then?"

His brother had a point. Lach's mind raced with possibilities, but only one made a lick of sense. "Torin's found a way to kill you, hasn't he?"

The sluagh frowned. "Torin seeks purity of race, and the Host is an abomination."

Now he had them. "Tell me more."

The sluagh sighed, leaned in, and began to speak.

Hours later, Lachlan felt the weight of all the planes on his shoulders. Torin was coming. He wouldn't stop until the planes bowed to him.

The sluagh left, racing away to the caves where his brethren hid. All around him was quiet. The Seelie kings spoke to each other in whispers, Dante at their side. The rest had an air of shock surrounding them.

War was coming.

"Son, you did well." His father sat beside him, his weathered face a mask of care. There was a long pause, as though he didn't wish to broach the subject, but knew he must. "How did you do it? How do you raise the dead? Is it a spell?"

Shim's eyes rolled. "He did it the same way I call forth fire. It's inside him. It's the powers we came into thirteen years ago."

"King Fergus," Beck interrupted. "I may not know the Unseelie, but grant that my brother and I know what it means to be symbiotic twins. Neither Cian nor I had a whisper of power before we bonded. Not a hint."

"Yeah, Beck here told everyone it was a myth," Cian added. "He still owes me a thousand gold on that bet."

The warrior king slapped at the Green Man. "Hush. This is no place for sarcasm. Tell them, Ci."

Cian became serious. "I would bet the kingdom I don't have yet that they've bonded. They're what? Thirty? By the time we turned thirty, we were beginning to fade. These boys aren't close to fading. They're powerful. What happened to your bondmate?"

Lach took a long breath. "She was trapped on the Seelie plane."

Beck nodded. It was probably a story he'd heard before. "She must be strong if you can still feel the bond."

"We've never met her, but we've dreamed of her since we were children." Shim watched the Seelie kings.

The Seelie kings turned to each other, a silent conversation happening in their heads. Lach knew because it happened between him and Shim. After a long moment, Beck looked over, his face tense. "How would you bond with a woman you've never met?"

"I don't know what it was like for you two," Lach admitted. "I only know that since I knew what the word *love* meant, I loved her. She came to me and Shim every night."

"In our dreams." Shim took over. "At first we simply played because we were young. We couldn't hear her. We just felt. She talked. She talked a lot, but we simply felt her presence. It calmed us each night, and we knew she was the one."

Lach remembered those times. Bronwyn had been a comfort even then. "We could see through her eyes. She's a strong broadcaster.

Sometimes, even during the day, Shim can see her. It's how we figured out who she was and where she lives. When we were young, we would see and feel her when her emotions were strong. There was a river by her house. Full of fish. She would swim with her brother, her mother watching on. She would strip down to her shift and throw her body in, a wild cry on her lips. She would look up as she floated on the water and wonder where her other brother was."

Lach was well aware of what he was doing. He was pulling from her memories. He was baiting the Seelie kings. But he had to prove his truth or they could side with his father. Bronwyn had to be saved before the war broke out.

Cian's body had tensed. "Tell me more about her."

Shim seemed to understand what Lach was doing. "She's the loveliest thing in all the planes. Brown hair and brown eyes. A sweet laugh." He turned to Dante. "You pulled her pigtails and called her a brat."

Dante's mouth dropped. "No."

Lach didn't wait for further denials. "We bonded with her on the night she died. We felt it. Shim could see it."

"I saw her run to her mother's room. She was so scared. I tried to reach out, but she'd taken a knife to her gut." Shim's hand drifted to his side, where he'd felt the knife sink into their mate. "She thought she was dead, and then you came, Cian. You held her. You told her you loved her. And she died."

Tears fell from Shim's eyes. He felt it more deeply because he'd been there with her. Lach often wished he'd been there, too, but someone had to ground them all.

Cian shook his head. "She died. Bron is dead. I couldn't save her."

The words slipped easily from Lach's mouth. "But we could."

The Seelie kings stopped, their jaws tensing. Their expressions were utterly identical, pained and haunted and beneath all of it, a breath of hope.

"I don't believe it." Cian finally moved, pacing the floor. He ran a hand through his hair. "I felt it. She was dead. I wouldn't have left my sister. I couldn't. I couldn't have left her."

"I don't understand any of this." His father looked almost as guilty as the Seelies.

Lach felt an ember of hope that they might finally believe him. "We've thought about this a lot. We've talked about it, asked some Fae who know about bonding, some vampires who understand consorts. They think Bronwyn is an incredibly strong broadcaster. I know that any bondmate could balance us, but you know that there's a difference between the bond and that perfect mate. Her mind reached out, even as a child, and she found us. We held to the bond. If Bron is a broadcaster, then Shim is a receptor."

Beck's face was a careful blank. "Let's accept the fact that Bron is alive somehow."

"She's alive," Shim insisted.

"How did you save her?" Dante asked.

Shim shook his head. "I don't know. It's all muddled. I remember feeling her die and grabbing on to Lach."

Lach didn't like to think about that night. It was a nightmare in his head, a collection of fear and pain. "It was the first time our powers manifested."

"The night of the fire," his father whispered, looking at the scars on Lach's face.

"Yes. We all almost died that night." He stared at his father. "We lost her for a long time. That was when we started to fade. We couldn't be sure she was alive. And yet the bond was there. It was like bonding over that distance broke the connection for a while."

Shim sighed. "And then one day, I was sleeping and I felt her at the edge of my consciousness. Every night the connection got stronger, and now I can feel her during the day when I concentrate."

"That's why you seem to be fading. That's why you lie around. You're seeing her." His father sat back and seemed to have aged twenty years. "Do you think she knows what happened to my Gilly?"

This was a piece of information they had withheld. They had thought about it, but with their father not believing them, it seemed cruel to tell him.

"Gillian's alive."

The room erupted in chaos. The news that the Unseelie princess was alive and potentially in danger somewhere on the Seelie plane lit a fire under the nobles' asses. His father sat, taking it all in. There was already talk of a raid, a quiet retrieval mission, even of hiring a hag to contact her. This was another reason they had kept quiet. Until they were ready to rescue their bondmate, they couldn't risk detection, and they worried their father would be reckless, thus costing both women their lives. Amidst all the discussion, the Finn twins walked away, quietly speaking among themselves.

He looked at Shim who nodded, understanding what they needed to do.

They stood up, moving toward the Seelies. It was time to talk to their brothers-in-law.

Even before they'd made it to the Finns, Cian Finn turned, walking their way with an angry look on his face.

"Why the hell haven't you said something before now?" Cian got right in Lach's space.

Lach had no intentions of letting the Green Man intimidate him. "Should I have walked around informing everyone that Bronwyn Finn is alive? Do you think that wouldn't have gotten back to Torin?"

Beck seemed calmer, but there was a cold look in his eyes. "You could have told us. We both have relatives on the Vampire plane. We've probably been in the same city at the same time, and yet you kept this a secret."

"We told our father," Shim argued. "Not her name because we understood the danger to her, but we explained the situation, and he refused to believe. If you hadn't seen what Lach could do tonight, you wouldn't have believed it, either."

"You bloody well could have tried," Cian spat.

"Tell me something, Prince Lachlan," Beck began with lazy menace. "Does my sister know she's a princess of the Unseelie Fae?"

There it was, that churning in the pit of Lach's belly. "The connection is difficult to explain."

"Yes, you seem to have that trouble a lot," Cian accused.

Shim was getting angry, his hands twitching. When Shim got angry, fireballs tended to descend from out of nowhere.

"Shim, calm down. Torching our brothers-in-law won't make the situation better."

His ever-more-reasonable brother smiled grimly. "It will make me feel better."

"I'd love to see you try it," Cian ground back.

Beck managed a laugh. "He's my calm half."

A kinship opened between them. "Shim is my happy half. I'm a righteous bastard."

"Well, I'm all sunshine and daisies," Beck replied, his expression relaxing. "Cian, stop overreacting. I understand how you feel, but you know damn well that I wouldn't have taken a meeting with the Unseelie until very recently."

"It wasn't like I didn't try," his father said, joining them. "I would have tried harder if I'd listened to my sons."

A fracture started in Lach's stubbornness. He knew it was coming from Shim, but he welcomed it. Being angry with his father hadn't gotten them anywhere.

"I still would have resisted," Beck Finn admitted. "Until we found our Meggie, we were the ones who were fading. I couldn't consider any sort of an alliance. It wouldn't have worked, and then I was only concerned with bonding with Meggie and keeping her safe."

"You can't hide anymore." The quiet statement came from Dante Dellacourt, who looked so much more serious than the entertainments on the Vampire plane had made him out to be. Lach never would have expected the vampire to give up everything to follow his cousins on what was likely a lost cause.

It can't be lost. It can't. Not yet. After he and Shim had gotten their bondmate out of Tír na nÓg, then it could all go to hell, but not before then. After Bronwyn was safe in the Dark Palace, the Seelie plane could rot for all he cared. They would close the Unseelie plane and live in peace. Let the other planes duke it out. This wasn't Lach's fight.

"I know I can't hide, Dante," Beck allowed. "The time has come." He turned back to Lach and Shim. "We were talking to your father about the plan Dante's come up with. In a week and a half, a formal group of ambassadors from the Vampire plane will be welcomed into Tír na nÓg. That means Torin has to open the plane."

Torin's hags had managed to shut off Tír na nÓg for over thirteen years. Some managed to sneak in or out. There were always cracks a smart Fae could slip through, but not an army, and that's what the Seelie twins would need. But if the magical walls were down, a crack in the veil that held the plane closed could be widened by a decent enough witch. Then a small force could get through. What had his father promised them?

"You intend to raid Tír na nÓg?" Lach kept his voice measured.

Cian took a deep breath, obviously calming himself. "We have to. Single assassins haven't done the trick. We tried that at first, and Torin always finds them."

Lach's father answered that one. "It's the hags. It's why sneaking you into Tír na nÓg won't work."

Dante agreed. "It's like a magical alarm system. At some point in time, Torin stole hair or blood from both of you. It contains your signature, like a scent to a wolf. The minute you step on the plane, Torin will know. So when it happens, it has to happen fast, because Torin will be ready."

William Roan, the vampire mercenary, stepped forward. "That's what I'm here for. I can sneak onto the plane and start gathering Fae supporters. I've been running small missions on the plane for years, gathering consorts for wealthy royals. It's been a small operation, nothing that could truly gain the pretender's eye, but I've made many allies. There's a network of Fae waiting to join the true kings when the time comes. Tomorrow, I'll take a small squad and begin rallying the troops. By the time we meet up, the kings will have the army they need. Including, we hope, a contingent of Unseelie."

Lach was about to point out the problems with that plan when Shim leaned forward. "We'll go with Roan. We'll find Bron and Gilly and bring them back."

"I don't think that's such a good idea," his father said. "I don't know that I want all of my children on that plane. It's too dangerous."

"And the plane is huge," Cian pointed out. "You could walk for days and never come close to her. Do you have any idea where she is?"

Shim's eyes went a little unfocused. He spoke, but not to anyone in particular. "She lives in a tower. It looks out over long fields of wheat. She works there, her hands pulling and plucking, working the plow."

Lach watched as Beck paled at the thought of his sister working in the fields like a commoner. Lach could tell Beck that there was still nothing common at all about Bronwyn Finn.

"It's almost always hot," Shim continued. "Lately when I reach her and I can see through her eyes, she's preparing for the harvest. Tomorrow there's a festival of some type. Bron helped put up a pole, and there are colored ribbons on the top. What do you think they'll do with those?"

"She's in the Tuathanas District. It's an agriculture district. They grow much of our wheat and the Festival of Threshing is celebrated with a maypole. The children of the villages dance around it. There is much merrymaking." Cian looked at his brother, a smile growing on his face. "It's perfect. It's quiet and rural and days from the palace. No one would dream of looking for her there. Or think anything of men on the road at that time of year. Many traders are on the road. Goddess, Beck, do you really think she's alive?"

"She's alive," Lach insisted. "And we're going to get her out of there before the war begins."

Beck nodded. "Yes. We have to put our plans aside. We have to save our sister, your sister."

Dante's mouth firmed. "No. Absolutely not."

Beck turned on his cousin, but Julian Lodge stood at Dante's side. "I agree with Dellacourt. You're not seeing the big picture."

"Our sister already survived one war. She shouldn't have to do it again," Beck insisted.

"We can't leave her there." Cian stared at the vampires.

The vampire mercenary stepped forward. "You won't get another shot at this, Your Highnesses. I know that negotiations will take a while, but if you allow the vampires to enter a full alliance with Torin, he'll have access to all their technology. Think about it. Do you want to go up against a guard armed with sonic weapons when you have a band of peasants at your back? Even waiting a month could be dangerous."

"It won't take us a month," Lach insisted. "All we need is a few days to get ready."

"I'll leave today," Shim promised.

Julian shook his head. "She's my niece, too, but we can't risk it."

"She's our sister," the kings said in one voice.

"And she's a princess of the realm. You can't have it both ways," Dante said, his face harsh. "You have to choose, cos. Choose now. You can be kings or you can be quiet family men who put their sister first."

Beck went red, whether with rage or shame, Lach couldn't tell. "You know I can't do that. Torin won't allow it."

Dante jumped on the words. "Then your choice was already made.

Damn it, Beck, it was made the moment you were born. You are not an ordinary man. I know it's unfair that you're not able to think of your family first, but you have a kingdom relying on you."

"More than a kingdom," Julian said quietly. "All of the planes are at risk. You didn't ask for this, Your Highness, but it is your burden to bear. The question is will you bear it or should we find another to take your place? I know I, for one, will not allow the planes to fall because your heart is too tender for the task."

A loud clap of thunder shook the walls of the palace. A storm was gathering outside, and it sounded brutal. Even the floor seemed to shake a bit. Lightning lit the windows, electrifying the sky. Rain began to beat on the roof though moments before there hadn't been a cloud in the sky. It seemed the rumors were true, and the warrior king could call the storms to his aid.

"Now who's overreacting?" Cian said with a hint of a smile. "You know they're right, brother. We can love Bron all we want, but we're killing her if we don't take our throne. We'll get our crown back or we will die. There are no other options. The time has come, and I welcome it. I want it to be over with so we can settle down with our Meggie."

"Or we'll settle her into a grave," Beck said, his voice tight. The rain softened, lessening to a gentle pattering on the roof.

"This life or another, we'll be with her," Cian said on a sigh. The kings of the Seelie Fae stood together for a long moment, their brotherhood apparent.

Beck nodded. He brought his deep gray eyes up to catch Lach's. "You'll go then. I don't really have to ask you, do I? You'll do it because she's your bondmate."

His father stood, a hand on his forehead. "I cannot let my heirs go. I love my daughter. The idea that my Gilly is alive fills me with joy, but I can't sacrifice my heirs. I will send others."

Julian put a hand on his uncle's shoulder. "Then Lach and Shim will find another way, and they will be alone."

Julian knew them well. Lach's mind was already working. Now that they knew where she was, there would be no holding them back. Shim would follow him. They would get on that plane one way or another. "We're going to find her, Father. You can't stop us."

"We will have her," Shim said, his voice deeper than before. His fangs had come out, and for once his brother looked savage.

If the evidence of their vampire half bothered the Seelies, they didn't show it.

"Save our sister," Cian requested.

A wild thrill went through Lach. Yes, the time had come. For the Seelies to face their fate and for him to meet his mate.

Chapter Three

Night fell, creeping across the fields like a mouse edging away from a predator. The shadows grew across the wheat until all was darkness, with only the silvery moonlight to illuminate the swaying crops.

Bron sat in her tower, overlooking what was left of her kingdom.

"We've been in tougher spots, you know." Gillian walked into the room, a fresh quilt in her hands. The days were still hot, the sun branding everything in its path, but the nights were beginning to cool.

Bron would be so warm between her Dark Ones. They would never allow the cold to seep into her bones. She stared at her bed, almost time to sink into sleep and a world where she was loved.

"I know." Bron answered Gillian, not wanting the older woman to understand her impatience to be abed.

Gillian placed the quilt down and stared for a moment as though assessing the situation. "Do you want to run now?"

It was a kindness to even offer. Bron forced her attention to the here and now. She owed Gillian much more than her life. "We have to have coin. I know that. I can handle Micha. He's a nasty old man, but I can manipulate him."

Gillian sat on the edge of the bed, her hands in her lap. "I tried to turn his eye to me so you wouldn't have to."

Bron rushed to her side. "Gilly, don't. I can handle him."

Gillian was so still, Bron thought she wouldn't say another word. "He didn't even look at me. Not that I wanted him to, but still. I know I'm not a youngling anymore, but I thought I had some charm."

Too, too often she sank into her own grief and forgot how much Gillian had given up for her. Gillian had lost her own kingdom. She'd been cut off from it as surely as if someone had taken it. All doors had closed because Gillian hadn't left her behind. She'd given up her youth. What would have happened if she'd been safe on the Unseelie plane when Torin had started his nasty game? Would she be married by now? Have a child?

She let her hand drift over Gillian's, feeling the calluses and scars that hadn't existed before she'd saved a dead princess. Her voice choked with emotion. "I think you're the most beautiful woman in all the planes."

Unshed tears made Gillian's dark eyes shine. "You haven't seen much, little one."

Bron shook her head. "I've seen enough to know I love you very much."

Gillian hugged her, a tight embrace. "And I love you. You understand that whatever I did, whatever reason I did it, I have come to love you, Bronwyn. I would place you first now."

"Why did you do it?"

Gillian sat back, taking a long breath. "I thought if I saved you, you could bring the kingdoms together. I intended to talk to my father and marry you off to my brothers."

A part of Bron was offended, but it was the childish bit that clung to shadowy vestiges of her former life. She was more practical now. "I was only fourteen at the time. I'm not sure I would have made a decent wife."

"Had I gotten you off the plane, you would have been brought up to be an Unseelie princess. I would have seen to it, and your brothers would have been welcomed. They would have had a place until such time as an army was ready. We weren't always two tribes, you know."

It was radical what Gillian proposed. "That was thousands of years ago."

"I know. I wasn't trying to unite the crowns, merely to have a closer relationship. We fight far too often. In the end, it will make us vulnerable. I've studied this plane called Earth. They are much like the vampires, though they've been closed off for so long, they don't understand the way the planes work anymore. I don't know they ever did. They do understand what it means to conquer. When the humans discover our secrets, I doubt they'll be content to leave us be. We will need each other. Whether it's tomorrow or a thousand years from now, we will need to stand together if we're to survive."

Gillian always thought ahead. It was, she claimed, the mark of a true leader.

"The humans could certainly take us now," Bron said with a sigh. "Is that why you were here in the first place? To negotiate a marriage?"

"I tried to negotiate a marriage between myself and your brothers," Gillian admitted. "I am capable of bonding, just as you are. I could have bridged the kings. But your father had already selected a bondmate."

Bron's nose wrinkled. "I think if Cian had known you were trying to push Maris out, he would have sent her over the edge of the moat. He couldn't stand her, and she hated him. I always wondered what Father was thinking selecting a mate who hated one of her proposed husbands. You would have been a better choice. Do you think they bonded?"

Gillian's mouth turned down. "I've heard rumors."

Bron leaned forward. "And you didn't tell me?"

"I didn't want to get your hopes up, and it could all be peasant rabble-rousing. We have no way of knowing. They say the kings have bonded and formed a true triad."

She sat back, her head spinning with the thought. A true triad. It was a legend. The story went that when a pair of symbiotic twins found their perfect mate, they came into godlike powers. In the past, some could call water to their aid, walking on it and forming huge waves to crush their enemies, while others had the power to talk to all manner of beast, building an army of predators. But it was merely a legend. If it had happened before, it was so long ago no one on either of the planes could remember it. Surely it was merely a rumor. Symbiotic twins were rare and powerful, but they couldn't control the elements.

Some could call forth the dead, bringing them back to life when his power merged with fire.

A chill crossed her skin. Where had that thought come from?

She shook it off. It didn't matter. "I pray the rumors are correct and that Beck and Cian have found their mate. I don't believe the true triad stuff. All I want is my brothers alive and happy and safe."

She hoped they were out there, perhaps on the Vampire plane with their cousin Dante, enjoying life. They didn't know she was alive. It was better that way. They could have their family without risking themselves. Even as the thought crossed her mind, she knew Torin wouldn't allow it. As long as Beck and Ci drew breath, he would plot to kill them. He had to.

And she had to stay alive. Because in the end, her brothers would be forced to come back to Tír na nÓg one way or another. She took a deep breath, the cool night air filling her lungs. That was a battle for another day.

"I'll deal with Micha. He'll want a grand wedding. He's intent on inviting the queen herself." Maris. Bron's fist clenched. Maris, the betrayer. Over the years, Bron had come to understand that Maris had been the one to open the palace gates and allow Torin's marauders in. Maris, who had pledged to love her brothers. Maris, whose corpse Bron intended to see tossed over her husband's.

Gillian stood, seemingly satisfied with that bit of news. "Excellent. A wedding like that will take months to plan. We can sell our crops and disappear. Perhaps a seaside province this time. I've long wanted to try my hand with a fishing net."

So she would be learning another skill. Well, she did enjoy a challenge. "We'll have the most profitable boat in no time."

Gillian nodded and left. Bron's heart raced a bit as she got under the covers and snuffed out her candle. She settled into the firm straw mattress, wiggling around until she was as comfortable as she was likely to be.

Moonlight streamed in, casting everything with a silvery glow. Bron closed her eyes and prayed for sleep.

* * * *

She walked into the room, white marble under her feet. This was the White Palace, her home. She knew it, even years later. It played in the back of her mind that it was probably different now. Thirteen years of Torin's rule had undoubtedly changed the place, but in her dreams, the palace was still her sunny home, unchanged, undimmed by faulty memory.

She turned her face up. This was the sunshine room. Oh, her mother called it the waiting room, where she and her ladies sat and sewed and chatted, but Bronwyn called it the sunshine room because it was always filled with light.

A familiar shape moved just outside of the light's reach. This shape hid in shadows.

Her Dark Ones.

"Are you coming out?" Bron called, teasing them a bit. She caught sight of one and then the other, their forms clinging to the edge of the light.

"Why don't you come back in?" They spoke in one voice, a slight echo in the words.

It was always this way. Come morning, she knew she would wonder why she never sat down and talked to them, but caught in the dream, she simply did what felt right.

They didn't love the light the way she did, but they would wait for her. She turned her face up to the sun, letting it warm her. The sun felt different here. In her village, it was always so hot during the summers, but at the palace the sun was a soft kiss on her skin, warming her gently.

"We can kiss you better than the sun. Come here."

She smiled, not looking their way yet. They grew surer and more dominant with each night. It was hard to believe that they had come to her as children. She'd been five and so shy of the boys who had called out to her in dreams.

She wanted to play with them now but not as children.

Her nipples tightened against the soft silk of her gown.

"If you don't come to us, we'll be forced to get you, sweetheart. It might not go well for you," the more dominant voice said.

"He's itching to spank you, love. Give him a reason." This second voice was gentler, but there was no mistaking his interest.

Nor hers. She could explore everything in these dreams, and lately, her interests had taken a distinctly disciplinary tone. She wondered if they would truly spank her. She wondered how it would feel.

"Yes, and you'll love it."

She felt a strong hand at her wrist and the scene changed. She was no longer in the palace, but some dark place where the marble at her feet was black and the room was dominated by an enormous bed draped with curtains.

Her Dark Ones stood by the bed. Twins. So alike she hadn't been able to tell them apart at first, but then she'd assigned them numbers. One was the rougher of the twins, though his hands were always gentle on her skin. Two had a sweet smile and liked to talk dirty.

"Where are we?" she asked.

One's brows rose. "We are where I want us to be. In our home. In our bed."

Never answers. She'd grown accustomed. They were dressed identically in dark leather pants. Those clothes were unlike anything in Tír na nÓg. The leather they made here didn't have the supple feel of the twins' clothes.

"You're beautiful tonight," Two said with a long sigh. "But I would love to see more of you."

One's eyes narrowed. "I thought we explained this before. You don't need garments around your men. You need only your own sweet skin."

She crossed her arms over her breasts. "You have no problem with pants, I see."

One's lips curved up in a wicked smile, his satisfaction a palpable thing. "A bratty mouth will bring you nothing but trouble, sweetheart."

He used that word often. *Brat.* She remembered her cousin calling her a brat when they were young. He would pull her pigtails lightly and laugh and call her *brat.* It was a phrase from the Vampire plane to speak of sweetly disobedient girls.

"I don't see why I should be naked when the two of you are clothed." She could feel the smile on her face. Her dreams had become more and more sensual in nature. In the last several years, since the dreams had flared back to life, each night they went a bit further. It had started with an embrace, their arms wrapping around her when she'd realized they were once again with her. Those dreams had been little flashes she couldn't seem to hold on to no matter how hard she tried. She'd clung to One and Two until they faded. Then gradually each had become more solid, the dreams lasting longer.

That was when the kissing had begun. What kisses they were. Long, slow kisses that seemed to last for hours. Only lips at first, and then One had boldly traced her lips with his tongue.

One was suddenly in front of her, his eyes warm as though he could read her thoughts. His hand came up, tracing her lips as his tongue had. "You like kissing."

"I like kissing you." She went up on her tiptoes, leaning in to brush her mouth against his.

He backed away, frowning. "Me? Who else do you kiss?"

She felt her eyes roll. Even in her dreams, men were difficult. "I'm twenty-seven years old. I have been caught by roving hands and held down for unwanted kisses. There isn't a peasant alive who hasn't suffered worse than me. I've had my guardian to protect me. Count yourself lucky that Gillian isn't in my dreams, for you would find yourself unable to kiss me."

"I think your guardian would show favor to our suit," Two said from behind her.

Bron sighed. She loved being surrounded by them. One moved back in, his hand cupping her cheek.

"I don't want another's hand on you," he said, his eyes serious.

She began to pull away because she wasn't about to take that, not even in a dream. "I am a virgin, but I'm not without the experience of a man nearly taking from me that which is mine to give. If it had happened, you would not touch me. Leave me be. I'll seek another dream."

He pulled her close. "Stop, brat. I didn't say that. I said I didn't want another's hand on you. You're ours. Our love, our heart. You can't expect us to be happy with such a thing." He tangled a hand in her hair. "I hate that we are not able to protect you."

She hated that they were not real. She wasn't stupid. They were a projection of her own needs. When she'd been a child, she'd needed companionship, and the Dark Ones had been there for her. Now, she needed love and protection, and her soul cried out for a lover she couldn't take. And her Dark Ones were here for her. They were her dream and her nightly refuge.

She sighed and relaxed, letting her hands slide on his muscular chest. His skin was warm and smooth, covering corded muscle. One was so overwhelming. Two was softer. She needed them both, but now she craved One's dominance. Her life was so out of control.

She wanted their touch.

"Kiss me," she said.

One frowned down at her. "You sound like a princess when you say that. Do you think you can order me around, Princess? Do you think I'm your slave?"

Two kissed the back of her neck, causing her to shiver. She couldn't be sure, but she would almost swear she felt the lightest scrape of something sharp along her skin. "I damn well am her slave, brother."

One reached out and smacked his twin's head. "Don't give up my game, brother. We both know who's in charge, but when we're bedding her, it's going to be us in the lead." He stared down at her, his deep, dark eyes pulling at her. "Princess, we're going to be your Masters in the bedroom. Do you understand what that means?"

"You want me to be a slave?" The term rankled.

"I want you to be the submissive partner, Princess. It's the way relationships work where we come from. There's a Dominant partner or partners and a submissive. It means we're to take care of you in all things."

What did it say about the enormous responsibilities of the last thirteen years of her life that when she fantasized about a relationship, it was with men who wanted to take the lead? Still, she couldn't let all of her control go. Not even in a dream.

"I can let you take the lead in this, but know I'm still my own woman."

He chuckled lightly. "I wouldn't have you any other way. You wouldn't be alive today if you were less of a woman than you are."

It was true, and she didn't want to think about any of that right now. She didn't want to think about the fact that she had to deal with the mayor tomorrow. The festival would be crowded enough that she could avoid him until she absolutely had to stand beside him and announce their engagement. She would play the demure fiancée and plead the harvest to keep from his company. As soon as the money was in Gillian's hands, they would disappear.

Micha was a momentary problem. Her Dark Ones were more important.

"All right then, you should tell me what you want me to do. You seemed to have enjoyed kissing me before." She directed her question to One since Two was once again preoccupied. His hands smoothed over her shoulders and down her arms as his mouth was again on the nape of her neck. The heat of his body surrounded her, and she could feel something hard pressed against her lower back.

His male part. His cock. She'd heard the village women giggle as they talked of their husbands and lovers. They often spoke of cocks and how much pleasure a cock could bring. Bron had watched the animals mate in the fields, but the women around her told her that making love to a man was very different.

This certainly felt different.

She rubbed back against Two.

"Hey. Don't you forget me." One pressed in, trapping her between their massive, muscular bodies. She was deliciously crushed in between them. "And I love kissing you. We both do. Now calm down and let us take control. We're getting closer. Can you feel it?"

Something did feel different. Their voices were stronger than before. Where they used to whisper, now they spoke in strong tones. Where the touches and caresses had once been light and soft as a spring breeze, they felt solid and real to her.

"I feel it. I want you here with me." She wanted to never wake up. She wanted to sink so far into the dream that it became her reality. Then she wouldn't have to worry about killing Torin or saving her people. She wouldn't have to find a place to hide Mags and Ove. She wouldn't have to plot ways to keep Micha's hands off her. She could simply be their submissive.

One kissed her, his lips strong against her own. She shivered when she felt his tongue trace the seam of her lips at the exact moment Two's fingertips began to pull down the bodice of her gown. The silky fabric skimmed her skin, and she opened for One's invasion. One kissed her like a ravenously hungry man, his mouth slanting over hers again and again. He rubbed his tongue along hers, a slow, silky slide that heated her whole body.

She felt it again, that slight flash of something sharp nipping at her flesh, but it was gone in an instant. Cool air kissed her breasts as Two worked the bodice to her waist.

One's head came up, and he stared down at her now-bare breasts.

It was only the second time she'd been naked in a dream, and in the first she'd been awakened by the damn rooster. She prayed dawn was far away.

"You're so beautiful," One said, his voice husky.

"So fucking gorgeous," Two whispered into her ear. "Think about how lovely these beauties will be when we dress them up."

Big, strong hands cupped her breasts, offering them up to One, who reached out and began to play with her nipples. She whimpered as he pinched them.

"That's right, love. That's a sweet sound." He rolled the nipples between his thumbs and forefingers. He would gently tug and then punctuate it with a sharp, stinging pinch that sent shivers of arousal to her pussy. Her nipples tightened, and her every inch of skin began to come alive. "It sounds like the princess likes our games, brother."

"She'll like the jewels I'll pick out for her nipples, too." Two nipped at her ear. "You'll be a good girl, won't you? You'll let your Masters dress you up. We'll bind you and hold you down for our pleasure. We'll pierce these gorgeous nipples and play with the rings."

"I don't know about that last bit." It was normal in some provinces, but she wasn't sure about it. Still, it was just a dream. "Maybe. Who knows what I'll let you do if you take care of me the way you've promised."

"Still making demands." One rubbed his nose against hers, the affection in the gesture making her heart skip. "I can't wait to feel the flat of my hand on your ass."

Two groaned behind her. "And I can't wait to sink my fangs in you."

She stopped. "Fangs?"

She would never dream of her Dark Ones with fangs. She'd never thought of them in anything but a funny way. Dante had fangs. Her husband would be *sidhe*, not a vampire. She stopped and tried to pull away.

"Hey." Two's hands tightened on her hips.

"Let me go." What the hell was happening? This wasn't her waking dream. When she thought about her Dark Ones, they were *sidhe*. They had some power, perhaps gentry royals. They would be her brothers' loyalists. They would help the cause.

They wouldn't be vampires.

"What's wrong?" One had tightened up, every muscle in his body taking on a tension.

It didn't matter. This was her fantasy, and she could utterly ignore anything she wasn't sure about. "Nothing. Touch me."

The fingers on her nipples tightened to the right side of pain. "You keep pushing me, brat. It makes me want to turn you over my knee."

Again, a very vampire-like attitude. It was okay. She'd loved her cousin, Dante. She'd adored her aunt and uncle and spent time on the plane. If she thought about it, she rather believed that it was where her brothers were, safe and sound with the Dellacourts. It was only predictable that she dream of vampires. Vampires wouldn't have to deal with Torin. Vampires were safe on their own plane.

It didn't matter. All that mattered was pleasure.

"Turn me over your knee, then," she said. "Just touch me. Any way you want."

One smiled, his lips turning up slightly. "Tell her what you want to do, brother."

Two's hands found her hips, pulling her back against his cock. "I want to eat you, love."

"What?" She wasn't sure how to take that. Was her dream becoming a nightmare?

One snorted, though he managed to make it sound regal. "Little virgin. He's talking about licking and sucking on your pussy. He wants to taste you."

She wasn't an idiot. She'd listened in on the women of the village. Peasant women were much more willing to talk than her former friends and handlers at the palace. The villagers could be bawdy and boisterous, and when a bit of ale was introduced, they could be very honest around a woman of marriageable age. She understood what he wanted. Yes, she wanted to try that.

"All right." The minute the words left her mouth, she was scooped up into Two's arms, and he began to walk toward the big bed.

She cuddled up against his massive chest. She felt small and fragile. She knew she wasn't. The last thirteen years had proven that beyond a shadow of a doubt, but it was so nice to feel protected and cherished even if it was only a dream.

He placed her on the bed. Somehow One had gotten there first. Two laid her down against One. Strong arms wrapped around her, the heat of his chest at her back. He nuzzled her cheek, kissing her lightly. His arms tightened around her.

"Stay still, love. Let my brother have his treat. He's waited so long to taste you." The words were hot on her skin.

Two pulled at the silk of the gown she wore, hauling it down her body until she was naked in front of them. She knew she would be horrified if this happened in her reality, but in the dream she felt sexy and beautiful. She loved the way Two stared down at her, his eyes widening as he took in her body.

She was perfect in this dream. She was soft, and her breasts were full. She was curvy the way beautiful royals were. Somehow her mind filled out her form to what it should have been. In the harsh light of day, she was typical of a woman who plowed fields for her existence. She wasn't gaunt, but she wasn't filled out the way a princess would be. She was a peasant and she looked it, but here she was everything she'd dreamed of being.

"You're so lovely." Two's fingers skimmed over her skin.

And they were amazing. Dark hair and eyes. Perfect faces with sharply masculine features. They were everything she could have dreamed of.

Two caught her ankles and very gently forced her legs apart.

"Leave them there." One whispered the command in her ear, his hands tweaking her nipples.

Two climbed on the bed looking like a big predatory cat. He got to his belly, his mouth hovered right over her pussy. "Can you smell her, brother?"

"She smells like she wants it," One replied. "Do you want it, Princess? Do you want my brother to shove his tongue deep inside you? Do you want him to taste every inch of your pussy? To stroke your clit until you come?"

73

"Yes." A simple answer, but it came from her soul. She wanted more than the orgasm. She wanted to feel connected to them, to sink so far into them that she never had to feel alone. She wanted this time when she could be Bronwyn again.

Bron gasped as his warm tongue slipped over her flesh. Her pussy lit up, beginning to pulse as blood rushed through her system. It was so intimate, so beautiful. She could feel her whole pussy soften. She was coming alive under his touch. She writhed as he drew his tongue over her clitoris.

Fingers tightened on her nipples, erotic pain flaring, making a sharp contrast to the soft pleasure at her core.

"You stay still. You don't want him to stop, do you? He'll stop, and we'll have to discipline you. If you don't behave, you'll feel the flat of my hand on that perfect ass of yours and then you'll suck us both and get nothing in return."

Despite the fact that everything inside her tightened at the thought of having One spank her, she didn't want to lose Two's tongue on her pussy. She was close, so close to something she'd never felt before. She'd played with herself, found comfort in masturbating, but this was something completely different. This was a massive quake where before she'd managed a gentle shaking. This was something utterly new.

One tortured her nipples while Two lashed her pussy with his tongue. Bron whimpered and cried, trying to float over the edge, but they kept it up. Two's tongue danced all over her pussy, lighting her up but never spending enough time to force her over that ever-elusive edge. Two gently pulled back the petals of her pussy, licking and sucking every inch of her flesh.

"You taste so good." The words seemed to sink into her skin. She felt his nose running over her pussy.

And then he speared her, his tongue fucking into her as his cock would. While he pierced her with his tongue, he pressed on her clit, and she went flying.

* * * *

She came awake with a cry of joy on her lips.

74

Bronwyn sat straight up in bed, her chest heaving as she tried to drag air into her lungs. Her hands were shaking, her nipples still peaked and wanting.

Tears leaked out of her eyes.

She was awake, and they were gone once more.

Loneliness swept across her. She could still feel their hands on her, but she was alone. Brutally, painfully alone.

She stared out into the star-filled night and prayed for sleep to take her once more.

* * * *

Torin Finn stood on the balcony of his palace, trying not to let the screams and cries get to him. Normally the wailing of the condemned was simply a sign that all was right in his kingdom, but today the sound seemed to have actual weight and motion, pushing at him. He had a fucking headache from that damn noise.

Why couldn't traitors die more quietly? Did they truly have to scream every time they were stabbed or cut or had their fingernails pulled from their bodies?

He sighed. It was because they were unworthy. They were not *sidhe*. *Sidhe* died properly. Even his own brother had died with a quiet dignity, his bright gray eyes widening as the sword went through his heart. Seamus Finn had died as a king should, with rage in his eyes and no cry on his lips.

Yes, his brother had died well.

"I'm glad I did one thing right."

Torin's stomach turned. Fuck, he wished his brother would go away. Thirteen years and his brother was still here, still a shade who managed to whisper in his ear.

"Shut up, Seamus. Why didn't you leave with your brethren?" The sluagh were gone. He'd had his guards check the caves near the palace. It was most likely a bad sign. Somehow they had heard of his plans to destroy them, but the one thing he had been happy about was the fact that his fucking dead brother would be gone, too. No such luck.

"I didn't become sluagh to join the happy family. When I died, I sent my wife on, but tied myself to this place until such time as you no longer breathe air." Seamus's form shimmered, a sure sign that he was emotional. Even then, his voice remained a hoarse whisper. "I chose to stay here because I owe my children."

Torin sighed. He'd heard this all before. Roughly three years after his successful coup, Seamus had shown up, having stored enough energy to make himself known. At first, Torin had thought he was going insane. Those around him still believed he was. Seamus was excellent at hiding from all others.

Seamus liked to show up at the worst times. When Torin was giving a speech, he'd catch visions of his brother's form. When he made love to his wife, Seamus stood and watched, those flint-gray eyes filled with judgment.

Torin hated his brother. Just like when he was alive, Seamus ruined everything simply by being around.

"My hags are going to make sure you never come back. They're working on it now. The blood of traitors will banish you to the underworld, and then I won't have to see you or listen to you prattle on ever again."

Seamus laughed. "I'll believe it when I see it. Even if you found a way to get rid of me, you can't get rid of the me who lives inside you, Torin. That piece of me will never fade until you join me in death."

Torin feared Seamus was right. Guilt weighed heavily on him, but he couldn't go back. He was too close to finishing off those annoying boys. The Vampire Government had declared them criminals. The word was that Beck and Cian had fled the Vampire plane and were seeking asylum elsewhere. Once they were caught and their bodies and that of the bitch they'd bonded to were hanged in the city square, the rebels would know all hope was gone.

Then he would take out all non-*sidhe* one by one if he had to. Including those disgusting, blood-drinking vampires.

All he had to do was kill two men.

"As long as they're out there, you aren't safe." Seamus seemed to be able to read his mind. His brother leaned against the marbled wall of the palace balcony, his ghostly eyes going out over the city. Beyond, Seamus could surely see the fires that had been set in the country in an attempt to quell the current insurrection. "These are small uprisings run by peasants. What would you do if one of the nobles gave the rebels someone real to rally behind? You didn't kill all of those with royal blood. The rebellions will almost surely continue since you don't know the first thing about running a country. Peasants don't like it when you steal all the food and leave them with nothing."

Torin's fists clenched. "Traitors. They're lucky I leave them alive."

Seamus's head shook. "Oh, brother, you've put them in the position where they have to choose between the king and their own lives—and the lives of their children. A king's worth is in protection and shelter, and you offer neither. You're a tyrant. It's why Father chose me over you."

Their father had chosen Seamus over the eldest, rightful heir. Torin had been forced to bite his tongue and plot revenge for twenty fucking years. "Our father was an idiot who would have had us make friends with the monsters. As you would. You were seriously thinking about a marriage between the Unseelie and your daughter. It's a good thing I did what I did or she would have been tortured beyond anything a girl should have to survive."

Seamus snorted. "You call all non-*sidhe* creatures Unseelie. It's ridiculous. There are plenty of *sidhe* who are considered Unseelie. And many helpful races who are as Seelie as me."

"The Unseelie are all half-breeds. Impure. Unworthy. I have plans for them." As soon as he'd dealt with the royal vampires, he would handle the Unseelie. Within mere months, he would rule three planes. Ambition burned bright inside him. He wouldn't stop until every *sidhe* bowed to him and his name was glorified for ridding the world of monsters.

A low wail pierced the night. Would the hags never be done?

"You allow a single incident to color your life, Torin. It was one group of goblins and trolls who nearly killed you," Seamus pointed out.

Torin turned away. He didn't think about the day. He didn't think about how the small band of monsters had delighted in beating him and making him bleed. "Well, I think they would all pause before attempting to harm me again."

"You're a big man, oh yes. King Torin kills brownies and gnomes." Disdain dripped from his brother's voice.

"Yes, and you embraced them all." Torin turned back to the ghost of his brother. "You were so fucking kind. You beat your own child."

If a sluagh could pale, Seamus did it. His form faded a bit. "I thought I was helping him. I thought I was correcting his bad behavior as our father corrected mine. I see things differently now. This side allows for a full accounting of all that is true if one is open to it. I hate you for killing my wife, but one good thing came from it. Beck was freed from my rigid morality. He can become the man he always should have been, and Cian can get over my ignorance. And they're both definitely better off without your bride."

Maris. Lovely, blonde, frigid as an iceberg. And seemingly as fertile. She'd been promised to the symbiotic twins, the bondmate who would have bridged them, but she'd loathed the idea. She'd been more than willing to help Torin in an effort to get out of a hated marriage.

At the time, she'd seemed a perfect bride. Thirteen years in, he'd given up going to her bed, but she still had her value. She was a bondmate but suspicious of psychic powers. She'd managed to make the other bondmates somewhat comfortable, until they had figured out he wanted to use their powers to enhance his own. "You didn't vet your pick properly, brother, or you would have known she hates non-*sidhe* as much as I do."

"Your Highness?" A throaty voice broke through the quiet. Una. One of his hags burst into the room.

And just like that, Seamus was gone. Torin had no doubt in his mind that his brother was still hanging about, listening in and gathering information to torture him with later.

"What is it? Do you have the spell?" They were working on a spell to kill the sluagh. He needed to be rid of his troublesome brother.

Una was one of the singularly least attractive women he'd ever seen. Even in her human form, there was an air of decay that hung about her no glamour could ever mask. On the surface she was in her middle years, a plain woman with fair skin that no one should really notice, but once he stared at her for too long, the wrongness couldn't be denied. Her sister Liadan had been the most skilled at glamour, but she was dead and the hags suspected the renegade royals had done her in.

Una shook that salt-and-pepper hair of hers. He noticed there was blood on her hands.

His head ached. The wailing wouldn't stop. Glannis, Una's remaining sister, joined her. Like the other hag, Glannis had streaks of blood marring her clothes and hands. Why were the stupid fucking brownies wailing when their torturers weren't busy torturing them?

The noise sounded like it was coming from the walls themselves. "I'm making a new rule. Cut the prisoners' tongues out before you start torturing them. I can't stand to listen to the bastards scream anymore. Why is it so loud? They're in the dungeon, are they not?"

Glannis wiped her hands on her skirt, seeming to not care that blood soaked the cotton. Her hair hung in clumpy strands, sweat dripping from her brow. "It would be rather hard to get any information out of them if we cut their tongues from their heads. Do you be expecting them to talk out of their arseholes?"

He didn't hesitate. He slapped her, adding to the blood on her clothes. Her head snapped back and a brutal cut opened on her lip. "You will watch your tongue around me, hag."

"Aye, Your Majesty," the hag replied, her tongue coming out to swipe at the blood on her chin.

The wailing reached epic proportions, threatening to shake the walls. Torin put his hands to his ears. "Go down to the dungeon and shut them the fuck up! Or I'll have your tongues."

Una shivered a bit. "It ain't the brownies."

He thought about plowing a fist into her face, but he still needed the bitches. "Then shut the goblins up. I don't care who it is."

Glannis pointed out the balcony toward the river that ran by the White Palace. "I think you should care, Your Majesty. It's why we came up here. One of the guards saw her."

Torin looked out, a cold chill invading his limbs. There was a single woman standing by the water's edge, a piece of clothing in her hand, a wash basin at her side. She got to her knees, soaking the garment in the river water.

"What in all the planes is that dumb bitch doing?" He turned away only to see his brother standing in the background, a wicked smile on his face. He ignored Seamus. "Get the guards. Tell them to shoot that woman and hang her corpse up for all to see. And shut that wailing up."

"The guards won't go near her," Una said. She wouldn't come out on the balcony. Una wasn't afraid of much. Her magic was based in blood. She killed with a perfection he'd seen in very few, but she was scared of a single woman washing her clothes?

The wailing. The washing. That eat-shit grin on his brother's face.

"*Bean sidhe?*" The words came out on a hushed sigh. Even speaking the name made his stomach revolt.

"It can't be too important." Unlike her sibling, Glannis didn't seem impressed by the legendary washer woman. "There's only one of them."

Una was nearly out the door now. "But they only wail for royal lines when death is near."

For royal lines. He knew the washer woman's tale. She was legendary across the planes. Some called her banshee, but here she was *bean sidhe*. The *bean sidhe* had three forms, the virgin, the mother, and the crone. Three forms of the same woman. She showed up before tragedies. She sang her song when a royal death was coming. He'd been smart enough to have his hags cast a spell over the palace three nights before his coup. The washer women had come—all three, but no one heard them.

Three would sing for a king. One for a prince or princess.

Or a pretender. Seamus's voice seeped into his head. *The* bean sidhe *know what you are.*

Could it be possible? Could the washer woman's wail be for him?

"Three would likely come for the outlaws. It's only one. It's a prince or princess. But we killed the girl." Glannis waved off the *bean sidhe.* "It's most likely the queen she sings for. 'Tis no great loss. You can take a new wife. A fertile one. The rebellions might die out if you had an heir of your own."

His coup had been carefully prepared. He'd taken no chances. He'd planned for years, including paying soothsayers across three different planes. Each had seen the same thing—Bronwyn, his ridiculous puffball of a niece, was the one who could strike the killing blow. Beck and Cian could take the throne back, but they couldn't kill him. Only that nitwit Bronwyn could.

But he'd buried her.

He turned to his brother. "You said you hated me for killing your wife."

The hags stared at him like he'd gone insane.

"Your Majesty, we don't hate you." Una looked around as though she could suddenly feel something but couldn't see it. Glannis glanced around, too, but neither could catch sight of Seamus, it seemed. Seamus showed himself only to his brother.

Torin didn't waste time on them. There were no explanations that could make sense, and he'd struck on something important. His brother's words came back to him. Seamus had lost his smile.

His brother railed at him for the loss of his throne and his wife. He often spoke of Beck and Cian. And he never, ever mentioned Bronwyn. Torin thought it was because a daughter was of no use outside what her hand in marriage could bring a kingdom. Seamus had ignored the girl except to lift her in his arms and twirl her around on occasion. He would pat her on the head and call her "little pixie." She was insignificant.

Or was she? His brother had changed since his death. He fucking loved everyone now. Everyone except his little pixie.

"She's alive." It was the only explanation. Somehow the twit had survived and laid out a body to be mistaken as her own. Perhaps that was why she'd set the fire.

Seamus shook his head, but he hadn't been a decent liar in life, and his turn as a sluagh hadn't fixed the problem.

Torin roared, the sound combining with the *bean sidhe's* wail. He put a hand to Glannis's throat and squeezed until the hag's eyes bulged.

"Find Bronwyn Finn."

Chapter Four

Shim stared out over the ocean. The temptation to grab the invisible thread that bound him to Bronwyn was nearly overwhelming. This was where the thread had always been its strongest. Here on the beach. Now, Shim understood why. There was a crack in the veil here that they would shortly slip through. It would lead them to Tír na nÓg.

The night before he'd felt so close to her. They'd drawn her in, bringing her to the chamber that would one day be theirs and stripping her bare. She'd been so beautiful, her skin nearly pearlescent in the moonlight. At first, she'd stayed in the bright light of day, her domain. In those moments when she'd turned her face up to the sun, she'd been a goddess, remote and untouchable, a true vision of pure Seelie beauty. But once they had her in their domain, she'd looked perfect—sexy and so fuckable that Shim's dick was still in agony hours later.

"Do you think she woke up?" Lach asked, joining him. Lach was already dressed for travel, in plain clothes and worn boots. Nothing that would give away the fact that they were royalty. It wouldn't work here in the Unseelie kingdom, but once they got to the Seelie plane, it was hoped they could blend in. They were, if anyone asked, merchants traveling to the agricultural provinces. That would explain the guard. Merchants had more rights than peasants but were far less interesting than nobles.

Though the sheer fact that they were traveling with a group of mercenary vampires, a gnome who thought he was the next coming of Lugh, and a young woman who could change into a wolf might hurt them in the blending-in department.

Shim sighed. The dream the night before had been the most vivid since their childhood. It had hurt when she'd disappeared. "I suppose so."

"You don't think she cut off contact herself, do you?" Lach asked, his expression blank, but that didn't work on the man who held the other half of his soul.

The smarter half. "No. She was right on the edge of a massive orgasm, Lach, so no I don't think she decided to cut us off. She woke up. It happens. Besides, as far as I can tell, she hasn't learned how to tune us out."

Shim turned. They'd been walking since daybreak, trudging back and forth along the beach, looking for something William Roan, the mercenary, called a weak point. He would stop every now and then, use his tablet to take readings, and then move on. Finally, they had stopped here. And then the waiting had begun.

Lach shrugged as though it didn't really matter. "I was wondering if she'd figured out something."

Shim sighed and looked at his brother. Though they had known all of their lives that this one woman was meant for them, he was sure that things seemed to be happening very quickly for Lachlan. "I had more control last night. Did you feel it?"

Lach nodded. "A bit, though I know you have the stronger connection."

And that was a point of contention between them. "Only because I had hold of the thread when she died. It connected us. It doesn't mean she's going to love you less. I think we should try to find a way to tell her, and I think we should show her your real face."

In the dreams, Lach's face was always perfect, freed from the scars of reality.

The unscarred side of Lach's head flushed a deep red. "So says the man with the perfect face."

"Damn it, she's not going to reject you."

"You heard what her brothers said. She was raised a princess of the Seelie. She won't want me. And I don't know what to do now that it's staring me in the face. I have to save her. And I can't let her go." Lach took a long breath. The night before, they had broken bread with Beck and Cian, who had been more than willing to talk about their sister. Bronwyn, they had explained, had always been a bit of a brat princess. Indulged by their mother, she had been raised to expect a perfect life. She should have never had a moment's struggle. They had no idea how she'd survived on her own.

But Shim knew. She was stronger than anyone gave her credit for. He could feel it. She was a different person than the child they had played through their dreams with. She was a woman who had fought for her life and was changed by the fight. She might have started life as a Seelie princess, as Beck and Cian Finn's sister, but she was his and Lach's woman now.

Duffy walked up to them, though waddling was perhaps a better word for what the gnome was doing. He was covered in plate armor, the very armor Shim had requested be made for his last birthday. It had been made as thin as could be, but it still weighed more than Duffy. Julian followed behind the gnome, slowing his normally long strides to match Duffy's.

Lach's mouth turned down in a frown. "Are you sure we should let him come along? I'm worried about him."

"We're going to be surrounded by vampires who know what they're doing," Shim assured him. He lowered his voice as Duffy got closer, not wanting the gnome to know what they spoke of. "You can't leave him behind. He would never forgive us. We're going after Bronwyn. Don't you think he'll want to see Gilly again?"

Duffy had loved Gillian for as long as Shim could remember. Duffy, for all his flirting, had been sweet on only Gillian, and he'd held that torch for thirteen years. Duffy wasn't foolish enough to believe his love would be returned. He'd told Shim time and time again, but Shim couldn't leave him behind.

Lach nodded tightly. "All right then. But I don't know about the vampires all knowing what they're doing. Why the hell is Dellacourt coming along?"

Julian lifted Duffy onto the ledge they stood on overlooking the sea. The gnome's armor clanged a bit, and he had to find his balance.

"Dellacourt's not so bad," Julian assured them. "And he won't let his wife go without him. I think you'll find Kaja helpful. You might know the district where your bondmate lives, but Kaja can pick up Gillian's scent. She'll save you days of looking."

"And it's very interesting when she turns into a wolf," Duffy added. "Did you see her earlier? She ain't got no clothes on when she turns back into a girl."

Julian stifled a laugh. "Yes, yet another reason Dellacourt won't allow his wife to venture out without him. Duffy's hit on her three times. You should watch it, little cos. Vampires take their consorts seriously."

Duffy smiled, a naughty grin. "It's okay. No one takes me seriously at all. That's when I swoop in and steal the girl. But after we find Gilly, I'll look after her. Won't have time for other women. She'll be needing a dedicated guard." Duffy looked around. "I don't understand why all the long faces. 'Tis a great adventure. We're going to another plane to rescue a princess. It's going to be amazing."

"It's going to be a miracle if we live," Lach muttered.

Lach had gotten all the mopey parts of their soul. Shim was a bit more worried than Duffy, but he could see the gnome's point. Shim got to one knee in front of Duffy. "I think Lach's worried that we have so little time to find them. Father has called for all the Unseelie warriors to gather in four days' time. At the end of the week, they will rip through the veil and invade Tír na nÓg before the vampire ambassadors enter. If we wait any longer, Torin could have access to vampire weaponry, and then we're all screwed. We have to find her, convince her to come with us, and get her back here before her brothers invade."

"There won't be any convincing." Lach frowned down at him. "She'll come or I'll tie her up and toss her over my shoulder."

"I taught you well," Julian said, slapping Lach on the back. "I rather wish I could go, but I'm rushing back to the Vampire plane. I've got a trusted employee spying on some officials. It wouldn't do to have them show up early. Taggart will ensure that doesn't happen. The Dellacourts and I are raising money and weapons to support your father and the Seelie twins. They won't go in alone. It's time to make our push. We'll take back Tír na nÓg or we will all die trying."

"Yes," Lach said, "it's the dying part I would like to avoid." He looked pointedly at Duffy.

Duffy's axe stood straight in his hand. He'd started to use it as a walking stick. "Don't worry none about it, Lach. I ain't letting no one kill you. The king himself charged me with protecting you both, but I would have done it anyway. I don't care that you got a kingdom waiting on you. You're me brothers."

Shim patted him on the back, his eyes meeting Lach's. They were of one mind when it came to Duffy. They would protect him. "I appreciate it, brother. Now, how much longer do we have?"

Julian gestured to the small crowd. "It's getting close. Come along now. Roan wants to talk to you."

Shim followed his cousin and Duffy, excitement growing. Before they reached the group, Lach put a hand on his shoulder.

"You have to stay with me."

A wealth of guilt washed across Shim. Since the connection between him and Bron had sputtered back to life, he'd spent more time holding on to her than he had dealing with things in this world. He'd left Lach to handle the day-to-day problems that came with being princes of the realm. He'd allowed himself to sink into his waking dreams of her, watching through her eyes as she lived her life. But all the while, Lach had been left out. How lonely had his brother become?

"I will stay in this world. I know it's important." He couldn't say anything else. An apology wasn't enough. It would never be enough.

"See that you do. It's getting harder and harder to pull you out. I can only imagine that you'll be able to feel her even more when we're on the same plane with her."

"I can handle it," Shim promised. "I'll spend all my time trying to keep Duff alive. Look at him. The vampire's going to kill him for sure."

Duffy had walked straight up to the lovely Kaja and taken her hand. The woman who had the power to turn into a wolf didn't seem to mind. She smiled down at him, speaking softly and clutching his hand. Dante didn't seem to mind, either. He looked indulgently on as his wife spoke to the gnome. But the minute he looked away, Duffy started staring at Kaja's ass. He turned and winked cheekily Shim's way.

"That vamp is going to figure out Duff's game and drain his ass." Lach had a smile on his face as he said it.

But the very idea had Shim thinking. *First blood.* His fangs popped out. They had waited a long time, but it would all be worth it. Bron was their mate. It was only right she should be their first blood, their only blood.

"Gods, hide those things," Julian said, shaking his head. "You're going to have the other vamps thinking you're an untried boy."

Shim stared at him seriously. In many ways, he was an untried boy. He was thirty years old, but he'd bonded at a young age. It had cut him off from many of the things young, wild Fae tried.

Julian's jaw dropped. "Are you fucking kidding me? After all the time you've spent in my club? After all the women I've sent you into private rooms with? You didn't fuck any of them? I paid a couple of them. Damn it."

Lach leaned in. "Do you have to announce it to the whole plane?"

Julian's voice lowered. "I'm sorry. I was sure I'd provided adequate opportunities for you to learn."

"We did learn. We know perfectly well how to top a sub and bring her to pleasure. Ask any of the women we've spent time with." Shim couldn't help but notice that the rest of the party was very politely ignoring them. Of course, vamps had excellent hearing. He wasn't ashamed. He would tell everyone. "We simply didn't cheat on our bondmate."

Julian's jaw tightened. "I understand, but there were other reasons for me doing this. You have goblin blood. All Unseelie do. Tell me you haven't thought about the mating fever."

It was a thing that happened sometimes with goblins who waited too long to mate. They would find a suitable female and go a little insane. Luckily female goblins were strong enough to survive the experience. Bronwyn was more fragile.

"It's not going to happen." Shim didn't believe it. He hadn't felt it before.

"We can handle it." Lach's words tripped over Shim's.

Julian cursed. "Then you've felt it?"

Shim turned on his brother. "What are you talking about?"

"It doesn't matter," Lach insisted. "It's not real. It's just every now and then I feel a bit out of control. But I'm fine. I haven't run out raping women."

Julian shook his head. "It will be different when you stand in front of her, and I'll be shocked if it doesn't transfer to Shim. When she's so close you can smell her and hear the blood in her veins, it will be different. I will pray to Danu for you, cos, and I will hope that Gillian's around. She might be the only one who can explain to your wife what's happening."

Julian stalked away, his anger evident in his every step.

William Roan cleared his throat as he walked up. "Your Highnesses?"

"Please, it's Shim and Lach. No titles." Shim tried to give Lach a minute to compose himself.

"That would be for the best," the vampire said. "We have only a few moments left. I want to explain exactly what is going to happen. We're working with the fact that Torin can't keep the Planeswalkers out."

Planeswalker demons were a type of being who came from a plane they called Hell. Shim had heard there were many demons, but only the Planeswalkers were commonly seen. If lore had it right, the other demons preferred their own plane and had a special affinity for the Earth plane. Planeswalker demons gathered energy from walking the various planes of existence. They knew where each door was and how to access it. They tended to keep very exact regimens, entering and leaving doors at the same times of the week or month. A smart man, and William Roan had proved himself to be very smart, could use the fact that no amount of magic could close the door to a Planeswalker, and for that brief moment when the door was open, there were cracks in the veil that kept the worlds apart. It was almost as though the walls of the planes, or dimensions as some called them, were separated by sheets, and when the sheet was opened in one place, it pulled taut or loose in others, leaving cracks.

Cracks a Fae could slip through.

"How long will we have?" Shim asked, looking around at the small team that had been assembled. It consisted of William Roan, his first in command—a vampire named Harry, two other soldiers named Gabriel and John, Dante, Kaja, and Duffy. Nine in all when he counted himself and Lach. They would have to move fast.

"A minute, perhaps a minute and a half." William grimaced. "I don't suppose I need to tell you what can happen if the veil closes on a person. It's not too late to back out. I've retrieved bondmates before. I have a system set up."

Shim's whole being rebelled at the idea. She was right there on the other side of some invisible veil. He couldn't leave it to anyone else. Shim could actually feel his brother's will. Now that they were standing on the other side, the door between them right there, the bond they'd formed with Bronwyn all those years ago was stronger than ever.

"No. We can't wait. If you choose to leave us behind, we'll find another way."

Lach leaned in. "And then we'll find you."

William Roan actually smiled at the threat. "There it is then." He sobered, his voice going low. "And I respect the hell out of you for the choices you've made regarding the princess."

Shim couldn't help the bitter laugh that rumbled from his throat. "That's a change. Most people look at us like we're insane when they find out we've never taken a woman."

Roan shook his head, some unnamed emotion choking his speech. "Don't let them tell you that. A man's worth isn't in how many women he's had. It's in how he loves the right one. You couldn't take another woman. You love this one. I respect you both for that, and I vow with my whole being to see you to your mate. I can only pray one day I find someone to love the way you love her."

Shim felt a deep connection to the vampire. It must be hard on him. He'd been promised so much as a royal. He'd been promised wealth and power and a long, long life with his consort, and all had been taken from him.

"We will follow you, Roan," Lach said, respect back in his tone. "Just tell us what to do. We've never been to Tír na nÓg."

William walked to the spot where he'd set his pack and tablet. "We'll enter here. We're going to line up as quickly as possible when the time comes. As soon as you're through, reach back and pull in the person behind you. We're going to be met by some allies on the other side. This part of the veil leads directly onto a ranch of sorts. It's run by two brothers who raise and train horses. They keep my packs and tools and vehicles hidden. I've already sent word and they have everything ready for us. We'll need to stay with them until darkness falls, and we can travel under the veil of night."

"Boss." Harry's sharp yell came before the tablet began beeping. "We have thirty seconds before the crack forms."

William grabbed his backpack, giving Julian a jaunty salute. "Lodge, I hope to see you on the field of battle in a week."

Julian flashed a wicked smile. "I'll be there. No matter what the Council says, a whole lot of vampires will be there. Try not to die, Dellacourt."

Dante grinned, grabbing his wife's hand. "My Kaj won't let me die."

Kaja shook her head. "I will not. It took me too long to train this husband. I do not wish to go through it again."

Dante shook his head before capturing her mouth with a soft kiss.

"I'll go in first, followed by Harry. The rest of you follow as quickly as you can." Roan's fangs were out, a sure sign that his adrenaline was up. His eyes moved, searching for something in the air in front of him. "There you are, gorgeous."

Gabe brought some kind of light and flashed it where Roan pointed. Sure enough, the light shimmered a few inches above the beach. It was odd, like the way the horizon seemed to shimmer in the distance on a very hot day, but this was close and small.

"It smells different." Kaja was scenting the air. "Dante, I smell fields and forests."

Dellacourt seemed to catch his wife's enthusiasm. "I smell an adventure. We have fun in forests, baby."

"It's going to be tight." Roan dropped to his belly. "Hurry." He put his hands through and suddenly his body began to disappear. One minute he was there and the next, his arms were gone, vanished as though they didn't exist. The rest of his body followed, swallowed up by whatever was on the other side of the veil.

Harry tossed a pack through and disappeared the same way.

Lach turned back to Julian. "You knew. This was here the whole time. You knew."

Julian's face was a careful blank. "The king wouldn't let anyone tell you. He didn't believe, Lachlan. No one did. Now get rid of your anger and prove us wrong. Your father is betting everything on this. His kingdom. His life. Forgive him and move on. You'll be happier for it."

Shim had figured it out the minute Julian had shown up, but he didn't struggle the way Lach did. He took his brother's elbow. "Go. We have to go."

Everyone else was gone.

Lach dove toward the crack, his big body disappearing. Shim turned to Duffy who stood there, axe in hand.

"Go, Duffy."

The gnome shook his head. "Ain't going 'til you do. Someone's gotta watch yer back."

He could be so stubborn. There were only seconds left. Shim didn't argue. He threw his body to the ground. "Grab my legs." He could already see Lach's big hands coming through, searching for Shim's arms to pull him along. "Grab my legs, Duffy!"

Shim could feel the veil beginning to close. There was a crack, and it felt like invisible walls were closing in on him. His breath caught in his chest. He was going to die like this, cut in half, so close to her and yet forever far away.

It felt like his arms were torn from his shoulders, but he was suddenly in a completely different place. The sun was brighter. The air warmer.

Shim sat up. He couldn't feel Duffy at his feet. "Duffy? He was holding on to my ankles. Duffy?"

And then the gnome appeared just as the crack between the two worlds slammed closed. Duffy was a small cannonball popping in from the other plane. He rolled and grunted to a stop. His helmet was askew and his armor out of place.

"Sorry. I almost forgot me axe. Wouldn't be nothing of a guard without me axe."

There was a rich laugh behind them, and Shim looked up. Two identical Fae twins stared down at him.

"Well, look at that. I've never seen a gnome warrior before, Max." The one who had spoken had a wide grin and a hat on his head.

Max looked to be the surlier of the two. "Well, that's the Unseelie for you, Rye."

Shim let his head fall back, dragging air into his lungs.

He was finally here.

Chapter Five

Lach stared out the back porch and tried to will the sun to go down. It had been hours and hours of waiting. Hours of listening to the Harper twins argue and crack wise. Lach was suddenly appreciative of his own brother.

A huge black dog lumbered into the yard, a gnarly stick in his mouth. The dog was roughly the size of a small pony, though it appeared the Harper twins liked to grow large animals. Their entire stock of horses were oversized and ran the range of colors from a brilliant red to blacks so dark they shimmered blue in the sunlight.

The rest of the group was huddled around the large table inside the *brugh*, enjoying a meal the twin's wife, Rachel, had cooked. It was a full table. The twins had five children, all but one larger than Duffy.

But Lach didn't want to eat. He wanted to move. He wanted to get started.

"You should eat, Your Highness, I mean, Lachlan." Roan walked out, followed by his vampire partner. They wouldn't enjoy the cabbage and sausages Rachel had cooked. He stopped, staring for a moment. "Unless you take after your vampire half. Now that I think about it, I haven't seen you or your brother eat."

Lach managed a smile. "I assure you, we're fine. We've had lots of meat, though the hunger for blood grows by the day. Cousin Julian made sure we had meal pills to fill those hungers."

Roan shook his head, his jaw tense. "Meal pills are nothing once you've had real blood."

"I'll wait for my wife, thank you."

Roan shook it off. "Sorry. Being near Rachel always gets my blood high. She's quite the consort."

Lach understood what he was saying. Rachel glowed, a faint outline around her body that let a vampire know her blood would strengthen him, elongate his life. A *sidhe* in need of a bondmate would have to get intimate to know if a woman could bond, but Lach had his vampire heritage to fall back on. Rachel Harper had a gorgeous glow about her.

"Don't tell Max," Roan said, his eyes searching the horizon. "Rye would laugh it off, but Max takes things far too seriously."

"How did you find them?" Lach was curious. Roan had a whole setup. He'd made a business out of stealing into Tír na nÓg.

Roan smiled. "I found the crack, and when I managed to get through it, Rye was staring down at me. He found out what I was doing, and I discovered that he and his brother and wife were rebels looking for a way to fuck with the pretender. Rachel had a sister who disappeared with Torin's guards. This whole village the Harpers live in is a wee bit radical. They're protected by the mountains and they have an intensely smart mayor. They've managed to survive relatively unscathed, but they intend to give Torin the fight of his life. We have weapons stashed all over Aoibhneas."

Aoibhneas. He knew the word well. Bliss. "Have you told them about the rebellion?"

Roan turned, and Lach saw Rye Harper walking up, his arm around his wife's waist. Max Harper followed behind them leading a ridiculously large horse with yellow eyes. He seemed to be muttering to the horse under his breath. Rye Harper had his eyes on Lach. The previously friendly cowboy had a serious look on his face.

"We're ready," Rye said. "We've been ready for thirteen years."

Rachel leaned into her husband. "Are they really alive?"

It was hard to believe how isolated Tír na nÓg had become. "Beck and Cian Finn are alive and well, and they have formed their true triad.

Beck has mastered storms and Cian is a Green Man. Your kings will be back soon."

Rachel hugged her husband and cried into his shoulder, clutching him. Rye Harper nodded toward Lach. "We'll be ready. Tell me something, are you really the Unseelie prince?"

Lach nodded. "I am."

"He is the Unseelie prince, but only half of him. You two should be happy you only share a face and not a soul."

Lach stopped and sighed because it had been the damn horse that spoke. The yellow eyes should have been a dead giveaway. A phooka. A potentially dangerous creature, but very powerful. They could often be chaotic, but the phooka had been known to band together with other creatures during times of hardship.

Rye laughed. "You have no idea how much I praise the day we weren't born symbiotic. I can't imagine having to be in his head all the time."

"You wish you had my brain, brother," Max shot back. He looked at the horse, narrowing his eyes. "Aren't you supposed to be undercover? Doesn't that mean not doing the whole talking thing? It tends to give you away, dummy."

The phooka gave a regal whinny. "I wouldn't walk around talking about someone else's intelligence, Harper. And the other horses hate you."

Max rolled his cool blue eyes. "I doubt that. Those horses love me. And you better love me, too. I could call the guards down on your nasty ass."

The phooka tossed his head. "I do not fear this, *sidhe*. I know far too much. Besides, you can grumble all you like, but you would not turn on an ally."

Max leaned in. "No, I wouldn't, but I could move your stall away from that pretty mare you have those nasty eyes on."

The phooka turned on him. "Don't you dare. Do you know how long it's taken me to convince her to let me close? I'm so close, Max. Have you seen her ass? It's the hottest filly ass in the whole province."

"Remember that." Max turned back to Lach. "You want to explain why we should trust you?"

Lach shrugged. "I don't care if you trust me or not."

Max huffed, his face betraying a bitterness. "Well, that's pretty much what I would expect from an Unseelie prince."

The *sidhe* walked off, after nodding to his brother and wife.

Rye gripped his wife's hand. "But you're going to help, right? I thought Roan said the Unseelie are going to back the true kings."

"My father is sending a force in. I am merely here to get my bondmate and get out. She is too important to risk." He looked pointedly at Rachel Harper. "I would certainly assume that you're not going to risk your bondmate."

Rye's face got red, his jaw tense, but the words that came out of his mouth were controlled. "My bondmate, my brother, my children, my town have all been at risk for thirteen years. I've been forced to raise my children under the tyrant's reign, wondering every bloody day if Torin isn't going to come for one of them. My oldest daughter, Paige, has great skill with magic, and I can't risk anyone outside of this community knowing it because Torin would take her and, if he couldn't warp her, he would hang her from the palace walls. So don't pretend that you know what it has been like for me. I'm sorry, Rachel. I thought I could do this. I'll be back."

Rye stalked off after his brother.

"Please forgive him. The last several years have been hard," Rachel said, smoothing back her strawberry-blonde hair. "At first, when King Seamus fell, we all held out hope that the Unseelie would come and save us. Many of us believed this would be the act that reunited our kingdoms."

Lach would have assumed the very idea would horrify the Seelie. "I don't think even King Seamus wanted that."

Rachel shrugged. "Seamus was a good king, but he was a royal. I have yet to meet a true royal who understood the plight of even the middle class. The best we can hope for is a king who has just laws and the means in place to oust sheriffs and mayors who take advantage. Torin simply takes without caring how it affects us. And he's systematically killing every creature who isn't *sidhe*."

"Then you're safe." He meant it to be somewhat comforting, but the minute the words came out of his mouth, a vision of Duffy being slaughtered because he wasn't *sidhe* assaulted his brain. He opened his mouth to call the words back, but Rachel Harper rounded on him, her pretty face red with anger.

"Safe? So I should allow the tyrant king to slaughter my neighbors, my sweet kin, because he's not coming for me? Let me tell you something, Your Highness, if you believe that he will be satisfied with killing only those who don't look like he does, you're a naïve idiot. When the brownies and goblins and trolls and pixies are gone, he will come for the rest of us. I will not sit idly by and pray to Danu that he not darken my door. I will not allow him to kill and rape and do as he pleases because he was strong enough to wrest the crown from his brother's head. I will fight. I will fight for my children. So you take your perfect bondmate and run back to the Unseelie plane. We do not need you here."

She began to walk away, and Lach realized how terribly he was handling his allies. "Mrs. Harper."

She didn't turn. "Yes, Your Highness."

"I apologize if I offended. I am not the diplomatic half." He wasn't sure what else to say. "I don't even know much about the situation here. It didn't seem to be an Unseelie problem."

She finally turned to him, tears in her eyes. "We're living, breathing beings, Your Highness. Call us what you will—Seelie, Unseelie, vampire. It matters not. We want the same things you do. We want our mates and our children to be happy. We want our dreams to come true. We're dying. How is that not everyone's problem?"

She sighed and walked away.

Lach watched her, wishing he knew what to say, what to do. It had been simple. Come to the Seelie plane. Get his mate. Get out. Let the war happen or not.

Two hours here and he knew he would have to make decisions he wasn't ready to make.

He felt his fists clench. His father had done him a grave disservice. Since that horrible day when Bron had died and Shim's power had surged, burning away half of Lach's face, his father had treated them both like they were fragile beings, not to be tormented with minor things like learning how to run the kingdom they would one day inherit. His father had lost Gillian, seen one of his heirs marred for life, and the other go into a fugue state. It was reasonable that he would be protective, but Lach now lacked the tools he needed. He knew nothing because his father didn't want to tax his frail system.

Dante stepped out, stretching his long limbs. He nodded Lach's way. "Almost time to head out."

There were still hours to go before they could begin. He didn't argue with the vampire though. Dellacourt had left behind a whole rich life to follow his cousins. Perhaps it was time to toss aside his preconceptions and start asking questions.

Perhaps it was time to become a king no matter what his father thought.

"Could you tell me about the situation here?"

Dellacourt's green eyes widened slightly. "Are you sure? You didn't seem at all interested before."

"I am now."

Dellacourt smiled. "Then take a seat, Your Highness. Consider this your first briefing."

Lach sat, and the vampire began to speak.

* * * *

The late-afternoon light was warm on her skin as she stood in the middle of the town square, music and laughter all around her. The Festival of Threshing. The agricultural provinces all had their own ways to celebrate the hard work of the season. Here there would be a small party for the threshing and a huge feast after harvest was done. But Bron wouldn't be around for the feasting this year. She would be on the road, these people she'd come to care about left behind.

Bron watched the children dance around the maypole, the colors blending, making a rainbow as the children bounced and sang. And her heart hurt because she knew how much Ove had wanted to attend. But the brownie was in hiding. Bron had been forced to leave her in a cold cave with her mother. Gillian had taken food and blankets, but it was only a matter of time before the guards thought to search for them. Torin's principles of purity had finally reached the outer provinces, and there was nowhere left to run.

Then stop running. You're of age. The time has come to fight. Gather an army. Be the princess you were born to be.

That angry voice in her head was becoming louder and harder to ignore. She wasn't a child any longer. Her brothers, it seemed, were not coming back. She was the only Finn left for a rebellion to build around. If she and Gillian left this province, how long would it be until something else sent them running again? How long before they ran out of places to hide? And how many of her friends would die along the way, without her defense because staying alive was all that mattered? Did she want to spend her life like this, hiding and pretending to be something she wasn't?

And that brought up the real question. Who the hell was she? She hadn't been brought up to be a warrior princess. She'd been brought up to be a fluffy wife. Time and hardship had molded her into something else. Something more.

Who was Bronwyn Finn becoming?

"Hello, my dear. Your dress is lovely, though I wish you had worn your sapphire-blue one." Micha's rheumy eyes took in her form, and she could practically see the old man salivate. He was dressed in his country best—a velvet overcoat that had been overly adorned with golden buttons and jewel-encrusted medals proclaiming some military service he'd never actually performed. Micha liked to steal such things from condemned prisoners and pass them off as his own, or so rumor had it.

One thing Bronwyn Finn was not about to become was the mayor's wife. She would fight like hell to avoid that, no question.

"I apologize, Mayor," Bron said with a yawn, already planning her getaway. "I suppose I wasn't thinking about such things as fashion. The harvest begins tomorrow. There was much to do this day to prepare. All the work has tired me."

His lips curled in a condescending smile. "Well, we shall have to make ours a particularly short engagement so you shall never have to work a plow again. Though I would say there will still be a bit of plowing involved in your life. Do not worry, dear. I'll be the driving force in that particular harvest."

It was all she could do to not show her disdain. She let her eyes go wide and innocent. She needed to be as virginal as possible so when she slapped him silly, she would have the perfect excuse of utter ignorance. "I did not know you planted your own food, Mayor. Well, that explains why you selected me as your mate. I can certainly help with your farming techniques."

The guards behind him laughed, elbowing each other. The mayor joined them. "My bride will need an education, will she not?"

"You're the man to give it to her, Mayor," one of the guards said. They stood behind him, two large men with swords at their sides. Bron noticed the long, distrustful stares of the farmers around her.

She felt herself flush. She wanted to show them exactly what her education over the last years had been. Swords and knives and hand-to-hand combat taught by a pair of open-minded goblins. They had taught her to fight dirty, to use her hands, her legs, her teeth. Anything to win the battle. They had taught her that the only true honor in battle was to stay alive.

There was a particular move they had taught her that she would love to practice on the mayor. It involved her knees and his balls. Yes, she'd been good at that move.

She pushed thoughts of crushing the mayor's withered old balls down and granted him a curtsey and what she hoped was a simpering smile. "I am sure to be grateful for any instruction you can give me, Sir Mayor, but now I must go and aid my sister. I have left her all alone to sell our bread."

The mayor frowned. "I don't know that I like my future wife in a stall selling her wares. I think, perhaps, your sister can handle this day alone, Isolde. Come and we will walk the grounds. I want everyone to see what a lovely fiancée I have found for myself."

He held out his arm in what she assumed was supposed to be a courtly gesture, and there was nothing to do but take it. Arguing with him would simply make her look like a fool and get both her and Gillian in trouble. She walked sedately beside the mayor as he waved to the people of the town. He stopped and talked to the more prominent members and ignored the peasants.

"We shall have to work on your priorities, dear," Micha said after leaving the town's richest merchant. "You seem to smile at the worthless and frown at the wealthy."

Because the wealthy of this town were complete asses. She took a deep breath and measured her response. "I am sorry. Perhaps it is because I know the working folk better."

Though her father had spent time with his subjects, both noble and peasant, he hadn't ever had loads of time to lavish on her. One of her fondest memories was walking with her father through the village on Saturday mornings. He would stroll through, waving at people, buying food from the merchants and trinkets. It was the only real time he ever spent with her and Cian, and sometimes Dante, when he visited. Her father hadn't been perfect, but he'd understood the value of all of his subjects.

The mayor shook his head. "I know. The Fae you consort with shall have to change. How you behave is going to reflect on me. I can't have you breaking bread with peasants. After all, the queen herself will be coming to our wedding."

The thought of being in the same room with Maris brought a smile to Bron's face. Yes, she had a few things to say to her brothers' former fiancée, and she would say them with the point of her blade. Being able to kill the traitorous bitch would almost be worth going through with the sham of a wedding.

"Ah, that has made you happy!" The mayor looked delighted. "Yes, you will love the queen. Such a perfect female."

"I would dearly love to stand in her presence," Bron allowed. Preferably close enough to slip a knife between her ribs, though it might not work since everyone knew the pretender queen didn't have a heart. It was said among the peasants she had sold it to a hag in exchange for her crown.

His hand covered hers. Soft and clammy, Micha had the hands of a man who had never worked a day in his life. "Well, dear, this gives me great hope. I worried for a while that you had no interest in court. Shall I fill you in on all the latest gossip?" He leaned toward her, a conspiratorial gleam in his eyes. "I have a spy in the palace. All of the mayors tend to. I talk to her through looking glass once a week." He put a finger to his lips. "Don't tell anyone, dear. Magic is getting a bad reputation these days, but this is a harmless thing."

Yes, it was harmless because it gained the mayor something, but not three days before Siobhan Hannigan had been jailed for placing a blessing spell on a newborn child who was struggling to breathe. The babe had survived, but both of her parents sat waiting trial, too, for hiring a witch. They probably wouldn't hold their babe again. Yet a spot of gossip was all right.

Still, she pretended to care because it kept his hands off her. "Tell me."

He looked around, leaning in and pulling away from his guards. "The rumor is that the princess might have survived the king's coup. My source said the king is initiating a countrywide search for Bronwyn Finn."

Bron felt her stomach lurch, her heart stop.

Micha rolled his eyes. "I think it's ridiculous. They buried the Finn bitch. She was a stupid child. She couldn't have survived. The king was very thorough when he liberated us. And if she did survive, she's more than likely with those brothers of hers, eking out an existence on some third-rate plane."

The world seemed to tilt, throwing her off-balance. Micha continued to speak, but his words seemed to come from someplace far away. What had happened? Thirteen years had passed and not a word of her survival had been heard. There hadn't been a whisper about her in all the towns and villages and provinces she and Gillian had sought refuge in. Thirteen years and now Torin believed?

Panic threatened to suffuse her. She felt that odd tingle that started in her hands whenever she was truly frightened. That tingle that always came before the fire.

Not now. Tears pricked her eyes. She had to get it under control. She couldn't lose it now in front of everyone.

Over the years, she had been truly afraid a few times, and each time a fire began. The first had been an overzealous suitor who had plunged his hands down her bodice. The chair beneath him had caught fire mysteriously.

Then there had been the vendor buying vegetables who thought she was a part of the bargain. His warehouse had gone up in flames.

Each time she'd felt her hands warm and tingle before whatever she was pointing at had caught fire. It frightened her. She knew not what it meant except her death if she was caught.

"Dear Isolde." The mayor clucked and hauled her close, his arm going around her waist. The guards chuckled behind her, making rude statements. She could smell the perfume he used to mask his odor. "I can see this news has frightened you. Please, my love, do not worry your pretty head. There will be no revolt. You are absolutely safe with

101

me. Bronwyn Finn is as worthless as her brothers. She's dead or as good as. She's no threat to anyone."

No threat. Useless. Yes, she felt it.

There was a loud shout, and the crowds began to move, opening up for the guard charging toward the mayor. The dancing stopped as a high wail could be heard. Everyone—peasant, farmer, noble—turned to the edge of the crowd.

The guard strode forward, the small body in his hands no impediment to his movement.

Bron gasped. Ove. She looked so tiny in the brutish guard's hold, her delicate feet dangling. The bastard had the wee brownie by her throat. Ove's eyes were bulging already as she struggled to breathe.

"Let her go!" Bron shouted, tearing away from the mayor. She thought about nothing but the fact that Ove couldn't last long. The guard's hand fit easily around her throat, and he could break her neck without even thinking about it. "You're killing her. She's a child. She didn't mean any harm. She only wanted to see the dancing."

She was barely two. A child in brownie years, not quite on the cusp of her womanhood. She was a baby who had wanted to come to the party, hold a ribbon in her hands while she pranced around the maypole with the other children. Bron knew what had happened. She'd snuck from safety, hoping to catch a glimpse of the party she should have attended. Ove didn't understand the principles of purity. Ove wanted to play with her friends. And now she was dying.

"Seize her!" the mayor ordered.

It wasn't until the guards grabbed her arms that Bron realized he was talking about her. She was brought back to the mayor. At the edge of the crowd, Gillian stood, shaking her head, her eyes begging Bronwyn to stay calm, to play her part. They were surrounded by guards, at least one for every five villagers, and food had been scarce. The villagers were weak. They would be no match for the huge guards.

"You will have to excuse my fiancée. She is a gentle soul who needs a firm hand to guide her." Micha's eyes narrowed on her, his mouth a flat line that promised retribution. He turned and looked at the guard who held the brownie. "What is that thing doing here ruining my party?"

The guard dropped Ove to the ground, her body hitting the dirt with a thud. The brownie dragged air into her lungs, her long fingers touching her throat. "I found the thing in the bushes watching the dancing."

The mayor sneered down at the sweet girl. "Take it away. Throw it on the fire. I don't care, but I want no further disruptions."

The tingling in Bron's hands was stronger than ever, and she couldn't deny it. Without thinking, going only on instinct, she called out to that power inside her and pointed at the guard who held a sword to Ove's throat. Fire sparked on the guard's tunic, a flash that erupted in all-out flames, engulfing him.

A hideous scream filled the waning day, and all eyes were on her.

The fire had come from her hands. She had held them up, and like a sorceress calling her power, she had directed it to her enemy.

The mayor gaped at her.

"Witch," he whispered.

And then a horrible pain hit the back of her head, and darkness took her.

Chapter Six

Shim felt her panic. It started like a hundred ghostly fingers brushing across his flesh, making bumps appear in their wake. He sat straight up in the chair he'd been occupying while drinking some of the tea Paige Harper had poured with a practiced hand. The young *sidhe* looked very much like her mother with strawberry-blonde hair and a wide smile. She appeared to be between fourteen and sixteen years of age, but she proved her maturity as Shim began to shake.

"Something is wrong." Her hands moved as though she could feel the air around her. "It's coming from the outside, but it's focused on you, Your Highness."

Someone had said the girl had a way with witchcraft, and it seemed that she was also sensitive to psychic episodes. But Shim didn't have time to think about it. He could feel Bron's heartbeat as though it was his own. He was suddenly out of breath, like someone had punched the air out of his lungs.

He heard Paige calling for her parents, felt Duffy's arm on his own, but Shim couldn't see him anymore. His vision was clouded, giving way to the eyes of his mind, going miles and miles away. He saw a small brownie on the ground, dirt swirling the earth beside her. A large leather boot reared back in a kicking motion.

"Damn it, Shim. Don't!" Duffy shouted, his hand coming off Shim's arm.

Shim tried to hold on, but Bron's pull was so great. She called to him, demanding his fire, his protection. Shim felt his power shimmer, skimming along his skin from someplace deep inside him.

Now his own panic began to take over. He remembered the last time he'd lost control. Lach had nearly died. His brother had been marred for the rest of his life. If he lost control here, in such a small setting, he wouldn't be able to save the men in the house. Much less the children. Gods, the Harper children were here.

He forced himself up, stumbling, not quite able to see the world in front of him. He tried to concentrate. Tried to force his brain back to this reality. It was so hard because he could feel Bron's emotion. She moved from pure terror to a rage that threatened to completely overtake him. He had mere seconds before the fire would no longer be containable. He could already sense it building. It would be a blast that flowed between him and Bronwyn, the flames shooting into both places. The Harper's nicely kept house would become their children's tomb.

And then he felt a calming presence. Paige. She put a hand on his elbow, whimpering a bit because she surely felt the heat in his skin. She was like a wash of cold water, quenching him briefly.

"Tell me what to do," she said.

Duffy's hand was suddenly in his. "Damn me, Shim. You're blazing hot. Come on, we need to get him outside before he blows."

"Blows?"

He heard Paige's shout through the chaotic mess of his brain. His world? Bron's world? It was hard to tell what he was seeing. He held on tightly to the power, but it was growing. Bron's need was overcoming his will. She was so strong, and she didn't know what she was doing.

He stumbled, forcing his eyes to focus on his feet.

"What's happening?"

It was his brother's voice. Shim could hear feet pounding and voices calling out, but he wasn't sure where they were coming from.

Bron was so angry. Her rage filled him. Years of impotent anger had been bottled up, and now it would not go away. His anger. Her anger. Their power.

"Damn it all." He felt his brother's hands on his shoulders. "Get away! Get away now!"

But his brother was still here. Lach had lost too much. Lach could die if he got caught in the fire, and it would be a big one. Grabbing on to the final vestige of his will, he pushed his brother away and ran.

He knew he was outside now, could feel the air on his skin as his clothes began to burn off.

He stopped, his vision utterly taken over by Bronwyn.

He saw a guard standing in the middle of a large crowd, a brownie child at his feet and his mercy. The guard had none. Bron's memories assaulted him. It was so much stronger than ever before. Being on the same plane with nothing between them but miles, he could feel her power. She transmitted so strongly, but not only could she transmit, she pulled power from him.

The fire built and Shim gave in to his instincts. He forced the fire into his hands, Bron's hands, and directed it in a thin line, trying to keep it away from the crowds. Once he let it flow, it immediately became easier to control. Flames shot from his fingertips. His skin was on fire, every inch of his body engulfed in flames, but he could control them.

The guard screamed, but the brownie Bron had been trying to save skittered away. A long breath came out of her body and then he heard a single word.

"Witch."

Shim fell to the ground, like a puppet that had its strings cut. The flames went out, and Shim was aware that he was alone again.

His hands shook as he sat up. Something was very wrong. The connection had been brutally severed. Bron was in trouble.

Shim struggled to his feet. His naked damn feet. As his power grew, he'd found his skin could handle the flames that engulfed him, though his clothes never survived.

"Holy crap balls," Dellacourt said, staring at the ground surrounding Shim. A perfect circle of burned grass had formed when he'd finally let his power go. "You've already come into your power."

Shim's voice was still shaky. "I think we mentioned that."

Dante pointed toward the woods where Shim could clearly see the line of fire he'd made when Bron had seized his power.

"It could have been worse," Lach said, handing him a blanket. "What the hell happened? I felt something. My power surged." Lach looked back at the porch where the Harpers stood staring. "I am so sorry. Do you have a lot of bodies buried close by?"

"What?" Rye asked. Then he took a startled step back, pulling his wife toward him.

A partially decomposed dog was trotting out of the woods, a large black dog running beside it.

"Quigley!" Rachel started trying to run toward the black dog. "Get away from that thing!"

One of the younger Harper children, a boy Shim remembered was named Patrick, stepped forward. He couldn't be more than seven, but he looked at his fathers with outrage. "That's Queenie! You told us Queenie went to the city."

His brother rolled his eyes. "Dummy, don't you know that's what Da says when one of the animals dies? He's too chicken to tell you so he pretends he took it to the city. Queenie got into a bad patch of berries and got herself poisoned. Da buried her in the woods."

"Well, it looks like Da was wrong." Patrick started to go out, but Rye held him back.

Shim wrapped the blanket around his body, his mind only half working. He looked at his brother. Lach had gone a pasty white. The dog wasn't the only thing crawling back from wherever it had been buried. There was a horse skeleton prancing and whinnying.

"Buttercup?" Max said, with a smile on his face. "Damn, but I would know that gait anywhere. Look at you girl! You can still run. What the hell is happening?"

"Shim is a fire adept. It's his special power." Roan stepped up, examining the ground beneath Shim's feet. "Lachlan is a necromancer. They came into their powers in a unique fashion. They bonded, but from a distance."

Dante nodded. "They should have more control once a full bond is completed. But I don't understand how it goes crazy like that. Did Shim mean to blow a path through the woods?"

"No. It was Bron," he explained. "She was afraid, and then she was angry. She pulled the power out of me."

Lach took a deep breath. "And mine always flares when Shim's goes crazy. I'm sorry. You'll be reburying corpses for days."

Shim's head was starting to clear. He was still shaky, but his ability to think and feel were coming back, and he didn't like what was left. Lach helped him to the porch. "Something's wrong with Bron."

His brother leaned over. "I know. I could feel a bit of it, but we have to get you calm and strong again before we rush off. Tell me what happened. I could feel it. I couldn't see it. I never see it."

Shim knew his brother felt cut off, but he didn't have time to deal with that now. "It's a jumble. I know she was trying to protect a brownie. A youngling, I think. Why was a guard trying to hurt a little brownie?"

Max Harper started to walk out toward the corpse formerly known as Buttercup.

"Damn, Max." Rye's eyes had widened and his skin had paled.

Lach shook his head. "The horse won't hurt him. It doesn't know it's dead. Same with the dog."

Rachel nodded, and the kids, with the exception of Paige, ran out to greet Queenie.

Rachel frowned, her eyes on her children. "You were told that Torin is systematically killing non-*sidhe*."

Shim leaned against the porch railing. "I guess I thought you were talking about goblins and ogres. You know, the rougher creatures. Brownies are helpful. Gnomes keep the gardens growing. How does Torin think he'll feed everyone?"

"He doesn't care," Rye replied. "I have no doubt he'll enslave a few, but he'll think that a little starvation will keep the lower classes in line. We can't rebel if we don't have the energy to fight."

"I don't understand what he's thinking." Shim couldn't quite wrap his head around it. Why would anyone want to upset the balance? It was one thing to kill an ogre who threatened hundreds of villagers, quite another to systematically wipe them out. Ogres played a part, too. The same with pixies and even sluagh. They all served a purpose. The flowers would die without the pixies. The crops would struggle without the gnomes. Ogres were predators who culled herds. And they were living, thinking beings.

What was happening with Bron?

"He called her a witch."

Lach's eyes went wide. "What?"

Rachel Harper took a long breath. "What do you mean? You can really see her? Hear what's happening to her?"

Shim nodded. "It can be confusing, but I know what I heard. There was a man there. He was dressed in rich clothes. He was older. Bron didn't like him. She was disgusted by him. He called her a witch, and then the connection was gone. I think she's unconscious."

He didn't like the thought of how that had happened. He'd felt her one minute, and she'd been gone the next.

Paige Harper had paled a bit. "Witches are considered bad here. At least for the last few years. Anyone with psychic ability is labeled a witch, and Torin deals with them the same way he does non-*sidhe*."

Rachel put an arm around her daughter, obviously lending her strength. "He's taken bondmates, especially the strong ones, and they disappear. We don't know if they're dead or if he's got them held somewhere. We've been safe here because we're so isolated, but we've lost a few when we leave the village."

Dellacourt spoke up. "According to the sluagh, he's trained a number of consorts to turn on their masters. He's turning over a hundred consorts to the vampire ambassadors. They're set to go off somewhere down the line, like a number of bombs he's planted."

Paige put a hand to her mouth, stifling a sob. She turned and ran back into the house. Rachel sent Shim an apologetic glance and then ran after her daughter.

Rye sighed. "Paige's best friend is a boy named Charlie. He's the sheriff's son. Well, Nathan was the sheriff until Torin took over. He sent another sheriff in. We killed that asshole, but Torin doesn't know it. Two years ago, Charlie disappeared. Nathan and his partner Zane and their wife Calliope have been searching for their son ever since. He could bond. He was very strong. They tracked him to the palace, but they haven't been able to get close."

Shim didn't know what to say. He knew what Torin would have to do to make the bondmates into his own personal timebombs. He would have tortured them. He would have warped them.

They couldn't get Bronwyn out of here fast enough.

"Do you think they'll kill her?" Lach asked, his eyes tightening.

"She's not dead." He would feel it.

Rye leaned forward, his weight on the porch railing. He watched his children play with a dead dog. "Did she take your power? I've heard it can happen with very strong broadcasters. Paige is a receiver. She's the one who sent Charlie's parents to the palace. She can still hear him every day. It sounds as though your Bron is a broadcaster. If she took your power and turned it on someone, then they could think she's a witch. There will be a trial, if she's lucky. If not, they'll hold a public execution at sunset tomorrow."

Shim closed his eyes, searching for the connection to Bron.

"Can you feel her?" Lach asked, desperation creeping into his tone.

Shim shook his head. "No. She's gone. She's not conscious, and she's not naturally asleep."

William Roan spoke up. "Most likely we can make it to her province by afternoon. If she's being held in the town center, then at least we'll know where she is."

Lach shook his head. "We need to go now."

Roan sighed. "No, Your Highness. We still have to wait until dark. It's far too dangerous."

Shim looked to his brother. This was a game they had played a hundred times before. Despite being princes of the realm, they'd had to deal with the fact that everyone thought they were damaged goods. This wasn't the first time they'd been overruled by a well-meaning protector. The truth was a prince's life was rigid, and there wasn't much freedom to it all. What freedom they'd had, they'd taken.

Lach nodded, obviously reading his brother's mind.

Shim turned to Roan. "I understand. Just try to make it soon."

Lach played the part they had designated for him long ago. "What are you talking about, Shim? We need to go now. She's in danger."

Roan watched them, his dark eyes taking in their argument. "Prince Lachlan, your brother is being reasonable."

Dante got in on the action. "We can't risk the two of you by running around in broad daylight. We all agreed to this plan."

He meant their father had agreed to this plan, and the Unseelie portion of this particular revolution depended on Lach and Shim's survival. If they had to, Shim was pretty sure Roan was ready to lock him and Lachlan up and they would go after Bronwyn without them. It would all be for their own good, but he wasn't having it. He wouldn't trust anyone else with his mate.

Shim let his face fall into the perfectly amenable expression he wore every day. "They're right, Lach. We would put Bron in more danger."

Lach shook his head. "You're such a coward, Shim. When she dies, when we end up holding her corpse instead of her warm, living body, it's going to be on you."

Lach stormed out, his boots ringing across the wood floor of the porch. He stalked toward the barn.

Dellacourt started to go after him.

Shim put a hand out. "Don't. I know my brother. He needs to be alone for a bit. Don't worry. He'll come around. He doesn't have a choice."

He watched as Lach disappeared. As they'd done since childhood, Lach would make the preparations needed to circumvent the people who would hold them back. Lach's bad reputation served their purpose. And Shim's served it as well. No one walked after Lach, preferring to praise Shim for his reasonableness.

Roan looked out over the yard where Max Harper stood talking to a desiccated horse, his face a mixture of horror and an odd sense of wonder.

"That horse." Roan nodded toward it. "How long has it been dead?"

For a long time as far as Shim could see. There wasn't a lot of flesh left, just sinew connecting bones.

"A year or so. Max loved that filly." Rye smiled.

Roan let loose a long whistle. "It should be delicate. It shouldn't be able to move like that. The bones should be brittle and break almost on contact. Yet that corpse is moving with ease, almost as it did when it was alive. Is that always what happens around your brother?"

Shim stared at the dead thing. He was beginning to follow Roan's line of thinking. "They weren't at first. The first creatures he brought back were very weak. They mostly were things like rats and vermin that lay where they died. But you buried the dog and the horse."

Rye Harper's eyes flared. "We buried that horse deep. Max didn't want the bears or the mountain trolls to get her. He dug for a day and a half. Our neighbors, Rafael and Cameron, helped us."

Roan whistled again. "That horse climbed from its grave when Lachlan's power called. It makes me wonder what he could do if he focused that power. Gives me something to think about." He started to walk into the house but put a hand on Shim's shoulder. "Thank you, Your Highness, for being so reasonable."

Reason had nothing to do with it. Shim gave the vampire a placid smile. He wouldn't be thanking him in an hour when he realized they were gone.

We're coming, Bron.

Nothing was more important than Bronwyn. Nothing.

* * * *

Torin walked into the room. Deep underground, he could feel the cold chill in his bones. This was the place of hags and their black magic.

"Why do you need me here, Your Majesty?" Maris asked, her blonde head held regally despite the cesspit they were walking into.

"I told you. I want my queen by my side." The hags had insisted that both royals be in attendance as they worked this spell. The spell that would lead him to Bronwyn Finn.

"She isn't alive. I identified the body myself." Maris had dressed for the occasion in all white, making her sure to stand out in the darkened chambers. His bride had always preferred white and sunny shades, saying they were Seelie colors. Torin rather thought it a clever disguise to mask her dark, brittle heart. Maris was a vision of loveliness amid the gloom. Her very tranquility was what had made her such an effective partner in betrayal.

"Your Majesties." Una greeted them in true form. They could be nothing less in this space. Her bland attractiveness had fallen away, and her truth made Maris stop and shudder delicately.

Glannis joined her sister. The hag's nose had grown by three inches, and her flesh sagged everywhere. Una was thin to the point of gauntness, her cheeks hollow and lips sunken in. When she smiled—he wasn't sure he should call it a smile—Torin noticed the hag had no teeth.

He'd rarely seen them in their true forms, not since that fateful day they had saved him from the ogres and set him on his path to purity.

Of course, what they didn't know was that once he'd won the day, he intended to get rid of them as well. But not until he had no further need of them. Until that glorious day, he hid his distaste.

"You've had hours and hours. What have you discovered?" Torin asked, wanting nothing more than to get this over with.

Glannis frowned, her skin sagging until he wasn't sure how she could see. "Bronwyn Finn is alive."

Maris gasped. "Impossible. I saw her body."

"This body, Your Majesty?" Una asked, gesturing toward the back of the cave.

A girl sat on a log, her youthful face illuminated by the firepit in the center of the cavern. She appeared to be fourteen or fifteen, a girl trapped forever in the first blush of her womanhood. She wore a fine overdress of sheer, pale pink silk. Her hair was pinned up in elegant braids. There was a sun-shaped pendant around her throat, the crest of the Finn line.

Maris stared at the girl, moving in closer. Torin had to give his bride credit. She matched her actions to her words. She wasn't a shrinking violet. She'd slit a few throats in her own time. His queen walked up to the girl and put a hand under her chin. She looked delicate in the firelight, the dead girl. There was no question she was dead. Her pretty gown was blood stained, and there was a hole in her belly. Yet she sat there as calmly as she could, as though she waited to be called into the temple or the schoolroom.

Maris looked at the girl before turning back to the hags. "Yes. This is Bronwyn Finn. I knew the little brat. I was forced to spend time with her after my parents sold me to the king. She used to call me sister. You think I wasn't sure? You think I didn't know the very Fae I was forced to live with for a year?"

Una's matchstick hand came out, a bony finger shaking. "No, Your Majesty. That's why it worked so well. You saw what they wanted you to see."

Torin stepped up. He wasn't sure what Una was going on about. His niece sat there, her blank face staring up at him. She was the only one he'd felt a bit of remorse about. Bronwyn had been a sweet child, seemingly harmless. She'd wanted hugs and presents from his travels. She'd been a bit starved for affection from a father who had been too busy raising a warrior king.

But he hadn't hesitated when he'd heard the prophecy. He'd sent his soldiers to kill the one person in the world who could take his heart. And now she sat staring up at him with nonjudgmental eyes, and he wondered who the brat would have become. She would have been married off, perhaps to the Unseelie princes if the rumors were true. She was better off dead.

"Speak plainly, hag. I tire of these riddles. We got rid of all the witches weeks before the coup. Maris sent the queen's personal advisor away herself. There was no one with magic here in the palace. Surely you're not saying that my queen was derelict in her duties."

Maris frowned his way. "I did as I was asked. I identified the workers with magical abilities and either killed them or sent them from the palace on various errands and then had them butchered. I did my job, Your Majesty. I rather fear that perhaps the hags did not do theirs."

Glannis shrugged, a rolling motion of her flesh. "We were unaware that there would be guests in the palace until after the battle. We were not allowed into these sanctified walls until the charms and wards against black magic were taken down."

"Yes," Maris said, latching on to the idea. "They weren't taken down until after the battle. So there was no magic in the palace until after Bronwyn was dead."

Una shook her head. "No black magic, Your Majesty. But white magic was always permitted in the palace of light, encouraged even. The very marble of the palace reflects good intentions and strengthens spells. Spells of protection. Spells that could hide a true face."

Glannis brought a knife to her arm. She stood over a pitcher that bubbled over with some foamy fog. The hag sliced into her own flesh, her expression never betraying the pain she must have felt, if a hag could feel anything at all. Torin watched as black blood oozed from her veins like some noxious oil and spilled into the pitcher. Glannis smiled, showing off blackened teeth.

"Fear not, Your Majesty." Her laughter cackled, bouncing off the walls of the cave. "I feasted well for the last days. I am filled with much blood."

Torin didn't betray his disgust. He simply watched as she squeezed her wrist until she was satisfied. He understood what the hag had meant. The hags feasted on the blood of traitors. Unlike vampires, they didn't take it directly from the bodies. They would slit throats and drain the creatures and drink down what came out. Glannis had had a bit too much. If brownie and ogre blood did that to a figure, someone should put the bitch on a diet.

Still, he watched as Una chanted over the pitcher. Witches, hags, priests. All the same with the bloody chanting. It bored him. He would outlaw chanting when the time came. It was all he could do not to roll his eyes as the hags called out to some dark goddess with an unpronounceable name. Religion. He would definitely get rid of that.

Finally, Una pronounced the spell done and brought it to the mute dead girl. She seemed so solid, but it was an illusion. If he stared hard enough, he could see a thin sliver of bone. It sat on the rock under the girl. Her form shimmered briefly, and the bone was solid. The hags had insisted on keeping one small piece of each dead royal in an ornate box. They had saved one of Bronwyn's fingers. They held a piece of the queen's skull. Only Seamus had been spared. His body had burned in the fire that had raged.

Una nodded before carrying the pitcher to the dead girl. "Reveal yourself."

She tipped the pitcher over. The ghostly fog spread like water falling. It engulfed the girl, and as the fog cleared, someone very different sat in her place.

This girl was thinner but of the same build. Her hair was shorter than Bronwyn's and not done up in elaborate braids. Her much darker hair was pulled back in a single bun, and her face had gone a horrible blue. There were distinct handprints around the girl's throat. She was dressed in plain clothes, the type worn by those who served the queen and her children.

Maris kneeled, staring at the girl. "This is not the girl I saw. This girl is named Eionnette. She was one of the girls who kept Bronwyn's clothes. This is not Bronwyn."

Glannis held her wrist and nodded toward the queen. "Yes. We rather thought that when we used the bone to bring back her image. Worry not, Your Highness. We've already tested the queen's skull.

She's dead. And, of course, you killed Seamus yourself."

"Seamus is very dead. I know that." Torin felt weary. Seamus was, once again, standing in the same room, his ghostly eyes passing judgment, though this time there was a hint of fear there, too.

"But his daughter is alive." Una passed a hand through the ghost girl and it faded with the fog, leaving behind a single small bone. All that was left of the girl.

Seamus's eyes flared, and Torin was pretty damn sure if his dead brother could kill, he would have his hands around the hag's throat.

Torin made a decision. He could scream and wail and beat his chest, but it would give his brother a sense of satisfaction. Seamus had known his daughter was alive. He'd hidden it for years. He'd hoarded the knowledge like a treasure trove of gold that kept him alive.

Torin had thought his victory over his brother complete, but there was one last battle to win.

He kept his voice calm, his demeanor kingly. "So Bronwyn killed her servant and ran?"

Glannis laughed, the sound more like a nasty cough than actual joy. "No, Your Majesty. Bronwyn Finn never showed a single talent for magic. It tends to start early. She would have shown an aptitude, and her parents would have placed her with a mentor."

Una tapped her nonexistent lips with a bony finger. "I've been thinking about the Unseelie princess, Your Majesty."

He gritted his teeth. It made perfect sense. She was the one they couldn't vet. She was the one Maris hadn't been able to keep out. "Then Gillian McIver is still in Tír na nÓg, too."

Glannis smiled. "Oh, yes, Your Majesty, and she's the reason why we're going to find them. The Unseelie have a particular magic about them, even when the magic is pure and white. It's a signature of sorts."

Maris looked up, her pale skin a rosy pink in the light of the fire. "You've found them?"

Una shrugged. "We've found a strong Unseelie signature in an agricultural district. We believe that the Princess Gillian saved Bronwyn and attempted to get her out of Tír na nÓg. If we're right, she failed, and Bronwyn has been hiding here."

She waved a hand across the back cave wall and a small map lit up, the provinces of Tír na nÓg flaring. There were two provinces

116

glowing with color, one stronger than the other.

"That's Tuathanas and Aoibhneas." Tuathanas was a bright red, but Aoibhneas was a pink. "Are they in both places? Tell me it's Aoibhneas. I hate those freaks. The mayor is an utterly insane man, but he turns out to be quite adept at both politics and defense. I would love a good reason to torch the whole town."

Maris rolled her eyes. It was a point of contention between them. "And where would you get your horses? Where would the palace get the confections we've come to love? Aoibhneas produces many of our luxuries."

"And many of our radicals." The sooner he killed them all the better.

"It matters not, Your Majesty," Una argued. "The princess is in Tuathanas. The color is much brighter there, and the Unseelie magic has been going on for much longer. I wouldn't be surprised if the other was caused by some passerby. It's strong but temporary. See, it's already fading, but Tuathanas is going strong. This is where to send the troops."

His brother's ghost was gone again.

Torin took a long breath. One last little girl to kill.

"I'll send the troops tonight."

Chapter Seven

"Will you be all right in here?" Rachel looked around the loft room. It was small, the floor covered in straw. There was a stove, a chair, a wooden closet, and a cot. Lach sat in the chair, leaving Shim no place to sit except the cot. "This is the place Max sleeps when he has a sick animal or when I get mad and kick him out of our bed. I can find some space in the house if you would rather. It's rough out here."

Shim shrugged. "We've been in worse. Sincerely, Mrs. Harper, we're fine out here. After what happened earlier, I'm happy you'll let us stay on your land at all."

Rachel opened the closet and pulled out a couple of woolen blankets, handing one to Shim and then Lach. "I'm just glad the dead things are dead again. I heard they popped up all over the village. Our healer ended up having to knock the mayor out with a sleep spell. He was walking around with the hidden vamp tech we've been gathering for the rebellion shooting corpses and talking about something called the zombie apocalypse. None of us knows what that is. We're lucky Caleb is damn good with that spell."

Lach had turned a bright red and mumbled an apology.

Rachel turned to him. "It's all right. The kids were happy to see Queenie again, even if they're mad at their dads for lying about the dog dying. It's really not a terrible thing. It could be quite useful when you think about it."

"I don't see how, but we thank you for the accommodations." Lach kept his voice polite, but Shim could feel the impatience coming off him. He would have to work to keep his brother from running the minute Rachel Harper walked out of the barn.

The sun had set. They'd eaten a small meal, but still Roan held fast to the after-midnight rule. Hours and hours of waiting. Hours when they were supposed to get some rest for the hard night ahead. Hours neither of them intended to spend. But they couldn't simply make a mad dash for it. They had to play it cautiously. For all they knew, Roan was watching them.

"Let me know if I can do anything else to help you." Rachel nodded as she stepped toward the ladder that led down to the barn floor. She stopped at the top, just as her feet hit the first rung. Her face turned down and her voice quieted. "Should I do anything for him?"

Shim held back a grin. Duffy was "patrolling" the barn, his axe on his shoulder. He'd sighed and gotten up from the dinner table when Roan had told them all to get a few hours of sleep before they headed out. He'd announced that he would watch over the princes. Shim had bet Duffy would be asleep in fifteen minutes. He'd always been able to sleep in the oddest of places, ever since they were children. If Duffy wasn't moving with a manic animation, he was snoozing, often against his or Lach's arm. "Don't worry about Duff. He's a tough one."

Rachel nodded and disappeared. The minute Shim heard the door close, he turned to his brother.

Lach was already on his feet, a pack in his hand. "I took one of the vamps' packs. He was already asleep. He won't notice it's gone until they're ready to go. By then, it won't matter. We'll be gone. It's got meal pills, a tablet, everything we could need. We'll find solid food on the way, but the meal pills should hold us."

It was exactly what he'd feared. Shim didn't move. "Lach, give it an hour. Roan is still awake. The Harper kids are running all over the place. And we need to get not only us but two horses out of here."

There was a gentle nicker from down below. "Why two, Your Highness, when one would be easier and so much faster?"

There was a sound like the rushing of water and then a man with shaggy black hair climbed up the ladder. Shim did a double take because the man wasn't wearing a stitch of clothing. He was young and very fit, but his hair was a wild nest of darkness, his eyes an amber yellow.

This was the phooka in his human form—a rare sight.

"Are you planning on killing us now?" Lach asked, no real worry in his voice. He had an amused air of expectation around him. It was a fair question. Phookas tended to hide their true form from all, though they had been known to imprint on *sidhe* from time to time, usually as younglings.

"Which of the Harpers do you belong to?" Shim asked, his mind making the leap.

The phooka grinned, a flash of sharp teeth. "Max. The idiot doesn't even know I've been around him most of his life. He saved me when I was a child. Some nasty *sidhe* killed me ma. I escaped in dog form, and Max took me in. He fed me and healed me wounds. I stayed with him for many years as a dog. Then I took hawk form and finally this one. I take the form needed to protect him. I came to him in my horse form a few months back. It's the first time I've talked to him." His eyes narrowed. "He doesn't make it easy to repay my debt. He's reckless and obnoxious, but he has a good heart. And the children." He sighed. "I've come to care for the little buggers."

Lach leaned forward, studying the phooka. "Or you're a tricky bastard and you're feeding us a huge line of crap in order to create chaos."

The phooka shrugged. "Or that. I don't care what you believe, but I'm your best bet to get out of here before those vamps shut you down. Poor little princes. No one ever lets you play. Do you honestly think you can rescue your princess without getting yourselves killed? You can't even control your own powers. You're as likely to torch her as save her, aren't you, Shim? Don't worry, your brother here can bring her back to life. Well, he can bring her corpse back. Do it quick, Lach, before she starts to stink."

Lach stood, his massive hands clenched into fists. There was practically steam coming out of his brother's ears, and that was Shim's job. "Leave us."

Shim put a hand up, a gesture to slow down. "Don't be so quick to judge. It's his nature. But it's also his nature to help his master."

Amber eyes rolled. "He ain't me master. He's me friend, and yes, I want to help him. I was only making a wee joke about the stinking corpses. Come on, man. It was funny. Like the dog today. Damn thing tried to wag half a tail."

The phooka laughed, the sound a bit maniacal, but he was right. Not about the half-tailed dog, but he was fast in his horse form and phookas were known to be hard to see unless they wanted to be seen.

"You know where Tuathanas is?" Shim asked.

Lach moved to sit beside him, a scowl on his face. "I'm sure he knows where everything is."

The phooka scratched at his scruffy head. "I do, indeed. And I swear on all that Danu's given me, I'm not lying. I want Torin out as much as the rest of you. Probably more since I don't have anywhere else to go. There's no kingdom waiting for me. There's only this farm and those Fae, and Torin will kill us all if something doesn't change. We've been safe here in the mountains. He hasn't had the inclination to attack, but he will eventually and we'll fall. So I'm offering you a deal, one time only, Your Highnesses. I shall carry you to the princess. I will be your ally. Me word is me bond. And I expect that you'll treat your ally with every due care."

The phooka's amber eyes burned in the dim light of the barn.

Lach looked at Shim and slowly nodded.

Shim took the phooka's hand. "Allies."

The phooka's hand tightened and his form wavered. "Don't forget it, Your Highness. Don't forget what we do to those who cross us. I'm the boogey man. I know what your fear is." He turned those burning eyes to Lach. "And his radiates off him."

The phooka changed, his hand releasing Shim's. His form shimmered and reassembled itself. Shim shuddered and shrank back at what he saw sitting in front of him.

"Ain't this what you both fear deep down?" The phooka's voice spoke, but it was through Shim's own lips.

Shim sat in front of himself, his smile wide and calm, but the rest of him was on fire, the flames flaring out and crackling, tendrils of heat and agony pointing like accusatory fingers.

"Look at me. I'm brighter than the sun and a whole lot more deadly. I can't control meself. I'll burn down everyone I love." The phooka changed, taking on Lach's likeness, but this was a different

Lach than the brother Shim knew. This Lach was sunken, all the light in his face gone as though someone had snuffed his candle out and what was left behind was a ruined, useless wick. Death hung on this Lach, a cloak he'd donned and wrapped around his soul. Maggots crawled on his arms, and a black-eyed rat poked its head from under his collar. "Lord of the Dead. Who could love you? Who wants a cold embrace when they could have a hot one? Is there an inch of you that truly lives, Death Lord?"

And then the phooka was a slight, wild-haired man again, his eyes narrowed. "Yes, I know what scares you both. Don't you forget it when the going gets tough and someone like me is easy to leave behind. Know that you can never really leave me. I would be with you for always and always, a nightmare under your bed."

The phooka smiled as though they had been having a pleasant conversation. He tipped his head. "Meet me in an hour out back, and be ready to fly."

The phooka disappeared, and they heard the rush of air and then a whinny signaling he was again a horse. There was the sound of hooves on the floor and then all was silent.

Lach got up and stared down at the floor of the barn. "I'm thinking once that fucker's dead, he's mine. How would you like that, phooka? How would you like dangling on my strings, dancing when I tell you to dance?"

Shim sighed. He was still shaken, but the truth was it was no surprise to him. "Leave him be. He didn't tell us anything we didn't already know. You're afraid of what I'll do, and I'm scared of losing you to the darkness."

Lach scrubbed a hand through his hair as he paced. "Why do you always find a way to be more reasonable than me? Though I still think I have the better idea. It can be hard on the road. Horses make good jerky. He'll have a damn hard time sneaking under my bed when the bastard's in my belly."

There was a long whinny, but Shim would have sworn that horse was laughing.

Lach sat down on the cot, his anger dissipating. "He has a point."

"His kind always does." It was the nature of the phooka and other tricksters like him. They knew how to go for the throat.

"Why would she ever want me? I make dead things crawl. I'm utterly useless unless you want to pet your dead dog one last time." Lach sighed. "Maybe that's why our connection isn't as strong. Do you think she can feel how cold I am?"

Shim thought about planting a fist in the phooka's muzzle, but they really did need him. "You aren't cold." He started to say something else, but then he felt it. Panic. Disorientation. Pain in his head like someone was taking a hammer to him.

Bronwyn was awake.

"I can feel her," Lach whispered, his hand going to the back of his head. "I'm going to kill those guards. Can you talk to her?"

"Only when we're sleeping, and you know how it is then." His heart was nearly stopped in his chest. Bronwyn was struggling. He could feel her panic and her intent. She was going to try to escape. In that one moment, she didn't care that she would likely be killed. She simply wanted it to be over.

Lach took a deep breath. "We have to focus. We have to get her to calm down."

Shim's hands were shaking. "I'm open to suggestions, brother. She transmits well, but she never listens."

"Make her."

Shim could feel Lach's will pressing on him. It was a palpable thing.

"What are you doing?" Shim asked.

"I'm opening myself up. I'm done letting this thing control me. We need power to connect us to her. Well, I know where my power comes from, and there's a trail of dead between us and her. I can feel it. I can use it to push my way into her head."

Shim took a deep breath and understood what Lach was doing. The phooka had shown them what they didn't want to face. They feared each other. They feared themselves. But what if they didn't have to? What if they could figure out a way to control it, to use their natural elements to fuel their power, and not the other way around?

Shim closed his eyes, trying to push Bron's panic aside. He felt the fire in the Harper's hearth. The power rushed along his skin. That fire led to another, a stronger fire, a bonfire somewhere along the road. It was all connected, a line of flame and heat that bounced to another.

Each one he grabbed hold of flared, possibly sending the Fae who sat around it reeling back a bit, but Shim kept control. The fire didn't bloom out, burning anyone. He could do this.

Lead me to her.

He breathed deeply, the smell of flames and smoldering embers filling his every sense. This was his home, given to him the day he'd bonded with his mate, connecting him to the other half of his soul.

"So many dead," his brother whispered.

Lach's power was a cold chill that ran up Shim's spine. His brother was so strong, but he feared his gifts. "Yes, so many dead who can lead the way to Bronwyn. Don't stop."

"I have her." Lach opened his mind and, sure enough, Shim felt her. The connection was right there, stronger than ever.

Shim grabbed it, letting go of his own hunt, the fires dying down for now. "Hold the connection. Can you do it?"

Lach's voice was firm and in control. "I have it. She's in a jail. There's a cemetery a short distance from it, but the place is coated in death. It's easy, Shim. I can see her. Gods, I can feel how scared she is. She's going to try something foolish."

"Stop, *a stóirín*." Shim put a wealth of power behind the word. He shoved every dominant trait he possessed into that one word, sending it over the line that ran from him to Lach to Bronwyn.

Nothing.

"She can't hear," Lach said. "But I think she can feel. I clenched my fists and she clenched hers, almost like she was answering me. She's trying to work the lock open. I think there's a guard right outside her door. They'll kill her, or we could lose her. She could run and we wouldn't be able to find her. The war is about to start."

Shim knew all the ways this could quickly go very, very badly. "We have to calm her down."

She wasn't listening, or talking didn't work the way they thought it did. This connection was new to them. To be able to communicate when they were all conscious was brand-new territory. But if she could feel, then Shim knew what to do.

"Hold the connection, brother," he said to his other half. "I know how to turn our mate's mind to something that won't get her killed."

* * * *

Bronwyn stopped. She shuddered, the cold threatening to overtake her. They hadn't even left a blanket in the frigid, dank cell they'd tossed her into. There was nothing but a cot and a bucket. She didn't like to think about what the bucket was for.

Her head ached. She wondered if Ove was even alive.

She had to get out of here. She had to. If she stayed the night, they would execute her in the morning.

Goddess, what had she done? She'd felt the heat in her hands, rolling up from her soul. She'd called it. It had been hers to command. Little Ove had been lying on the ground, her fragile body seconds from being kicked apart by brutal feet. She hadn't thought. She'd acted and the world around her had gone up in flames. It had been natural. She hadn't feared the fire.

But she was afraid of the cold she felt now.

She had to ignore it. She was scared. Sure she was. She was locked in a prison. She had every right to be scared. Her head throbbed. What had happened? She remembered everything up to the fire coursing through her veins. She was a pyromancer. It was the only explanation. She needed to come to terms with it. It could help her enormously.

She was done. Watching sweet Ove lie there in the dirt had crystalized her resolve. She needed to stop hiding. One way or another, she was going to be Bronwyn Finn again. In life. In death. If Torin was looking for her, maybe it was time to make herself available to the rebels. Gillian was wrong. Her only job wasn't to stay alive. Her job was to fight.

She looked around her small cell. They hadn't placed her in the jail, but in the private cell of the sheriff's office. A thick oak door with a small rectangular hole stood in the way of her and freedom. She had to get out. Staring at the door, she tried to call the fire forth.

Nothing.

Her palms were cold, not hot. And she could feel them flexing almost as though they weren't her own. Her hands clenched of their own volition. And yet there was something about it that felt almost soothing, like a hand reached out to embrace her own.

She ignored it. She was alone. No one had hugged her or touched her in years. Gillian would pat her hand or her back. Ove hugged her, but it was for the brownie's comfort. It had been thirteen years since she'd really felt compassionate hands on her body.

Except in her dreams. But she wasn't dreaming now.

She got to her knees in front of the door, trying to peer out the keyhole. She could fashion a lockpick. She'd been taught by the best thieves. She simply needed two pieces of flexible but strong material. Her hands felt around the material of her dress. There was a pin that held her neat apron to the tunic. It would do. She pulled it out. Flexible and easy to work with. She could scrape the pins of the lock with it. Now she needed something more solid to hold the lock in place.

Sweet heat invaded her veins.

Bronwyn.

Her name rumbled along her skin. A dark, sensual masculine tone echoed in her brain. It said her name over and over. It wasn't an unpleasant thing meant to draw her attention, more like a monk whispering a prayer over and over.

Except the low feeling in her womb didn't remind her of any religion.

She struggled to breathe. Her pussy was warm. Except it wasn't a pussy.

Bronwyn sighed and closed her eyes. What the hell was happening to her? A cock. She could feel a cock as though she had one herself. It was a wonderful thing to have a cock. A cock was the center of the whole world.

Bron felt her head roll back, her focus scatter. She couldn't concentrate on the door. How could she think about anything but the warm feeling in the center of her body? Stumbling back, she held her hands out, trying to find that cot. Her feet felt dumb, her whole body being taken over by sensation.

What in all the planes was happening to her?

Calm down, love. Let it happen.

The words flowed over her. She knew that voice. It was the voice of her Dark Ones. They often spoke as one, their tone flowing in and out. She knew it well. Tears pricked her eyes. She was still asleep. She was dreaming. The whole incident with Ove had been naught but a terrible nightmare. It was still the night before the festival, and she had time.

She fell back on the mattress, worrying because this bed wasn't hers. It was hard and unyielding, made of wool. Her sheets were of a soft cotton. They had brought them when they left the last province, she and Gillian. Those sheets had been easy to slip into their packs. A reminder of the home they had enjoyed for a few years.

So many "homes."

She gasped. A hand circled her dream cock. Strong fingers tightened around masculine flesh. No wonder men became obsessed with such a thing. She felt lit from the inside out. That hand laid a light touch along her cock. Her cock? What sort of dream was this?

The kind that keeps you out of trouble.

That voice echoed through her head like a shout from the wrong end of a long tunnel. She tried to call back but was robbed of her breath as that dream hand grasped her cock and began to squeeze with light pressure.

She fell back on the cot, not giving a damn about the scratchy wool on her back. It could be pine needles for all she cared. This feeling was glorious.

Yes, love, give in. Let us help. Let us find you.

Her ears only caught a part of what her dream voice said, but the sensation ruled her core. She felt her cock and balls, both so, so sensitive. Her balls were tight against her body. They always were when she was around. They drew up at the very thought of being close to her. She was beautiful. So fucking gorgeous. They didn't need to truly see her. They knew what she was because their souls had meshed. They had mingled in dreams since childhood. A lovely tangling of their bodies was a simple next step.

She felt the moon on her face, the light a gentle slash across her eyes. Were they feeling the same moon on their faces?

She groaned, the sound masculine and deep to her ears. She wasn't hearing her own voice. She was hearing his.

Shim, love. My name is Shim.

She fell back against the cot. Shim. Was that his name? Her Dark One? This connection felt different. There had always been a gauzy, dreamy quality to the connection before, but this felt so real. His voice wavered a bit, but there was a solidness to it that had never been there before.

Bronwyn. My name is Bronwyn.

There was a low chuckle. She could feel its warmth like he was beside her and his breath could heat her skin. *Yes, love. You're...Always known.*

She wanted to hear him, everything he said, but there was a maddening disconnect. And then she felt a surge of arousal. It took her breath away. What was he doing?

She needed to get up. She needed to get away, but he called to her. Perhaps she was still dreaming. Yes. She was dreaming, and this was her precious time. She wasn't about to waste it with plotting and planning that wouldn't come to fruition. Bron took a long breath and mentally reached for Shim. Shim. She loved his name. For so long she'd dreamed of him and his twin, but they had no names. Shim. It made him seem real.

And Shim was a dirty boy.

I want to touch...breasts. Touch...

How could she even think when his hand kept stroking his cock? A cock was a marvelous thing. Long and thick, it was like a lightning rod that attracted pleasure. Shim's heartbeat was steady and strong, his hand moving up and down. An image struck her, slamming into her head with gentle force.

He wanted to spread her legs. He wanted to take that cock and enter her body, joining them together.

They would be naked, not a stitch between them, only warm flesh that fit together perfectly. He would cover her, his chest to her breast, bellies rubbing, legs entangled. Even their toes would kiss. His mouth would sink onto hers, his tongue fusing them together as his cock laid claim.

Her whole body relaxed.

Touch...

He wanted her to touch herself. Her breasts. She put her hand to her breast, his satisfaction pulsing across their connection. He wanted to hold her breasts in his hands, cupping them, playing with the nipples.

It wasn't enough. Without opening her eyes, she undid the buttons on her bodice, the cool air caressing her breasts. Her nipples tightened.

Ours.

She pushed the sides of her bodice away, cupping her own breasts. She didn't feel her hands. She felt big, masculine hands on her body. She pinched her nipples, the image of what Shim wanted playing in her brain. He wanted to own her nipples. He wanted to roll them in his fingers, dress them up with jewels.

She pulled at her nipples, feeling the heat of his mouth. This was what he wanted. Shim wanted to suck her nipples. He would start with kisses, like pixie wings on her skin. He would cover her flesh with soft kisses, and then she would feel the long, slow lick of his tongue.

Yes, love...what I want...

She sent the image out. She wanted it, too. She wanted his mouth on her, devouring her like a treat after a hard day's work. His tongue flicked around her nipple, making it a hard nub. It stood straight up, pointing to his mouth, begging for more.

The rough edge of his teeth dragged along her nipple. It was a wickedly decadent feeling, running on the right side of pain. He bit at her nipple and then sucked it into his mouth with lavish affection.

It felt so good. The sensation raced from her nipples to deep in her pussy where an ache had begun.

And all the while she felt the tug on his cock, his strong hand running the length. There was a wetness at the tip. His seed. That's what the women called it.

Cum, love. That's...cum.

The head of his cock was covered in a silky fluid. It eased the way of his hand to stroke from bulb to base and back in an easy, slow motion. He loved this. He did this often, and when he did, he thought of her. When he stroked his own cock, it was always with her pussy in mind. He would close his eyes and see her, as she was in their dreams. She would be over him, her breasts bouncing as she rode him like a horse. She would be under him, covered by his body, open to him. She would be tied up and awaiting his pleasure, her ass in the air.

Such images assaulted her, making her gasp at the sheer eroticism that played through his mind. He'd thought up a thousand scenarios, a thousand ways to have her. It was his pastime—dreaming of ways to fuck her.

He had so many plans. He would dominate her. He would take care of her. He would fuck her over and over and over until she could always feel him inside her. Until he could be a thousand miles away and still feel his cock in her pussy.

He was hot. So hot. His touch sparked across her skin, little flames licking at her.

This was where her fire came from. It came from Shim.

She moved on the bed, restless and alive. She felt more alive than she had in years. Her whole body was awake, but she was missing something.

Where is my other Dark One?

Did he have a name? His face was the same as Shim's. Why wasn't he here with her?

Hush, love…holding the connection…holding…pissed he can't join in…

Shim moved down her body, kissing her breasts and the valley between them. He wanted to see her tied up. It was an odd image, one she might turn away from, but she could feel how much he wanted it. He wanted to see her wrapped in thin ropes, the ties elaborate, reminding her of the tortoises who lumbered down the road from time to time. He would bind her and then take his time creating the design, her body his canvas. He was an artist with the rope, spending hours and hours practicing on women in some odd place. She could see it as though sharing his memories. An elegant place not of this plane. The Vampire plane. It had to be. There was no other place with lights that carried no flame, wood that wasn't wood under her feet. Shim would tie the women up, but he never touched them for his pleasure. That was reserved for her and her alone. Everything was for her. All the training, all the pain. To be with her.

Tears pooled in her eyes. What a lovely dream she was having.

Not…don't…listen, Bronwyn…

She shook her head. She didn't want to argue. She could feel the connection waver. She grabbed it with her mind. She didn't want the dream to end. She didn't want to leave this place where she could feel Shim. All that was waiting for her was pain and heartbreak and death. This was where she wanted to be. If she could she would sink into this place and never leave them.

She sent him an image of what she wanted. Him. The other him. One and her Two. Shim cuddled to her front and her other at her back.

She wanted a name for him.

Lachlan.

It whispered through her body, like a cool thrill going up her spine.

Shim and Lachlan. Her Dark Ones.

They would surround her, making her feel so petite. She wouldn't have to be a princess with them. She didn't have to be strong. She only had to be theirs.

She could feel Shim's deep pleasure with the image. It was what he wanted, too. The three of them together. The halves of his whole finally combined through her mind, her soul connecting theirs.

They would almost flow into one another, their pleasures combining.

Shim took over. His breathing picked up, sending her heart racing. He was close. His balls, so heavy and aching and infused with power. They didn't swing anymore. They were drawn up, ready to spill inside her. He wanted that. He wanted to fill her.

There was a tingling at the base of her spine, so wild she jerked slightly, but then she knew what was happening. Shim was coming, finishing, completing the cycle they'd begun.

Bron's heart nearly stopped at the pleasure. Relief cascaded through her like a giant river as he spilled his seed. She could feel Shim's joy in the act. In his mind's eye, he pumped in and out of her pussy, grinding against her, giving her everything he had. He squeezed his cock, wringing every ounce of pleasure.

She dragged air into her lungs, blood pumping through her body in a pleasant pounding rhythm. She was happy and lethargic and she felt so, so good.

And then a hard voice echoed in her head. He practically screamed as though he wasn't sure she could hear.

Stay where you are! We're coming for you.

Bron came awake. She sat straight up in her cell, the moonlight streaking through the high bars the only illumination.

Her head hurt again. Had she actually been sleeping? It had been so different. They'd spoken to her, telling her their names. She'd felt his pleasure.

Symbiotic twins. She laughed a bit ruefully. Well, of course, she'd dreamed up a set of symbiotic twins. She missed her brothers. She was in a horrible position and symbiotic twins were powerful. Tears squeezed out of her eyes. She was alone again. She could still feel her nipples throbbing and the wetness of her pussy. She acknowledged for the first time that she might be a little crazy.

"Uhm, are you finished with all that…whatever you were doing?"

Bron gasped and sat up, pulling the flaps of her bodice together. Dear goddess, she'd been caught masturbating. She looked up and saw a guard staring through the cell door. There was a small window that opened from the opposite side. The guard shoved a tray of food through the slot in the door.

She remembered him from the day before. She'd fed him while he stood guard for the mayor. Now he was her jailor. So much for kindness.

She pulled her dignity around her. Well, whatever dignity she had left. Now he probably thought she was a whore along with being a witch. She carefully schooled her features. No matter what she was accused of, she was still Bronwyn Finn. If she was going to be burned tomorrow, she wouldn't let her fear show.

She forced herself to stand and walk across the cell. Her legs felt wobbly, like a newborn lamb learning to walk. Crossing the cell floor with small steps, she held her head high. She grasped the wood tray. There were slices of bread and an apple that been quartered. Nothing else. Still, she took it.

"Don't forget this, Isolde." The guard regarded her seriously through the small window, his hand pressing through the slot. He offered her a small, folded piece of parchment.

She took it, placing it under the tray so anyone else looking wouldn't be able to see it.

"Eat well, witch. Tomorrow you burn."

The window slammed closed, and she heard the guard's boots ring down the hallway.

Bron forced herself to eat the bread and the apple. She let an hour go by and then two. When she was sure no one was watching, she finally pulled out that slip of paper.

Trust Niall. He's working with us. I won't let you burn. G

Niall? She stared at the door. The guard. The one who had looked pissed when the mayor had talked about purification. The one who had told her to hide the brownies.

The one who had passed her the note.

Bron tore the note into tiny pieces, taking her time to make sure no one could ever put it back together. She shoved it into the seams of the mattress and lay back.

Her head still hurt, but her heart was worse. She would follow instructions. She would trust Niall, but she wanted her Shim and her Lach, and they didn't really exist. She was damaged. So damaged.

She closed her eyes, but sleep wouldn't come.

Chapter Eight

The light streaming in from the high window brought Bron out of the restless sleep she'd finally found sometime before dawn. She sat straight up on the hard cot and tried to remember her dreams.

She could only remember one, but it had been a little wild. Shim and Lachlan. They had names after years and years of dreams. Odd. She'd never heard the name Shim before, and she wouldn't have picked Lachlan. She'd always liked Padric and James.

She stretched and saw a wooden tray. A guard must have brought it in this morning while she slept. A wooden mug of water and a dry crust of bread. Her last meal.

She shuffled over and sipped the water, her throat a parched mess. She couldn't even look at the bread, her stomach churning at the thought. She put down the mug. Even the water tasted bad here.

She shook her head, trying to gather her thoughts. What was happening to her? Her mind flew back to so many years before. She'd been just a child, listening in on her parents talking. Her father had worried that Bron was touched in the head. Her mother tried to argue that imaginary friends were normal for a six-year-old. Her mother had touched her father's face and asked him to spend more time with Bron and Cian. She vaguely remembered her father saying something about them not needing his steadying hand the way Beck did. Then her father had been gone and her mother wept.

Bron had stopped talking about her Dark Ones that day. Even at six she'd known something was wrong, despite what her mother had said. Six-year-olds might have imaginary friends, but the Dark Ones didn't seem imaginary.

And now she was twenty-seven.

She could still feel Shim's hold on his cock. He'd gripped it with the confidence of long use. She could practically see him winking at her flirtatiously.

We're coming, Bron.

That voice in her head was accompanied by the candle at her bedside flaring to life. But she'd blown it out.

Mad. It was the only explanation.

She forced herself to take another drink and then tried the bread. If she had any chance at running, she would need some strength. After taking another small sip and chewing through some of the bread, she turned to the window.

Something was happening outside. She stood on her small cot, straining to see out the window above her. Grasping the bars that covered the window, she went up on her tiptoes and could barely see the courtyard outside. Guards worked, hauling logs into the clearing. They were directed by the sheriff to place them in a circle surrounding a giant pole.

The maypole. *Bastards.* Yesterday it had been decorated with colorful ribbons, the center of the children's joy. Today it would be the center of the bonfire that would take her life. They would bring her to the pole, and the executioner would tie her down and they would set her on fire.

She stared out, recognizing a few of the guards. They had laughed and danced with her at the festivals and now they would be the ones who lit her body on fire, the final payment for defying the pretender.

There was the sound of footsteps coming down the hall. Loud and lumbering. Not Niall. Bron slipped back down to the bed. She'd been so afraid the night before, for Ove, for herself. Now there was a horrible nothingness as the window in the door opened, and the mayor's puffy face showed through the opening.

"Traitorous bitch."

Yes, she would likely hear a whole lot of that. "Tell me something I don't know."

His face twisted, contorting into a mask of fury. "I'll tell you something you don't know. I've placed wards around the village. No magic is going to save you."

She hadn't expected it to. It was standard procedure to ward the jail against all magic. The sheriff certainly didn't want prisoners to be able to escape death by way of witchcraft. Bron wouldn't be surprised if Micha had the whole damn village warded after yesterday. "I didn't expect it to. I don't truly understand what happened yesterday. I know you won't believe it, but I don't care. I didn't mean to torch your guard."

"He died, you know."

She was surprised to not feel a thing. It had been the guard or Ove, and Ove hadn't done anything wrong. In that moment, she would have killed anyone who was going to try to hurt the innocent youngling. She would do it again. She would never be able to sit by and watch. If she hadn't felt that power surge, she would have attempted to stop the guard in some other way. She would never be able to sit idly by and watch as someone was killed for no reason.

But that's what you've been doing for thirteen years, Princess Bronwyn.

"You don't even care. I never knew you at all. Know this—I'll find that brownie and I'll throw her on a fire, too." Micha huffed as though he'd expected something more. Some groveling perhaps or offers of her body in exchange for a bit of mercy.

That wasn't going to happen. She wasn't stupid. After what had happened yesterday, there would be no mercy for her. She was happy someone had thought to hide Ove away. "What do you want, Micha?"

"You should call me by my rightful name, you ungrateful bitch."

Why wouldn't he go away? Shouldn't the hours before her inevitably horrific death be quiet and peaceful? She could try to go to sleep and see Shim and Lach again. Maybe, if there was a place beyond this one, maybe they would be real.

Selfish. So selfish. You want to die so you don't have to fight.

The voice inside her head was getting obnoxious. Well, the voice that seemed steeped in guilt. She apparently had a whole bunch of voices inside her head. "If you aren't going to tell me what you want, then feel free to go away."

"I want you to tell me where your bitch sister went to."

That had Bron sitting up and fast. She was definitely still capable of feeling something. Gillian had slipped her a note. Goddess, the last thing she wanted was to get Gillian killed. "She doesn't have anything to do with this."

His eyes narrowed to slits, making his irises look like endless dark. "I doubt that. She's already managed to kill three of my best guards."

Gillian? "I don't believe it."

"It was her or her friends. Tell me where she is and I'll make your death painless. I can have the healer brew a tea to ease the way. You won't feel the fire. You won't feel anything. All you have to do is tell me where Gillian is. Isolde, you don't want more deaths, do you?"

She didn't want them, but they would come. They would come whether she stood up or not. They would come if she escaped. They would come if she burned. She'd spent thirteen years believing that staying alive was all that was important. But weren't some things worth dying over?

She thought about the note Gillian had sent through Niall. She knew exactly what Gillian would do. She would run. Bron wasn't sure how she'd convinced the guard to help them, but Gillian would sacrifice anyone she had to in order to ensure Bron's continued existence. Gillian would save her and move on to the next far-off province, hiding and concealing their identities.

They would wait. And for what? For her brothers to return? For Bron to grow up? She was twenty-seven. She wouldn't get any more ready to become the focus of a revolution.

"I'm not telling you where she is. I won't say a word. Not about my sister."

A plan was ruminating, forming in her brain. A really bad plan, probably, but a plan. She'd waited long enough. It was time she gave to the cause. Gillian seemed to think that Bronwyn was the cause, but Bron knew differently.

Ove was the cause. Everyone who had been hurt by the pretender was the cause. Bronwyn was merely a pawn, and it was time to make her move. The pawn could take the king if it was played correctly.

"You're stupid, Isolde."

"I'm not Isolde." She finally got up and walked to the door. Her feet felt a bit unsteady, but she caught her balance.

"What are you trying to say?"

She gave him a feral grin. "Figure it out, Micha. Think for a minute, and it'll come to you."

He stared at her, his face a blank. "Isolde, tell me where your sister is. The fire will make you scream."

Would it? She *was* fire. It leapt from her fingertips. It had a place in her heart. "I'll take that chance."

"Isolde…"

"Don't call me that." She couldn't stand it. It wasn't her damn name. It wasn't her place. "Call me by my name. Call me Bronwyn."

He took a quick step back, a gasp on his lips. "You're lying."

"I'm not." She wouldn't go down quietly. Whether Niall saved her or she died in the fire, it didn't matter. She needed to have her name. There was power in her name. "Call me by my name. Call me Bronwyn Finn."

His head shook. "You'll burn then, dumb bitch. If you think for a second I'll tell anyone what you've said, you're wrong. I wouldn't let anyone know I planned to marry someone who is utterly insane. You're a stupid girl. You're not a princess. And if you think that this ploy will buy you time, you're wrong. I stood up in front of a crowd and said I wanted to marry you. Too many people know. I won't go down with you. No. You'll burn before you can even open your mouth and spout such vicious lies."

She stared at Micha through the window, its bars mocking her. She was in a cage, but then she'd been there for thirteen years.

What could she do? She'd been quiet for so long. She'd hidden her existence. It had kept her alive, but now she saw a distinct problem with it. No one would believe her. She'd been a child when she'd gone on the run. She was a woman now, and no one with the exception of Gillian had watched her grow. She looked like her father. Gillian said it, but did anyone remember? The knife. It had the Finn crest on it. Did it prove a damn thing? There were only two weapons made with that crest—the sun and the moon. Beck had the sword. She was sure of it.

He wouldn't have left without their father's sword.

And the knife had been used on her. She'd pulled it from her body. Torin had to have taken it from her father's body. He'd given it to his assassin to kill her. Her own father's knife. It was her only proof beyond her face. It was still in its hiding place in the tower. "I am Bronwyn Finn. I was born in the White Palace and I died there. I was given a second life. I am my father's daughter."

A huffy laugh came through the window. "Those can be your last words, though no one will believe it. Good luck, Isolde. When you're nothing but ashes, your sister will run. You're nothing. Nothing at all."

The window slammed shut. She was so much more than nothing. She was the revolution, but perhaps she'd waited too long. Leaning against the door, she felt her head swimming. Not enough sleep. Not enough food. Not enough life.

She'd spent too long in her dreams. She'd wanted to be somewhere else for so long she'd neglected the here and now. Shim and Lachlan were dreams. They were a way out of her destiny, and now that she was finally ready to face it, she would probably get her ass fried in a fire.

Her brothers wouldn't know. They would always think she'd died at the palace. They wouldn't know she'd been burned at the maypole—the stake. Half an hour passed, the minutes running by like molasses dripping off a spoon toward a well-cooked piece of bread. She drank more water. Ate the last of the bread. Slow. So slow. She was able to go over most of her life. She was shocked to realize how much of it she'd spent in dreams. When she looked back on her life, she saw the times Cian had played with her and her mother had rocked her, stroking her hair during thunderstorms. She remembered holding her da's hand as they walked through the streets of the village. But mostly she saw Shim and Lach. She saw them as children, laughing and playing through fields of golden wheat and swimming on a pebbled beach, the ocean water foaming around them. There were mermaids in the waters, but they didn't need to worry about it because mermaids only called to the unfaithful and the unwary. They played and played, telling secrets and stories. Stories she'd heard but could barely remember the next day. When she'd begun to gain her womanhood, the dreams had changed. Her Dark Ones had started to touch her. Little glancing strokes at first and then a kiss here and there. Her cheeks and her forehead and sweetly enough, her nose. Finally they had pressed a mouth to hers. A tongue had caressed and then…

Death.

So long was the darkness. The aloneness. It was worse because for so long she'd been with them. And then the connection had been cut as though it hadn't existed.

Years had passed. She'd run and run. So many provinces. So many new faces.

She'd been scared, reaching out every night for that connection she'd counted on all her life. Nothing, until one night, a tendril had reached back, like a light in the darkness. She reached for it and finally she'd seen them. They hadn't been solid at first, but she'd felt a touch, a caress that made her skin light up.

She'd been twenty. Six years had passed in loneliness and then another three in a frustrating reaching. She would grasp and then the dream would be gone, like a ghost that had never really existed. Every morning she'd awakened aware that she hadn't gotten what she wanted and then…

That kiss.

Her whole life, the happy part, played out in a long dream.

She'd given up everything for a damn dream.

There was a scratch at her door.

"They're coming."

Niall's voice.

"What should I do?" She kneeled before the door. It was time to make her play, but she felt so tired. Her hands shook slightly. The world was a bit fuzzy. Was she starting to panic?

"I don't know." The words were hesitant. "They're coming early. It was supposed to happen at noon. It's only ten."

Micha was running early. He probably thought that if he could get rid of her, Gillian would stop her assault. He would burn her before the township was up and able to protest that she hadn't had a fair trial. She hadn't even seen the town magistrate.

She'd made a terrible mistake. Micha had upped the timeline because now he didn't want her talking. Goddess, she was terrible at this. Horrible. She didn't know what to do except to try. She wouldn't be walked to her execution calmly. Dignity wasn't going to help her.

Besides, no one had gathered. No one would bear witness. And no one would help her.

They had all turned their backs.

She would fight until the flames took her.

"They're coming, Your Highness. Please don't call attention. I have a plan. Someone has run to tell Gillian." Niall's voice was thin through the cracks of the door, and then the only sound she heard was the hard thud of boots against the floor.

The door slammed open, and she was faced with two of the largest guards in the village. They were each a foot taller and had a hundred pounds on her, but they were armed to the teeth as though she was the most dangerous criminal on the plane. They each held a sword and had knives at their belts.

She knew how to use a knife. She could certainly get one of them, but could she get both?

Niall had begged her not to draw attention. There was some plan in place.

Your Highness. Goddess, Niall had called her "Your Highness."

"Isolde, are you going to come quietly or should we cut out that pretty tongue of yours right here?" Arik, the older of the two guards, asked.

"I think we should have a bit of fun with her before she goes out. Seems a shame to leave this life without ever knowing the touch of a man." Tir leered at her.

Arik held out a hand. "Don't touch that one. You weren't here yesterday. It's best that one goes out in the flames. Come on, wench. Time to go."

Bron took a deep breath and made her decision. She would give Niall some time. He knew something. Gillian had brought him in on the secret, and that meant Gillian trusted him. She nodded to her captors and smoothed out her dress before stepping forward to follow them.

The hallway was utterly silent as they moved toward the stairs that would lead them up and into the main hall. She followed Arik, who lumbered in front of her. All the long walk, she could feel Tir's eyes on her. She began to feel an ache low in her gut. Fear? It was a horrible rolling sensation.

"We'll get a hot fire going for you, witch." Arik's voice echoed off the stone walls.

"But not so hot it won't take a little time to work. Wouldn't want you going out too soon, now would we?" Tir said with a hollow laugh.

"Wouldn't want to disappoint the crowd." Bron frowned, her feet shuffling in front of her. One foot in front of the other. She had to get through each moment. She tried to focus. Her skin felt hot. Was it starting again?

Arik stopped at the bottom step. "Ain't no crowd. Heard they was too afraid of you. The mayor is trying to calm them, tell them he has you under control. I'm sure by the time the magistrate passes sentence, they'll come out in droves and see you ain't nothing to be afraid of."

But Tir was frowning. "I heard they wouldn't come because they love her. She gave a lot of people in this village food. That sister of hers healed a lot of Fae."

Arik's eyes went hard. "That's the way witches work. They bring you in. Who knows how many she really hurt? My neighbor lost two cows last week. I bet it was her."

Tir seemed to pull his energy back around him. He nodded. "You're right. Me ma's wrong. She'll see when the witch dies and things get better around here. Move it, Isolde. Don't think because a few of us are too stupid to see that you're evil, that they're going to help you. More's like those who don't come will get punished."

She found a comfort in the fact that they were rebelling, even if it was in a quiet way. The people of this village seemed so deeply content with the status quo, but perhaps that was because Torin hadn't really touched them yet. Things were changing. Bronwyn simply had to find a way to live long enough to see it happen.

She tried to focus on the heat that threatened to take over her body. It needed to be in her hands, not low in her gut.

Arik turned back around and had a foot on the first step of the stairs. Bron began to follow. There was nothing else to do. The corridor was narrow and didn't lend itself to fighting. But if she could start a fire, maybe she could run.

Bron heard the guard shuffling behind her. He gave a soft grunt, and then there was a hand on her elbow. She turned and looked into Niall's brown eyes. He held a finger to his lips, an obvious request for silence. Tir was on the floor, his body in a crumpled mass. Bron checked her gasp.

Niall held a blade in his hand, the knife slick with blood. Tir's blood.

The enormity of it grasped her. Niall was killing to protect her. Did she want that responsibility? Did she have a choice? The choices she would make if she pursued this path hit her squarely in the gut as Arik moved up the stairs and Niall stalked him.

Bron clung to the side of the wall, her eyes moving between Tir's body and Niall's arm as he reared back. The burning sensation hadn't gone away. What in all the planes was happening to her? She had to think.

She made the decision. There would be no going back. There would be blood and death, and she could not shrink from it. She would eat the guilt because that's what it meant to be a leader.

Niall slit his throat, the knife moving in utter silence. He held Arik against his body, his arm around Arik's shoulders in an odd approximation of intimacy. Niall brought the larger man to the ground. He never had a chance to shout or say a word.

Her protector eased him to the floor and held the blade at his side. "Your Highness, I need you to trust me."

"Gillian told you. Gillian trusts you."

His face contorted in confusion. "Gillian? No. Gillian knows who sent me. I talked to her yesterday. I knew she wasn't your sister so I figured she had to be the Unseelie princess who went missing."

Bron stared at him for a minute. "Who sent you? Who told you my name?"

Niall's eyes were on the stairs above. "You have to play your part, Your Highness. We don't have another way out. Just take a deep breath and follow my lead."

He took her elbow and started to escort her up the stone steps. But she had a few questions. If she was going to be the center of this revolution, she was going to start playing the part.

"If Gillian didn't send you, who did?" Bron could feel the sweat on her brow, the ache in her gut. But it wasn't her gut. Not really. It was lower, deeper—an ache with only one cure.

Niall stopped on the second stair. They were still so close to the bodies, but it didn't seem to bother Niall. He simply stared at her for a moment as though trying to decide how much she could handle. "You don't remember me. Niall Younger. My father was the stableman. He took care of the horses for the White Palace. I worked with him. I took care of your pony."

Her mind raced, and she saw a young man, only three or four years older than she. Brown hair and bark-colored eyes, and a soft hand with the horses. His father had taught her to ride.

"I remember you. You had a brother named Walter."

His face turned down. "Walter and me dad died long ago. I was left alone in the palace, but I found a friend. A shade. A sluagh. He taught me how to live, gave me information on where to find food and who would protect me. He sent me to the cook who helped me. I was only fifteen. The cook gave me a place to stay, and the sluagh gave me a purpose. He taught me how to fight, how to be a guard. He whispered to me who to get in good with so I would have my choice of assignments. And he gave me my reason to live. To find Bronwyn Finn. To locate his daughter."

Bron felt locked in place, the whole world spinning. Her father? "My father can't be a sluagh. He would never."

It was beyond comprehension.

"He had no other choice. When the light came, he didn't walk into it. He couldn't because he had work to do. His children still needed him. He stayed for you. He molded me into his emissary. As far as I know, only Torin and myself have ever seen him. He's not haunting anyone but his brother. He had a different use for me."

"My father turned sluagh, and he knows I'm alive?" It didn't add up in her head.

"He saw the Unseelie princess make her way out of the palace with you. He would have followed, but he was weak at the time. He was tied to the place of his death. He still is for some reason. When the other sluagh left the plane, he wasn't able to move past the caves. He's bound to Torin now. He can only go where Torin goes. So he trained me to find you. I've been moving up in the guard, and I've served ten different noblemen, all the while looking for you. I knew I had finally found you a couple of days back, but I wasn't sure how to get you out of here. Now I don't have a choice. Gillian is talking to the villagers. She's trying to find a way to get you off the plane." He stared at her for a moment. "That is not what your father wants."

"What does my father want?" Her father had ignored her with the exception of pats on the head and telling her she was pretty and a wee bit insane. What could her father want for her to do?

Niall took her by the arm. "Lead them. Take your crown back. Your brothers are gone, and it seems they will not be coming back. You're his blood. That crown is yours. I am going to take you north to Sir Giles's province and then on to Aoibhneas."

The mountain province. She hadn't been to Aoibhneas. It was difficult to get to and rumored to be an odd place. The Fae who lived there had always been outspoken and considered a bit difficult. They were strong fighters and used the land to their advantage. Aoibhneas. She could make her stand there. The rebellion could start there.

She could gather Fae along the way. Yes, it could work, or even if it didn't, at least she would have tried. At least she could say she had finally stood up. If she could only get her legs to work.

"We must tell Gillian. And I have to take the brownies with me."

Niall's voice lowered to a deep growl. "Not possible, Your Highness. I am taking you to Sir Giles where he will make arrangements to see us safely to Aoibhneas. This must be done with the greatest of secrecy. Time is of the essence. And under no circumstances are we to tell Princess Gillian of our plans."

Not tell Gilly? Bron tried to pull away. "I can't leave without my sister."

"She is not your sister, and as far as your father and I can tell, she has a completely different agenda than our own."

"She's saved me time and time again. She raised me. She trained me."

"Because she always intended to take you to the Unseelie plane. This is not her fight. You're a bargaining chip for Gillian McIver. I would have completely left Gillian out of the planning if I could have. As it stands, she only knows I'm trying to help. We're going to keep it that way. You cannot leave the plane. There must be a Finn in Tír na nÓg or all is lost."

There was a shuffling upstairs, and she heard a male voice call out. "Guards? Where is the witch?"

Niall's jaw firmed, and he took her elbow. "Follow my lead, Your

Highness. I will protect and defend you with my life. This I vow. I will see you on your rightful throne and not that of the Unseelie."

He began up the stairs, stepping around the bodies of the guards he'd killed. Bron's mind was racing. What was going on? What did he mean about Gillian? Gillian had been trying for years to take Bron to the Unseelie plane, but that made sense. It was her home plane. Where else would Gillian go?

She followed Niall into the main hall, her eyes on her potential ally. Niall was a handsome young man roughly her age. She tried to remember him. His father had been kind enough, but all she could remember of the boy was a shy lad who brushed her pony's coat and gave her carrots to feed it. Could she believe him? Did she have a choice?

"Hurry along now." Micha stood frowning. There was a circular disc around his neck, tied with rough twine. It didn't fit with Micha's normal elegant dress. The mayor pressed a second one into Niall's hand. "Wear this. It's a ward to protect you from the bitch's magic. And hopefully the potion has started to work."

"Potion?" Niall asked. His eyes took in the room. Three guards stood at attention, Micha's closest men. The door to the grounds stood open, and the sounds of workers shuffling as they built the great bonfire wafted in. Already Bron could smell the scent of the oil they doused the wood in.

Micha shrugged. "I had one of my house women concoct a dampening potion. It should keep her calm and compliant. I slipped it into her water this morning. She should be a mess by now. It's actually an aphrodisiac, but it has the added benefit of making the user very submissive." His eyes found hers. "Did you think I'd give you your last words? Not a chance. I have too much at stake. But you shouldn't be able to talk at this point."

She tried to back away.

Micha grabbed a vial off his desk. "Hold her."

Niall stopped, obviously not sure what to do. Poor Niall. None of this had gone how he'd planned. She was sure he'd hoped to slip her out of the province with no one the wiser. Now he had to get her away from more guards and deal with a drugged princess. He was forced to watch as one of Micha's personal guards held her and forced her head back.

The substance was vile, and she recognized the bitter taste. There had only been a hint of it in the water. This was undiluted. It raked through her system, burning as it made its way down her gut. The effect was almost instantaneous. A horrible ache, so much worse than before, grabbed her.

She needed. She needed them.

"Shim. Lach." She could feel her head lolling back.

"That's better." Micha's muddy eyes looked down at her. "See, my dear, now you're compliant, more like the lady you should have been."

"Hurts." She seemed to only be able to speak single words now. "Shim. Lach."

He shook his head. "Are they your lovers, dear? I should have known you would be a whore, too. I should have taken you and left it at that. You ungrateful wretch. You don't deserve to be my wife. Go and see if the fire is ready yet and bring the magistrate. Our witch has confessed."

She felt her body falling and the cold stone floor against her skin. Her head ached, a sharp pain, but it was nothing compared to the fires that licked at her body. Fire. Fire should be sweet, but now it was only pain. Shim. Shim was fire. Like a shimmer. Lach was cool like a lake. Yes, that was where she'd gotten their names. One mystery solved. Would she see them soon?

"Your Highness, I am outnumbered." Niall lifted her off the floor where they had simply tossed her like she was a piece of garbage. Niall's words were whispered against her ear, so small she could barely make them out.

She wanted to kiss him. She wanted his lips on hers, his cock sliding deep. That would quench the fire. Her eyes would close, and she could pretend he was Lach or Shim.

Goddess, it was cruel to die like this. To know this ache and know what it meant. She would die a virgin, fire torching her from the inside and the outside.

"Your Highness, you must tell me where the knife is."

Urgency flavored his command. He was so close, his skin hidden under layers of clothes. Shim. She'd seen him without his clothes. And Lach. So beautiful. She needed flesh against hers. It was all she wanted now. Shim was close. She could see him. He was holding her.

"Shim. Kiss me."

"Damn it, Bronwyn." There was a shuffling as he looked down at her. His eyes shifted to dark blue. There he was. But his words made little sense. "I need to know where the knife is. It's the only proof. I can't save you, but I have a job to do. If I can't save you, I have to find someone else. That knife is proof. Please. You owe the kingdom."

Kingdom? What kingdom? Why did he care about the kingdom? She hurt. She ached. She couldn't even breathe. "Kiss me." Why wouldn't he kiss her? Lach liked to play vampire games, but Shim was always so quick with kisses. She needed both. Where was Lachlan?

Her body shook. Niall wouldn't leave her be. "The knife. Where is the knife?"

He kept talking about the knife. He urged her. Told her they were coming. The words didn't make sense.

"The tower. In the tower." That was where she'd hidden the knife. The knife had been her father's. The knife had killed her, blood tumbling from her body until nothingness had swallowed her up and then fire had brought her back. A phoenix. She'd been a phoenix, born anew.

They had given her wings.

"Where in the tower?" Niall asked the question with obvious impatience. "I'm out of time. They're coming back. I'll have to find it myself. I am sorry for this, Your Highness. I wish you good luck in your journey."

And she was back on the floor. Alone. Abandoned. A cramp hit her. She needed to touch herself, but she couldn't make her damn arms work. A journey. She was taking a journey.

Into death.

Rough hands pulled her up, dragging her when her feet wouldn't work. Tears streamed now. The world was a chaotic mess, and she couldn't feel them. They were always there, somewhere in the back of her mind. She no longer cared that they were an expression of what was wrong with her. They had been the best part of her pathetic life, and she couldn't feel them. Real or not, she wanted them here.

"Lachlan." Someone was screaming his name. "Shim."

She could smell the fire. So close now. Her head snapped back.

Someone had slapped her. Blood. She tasted it even as another seizure hit. The agony was unimaginable, a body that cried out for solace and would get not an ounce.

Rope bit into her wrists, the only thing holding her up.

The guards laughed. Called her trash. Better off ashes. That was all she was to these men. Nothing. She meant nothing. Her dreams and madness meant less than nothing. They would lash her to a pole and burn her then sweep up her ashes. It would be as though she hadn't lived.

Bronwyn Finn had died so long ago, and now this girl, this woman she'd become, would be gone, too. Ashes burned in the fire, sent to the wind. The ache in her gut…pussy. It was in her pussy. There was no way to deny it now. The ache in her pussy superseded all other pain. What a horrible way to die—all her sweetness dissolved and she was left with only a raw ache as the sum of all her years.

Lachlan. Shim. She called to them. She didn't know if she cried out loud or if it was only in her head.

She felt the heat of the fire and prayed she would see them soon.

Chapter Nine

The phooka stopped at the edge of the forest, his mighty hooves kicking up dirt. Beyond the copse of trees, there was a small village. Bron's village. They'd ridden all night, never letting up. Lach wasn't close to tired, as though something as inconsequential as fatigue couldn't touch him now.

But fear could.

Lach dismounted from the phooka's enormous back, his boots thudding against the forest floor. Something was wrong. He could feel it. Or rather not feel it.

He didn't have the same connection to Bron that his twin had, but since he'd been on this plane, he could feel her like a whisper in the back of his head. Now the noise was gone, as though someone had turned it off. It had happened a few minutes before, but it scared the crap out of him, as his vampire cousins would say.

"Something's gone wrong." Shim stood beside him, one hand on their steed.

Their ridiculously obnoxious steed who talked way too much for a horse. "Aren't you the smart one, Shim? The king is slaughtering Fae and you're only now figuring out that there's something wrong."

Lach rolled his eyes. "Shut up, phoo."

Shim ignored the phooka utterly. "A couple of minutes back, I lost touch with Bron."

"Could she be sleeping?" Lach couldn't imagine it. She had to be terrified. They had no idea what had happened after she'd been called a witch and lost consciousness. But the humming in the back of his head had been there, an oddly comfortable sensation. He felt bereft without it.

But he thought he would know if she'd died.

She couldn't die. Not when they were so close.

Shim shook his head. "She was sleeping earlier. I could feel it. You have to get used to the connection now that it's strong enough for you to feel it. When she's sleeping, the hum changes."

Yes, he'd noticed it. "It's like it's muted and calm, and when she wakes up there's a liveliness to the sound."

"That's right. But now there's nothing. She was awake and moving and then nothing."

Lach thought back to those last few moments. His brother was wrong. "Not nothing. She was confused."

The phooka huffed and tossed his head back and forth. "Perhaps the princess was drugged." He sniffed the air. "I've heard that sometimes executioners are kind. They drug the ones they set on fire. Smells like they're already at work."

Panic, pure and unadulterated, raced through his veins. He started to run toward the village, but his brother's hand stopped him.

"Don't you dare. This is my element, not yours, brother." His eyes closed briefly. "I can feel it. The fire. Idiots. They can't kill my mate with fire." He looked up again, and his normally dark eyes had gone a distinct reddish orange. "Stay away from it. We both know it can burn you."

"And we both know that a sword can cut you in half." Lach looked to the phooka, who had far better senses than either of them. "How many people are out there?"

The phooka took a long breath. "Many. At least twenty. By the horrible smell of them, I would say almost all men."

And men would have swords. Two against twenty.

Or were they just two? What had Roan said back in Aoibhneas? That the dead Lach brought back were powerful. Chaos. Perhaps chaos could be their friend for once.

"Can you grab the fire? Keep it from her?" Lach asked.

"Already done, brother. Though I doubt anyone knows I have control. I can't see anything, so I'm simply keeping it in a circle. How do I know she isn't burning already?"

"Because I don't smell the divine scent of roasting princess yet, Your Highness. No way I would miss that. Control the fire. I'll see what I can find out." The air around the phooka shimmered, and the horse became an odd-looking creature. What spoke to him was a combination of a large squirrel and a creature Lach had seen in vampire DLs. A lemur. But lemurs were slow, and the phooka was not. He scampered up into the trees using long claws. The leaves above their heads shook, delicate green shells raining down on them.

Lach's whole body was on edge. Bronwyn was in that village. She was close, so close. It was everything he'd wanted since that first moment as a child when he'd closed his eyes and seen her in his dreams. She'd been a girl, even younger than him and Shim. In that first dream, he remembered them all looking at each other as though wondering what to do and then Bron had shown them a game. A silly thing. She threw a pebble and then hopped and skipped to pick it up. Unseelie games tended to involve blood and often death. It had been a sweet thing to spend time with the wide-eyed girl.

When they had awakened the next morning, they had laughed about sharing a dream.

They were still dreaming of her when they'd turned sixteen, and Lach had known that somehow, someway Bronwyn completed him.

And then he'd seen a picture of her and set the idea in his father's mind to merge the tribes through marriage.

"I can't stand this waiting," Shim said.

He hated it, too, but finding Bronwyn wouldn't mean a thing if they didn't live through the experience. They needed to stay calm. Rushing in could be bad for Bronwyn, too. What they really needed was an army.

An idea played at his brain. He needed an army, but his father had ensured their army wouldn't follow him. He hadn't meant to, but he'd treated Lach and Shim like fragile idiots for so long, no one would follow them. No Unseelie alive would follow a fragile king.

He opened his senses and found that cold place deep in his center where his power resided. He couldn't have a living army. Roan was in charge of the men he'd brought. But there was more than the living to consider.

"Damn me, Lach. What are you doing?" Shim's eyes were wide.

He felt for them. The dead were everywhere, as much a part of the land as the living could ever be. The dead were oddly eternal, shifting from one form to the next. From living to corpse to food and fertilizer, and in their own way, right back to living.

But Lach wanted the corpses. Yes. They would do nicely.

"Getting us some backup." He called to them, reaching out with his mind, tendrils of power flowing like a cool river, sweeping up the dead in its wake.

He ignored the smaller creatures. Rats who had died crawled once more, birds flew, and cats hissed from long-dead mouths. But Lach was concerned with the mausoleums. Yes. His power sought the places of the dead.

He'd always fought the power, but now he embraced it. He opened himself to it, welcoming the rush of sensation that came with it. He knew them. As he called to them, so did they speak to him.

Sir Bran Jenkins lay on his cold slab, a sword clutched in his hands, placed there by his sons and his widow that he might fight on in the afterlife. Sir Bran wanted to fight. It had run through his veins, and though he no longer had blood, the desire clung to his bones more strongly than any shroud.

His sons, both taken not long after, lay in the crypt close to their father.

A family of warriors with nothing left but useless swords that would never again sing with the heat of battle.

Then fight, Sir Bran. Take up your sword. Wake up your sons. Fight for me.

He called to them, sending his message out to the quiet mass of dead. Ears long since past hearing listened, perking up, ghastly smiles forming on lipless faces. Lach felt them rising from their stone beds or clawing up from the ground.

And he heard the cries of the living who had the horrible fate of coming into contact with his army of dead.

The phooka scrambled down the tree, his long tail twitching, amber eyes enormous in the afternoon light. "You've been busy, Your Highness. It seems the dead walk again."

"The dead fight again." Lach corrected him.

"Whatever they're doing, it's working. Go quickly, Your Highnesses. Your princess is in a bad way. She's surrounded by fire. The flames refuse to touch her, but I cannot say the same for the smoke. The battle is all around her. Hurry."

Shim took off, sword in hand. Lach followed, his mind working in two directions—saving Bronwyn and keeping control of his creatures. He could feel them fighting, sent images of guards. Kill the guards. Leave everyone else.

They raced past buildings, small structures, the place markers of a small, poor village. Mud huts and thatched roofs surrounded them. Bron had lived here, was dying here, when she should have had two palaces to choose from.

All around him there were sounds of battle. Grunts and groans and the creaking of limbs as they moved, trying to protect hearts and heads and bellies from opponents' swords. Screams could be heard over the clanging of metal against metal. Cries of terror. Pleas for the dead to go back to their graves.

Lach felt the heat from the fire before he could see it. He stopped in his tracks, his mind flying back to that day. He didn't remember much except the heat and pain, and the deep need to save his brother from both.

He couldn't go there. He forced his attention to the present. Even that one small lapse had cost him. His corpses had fallen to the ground. The guards who remained stood staring down as though utterly surprised by their victories.

Bron. Bron was in the middle of it all. He saw her for the first time. Her skin was pink from the heat, sweat coating her as she hung limply from the pole they had attached her to. Lach clutched his sword, his heart threatening to fail. Her black hair hung around her face, lips as red as any rose but just as unmoving. They were too late.

Shim elbowed a guard who seemed to realize that the dead were not the only opponents.

"Get back to yer houses." The guard shoved at his brother, but before Shim had hit the dirt, the guard was on fire, his tunic going up like a torch.

Lach clutched the sword in his hand. It was mostly for decoration, though both he and Shim had received instruction. But now, as the world seemed to crash around him, instinct coursed through his body. His corpse warriors were reviving now that he had control of himself. He would kill them all. They had taken his princess, his mate, the only woman in the world who could bridge the halves of himself. They had murdered her and now they would pay.

Rage rose, adrenaline coursing through him. He sent it out, his corpses popping back up to the horror of the guards. Finally, finally Lachlan knew who he was. He was the warrior, never tested, never allowed to battle as was his right. Never allowed to slaughter his enemies.

"You, young *sidhe*. Take up that sword. Defend me," said a sweaty man in clothing far too elegant for an agricultural town. "The witch has done this. We must kill the witch."

Lach didn't even think about it. He skewered the repugnant man, thrusting his sword deep into the man's belly. He wore a broach with what appeared to be the village's crest. The mayor, perhaps? It didn't matter. He'd had a hand in Bronwyn's death.

He could kill the whole village. He pulled his sword free as a large guard attacked. It was easy now that he gave in to his purest instincts. He'd fought for so long. He'd fought the death magic, and he'd fought this deep desire that formed the core truth of Lachlan McIver.

He was an animal, an instrument of pure death.

Lach let go. There was nothing but vengeance now. He would fight and fight until someone put him down. This plane had taken his Bronwyn, and it would run red with blood. He wouldn't care who he killed as long as he continued to kill.

He moved his sword. Somewhere in the darkest recesses of his mind, he realized that his warriors were following him now. When he moved his sword, slicing through a guard's neck, his warriors did the same, a grandly choreographed dance of death.

Something warm and rich-smelling coated his hand. Blood. Sweet blood. His fangs were out, practically crying for a taste. Another part of himself buried. Lach felt something hit his back. An ache began but he ignored it. He reached around and tossed the man aside, his big body hitting the dirt. He was vulnerable, helpless, his throat wide open because his helm was gone. It would be so sweet to drain the guard dry, to drink him down until his legs stopped twitching, his blood strengthening Lachlan.

But he wouldn't. This piece of him would remain buried no matter how insane he went. There would be no first blood for Lach. There would be no first woman. There would be no sex.

His soul's mate was gone and with her all that would have been sweet. Now there would be only death and wasted blood and revenge.

Lach's sword thrust again and again. Two guards and then three attacked, ignoring the corpses. Pain bloomed in his side, but he pushed it away. The savage joy of battle was all that mattered. They all fell to his sword and one to his bare hands. Oh, he enjoyed that one. He loved the cracking of bones and the splitting of skin.

He'd hidden it all because he'd feared his mate would think him a monster, but his mate was gone and the worlds could quake for all he cared now.

He felt drunk—on the death, on the blood, on the power. He was Lachlan McIver, King of the Dead.

"Well done, Your Highness." The phooka sat on the thatched roof of a house directly in front of Lach. He could see eyes staring at him. Terrified villagers who hid behind their shutters and likely prayed he took no notice of them. "You killed them all. No more guards left to eviscerate. Are you planning to start on the farmers? When you kill them all, you can move on to the children."

His sword trembled as his hands shook. The need to kill was an actual presence in his system. It flowed through him, warring with all other instincts. Lach could feel his corpse warriors standing behind him, waiting for his next command. Waiting for him to tell them who to kill next.

The phooka wrinkled his nose, his tail twitching. Claws dragged along the roof making a nasty scratching sound. "There are four right in here, Your Highness. Four souls for you to take. A man. A woman. Two children. Think of the blood. Think of the screams."

Something about the little devil's voice made him shiver. Or the fact that he could suddenly see himself slaughtering children. This was why he'd shoved his warrior half so far down. He was a monster.

"Lachlan!"

He let his sword drop, turning. His heart was pounding. Bron was dead. None of it mattered. If he continued, he would kill the families in their houses. He would plunder and pillage and then call their dead bodies to serve him.

And it wouldn't bring her back.

He looked at his brother. He'd failed Shim as well. Without their mate, Shim would fade. Lach would go mad. He would have to be put down.

He'd failed everyone.

Shim stood in the middle of the square. The fire that had previously burned there was gone, only ashes surrounding the pole where they had bound her. He'd always envisioned her in bondage, his hands tying her lovingly to prepare her for play. This was a perverted vision of what should be loving.

Bronwyn's delicate body lay in Shim's arms, her limbs utterly limp, her head falling back. The sword fell from his hand. If another attacked, he would let death come. He would join his mate.

Shim hoisted her up, cradling her to his chest. "Lach, we have to go. Where are we going to go? We need a healer. Something's wrong with me."

Everything was wrong. Bron was gone.

"Lachlan? Shim?" A feminine voice cut through his misery.

Lach turned and, for a moment, his heart softened. She wore different clothes, peasant clothes, but he knew this woman. She was his sister. His Gilly, the girl who had laughed with them, brought them their first horses.

Saved their bondmate.

He'd failed Gillian, too.

She stood there, staring between them, dark eyes confused as though she couldn't believe they were here. "Where is the army? Father sent a force. He had to send a force, right? Where are they? We need to leave."

"I'm not leaving, Gillian." Lach's heart felt like it would burst with the agony of what he felt. "You have to put me down. I can't handle breaking with Bronwyn. Please, Gillian, if you ever loved me, kill me now. Save these people."

Gillian's mouth dropped open. "Goddess, Lach, you're being ridiculous. Now tell me where the army is and how we get off this plane. We can have our family reunion later, brother."

Shim had fallen to his knees, taking Bron with him. "She smells so damn good. I can't resist. Lach. I need her."

He watched as his brother's eyes bled to pure black, and the whites pushed out. Shim's fangs lengthened until they filled his mouth, tipping over his lips.

Mating fever.

How could Shim have mating fever for their dead mate?

Bron's hands shook lightly, and then he heard it, a soft, sweet moan.

And he smelled it. Her scent. A breeze blew it, the delicate scent of her life wafting over his senses, filling him, and he was overcome.

His fangs pulled. His cock hardened. His focus dimmed to one thing and one thing alone.

Her.

The mating fever took over.

* * * *

Shim shook, his every sense open and overflowing with her. Somewhere in the back of his head, he knew what this was.

His goblin blood was calling. He was proudly Unseelie. It meant his blood was mixed with all the Fae of the planes. His mother had been a vampire. His father a mix of *sidhe* and goblin and brownie. It was the goblin he felt now. The goblin need to mate with the perfect female rode him.

Bron shook in his arms. Why had Lach thought for a second she could be dead? Fire could not kill Shim's mate. Death could not take Lach's. Had he gotten every bit of optimism between them? It was obvious that Lachlan had gotten all the fighting skill. There were dead bodies everywhere, some fresh and some seemingly ancient. They lay around the courtyard, though despite their placement, it still seemed to Shim that they lay at Lach's feet waiting for the moment when their master called to them again.

Bron moaned, her eyes fluttering open only to close again.

His cock stood up straight in his pants. Just being near her, smelling her, touching her was driving him crazy. He had to try to focus on anything but her. She filled his senses, his world. Someone was saying something, but all he could do was stare at the woman in his arms. His mate. His bridge.

He wiped away a smudge on her face. She was so much more slender than she'd been in her dreams, her hands callused and her face slightly red from time in the sun. Thirteen years of running and being forced to work like a peasant had taken their toll, but she was still so beautiful to him. He would coddle her and cosset her and feed her. She wouldn't have to worry again. He would take her off this plane, and she would never fear for her life or work a plow or go hungry again. She would be his sweet wife, protected from all the bad things of the world.

Of course, one of the bad things of the world appeared to be his other half. Lach stood staring down at them, his body covered in blood, his eyes huge and foreign in his face. The goblin blood was working in his brother's veins, too.

"She smells so good." Lach got to one knee, seemingly dazed by the sight of her.

"Lachlan, you can't touch her right now. You're covered in blood and we're out in the open." A firm, feminine voice broke through his haze. "You two have mating fever. This isn't the time or the place. Take a step back and let me get Bronwyn someplace safe."

Shim heard the growl coming from his own throat. He felt feral. The blood, the heat, the closeness of his Bron. He suddenly realized he didn't want anyone else around. He wanted Bron. It was past time to take her. She fucking belonged to him. She'd been promised to him since the moment of her birth, and he wouldn't allow one more thing to come between them.

Lach's huge dark eyes focused on their mate. "Bronwyn." Lach touched her hair before letting his hands float, skimming across her skin, pausing at the vein in her neck. "She's alive."

Shim nodded, ignoring the fact that a crowd seemed to be gathering.

"Our sister is here. Gillian's alive." Lach said the words, but he was wholly focused on Bron.

"Shim, please think for a second." Gillian had moved in closer, delicately moving around the bodies of the fallen. "You can't take her here."

"She is ours." Lach spoke around the fangs in his mouth. "We'll take her where we want to. She belongs to us."

Yes, his brother was definitely feeling the fever, and now some of Gillian's words were breaking through. Bron was hurt. Bron wasn't even conscious. Did they intend to push her skirts up right here on the battlefield, the dead all around them?

It would prove once and for all what animals they were. Yes, when her brothers discovered how they had treated her, they would be welcomed with open arms.

Lach's face was in her hair, breathing in her scent, letting it flow around him. Lach growled, his hand moving to her breast. If Shim didn't stop him, the fever would take control, and there would be no controlling the warrior half. The dead all around them proved Lach was capable of giving in to the beast that lay inside their soul.

"Please, Shim. I understand the fever, but Bronwyn will not. As far as I can tell, she doesn't even know you're real." Gillian took another cautious step forward. "Please. If you give in to the fever, you'll take her with not an ounce of thought to her. She's a virgin. I made sure of it. I've protected her for thirteen years because I knew she was your mate. Trust me. Take her back to the tower. Give her and yourselves some privacy."

Bron's eyes fluttered open. Shim stopped, terrified that the next sound would be Bronwyn's scream. Brown eyes looked at him. She seemed unfocused, shaky. Her hand came, brushing his chin. "My Shim?"

His heart leapt. "Yours."

"Lach?"

Lach kissed her forehead. "Is here now, love."

"What is wrong with your eyes?" She tried to sit up.

Before Shim could explain, she doubled over, her knees coming up and a low wail moving from her mouth. Pain was etched on her face, her hands stiffening into fists.

"Please make it stop. Why won't it stop?"

Shim looked to his sister. "What's wrong with her? I can't feel her.

I should be able to feel her. We're bonded but there is nothing connecting us now."

His sister seemed to be treating them like dangerous predators. She moved forward slowly, holding her hands out to show she had no weapons. Even though she moved cautiously, he found himself clutching Bron tighter, and Lach bared his fangs.

"I am not taking her from you. Damn it. Calm down both of you. You're scaring the entire village, and we seem to need them as you did not bring an army with you." Gillian stood in front of them.

"They left the army behind." The phooka had moved from his perch on the roof to the pole that had held Bron. He hung there, his claws sunk deep. "Though I wouldn't call it an army exactly. More like a small unit."

"And they brought along a little devil." Gillian frowned at the phooka before turning her gaze back to her brothers. "Do you not know what that is? It's a trickster. Did he trick you away from Father's men?"

Bronwyn was moaning softly, tears squeezing from her eyes. Shim wasn't in the mood to hear about his choice of vehicle. "Tell me what is wrong with our mate."

Gillian got to one knee. "Bronwyn. Bronwyn, did they give you anything? Did they put something in your food or water?"

Bron bit her bottom lip and forced herself to nod. Her mouth opened as though she was trying to speak, but her body convulsed again.

Even Lach seemed to come out of his fever long enough to be worried. "What's wrong? What did they give her?"

Gillian ignored them both, putting a hand to Bron's forehead and feeling it. "She's burning up. I suspect they gave her something to quiet her, but it wouldn't explain why she's in such pain."

Shim leaned over, looking into her face. "Tell me how to help you, *a chumann*."

One hand came to his head, her fingers soft on his hair. "Kiss me."

Her mouth came up, touching his, lips pressed to lips. He felt like he was falling into a dark well and Bron was the only spark of light. Her soft moan had his cock leaping in his pants. An aching want suffused his body with desire. His heart sped up, and a horrible pain began in his cock.

He needed. He fucking needed her.

"Damn it." Gillian stood and turned back to talk to someone. Shim didn't care. He knew what she needed now. Her body was calling to him. That bright, shimmering line that connected them was starting to come back.

"It hurts. She's hurting so much." Lach felt the connection, too, their minds opening to each other now that Bron was awake again, but the connection was marred by her pain, her outrageous need.

Gillian stepped forward again. "Pick her up. We need to get her inside. We have no way of knowing until we do a count if you killed everyone you should have. Reymon has a house close by. He's willing to give it to you for the time being. I'll keep watch for this squad of men who I have to hope will be smart enough to follow you."

Through his haze, Shim managed to get up and haul Bron with him, her slight weight nothing against his strength. She clutched at him, her eyes fevered with desire. She pushed at his shirt, trying to get her hands on his skin. Shim couldn't help it. He needed her so badly. She was the fever in his blood now. He kissed her, his tongue plunging deep.

He needed to get her away from here. He had to protect her, and he couldn't take her here. It was too open. He didn't want eyes on them. This was his bonding time.

But if he didn't get inside her soon, he might burn down the village around him. Already he could feel the need to unleash his power. He would lose control if he didn't satisfy Bron's desire.

Lach was at his side as he began to move toward the small house Gillian pointed to. The door opened, and a woman pointed them to a back room. The house was a storefront. Candles and herbs covered the shelves. The man named Reymon gestured them through to narrow stairs.

"Our bedroom is small, but the bed is comfortable. 'Tis an honor to host your first night, Your Highnesses." Reymon nodded. "We've hoped for this for so long. The Unseelie will finally come."

He didn't want to think about the man's enigmatic words. He wanted to take off his wife's clothes and be with her finally. She mewled and twitched in his arms. Lach went up the stairs first, checking the bedroom and finally turning.

"Leave us, sister." Lach nodded toward Gillian, who stood in the doorway.

Gillian took a deep breath as Shim set Bron on the bed.

"Take her. Make her yours," Gillian said. "Bond fully with her so there can be no question from the Seelies that she belongs to our clan. Impregnate her if you can. And do it quickly. We need to be gone from this plane by the morning. I'm going to go and clean up the mess the warrior half left. And brothers, it is good to see you and to see just how powerful you've become. When the time is right and we unite the tribes, you will be the true Kings of the Fae. I honor you, brothers, and the woman who will bring the Unseelie into ultimate power."

Gillian turned and walked out, the door closing behind her.

Shim looked down at his wife, the woman who would be his queen.

"Kiss me." Her words were fevered, her eyes desperate. Her body tightened as though the pain forced her to clench her every muscle. "Please. Please."

He couldn't resist her. Didn't want to. Wanted to inhale her, to taste her, to take her into his body and to put himself in hers. He needed to merge with her. The world around faded away until all he could see and taste and touch and feel was her.

Shim gave in to the fever.

Chapter Ten

Bron thought she'd died and gone to the Summerlands. They were here, her Dark Ones. Shim and Lach. She'd called to them as the fire had started and when she'd opened her eyes again, they'd been here. Surely this was her reward. To be with the men from her dreams.

And then the pains had struck again.

She was still here in Tuathanas. She was still dying. She could hear Gillian saying something that she knew should disturb her. Something about crowns and thrones and playing her part. The words burned into Bron's brain, but she couldn't filter them now. Her gut seized. She cried. That was the worst. She couldn't stop crying.

Was she dreaming again? She heard someone asking for a kiss. Pleading and begging for a kiss.

"Hush, *a chumann*." A deep voice forced her from her panic. She opened her eyes, her pussy still burning, and saw him staring down at her. It was Shim but not as she'd dreamed him. This Shim had eyes as deep as the sky just before night swallowed up the day. There was no white to his eyes, merely a deep and never-ending midnight. And fangs. They were small, the size of a royal vampire's, and ever so slightly curved. "I know what you need. You feel the fever, too."

Yes, fever. She felt it. It was low in her belly, in her pussy and her breasts. But it was also in her head. Something else was happening. She could feel her Dark Ones. They needed, too. They needed to possess her, to be one with her.

"I want to kiss her. You've had your turn." Another voice called to her. She turned and saw her other. Lach. She'd named him Lach. Her heart seized. Lach's face was the same as his brother's except for the scars. It didn't mar his beauty, but it did speak of a pain he'd suffered. She reached up and touched him. He tried to turn away, but she held him fast, placing both her hands on his skin. One side was so smooth, perfect, but the other had three long scars forming hills and valleys, a road map of the pain he'd suffered. Burns. Lach had been burned.

For her? She remembered the fire. Had he rescued her? His eyes turned down as though he was waiting for her to send him away. She leaned over and placed a kiss on the longest of the scars. She started at the bottom, at the hard line of his jaw. She kissed him, over and over, a slow brushing of lips to scarred flesh. She kissed all the way to just right of his eyes. While she pressed kisses to Lach's face, Shim's hands moved on her back. She could feel an insistent tug at the ties of her dress. Yes. She didn't need the dress. She needed to be skin to skin with them, pressed to their bodies, feeling their hearts beat.

Lach's hands came up, covering hers. There was a predatory light in those midnight-blue eyes of his. "You accept me?"

What an odd question. How could she accept something that had always been? He was a part of her. Of course she accepted him.

"Say it, Bronwyn. Say you're mine. Mine to protect and love."

Bron nodded. She would agree to almost anything to keep this dream going.

His hands tightened. "Say it."

"I'm yours." He seemed to need to hear it. It didn't matter. It was true. She'd always been his. In life. As she moved to death. She was theirs. They had claimed her heart so long ago it was difficult to remember a time when she hadn't had them in her dreams. It was only right that they be with her as she left this life. If she held on to them as she died, maybe she could pull them with her, be with them in what came after.

"Mine. Fucking mine, *a chumann*." Lach stroked a hand in her hair and wound it through his fingers, tugging back lightly. He looked fierce as he straightened his body, towering over her. "Mine. My princess. My mate."

"Our mate, brother. Or are we going to have a problem?" Shim was at her back, his voice a hard grind against her ear.

"I want my fair time. You've held her. It's my time."

"I had to hold her. I had to protect her while you were busy slaughtering everyone in town."

"I killed the men who tried to burn our mate," Lach insisted. "I make no apologies. If you have a problem with me perhaps we should fight and see who gets to take her first."

She felt Shim back off. Lach's aggression was practically pounding through the room.

"We're not goblins." Shim's tone had gone steady as though he knew he had to find a way to be calm. "We're not going to fight to the death over our mate. Calm yourself. We're still *sidhe*. We're still brothers. Negotiate."

All the while they talked, hands were on her. Lach pulled her to his body, tugging on her hair and taking her lips. He kissed her, groaning into her mouth, the sound rumbling along her skin. Shim's fingers tugged at the shoulders of her dress, pulling it down and smoothing over her arms. This was what she needed. Hands on her body. A mouth on hers. Their cocks sliding inside.

Lach's tongue plunged deep, dancing against her, his mouth dominating. He came up for air, his hands on her hips, drawing her in. She gasped as she felt the hard line of his cock. Lachlan's cock was nestled against her belly. It wasn't where she wanted it to be, but it was there, so close she could feel it. Only a few layers of clothing.

"Please. It hurts." Another flare of pain caught her.

Lach's hand pulled her skirt up and she felt his palm on her thigh. Rough skin, so unlike the slimy feel of Micha's hand on her flesh. This touch thrilled her.

"I'll negotiate, brother. While I take care of our mate. Show me her breasts." Lach's voice was low in his throat, the rumble deep and commanding.

"Touch her. She needs hands on her." Shim pushed the bodice of her dress down while Lach's hands climbed up her leg.

Her nipples peaked in the cool air. Where was she? She wasn't in the White Palace. Why had her dreams brought her to this place? It was small, the bed made of straw and ropes. A merchant's bed. Did she know this place?

"I'll take her body first," Lach offered.

"Only if I get first blood," Shim shot back.

Blood? Why were they talking about blood?

Her breasts brushed Lach's chest, her aching nipples chafing against the rough wool of his tunic. Lach's fingers slipped under the gathered band of her undergarment. She trembled as his fingers teased at the outer edges of her pussy.

"First blood, then." Shim agreed to whatever they were talking about and then cupped her breasts in his hands, holding them up for his brother's perusal. "These are ours. You're gorgeous, *a chumann*. So fucking beautiful."

His words were as seductive as the hands on her breasts. She'd only ever touched herself there, pretending to be one of them. She'd cupped her breasts deep in the night and pulled at her nipples, imagining it was Lach or Shim tugging at them. She'd dreamed they would call her beautiful, though she knew it wasn't true. But in their eyes she was lovely because she belonged to them. Now, in the most vivid of all her dreams, she truly felt beautiful.

She opened her legs and tried to force those teasing fingers inside.

Lach abruptly pulled away. "Stay still, Bronwyn. You agreed to be mine. That means we play things my way in the bedroom."

She pushed away from him. What was he talking about? She was in agony and he wanted to place rules on her? So many fucking rules. *Don't tell anyone your name, Bronwyn. Don't get too close, Bronwyn. Don't say a word. Don't fight. Don't fight. Don't fight.*

Lach grabbed her wrists, pulling her close. "Don't do that, love. Don't push me now. I'm on the edge. I killed twenty men to get to you. I don't want to lose control again. Obey me and everything will be fine."

"Touch me and everything will be fine," she demanded.

He let her go and turned away.

Shim wrapped his arms around her waist, pulling her back into his arms. "Hush, Bron. He doesn't understand. He can't feel you like I do, but I promise, he's not trying to hurt you. He's worried that if he loses control he could hurt you. It's his nature. He's the dominant half, but I have my job, too. I know what you need."

Shim's left hand made its way to her thighs and straight to her pussy. He didn't tease or play. He went straight for her clitoris, rubbing the plump nubbin.

Blessed relief. She wasn't completely there yet, but oh she felt so much better. She couldn't help it. She rolled her hips, rubbing against his fingers.

"Then tell me what she needs, brother." Lach stood above them, staring down. "I'm so close to the fucking edge. She can't fight me. It will send me over. I already want to tie her up and spank that ass of hers. I need to dominate her. It's like a fire in my gut."

Bron let her head roll back against Shim's shoulder. Everything sounded good now that he was touching her. The drug was still in control, running through her system, but now she was getting the antidote. Shim's long fingers slid around her pussy, rubbing her clit and then foraging inside. It felt so good. It calmed the fire. She was moving toward something wonderful.

"And you can dominate her, after she gets what she needs."

"Just fucking tell me, Shim. I can't read her mind the way you can."

Shim kissed the shell of her ear. "I can't read her mind. We bonded too far away. We need to be close like this and rebond. Then I'll know everything, but I know this much. She needs to come. She can't think or obey until she comes. Whatever they forced on her, it was partially an aphrodisiac."

"Ah, like the vampires make for their orgies so a woman can come for hours." Lach's eyes narrowed.

"Yes," Shim replied. "But the vamps got it from the Seelies. If we can give her a few orgasms, I think you'll discover she'll be deeply submissive."

Lach nodded. "Let me help."

His hands found her nipples, rolling them between his thumbs and forefingers. Bron whimpered at the sting of pain that shot like an arrow straight to her pussy. She couldn't breathe. She was right on the edge.

"Come for me. Come for us." Shim's thumbs rotated on her clit as his fingers plunged deep.

Bron tripped over the edge. That wonderful word "orgasm" finally meant something to her. It meant relief, pleasure, and an overwhelming sense of finally belonging.

She belonged with these men. Her dream men.

The pleasure washed over her, suffusing every cell of her body with a delicious sense of languor. She slumped down, unable to hold herself up for one minute longer. Blood pounded through her body. The only thing holding her up was Shim's strong arms around her waist.

So sweet. After what seemed like hours of agony, the very cessation of pain felt like the purest pleasure. Her skin felt deliciously alive. A smile curled her lips up.

"See." Shim's cock nestled against her ass. She was half naked, her breasts bared to them. Lach's fangs were out, his hands still rubbing her breasts. "So much better. Don't you feel better, my princess?"

She sighed, groaning as Shim's fingers slipped from her pussy. She didn't want them to leave. She liked how it felt to have some piece of him inside her. "I want it again."

She could take her time. They could linger over her, giving her round after delicious round of pleasure.

"Not this time, love. Don't you think it's our turn?" Shim nipped at her ear.

Their turn. Her turn. Did it matter as long as they kept touching her?

Lach's hands were back in her hair. "Get her clothes off. Now, Shim. I can't wait. It's killing me."

Shim chuckled. "He's such a pain in my ass. He thinks I don't feel it, but he's wrong. I feel it every bit as badly as he does, but I'm the intellectual half. It's my lot in life to be forced to forever deal with his drama."

This wasn't how she'd imagined they would speak. "You talk so oddly."

"Hold your arms up, love." Shim pulled the dress over her head, freeing her from the burden. "I talk the way I do because I spent so much time on the Vampire plane. Our mother was a vampire. She wanted us to have close ties to her people."

She still felt like she was floating, but sparks had already begun in her pussy again. "My cos is a vampire."

"Yes, Dante. We've met him." Shim's hands skimmed down, dragging her undergarments along.

Of course they knew Dante. They lived in her head. Dante was there, the funniest of playmates.

"He annoys me, but his consort seems nice," Lach allowed.

Consort? Dante wasn't old enough to have a consort. Confusion began to set in. And so did pain. She doubled over, crying. She'd hoped it was gone, but it was back, that fire in her loins. The burning flared and she couldn't help but cry out her despair.

"Damn it," Shim cursed. "Whatever they gave her, it was strong. She needs another orgasm. Lie down, love."

Lach picked her up. "Who did this to you, *a chumann*? Give me his name."

A fine tremor went through her. The fire was building. "Micha. He wanted to marry me. He was angry when I showed my true self."

Oh, she needed the touch again. Lach laid her on the bed, staring down at her as Shim stripped off her undergarment. Naked. She was naked in front of him. His eyes latched on to her pussy.

"Where is this man? I will have his heart on the end of my sword." Lach pulled his shirt over his head revealing a perfectly sculpted chest. His torso was covered with golden, sun-kissed skin pulled over taut muscles. He was so masculine.

"He's the mayor. He didn't want me to tell them who I am." No one wanted her to tell. Certainly not Gillian. Gillian. She'd been here. She'd said things that made no sense.

"A small man, older? Did he wear a golden broach and order everyone about as though he owned them?"

Her legs moved restlessly of their own accord. "Yes. He put the solution in my water and when it didn't work, he forced it down my throat."

Lach pushed his pants down, freeing his cock. Bron's eyes widened. A cock. She'd seen them before on small boys bathing in the river and once when she'd accidently seen two peasants making love in a barn, but Lach was so much more. His cock was long and thick. It was almost purple, like a ripe plum sitting on a thick stalk. Lach wrapped a hand around his cock, stroking firmly.

"Spread your legs, love. If you want me to take care of you, you have to give access." Lach didn't wait for her to obey. He took her ankles and forced them apart, leaving her pussy on full display. "If he was wearing a purple tunic and that gold broach, then you don't need to worry about him ever again, love. He's lying in the town square and he won't get up unless I tell him to. Gods, that's a gorgeous sight."

He reached down and touched her, his finger running from her navel down to her core. He delved inside, running all over her labia and pussy.

His cock jumped. She knew it wasn't true, that it was only her imagination, but the idea that Micha had gotten what was coming to him gave her comfort. Micha had cut a swath through the district, taking advantage of anyone he could. The plane would be a better place without him.

"Lift up, *a chumann*." Shim was getting in behind her, sliding his naked body under her own. Warm flesh surrounded her.

Lach pulled his fingers free and did something that made Bron gasp. He stared for a moment at his fingers, coated in the cream of her arousal. Then he shoved those fingers into his mouth and licked them clean.

"He thinks you taste good." Shim's hands were once again on her breasts.

"He knows you taste good," Lach said.

Bron shook her head. They were wasting time. The fire was building. "Please. Touch me."

Lach settled himself between her legs. "I will, love. I'll touch you. I'll make you come. I studied. I learned everything just for you."

She was about to protest again, but he leaned over, his whole body on the bed, torso down. His face was close to her pussy. She couldn't imagine what he was planning and then he licked her.

What a feeling. Perfection. Arousal swelled, puffing up her pussy, her clit poking out its hood and throbbing for his touch. He stroked her, a long lick of his tongue that lit up every inch of her pussy. He speared her with his tongue. It was like a cock. He was fucking her, but with his tongue, tasting her essence. It was so intimate. She was on his tongue. He was in her pussy.

Lachlan licked and sucked and lit her up like a firefly pulsing with energy and life. He held her down, his hands on her thighs, pressing them open. Shim held her arms, keeping her still for his brother's tasting. And Lach feasted. His tongue was everywhere. He sucked at her labial lips, lavishing affection there. He ran his nose along her pussy, breathing deeply as though he wanted to inhale her, to make her his every breath.

But as he breathed her in, she lost her own. It felt so good, that soft but strong tongue delving deep and then worrying her clitoris.

Something sharp scraped against her neck. Shim. He squeezed her nipples to just the right side of pain. "Do you like the way he eats your pussy?"

Such a dirty phrase and yet it sounded good to her ears. She was Lachlan's feast, her pussy a sweet treat for his tongue. "Yes. I love it. It feels so good."

"He's going to make you suck his cock, love. He's going to put that monster to your lips and make you lick and suck him and swallow him down. Do you remember what cum is?"

He'd explained it to her in a dream, but she'd also heard the village women speak of it. "It's white. It seeps from a man's cock."

Lach nosed her, making a low groan.

"Yes," Shim said as she felt that scraping against her skin. It made her shiver and moan. "It's what a man injects into his mate during sex. It's what we want to give you. It's what will make you pregnant. We're going to love tasting your sweet cream, but we'll want you to taste us, too. You'll suck our cocks, let us shoot our cum deep inside you."

His words were intoxicating. She wanted to do exactly what he said. She wanted to taste them. It seemed such a foreign idea, but the intimacy of having her Dark Ones in her mouth, in her pussy, was overwhelming.

Lachlan was using his fingers now. Strong digits stretched her and moved inside her while his tongue licked at her clit. "She tastes so good. She's making me crazy." He nuzzled her inner thigh. "Gods, brother, I can hear the blood. She has a vein right here. We can feed from our mate and smell it when she comes."

Their mother. They'd mentioned their mother was a vampire. How was that true? It didn't matter. The drug flared in her system and all she wanted was to come again, to quench the fire. Shim's tongue licked a line of pure sensation from the base of her neck to her earlobe.

"I want to taste your juice, too. But that's not the only thing I want to taste, *a chumann*," Shim said. "Make her come, brother, so I can have my time."

Lach sucked her clit into his mouth and she went flying. It was stronger this time. The drug seemed almost banished from her system, but she knew it would come again. She would feel the ache and the fire, but she was no longer afraid. Her Dark Ones were here. They would care for her. They would give her what she needed to fight the ache.

Lach kissed her pussy one last time before getting to his knees. His cock bobbed, standing straight up, almost touching his navel. Those fangs were out, but now she wasn't afraid of those, either. Now they just made him look feral and magnificent.

She felt so good, but it was already building again, a tiny, hurtful flame that would engulf her once more. How long could she endure it?

Shim turned her, moving her body until she looked into his perfect face. She couldn't see Lach, but Shim held her fast.

"Now it's my turn for a taste." He licked his fangs as Bron got lost in his never-ending eyes.

* * * *

Shim felt it the moment he caught her. His eyes had widened, his vision expanding and shrinking at the same time. He could tell the expansion because his peripheral vision widened, but it didn't matter because his focus shrunk to one thing and one thing only. Bronwyn.

He opened that place deep inside—the royal vampire's legacy. He drew his prey in, a primal part of him calling to her. It was how a royal fed. A royal didn't drag down his prey. A royal made the prey beg for his bite.

"What's happening?" Bron's voice sounded half strangled in her throat.

Shim could hear her heart beating like the fast-running metronome in his old vampire tutor's piano lessons. Shim had mastered the piano with ease, but Lach had threatened to take an axe to the damn thing. *Thud. Thud. Thud.* A seductive beat promising nourishment for more than his body. Bronwyn's blood would fill his soul.

First blood.

It was sacred, or it should be. Shim knew there were many vampires who took blood as often as they took sex, but he wanted both only from his mate. Perhaps it was that they had been together since they were children, and before he'd even understood the word love, he'd been in love with her. Perhaps it was a function of his personality, but Shim had always known if he couldn't have Bronwyn, he would die alone, like a sad monk waiting for the day he could join his god.

He felt a bit of his brother's desperate need to dominate as he tugged Bron's hair to one side, exposing her neck.

"It's a way to make the bite painless." Lach sat back on his heels, watching them. He had his hand on his cock, caressing it. Shim knew exactly what he was doing. The mating fever was strong, probably stronger in Lach than in Shim himself. If he didn't keep his cock engaged, he would fall on Bronwyn with no thought but to pound himself into her, to imprint on her.

They had to take it slow.

But she was ready for this. Shim ran his nose along her neck. He'd seen this act performed before. Cousin Julian had forced him to watch it, to learn how it was done. Shim remembered how frustrated Julian had been that he and Lach wouldn't feed, but now it was all worth it. His first blood would be her blood.

Bron's eyes were caught in his. He felt like he could see all the way down to her beautiful, innocent soul. She was so lovely in her natural form. He'd wondered if she'd been like Lach, projecting a perfect image of herself, and it had been true. She was thinner in her real form, a bit more careworn, but still so perfect she made his heart stop. He and Lach would take better care of her. They would feed her and coddle her until her curves filled out and her eyes danced with mirth as they had when she'd run through their dreams as a child.

"This feels so good," she murmured.

The vampire connection of predator to beloved and honored prey was working in a way he hadn't expected. The drug wasn't as strong as this power, made even stronger through the shared connection of his brother. He drew her in, away from the pain, away from the fear, into a place that was just for the three of them.

His fangs were so big, he could barely talk through them. Like his cock, they were long and hard for his mate. And like his cock, they demanded to have their way. "This, love, is going to feel even better."

He drew her close, loving the way those nipples poked at his chest, brushing his own. He'd enjoyed tugging on them and couldn't wait for the day when they would take her and have her nipples pierced, adorning their sweet submissive as she should be.

Running on pure instinct, Shim drew back. He knew exactly where to bite. The long, thick vein in her neck practically pounded, calling out to him to open it and drink his fill.

"Take her, brother." Lach's hand was on her back as though he couldn't stand not touching her. "Bring her closer to us."

"I love you, *a stoirin*." It was nothing less than the truth. Shim reared back and his fangs sank into her soft flesh.

He took his first drag and finally understood why vampires jealously guarded this tradition. It was a secret thing, somewhat shameful in the modern vampire world, but Shim had never experienced an intimacy like it.

The blood flowed into his mouth, coating his tongue. It was the richest taste. No food, no wine, no drink at all would ever compare to the way she tasted. Like the deepest flavor, the most forbidden.

Shim felt her sigh and relax in his arms, her heart a clear beat in his head. He knew everything about her body in that instant. He knew her heartbeat was rising with each deep drag. Her pussy, already soft from Lach's lavish affection, was throbbing in time to her heart, her clit pulsing. Her head was foggy with desire, her thoughts of them covered in a lacy haze.

He caught small visions of her life, but mostly he felt her joy at being there with them. Her Dark Ones. Her One and her Two. Her Lachlan and her Shim.

So much running. So much hiding. So much of the before had been burned away by that one moment when the knife had cut through her belly and ended her life.

She didn't know. She didn't remember a thing about what had happened. She didn't recall how he'd reached across the planes and poured his life into her.

Gods, she didn't think he was real at all.

Bronwyn gasped and gripped his body, holding him as she quaked. The pleasure was so new to her, and she held fast to it like a drunk with the first taste of liquor. Bron didn't have a single shield. She transmitted her pleasure to him, the feeling going straight to Shim's cock. Her womb shook and quaked, sending pleasure coursing through her body and into his.

Shim's cock was gripped with her heat though she didn't lay a hand on it. Spasms ran through his belly and shook up his spine. He pulled his fangs out of her neck as the orgasm crashed into him. His cock pulsed out waves of cum, coating her belly as he thrust helplessly against her.

He finally fell back against the bed, taking her with him, wrapping himself around her.

"It's not enough," she whispered. "I loved it, but it's not enough."

She needed. He finally understood. It wasn't merely the orgasm she needed. She needed to be filled. She needed them to fill her up and let her know they were real and she wasn't alone.

He looked to his brother. "She needs you. Make love to her. Make her ours."

Chapter Eleven

Where was the fucking mating fever when he needed it? It had been riding him hard, and then he'd had a handle on it the minute he'd felt his brother feed and share Bronwyn's orgasm. Now it had deserted him and he was left with plain desire and overwhelming insecurity.

Lach stared down at Bronwyn. She looked soft and so damn sweet in Shim's arms. There were two perfect, delicate holes on her neck. They had already closed, but the temptation was right there to lean down and sink his fangs in, too. First blood.

He was made of the monstrous things of the planes. Unseelie *sidhe*. Vampire. Goblin. Sometimes he feared the scars on his face had finally unmasked him for what he was, as though his ruined face was an outward expression of his inward soul.

King of the Dead. What right did he have to take a creature who was so stunningly, gloriously alive?

Her eyes fluttered open and a smile crossed her lips. "It's not so bad now."

Shim kissed her. "I'm taking some of the pain, love. We're bonded. Not fully. That can come when you're not under the influence of herbs and potions, but we do have a bond. There's a piece of me inside you. Haven't you always been able to feel it?"

Shim belonged. Shim had been the one to save her. Shim had sent out a piece of his soul across the planes and placed it deep inside Bronwyn, giving her life where it had been taken.

All Lach had managed to do was save his brother from a fire that wouldn't have hurt him. All Lach had done was ruin his face and sit idly by his brother's bedside, hoping he would awaken once more.

"There were years when I couldn't feel you. I hated those years." Her hand drifted up. It didn't matter that Shim was taking some of her pain. Bronwyn was still under the influence of that potion. Her legs moved restlessly. She sank her hands in Shim's hair, pulling him down for a long kiss. "I was alone without my Dark Ones. Don't leave me again."

"Never," Shim replied. "We'll take you back to our home."

"The Dark Palace." Her feet tickled at his knees. He couldn't help it. He had to touch her. Her ankles were delicate, seemingly incongruous against his big, rough hands. "Will you carry me away to your bedroom? The one with the huge, soft bed?"

They had started taking her there in their shared dreams the year before, gently herding her toward what they wanted. If they couldn't have her in real life, they'd decided, they would take her in their dreams.

But now she would come with them. They would have her in their wing of the Dark Palace. She would be their princess. She would live with them and know that no one respected a word they said because their father thought them fragile.

"He won't think you're fragile when he hears how you raised an army of dead and took out the entire village guard, brother." Shim laughed as he kissed the top of her head. Shim seemed as drugged as Bron now, his hands stroking as though they couldn't stop moving over her skin.

Lach was not immune to whatever Bron and Shim were sending out. His cock was still throbbing. If only his brain could shut down. And it wouldn't happen as long as his brother kept eavesdropping. "Get out of my head."

Bron laughed a little. "You're both in my head. Be nicer to one another."

Lach's hands moved up her legs to her knees. He couldn't help himself. Her skin called to him. He knew he should stop. He wouldn't be good for her. She was a beauty, meant for the finer, sweeter things in life. She was small and delicate. How would she survive in his world thick with ogres and goblins and trolls, all who would test her mettle before accepting her as a royal? Sweet Bronwyn shouldn't have to deal with a beast like himself.

He wanted to dominate her. He wanted to be rough and fuck her until she screamed out his name and begged his mercy because she couldn't handle one more bit of pleasure. He wanted to place a collar around her throat as vampires so often did with their consorts—a symbol that she belonged to him. How could he tell her of his dark needs? The need to shove his cock in her pussy, up her ass, in her mouth. Anywhere it would fit. He wanted to fill her every hole.

"See, those are much more helpful thoughts, brother." Shim's eyes were shuttered, his fingers on her breasts. "Let go of all that angst and revel in our bonding time. We won't get much of it until we take our princess home."

"Stay out of my damn head, Shim. You're trying to influence me."

"No." His brother shook his head. "She's influencing both of us. She's so damn strong. I don't think she even knows how strong she is."

Bronwyn smiled, pride in her voice. "I'm very strong. I can plow a whole field in a day."

Both he and his brother shuddered. The thought of their mate in the fields was horrifying when she should have had an easeful life.

Lach found himself between her legs. Close. So close. His cock nudged her. This should be the extent of her duties, taking care of her mates' cocks.

"You will never have to do that again," he promised.

Her eyes found his. "But I'm good at it."

He rubbed his cock all along her labia, stopping just short of penetration. He was trying to be patient. Trying to prove he wasn't an animal. Perhaps she'd been too far gone to see his killing spree, to witness his dark power. "You're good at this. Good at making us want you."

She laughed. "All men want a woman. Even I know that, Lach."

"I've only ever wanted you."

Her smile turned slightly sad and she cupped his face in her hands.

"Of course you have. And I only wanted you. What does it say about me that I only ever wanted a dream?"

"I'm not a dream, *a chumann*." He was more of a nightmare, but it no longer mattered. She was too close, and he had to have her. He would protect her. He would be a barrier against the harshness of his world, but he would have her. She'd been promised to him. If he was half a man, he would walk away, but he would take her as his comfort for all he'd sacrificed.

He'd do everything he could to make up for the fact that she'd married a monster. He would be *her* monster.

"You're my dream." She turned to him, placing her hands on his shoulders. It was a submissive gesture of pure acceptance. Her legs were open, spread wide to accept him. Her eyes were focused on his. Every reason to wait faded away.

He could feel her heat. His cock was surrounded by it. Her pussy was slick with the juice of her orgasms. Cream coated him as he thrust against her labia.

"Bron, are you sure?" He didn't know why he was asking or what he would do if she said no. But he had to ask. He loved her so much. His whole life had been about wanting her, loving her. He had to know he was welcome.

"Please. I've waited so long. Too long. Let me have this before the after."

He wasn't sure what she meant, but he understood the word *please*. He could never deny her. He let the fever have its way. The need to mate was a rolling churn in his gut.

Lach laid his body on hers, holding not an ounce of his weight off. He sank into her. Chest to chest. Belly rubbing belly. Legs tangling. He touched his nose to hers—a sweet turn of his face. He nuzzled her, savoring the sensation. Thirty long years without her. Thirty long years trapped in his body without her to share himself with. This was what he'd longed for. To be here, coupled to his soul's mate, the woman who bridged the halves of himself.

His mind sought hers. It was there, the connection between them that existed because of the day she'd died. He grasped it. It wasn't the full bond, but he could strengthen it. He let his desire flow. He let her know what he wanted.

Her tied up. Her at his mercy. Her round ass pink from his discipline. Her pussy weeping for his cock.

"Yes. Yes." Her lips hovered under his.

He kissed her, surging into her mouth. Her tongue curled around his. She softened under him, her legs cradling his hips.

One thrust and he would be inside her. He would be where he'd wanted to be for thirty years.

He kissed her one last time and then pulled himself up, shifting his hips and poising his cock at her entrance. His eyes came up. Shim was behind Bron, his body cradling hers. Their eyes met, a long look between them. Shim was here with him. The two halves of his whole complete through this woman.

He thrust up gently.

Tight. She was so tight. Her pussy was wet, but it seemed so small.

"Don't stop." Bron was biting her lip. "I want this. Don't let me go without knowing this."

She wasn't going anywhere without him. He shifted his hips, his dick a huge presence in her virgin pussy. She gasped and strained, trying to accept him. The sounds she made went straight to his cock, swelling him further.

He pressed in, needing to get deep.

"Softly." His other half was right there. Shim had always been there, but now he felt closer than ever, able to access the other side of his soul.

Lach leaned back over, kissing her lips. "Let me in, *a chumann*."

My darling. My sweetheart.

Her arms drifted around his neck, her ankles locking around his waist. She relaxed. "You're already inside me."

He was. One firm push and he drove deep. Shim grimaced and then Lach felt it. Shim had taken her pain and shared it with Lach. The bastard. Flesh tore and swelled and stretched to accommodate his too-big cock, but Bron had felt only pleasure, the pure joy of his cock sliding home.

She shook slightly, her eyes drifting closed.

"Don't. Look at me. Be with me." He couldn't stand the thought that she would think of anyone else.

Stark brown eyes held him. "I'm always with you."

Always.

"Don't stop. Please, Lachlan."

He pulled out, every inch a deep drag on his cock. So good. She felt so good. Perfect. This was sex. This was making love. This was only possible with Bronwyn. He'd waited and his joy was boundless. The waiting had been worth it because this was everything he'd hoped for.

Every muscle in his body felt alive. He foraged back in, gaining ground. Pull out. Push in. An inch here. An inch there. Almost, and then he sighed and finally sank in to his balls.

Heat surrounded him.

Bronwyn groaned. "Yes. It feels so good."

She was feeling his pleasure. He pushed it outward, instinct guiding him. "You feel so good. This is how I feel, love. This is what you make me feel."

And he felt everything. Shim had relented a bit, allowing her feelings to flow through the room. She was stretched, the feeling not quite comfortable, but she loved it. She was full where before she'd been so empty. She loved being surrounded by them, loved the fact that there was no part of her they weren't touching. She'd been so alone. He'd had Shim, but she'd been alone and she'd needed them. Those long years when they hadn't been able to feel each other had stretched out, a desert plain she'd been forced to cross.

Her hips moved up, trying to keep him inside.

He thrust faster, losing himself in the rhythm. So new. Every feeling was new and fresh and better because it was shared. He loved the way she was open, sharing her senses, her feelings. Her nipples throbbed against his chest. Her heart pounded in time to his own.

He felt it, the connection, deep and pure. She flowed into him and he into her, mingling down to their souls. Never before had he felt so connected, not even to his brother who held half his soul.

His spine shivered, Bron gasping as she felt it, too, and then he dropped over the edge. He didn't think about anything but the pleasure that bubbled up and overflowed. He came, thrusting deep and holding himself hard against her. Bron was with him the whole way, her body convulsing under his, bucking up to take more and more of him.

He thrust until he had nothing left and then collapsed on top of his bondmate, his bride, his love.

She was finally theirs.

And she was asleep.

Shim stared down at her, his hand tenderly stroking back her hair. "That did it. She can rest now. The potion burned itself out. She's going to be all right. We can perform the full bond when we get back to Aoibhneas."

Lach rolled off her but had no intention of getting up from the bed. He might never leave it again. He cuddled her close, reveling in the heat and scent of their intimacy. His cock was already hard again, but Bron sighed and settled her head on his chest. Sleep. His bride needed sleep. They wouldn't set foot out of this room until Bronwyn was well and ready to travel.

Roan would just have to see things his way. He wouldn't be far behind, but Lachlan was done listening to him. The warrior king was ready to take his rightful place, and his first duty was to protect and care for his bondmate. "Let's rest for a bit and then I'll go speak to our sister. Roan should be here by then. We can make arrangements to safely take her back to our plane."

"She'll be happy to see her brothers." Shim sighed, his hand going around her waist. "She will not be happy that they're going into war."

Lach shrugged. It didn't matter. He had his Bron. A guilty feeling settled into his gut. This plane was Bronwyn's home. She might not want to leave it so easily.

And this plane had nearly burned her to death. It didn't matter. She'd promised to obey him, to submit to him, and he wanted her safe.

Shim settled in on the other side of Bronwyn, nuzzling her neck. "We don't have to worry about it now. I just want to hold her."

Lach let his eyes drift closed. He didn't need to dream this day. He had her in his arms.

* * * *

Bron came awake slowly, in small snatches of reality laced with the sweetness of the dreams she'd had.

She kept her eyes closed. She didn't want to leave this place where she'd grabbed her Dark Ones and held on for dear life. When she opened her eyes, they would be gone again and she would either be in the after or still in her dank cell awaiting that time when the executioner would call her name.

A shaft of sunlight was warm on her face and she tried to turn. She tried but she was caught. Her eyes flew open, and she looked into seriously blue eyes.

"Hello, sunshine."

Bron sat up in bed and screamed.

There was movement behind her as something large banged to the floor. A man. Another man. She was in bed with two men.

"Bronwyn? Bronwyn, love, you need to stop. Someone will think we're killing you, and that isn't going to be good for anyone." The dark-haired man cajoled her as though it was perfectly normal for her to be lying in bed stark naked with two men.

"We're not killing her, but damn me I think I might have broken my tailbone falling out of bed. Who thought this place would be big enough?" The second man brushed a hand through his hair and then stood, his enormous male organ bouncing and pointing straight at her. He frowned down and made no move to cover himself. "What's wrong, *a chumann*?"

What was wrong? What was wrong? She'd gone utterly mad. That was what was wrong. All of her life she'd been told she was insane, and now she knew it to be true. She'd lost her mind and now she was pulling her dream men straight out of her head.

"Where am I?" She clutched the sheet to her chest.

The man who had fallen to the floor stared at her, his eyes narrowing in obvious irritation. He was his brother's twin, but three long scars marred his face. Why did she remember touching those scars, kissing them and feeling this man melt underneath her tenderness? He didn't look like a man who needed tenderness now. "You're with your mates. Is there a reason you're hiding those breasts? They belong to me, and I want to see them."

And her dream men were suddenly unreasonable pricks, so all she could think was that she had a masochistic inner soul. "I was in my cell at the jail."

"Yes," the other one said, his hand on her shoulder. She pulled away. He sighed and continued his explanation. "You were in your cell, but they gave you a potion and took you to the square."

Vague, nightmarish images floated back to her brain. She'd been dragged and drugged and bound. She had an image of someone calling her "princess," but then he'd fled and left her to the wolves. Micha had been there, snarling at her, forcing poison into her veins. And then the flames had come. She'd cried out for someone to save her, and that must have been when her mind had broken. Bron took a long breath. What had really happened? Had she gotten away or was this what happened to the dead? Were her ashes already floating in the wind?

"She doesn't believe we're real."

"How can she not believe we're real? We've been in her dreams since she was a child."

The unscarred one shrugged. Shim. She'd named him Shim. "I don't know. Only Gillian believed us. Perhaps she had no one to believe her, no one to help figure out what was happening."

Bron drew her knees to her chest. "Gillian's here?"

"She's downstairs," the one she'd named Lach replied.

There was something about Gillian she needed to remember, but she couldn't quite catch it, and she kept getting distracted by man parts. They were everywhere, and neither man seemed willing to do a thing about it. "Shouldn't you cover those things up?"

Those things had given her such pleasure, sinking deep inside her. It was all a dream, of course. Except she was really sore. Really sore. Her body had a pleasant ache.

Shim smiled and gave her a wink she found all too sexy. "I don't want to cover it up. I'd rather use it on you, love."

Something heated up inside. Mingled in with the nightmare images were other softer, sweeter memories. Lach working over her, sharing his pleasure with her. Shim kissing her neck, lavishing affection before he sank his fangs deep.

Fuck it all, he'd bitten her. She shot off the bed, practically jumping toward the mirror. She stared at herself. There it was. Her neck was smooth and unblemished with the exception of two perfectly delicate marks. She'd been fed upon, and if she remembered correctly, she'd liked it.

What in all the planes of existence was happening to her?

"You're vampires." It was the only explanation. They were royal vampires. There was only one problem with the scenario. She turned to them, still trying to pull the sheet around her. "Why did you bite me? I'm not a consort."

"Like hell you're not. You're a consort. You're our consort." Lach threw his brother a furious stare. "How can she not know this? Are you trying to tell me that we've been pining for her, looking for her for damn near thirteen years, and she thought we were some masturbatory dream?"

Shim seemed the more reasonable of the two. "You know how hard it was to talk in those dreams. I would go in thinking I would explain everything to her and it would all drift away and we would simply be there." He turned to Bron. She was pretty sure now the enormous, bobbing cock that jutted from his center was simply in its natural form since it never wavered. How did he walk around like that? "Your parents never told you that you could bond? Your vampire cousins would have been able to see your glow."

Her father had never mentioned it, but she did remember Dante teasing her about glowing. She hadn't understood. She'd been kept so ignorant. "My parents didn't tell me, but then they didn't tell me much. They probably believed me to be far too young."

Lach frowned. "You weren't too young to know the truth. Didn't you understand that Gillian came to your plane with the express purpose of securing your engagement to us?"

Gillian. Gillian, her mentor. Her savior. What had Gillian said as the fires had died down? As Shim had carried her?

When the time is right and we unite the tribes, you will be the true Kings of the Fae. I honor you, brothers, and the woman who brings the Unseelie into ultimate power.

It was like a punch to the gut.

Impregnate her if you can.

Gillian, the woman who had rescued her, had given her over to two men she didn't know. She'd offered Bronwyn's body and womb and, more importantly, her royal blood. Gillian had come to the palace that day so long ago to secure Bronwyn's hand for her brothers. Her brothers—the Unseelie princes.

She had to hand it to Gillian. She was tenacious. She'd guarded Bron's innocence. Bron had believed she guarded her because Gillian had loved her, but now she knew it was because she'd been protecting her brothers' property.

"I'm not a virgin anymore." She'd hated the state, wanted to rid herself of it night after night in her dreams. She'd wanted her Dark Ones. They'd been her safe place, her haven.

Reality was brutal, and they had always been a lie.

Lach walked up to her. "No, you're not. And neither am I."

She snorted. They were gorgeous. They were princes of a plane known for its hedonism. Her own brothers had worked their way through every pretty *sidhe* female in their village by the time they were sixteen, and likely half the Vampire plane. "Yes, well, I'm sure you lost that a long time before."

He caught her shoulders and forced her to look into his eyes. "No. I waited. No sex. No blood. Just years of longing and waiting and hoping to find you. I don't know what you believe, but you better believe this—you were my first woman. You will be my last woman. There is no one in all the planes for me except you, Bronwyn McIver."

In his mind, they were already married. McIver. The name of the Unseelie royal family. She closed her eyes. Could it be true? She'd never thought she could bond, never been tested. She reached out with her mind and sure enough, there it was, the bond between them. Had it always been there and she'd been too stupid to realize it?

"I am still a virgin since you passed out after Lach fucked you. Could we perhaps do something about that? It's a terrible state and this thing won't go down and gods, your breasts are so lovely, Bron." Shim smiled, his eyes fixed on her chest.

Damn it. She'd lost hold of her sheet.

Before she could bend over to grab it, Lach had it in his hands. He tossed it away.

"You don't need that around us, wife. I don't want a damn thing between us. Shim, we should stop trying to talk to her. It's obvious she isn't listening." He grabbed hold of her hands and pulled her to his body. "This is what we need."

His mouth came down on hers. She would have fought if he'd slammed against her, but the damn man was smart enough to be tender. His lips barely brushed hers. When he spoke, she felt the words like a whisper on her skin. "I love you, Bronwyn. I've loved you all my life.

Please don't fight us now that we're finally here. Haven't we lost enough time?"

His need hummed through her brain, and she softened against him. His lips played on hers. He wasn't aggressive though she felt that in him. He was sweet and tender, and she was falling for all of it.

"Crap and fuck me mother, you really do have a girl in here!"

Bron jumped back and screamed, a strangled sound. There was a gnome climbing through the window, his small leg hoisted over the sill.

Shim groaned and fell back on the bed. "You have the worst timing, Duffy."

The gnome named Duffy grinned, lechery in his eyes. "I think I got real good timing, me brother. Perfect timing, actually. Hello there, darling. Did me brothers bother to mention me? Probably not since they ran away with no thought to me."

The gnome frowned and then sort of lost his balance and almost fell out the window. Lach caught him with one hand and dragged him back in, setting him on the floor. He tossed Bronwyn the sheet. "I did think of you, Duff. We both thought about how much you snore as we stepped over you on our way out."

"It was just a little nap," Duffy protested. "And Roan is going to kick your ass when he finds out you're holed up with some village cutie when you're supposed to be looking for this princess woman. Not that you aren't a fine specimen of womanhood, lovely lady. I'm actually surprised. I thought you two were all about the waiting." The gnome winked. "I'm their brother. Don't let the size of the man fool you. I'm actually quite creative. And these two are all spoken for. I'm totally available."

Shim and Lach stared down at the gnome.

"Fuck me, she's Bronwyn Finn, ain't she?" The gnome got to one knee. "Your Highness. I am so sorry I just had that fantasy about sticking me face in between your bosoms. I did not realize they were royal bosoms since they seemed so very, very nice and not at all high and mighty. Not that they aren't mighty..."

Duffy's words were cut off by a light slap to his head by Lachlan. "Shut up about my wife's bosoms, Duff. She's going to be your queen. Show her due respect."

Duffy huffed, his small face beaming with innocence. "I totally respect her bosoms."

Shim sighed and moved to pull on a pair of pants. "There's nothing for it. If Duffy's here, then Roan will charge in soon. Let's allow our Bron to get dressed and perhaps we can talk over a nice meal. Are you hungry, love?"

She wasn't, but she would do almost anything to get a moment to herself. They were overwhelming her. The events of the day had wreaked havoc on everything she knew. She needed a moment to process her own thoughts. She needed to take stock. And she really wanted the comfort of clothes. Sympathy. She could play on their sympathy. "Please, Shim. They did not feed their prisoners well in the jail."

Sure enough, both of the men paled and scrambled to get into their pants.

"I'll bring something up to you. You rest. We'll have to move by nightfall." Lach tugged his shirt over his head. She couldn't miss the blood stains.

"Move? Where?"

"To Aoibhneas." Shim shoved his feet into boots and then handed her some clothes. They had carefully folded her dress. "There's a gap in the planes. We can get back home. We can make sure you're safe."

She opened her mouth, but Lach was in front of her, staring down, his dark eyes full of will and command.

"No arguments. You will go home." He softened slightly. "Let's discuss it when you've had something to eat. Sweet Bronwyn, please don't look at me that way." He was quiet for a moment, his eyes sliding away from hers. "Does my face frighten you?"

He was worried about a few scars? The scars on his face didn't bother her at all, though she wondered how he'd gotten them. They looked a little like burns, as though sparks of fire had driven across his face. But they were small things compared to how perfectly lovely the rest of him was. "Your face doesn't scare me, but everything else about this does. I don't know what to think. And I'm not leaving my home plane. If you know who I am, then you have to know I cannot leave here. My people have need of me."

And she'd ignored that need for far too long. She'd just now decided to stand up and become the princess she should be. If her brothers couldn't reclaim their throne, then she would do it for them.

"Yes, your people have need of you." Shim ran a hand down her arm. "They need to meet their future queen."

There would be no talking to them. They obviously had their minds made up, and she wasn't sure they would tell her the truth even if she tried. Gillian's words were odd to her, but it seemed to Bronwyn that her mentor had political ambitions. She'd said something about uniting the Fae under Lachlan and Shim. Their marriage to the last Seelie princess would go a long way in securing those rights. She wasn't even sure Beck and Cian were alive, but she had to protect their throne just in case.

Lach's face was long, his disappointment obvious. "Come, Shim. I will deal with Roan. You can secure food fit for our princess. And Bronwyn, we will work this out. You no longer have to worry. Your men will take care of you always."

"You did a wonderful job, love." Shim kissed her hair. "You stayed alive."

He winked and followed his brother out the door.

"Duffy!" Lach shouted.

Duffy jumped to his feet. "Kind of hoped they would forget about me. Don't you worry none, Princess. I'll be standing guard. I won't let no one else ogle the royal bosoms."

The door closed. She was alone. She could breathe.

What had happened? Could she even believe her eyes?

"Hello, Your Highness."

She started. "I really wish Fae would stop climbing in through my window."

The small creature with the huge bushy black tail seemed to laugh. He had enormous eyes and what looked to be sharp teeth. His clawed feet clung to the windowsill. "You will have to excuse me, Your Highness. I wanted to see what all the fuss was about…and to beg a moment of your time on behalf of my family."

"I don't know what I could do for your family." She was almost certain the creature was a phooka, though she'd never seen one up close. A phooka could be a dangerous thing, but sometimes they bonded to other beings and became incredibly loyal. A bonded phooka would burn down the plane for its "family."

The phooka's eyes narrowed to slits. "You could do a hell of a lot more than you're doing now, Your Highness. Has cowardice been good to you?"

The words hurt because she saw some truth to them. "Please go away."

The laugh that huffed from the phooka's mouth couldn't be termed humorous. "No. Not until you learn a thing or two. Tell me something, Your Highness. What gives you any right to wear a crown? Is there anything about you that is meaningful besides the fact that whatever brat you spill from your thighs will have royal blood?"

The creature was pulling at her every nerve. "I have done nothing to deserve your scorn."

"Oh, yes, you have done nothing and doing nothing absolutely deserves my scorn. You ran when the palace fell. I can forgive you that. You were a child. But a woman stands before me now. A woman who has done nothing while her people are slaughtered, while innocent bondmates have been taken to Torin's hags and tortured and turned into weapons to be used against our once allies. You are a woman who has done nothing while her kin have suffered, fought, and died rallying behind her family name. Did you know your cousin Keir died?"

Her sweet cos Keir had only been a few years older than she was, but she knew the story. After Torin had killed her father, Keir had raised an army.

And his army had been slaughtered, Keir along with them.

"Other revolts have been started, all under the Finn banner," the phooka continued. "But Bronwyn Finn hid and plowed her fields and kept her head down. You still have a head. Many of the brave ones don't."

"What is your point? If it's to make me feel bad, then you win."

The phooka's yellow eyes seemed to glow with righteousness. "My point is that it is past time for you to be a woman. My family has a daughter named Paige. She's already made a heart bond with a young man named Charles. Charles was taken and sent to the palace because he could bond. Paige has been placated by the fact that the boy's fathers are promising to free him. If they cannot, then I fear Paige will try herself because my young Paige is more woman than you can ever be. And she will die and that will break my master's heart forever. I fight for the ones I love, Bronwyn Finn. It is too bad you cannot say the same."

"You will call me *Your Highness* and you will keep a civil tongue in your head around me. Is that understood?" If she was going to do this, she would do it right. No one of sane mind would follow a mild-mannered peasant princess, but she remembered her father's arrogance well.

Her father. He'd become a sluagh and left instructions for her. Sir Giles. Niall wanted her to go to Sir Giles. She sought her memory. Sir Giles was a landholder not too far away.

Who should she trust?

"Now that sounds more like a royal who might be worth something." The phooka's mouth curved up in an approximation of a smile. "You know if you stay here, your husbands will cart you back to the Unseelie plane and you'll spend the rest of your life spitting out their heirs. I've spent some time with them. I've got no doubt they want you, but they will keep you in the palace, away from anything to tax your lovely brain. You'll be their sweet wife, coddled and loved and marginalized. Is that what you want? Or do you want more?"

Perhaps once she could have been satisfied with being a wife and a mother as her own had been, but she'd been changed. Pain, loss, and work had transformed her.

She didn't want to sit on the sidelines as her mother had done. If she wore a crown, it would be because she'd earned it. She'd already given her blood. It was time to give more.

Shim and Lach. They had been in her dreams for so long, but she had to deal with reality. Reality was the Seelie plane and Torin.

"Help me escape."

The phooka practically purred. "It will be my greatest pleasure, Your Highness. I am your servant."

"Turn around. I need to get dressed."

The phooka turned. With shaking hands, she dressed. When she was ready, she looked at the bed where she'd lost her innocence. Given it. No matter what potion she'd been under, she'd wanted them. She'd loved them.

The phooka guided her out the window, and Bron wondered if she would ever see them again.

Chapter Twelve

Shim stepped off the final step and into the small store, his eyes on his sister.

Gillian looked so different than he remembered her. Thinner. Older. Wearing practical clothes where once she'd preferred gloriously feminine garb. Gillian McIver was a few years older than he and Lach, but she'd always seemed much more mature. After their mother had died, Gilly had run the household. She'd taken care of everything, including certain political situations. The Unseelie plane had lost a valuable royal when Gillian had been caught here. His sister stood looking over maps, her eyes serious as she spoke.

"We will need to move out after dark. The guards are dead, but at least five got away. There's no telling where they ran to or who they will tell. I can only promise that someone will talk and reinforcements will be sent." Gillian straightened up.

William Roan stood in the small store. The floor had been cleared out, and a large table brought in. Maps and vampire technology covered the table. And yet William Roan seemed to have eyes for only one person in the room. The vampire's whole being was focused on Gillian McIver.

Fuck. He should have thought about it, but he'd been utterly overwhelmed by being close to his bondmate.

"The vampire wants our sister," Lachlan whispered. "I didn't remember how bright her glow was."

Gillian glowed. He could see it because of his vampire blood. It told the royal vampire which beings contained blood that would elongate their lives. It called to the royal.

Shim's protective instincts flared.

"Don't," Lach whispered. "Not yet. Give Gillian a chance to deal with him. She's done an amazing job here. She's not a delicate flower. She's survived and kept our Bron alive. She deserves our respect." Lach stepped forward. "Sister."

Gillian's smile grew vibrant. She opened her arms. "Lachlan!"

Shim watched William Roan as his sister embraced his other half. The vampire studied her like a hungry predator, his eyes following every move she made. And Shim would swear the vampire's fangs were out.

Gillian embraced Shim, hugging him to her. "Brother, I thought I might never see you again."

"Yes, I thought the same," Roan said, every word a silky threat. "Imagine my surprise when I went to wake you so we could leave Aoibhneas."

Lach let his sister go. He didn't back down an inch from Roan. "I believe I mentioned that we should leave earlier. It was a good thing or our bondmate would be dead."

Gillian straightened her shoulders. "His Highness, the Prince of the Unseelie Fae, is correct. Her Royal Highness, the Princess Bronwyn, would be dead if her mates had not saved her. You were late, mercenary."

"I was attempting to keep the princes alive. Torin has guards on the roads. He has spies everywhere. I don't doubt that the events of the day will reach his ears soon. His Royal Highness has created a huge clusterfuck for my men." Roan leaned across the table. "There is a reason your father put me in charge."

Gillian laughed, a short, sharp sound that made Shim wonder what the vampire had done to set his sister off. "Is my father paying you? He shouldn't."

The air practically crackled around them. Roan's eyes got dark and big. The damn vampire wasn't even trying to control himself. "Your father and I made a deal. I don't get paid, Princess. I get a boon. Your father intends to make sure I get what I want."

"I'm sure someone of your stature will want gold," Gillian shot back. "That's what you poor vampires want."

"If you think that gold is what a vampire cherishes, you haven't spent enough time on our plane. Understand this, Princess, I mean to get what I want," Roan shot back. He shook his head and seemed to calm a bit. "Prince Lachlan, would you like to explain why you and your brother chose to run away from the guard your father sent?"

"I think they were just horny." Dante Dellacourt had a smirk on his face as he leaned against a wall.

"Well, you would know." Lach seemed to be in a ridiculously good mood. Shim had never seen his brother so relaxed.

Dellacourt stood up straight. "Is my cos all right? Goddess, I can't believe Bron's alive. Can I see her?"

"Bronwyn is fine. She's perfect. And she's tired. She'll be down in a little while," Shim replied, though he wasn't completely sure she was fine. She'd seemed very disconcerted. They needed to talk, but he would prefer to do so while they held her, bonding with her, skin to skin. It was necessary. They had been close to her mind for so long that she didn't trust the physical presence. "Though she's sure she's lost her wits."

Lach put a hand on his shoulder. "She was confused by the potion."

"Potion?" Dellacourt asked.

Gillian took her eyes off Roan and frowned Dellacourt's way. "Your sweet cos was nearly executed today for being a witch. It was only my brothers who saved her."

"As was right. We're her husbands," Shim pointed out. "And we knew she was in danger. We're bonded. We can feel her. Dellacourt, tell me you can't feel your consort."

Dellacourt frowned. "Most of the time, though she's good at shielding. It pisses me off. She tends to do it when she wants a spanking. But I understand what you're saying. I can feel my Kaj." He smiled a bit, his eyes losing focus. "She's happy right now. She's also curious about the village around her."

Shim turned on the vampire mercenary. He didn't understand them. He couldn't. "See? You don't have a consort. You don't have the bond. You can't understand."

Roan laughed, a disdainful huff. "No, Your Highness, I don't have a consort. I haven't had the cash or the connections to keep one. But that will change." His eyes went right back to Gillian.

She hugged Shim. "Stop baiting the mercenary, brother. I will try to do so as well. He's only here to help. And I'm grateful since otherwise we have nothing but you and Lach to protect our precious Bron." She smiled, her face vibrant. "She's wonderful, isn't she? When I first came to negotiate your marriage, I worried she was far too young and spoiled, but she's been magnificent through all of this. You should know I have come to love the girl dearly, and I will kick both of your asses if you cause my Bron a moment's pain."

Shim liked that his sister was so protective of their wife. "We love her, Gilly. We've been lost without her."

"But we have some work to do with her. I'm worried she's angry at you," Lach said, his eyes going back to the stairs.

Gillian sighed. "I am sure she will be. I thought it best to simply be her guardian. We kept to ourselves. We've met so many nobles here who would have used her as a rallying point."

Dellacourt's foot tapped as he thought. "Not just a rallying point, I would suspect. Bron is the last Finn on the plane. And she's female. If I were a betting man, I would lay a lot of gold on the fact that noble families here would see her as a way to take the crown. Oh, wait, I'm actually quite a good gambler. I also bet that's what you were doing here in the first place."

"I was attempting to negotiate a proper, advantageous marriage for my brothers," Gillian replied. "When the coup occurred, I protected the princess. She died. Do you understand that, vampire? She was dead, but my magic brought her back to life. I was the one who used magic to cover up the fact that she was alive. She's here today because of me."

Gillian was wrong about her magic. It had been he and Lach who had brought her back, but Shim kept his mouth closed. Gillian needed all the help she could get with the vampires.

"And you intend to use her to unite the crowns." Dellacourt's voice was without a touch of emotion. Bland, even. But there was a shrewd ruthlessness in the vampire's eyes that let Shim know he had an angle to play. "It might work except for one small fact you've overlooked."

"Really? I don't think I overlooked a thing. When Torin falls, and I will see that bastard fall if it is the last thing I do, Bronwyn will assume the crown and my brothers will be kings. My father will step down and the triumvirate will rule both planes." Gillian made her announcement with a brutal practicality.

"That will be interesting to see." Roan crossed his arms over his chest and smirked, his fangs peeking out.

Dante sighed a bit before making his point. "I believe Their Majesties, Beckett, Cian, and Megan Finn, will have something to say about that when they reclaim their throne. Or were you planning on Bronwyn going to war with her brothers? I assure you I love my cousin, but I will not allow her to claim her brothers' rightful throne. Certainly not when she would be an Unseelie puppet. But then your brothers would be puppets, too. You want to be the power behind the throne."

Shim stared at his sister, Dellacourt's words sinking in. "Gillian, Lach and I have no intentions of fighting with the Seelies."

"We're taking Bronwyn home. We're going to make sure she's safe," Lach said. "Her brothers can have this plane."

Gillian rounded on them both, her eyes alive with fire and anger. "Where is your bloody ambition, brothers? I don't care that the Finns bonded or that they think they can waltz in after thirteen long years and reclaim their throne as if they never ran."

"They had to run," Dellacourt argued. "And don't think they haven't tried to fight."

"Well, as I've been alone and protecting their sister, you'll have to forgive me for saying that they didn't try hard enough." Gillian's fists were clenched at her sides. "I have fought and protected her. I will not allow them to come in and claim that which I have sacrificed for. I will speak to Father. He will see reason. If my brothers don't want the crown, I'll take it myself. I'll take it by right of blood. I'll bring an Unseelie army back. Father will support me."

"Your father wants you safe," Roan said, his eyes hooded.

"My father trusts me, vampire. And you have nothing to do with it." She dismissed him utterly.

"Your father promised me a boon if I carried this off," Roan said, his words a silky menace. "Would you like to know what that boon is,

Princess? Your father has spent too much of his time mourning. He needs someone to come in and train his forces in modern warfare. He would feel so much safer if the general of his army was also his son-in-law."

"Bloody hell, Roan. Did you have to tell her that now?" Dellacourt asked, cool green eyes rolling.

Shim knew he should be shocked, but he wasn't. Gillian was a royal. She wouldn't be marrying the stableboy. She'd planned to offer herself as bondmate to the Seelie twins. She couldn't be shocked that their father offered her up to the man who would save her.

Except she obviously was. "No. My father wouldn't do that."

Roan didn't move, but there was a certain satisfaction in his stance. "Your father wants you safe, consort. I have done the king and your cousin Julian much service and will continue in the future. And you will be my reward."

Gillian turned to Lach. "Brother?"

Lach reached for her. "Gilly, I'll talk to Father, but you have to see that this plan of yours can't work. It would mean all-out war between the tribes. I don't want to war with my wife's family. Honestly, much of the hatred between us seems very silly now that I've walked the plane. They are Fae. We are Fae. We can coexist."

"This isn't our war, sister," Shim said. "We thank you for protecting our mate, but it is our turn to protect her and you. We will go back to our plane, and if the Seelies win the day, we will open relations with them."

"And you would call yourselves kings." Gillian shook her head and turned to Roan. "You will never touch me."

"We'll see about that." Roan didn't move as Gillian strode out of the house.

Lach stared at the vampire. "Find another consort."

"Your father was explicit, Your Highness." Roan's eyes were on the door that Gillian had slammed with vigor. "If I see you all safely back and lead the Seelies to their glory, my lieutenant and I will claim the princess and take over your father's armies. King Fergus doesn't want to unite the tribes under one crown. He merely wants good relations with them. He knows what it would cost. It would cost blood and death and pain unimaginable. Your father is a good king. And your sister is far too ambitious. I worry she's going to cost you your relationship with your bondmate."

"She's pissing me off, that's for sure," Dellacourt said. "You can't believe for a second that Bron will turn on her brothers."

"I don't want her to." Shim ran a hand through his hair. He hated politics. Politics always seemed to get in the way of doing what was right and just. "Give Gilly time but know this. I care not what my father promised you. If Gilly doesn't want you, I'll fight to make sure she's happy."

"I'll make her want me," Roan said with perfect arrogance. "I'm not a stupid man. I can handle your sister."

"I don't know about that. A smart man wouldn't have laid out his plan," Dellacourt said.

"This gives her time to get used to the idea. If I sprang it on her before the wedding, she might pull my fangs out. I rather like my fangs." He sighed and turned to Shim. "Though I would keep my mouth closed about your plans around your bondmate. After everything I heard, I doubt she will be happy fleeing the plane. She cares about these Fae. She was in jail because she tried to defend a brownie. The villagers truly care about her."

She hadn't seemed happy about the idea. And they hadn't even told her about her brothers. Guilt ate at him. He'd been far too busy fucking her to see to her welfare.

"We should have talked to her." Lach seemed to easily pick up on his thoughts.

Though the full, deep bond hadn't been performed yet, Shim was finding it so much easier to know what his brother was thinking now that Bronwyn was near.

"We will. Let's feed her and let her clean up and then we'll talk to her about our plans. And no dictating. Your 'I'm the dominant one and you will obey me' bit is going to get both of us in trouble. Let me handle her."

Lach frowned. "It should be easier than this."

"Women are never easy." Dellacourt smiled. "They have all these feelings and shit. Of course they also have boobs. Gods, I love boobs. Kaj has the most sensitive breasts. Really, I can get her to orgasm just by tweaking her nipples the right way. Where did my consort go?

Damn it, she's shielding again."

Shim sent out his own plea, a pulse of comfort for Bron. There was a flare of panic from her, and then it was like a wall came between them.

"What was that?" Lach asked.

"I think our wife just learned how to put up shields of her own."

Roan started folding up his maps and locking down his tablet. "Well, deal with her. We're going to have to take another route back to Aoibhneas. We ran into some of Torin's men. They were tipped off to some odd behavior in the forest. Two men and a phooka."

Shim wasn't going to be made to feel guilty about that. It had saved Bron. "Tell us when and we'll be ready to go. Just know that Bron is our main responsibility."

"And your sister is mine."

There was an odd comfort to the fact that the vampire would protect his sister. Shim was just worried about who would protect Roan from Gillian.

Shim hurried his preparations. He and Lach found some cheese and soft bread and fruit. The owner of the house was more than happy to provide for them. She spoke about how kind Isolde had been to her and all the villagers. And how they would all follow her now that her true identity was revealed.

Shim was grateful, but the woman's words also frightened him. He didn't want Bronwyn caught up in the fight. He wanted her safe.

"The sooner we get her out of here, the better," Lach said under his breath as they mounted the stairs.

"Her brothers can handle this fight." It was their crown, after all. Bron's crown waited on another plane.

Duffy's eyes were closed when they reached the door. Lach chuckled and poked at their adopted brother.

"I weren't sleeping. I was just resting." Duffy looked up at them. "I need me rest. I think I might have a vampire to kill."

Shim sighed. Fuck all. Duffy couldn't be pleased about the engagement. "Brother, you knew you couldn't marry her."

He shrugged and closed his eyes once more. "Always knew. Don't mean I won't protect her."

"Well, rest up. We move out tonight." Shim opened the door and realized that Bron hadn't waited.

Bron was gone.

* * * *

Bronwyn promised herself that when she made it to her tower, she would change into good old peasant clothes. Her second-best dress was hardly making it easy to run through the fields. It seemed to catch on everything as though invisible hands were trying to reach out and grasp her and pull her back.

She felt the tug of Lach and Shim. By now they had to know she was gone. The phooka had stayed behind to create some chaos, but before he'd left her, he'd taught her how to throw up some mental shields. According to the phooka, she was wide open to the men she'd dreamed about most of her life.

She pulled her skirt free of a branch. It tore. Like everything else in her life right now.

And she hadn't even known they were real. They had spent their whole lives understanding that she was a real, actual living creature, but Bronwyn Finn had walked around thinking she was insane. And everyone else had thought she was crazy, too. And now they thought they could just walk in and take her virginity and her blood and cart her off to goddess only knew where.

And that damn dog wouldn't stop following her.

"I don't have anything to feed you." She stared back at the animal. It was a pretty thing. She. For some reason Bron was pretty sure the dog was female. There was something delicate about its features. The dog, who might also be a wolf, sat back on her haunches as Bron found herself snarled in a bramble bush. "You don't want to go where I'm going. So shoo. Shoo, dog."

The dog snorted, her muzzle lifting in a fashion that made Bron think she was laughing. And it didn't move until she did, then the dog simply trotted along behind her.

"Fine, but you'll see. I'm going on a long journey." She rounded the final curve and her tower was close. It was tall and dominated the countryside. It had been her home for almost four years.

It had been her prison.

"She didn't care about me. Not really. I think that's what hurts worst of all." Bron watched for a moment trying to figure out if anyone was in the tower. She thought not. The phooka had claimed the others were all still in the village waiting for the best time to flee back to the Unseelie plane.

The wolf sat beside her and gently nuzzled her hand as though asking her to continue.

"You're a weird wolf or dog or whatever you are." She stood up and started to move. She only needed one thing really, but she would change her clothes, too. She needed the knife. She couldn't leave without it.

The wolf barked, an impatient sound. Well, maybe the phooka wasn't the only strange creature she would meet today.

"I've spent almost half my life with Gillian, and I just found out she never cared about me at all. Not the real me. She only saved me because she wanted me to marry her brothers. She told them to impregnate me so their claim would be indisputable."

The wolf growled low in her throat.

Bron stopped and looked around for the threat. The courtyard was completely empty. Then she realized why the wolf had growled.

"You didn't like the sound of that. Did you? I didn't either. They used me. Gillian pretended to care about me and protected me from men only because she wanted me to be a virgin when her brothers took me."

There it was again. The deep growl.

Bron got to one knee. She wasn't sure how, but this wolf understood what she was saying and seemed to empathize. She was pretty sure no one else would. Everyone else would say that was what royals did. They traded their daughters and sons in exchange for treaties and alliances and land. Her own brothers' engagement had been made in an attempt to bring Maris's family's great wealth of resources into the Finn family line.

"I know I should have understood that any marriage I make will not be one of love, but I've lived as a peasant for far too long. I've watched the way they live and how many choose mates based on love and affection." She reached out and stroked the wolf. Maybe it wasn't so bad to have a companion, even one who couldn't talk back. "The real problem is that I've loved those men all my life, and I didn't even know they were real. I loved them. Never wanted anyone else. And all they want from me is an alliance."

The wolf seemed to shake her head, but then she growled and got to all fours, the hair along her spine standing straight up.

Bronwyn stood to face whatever was coming her way.

Niall. He walked out of the tower, placing something in his pack. The guard had changed into what looked like traveling clothes, divesting himself of his armor and cape. He wore suede pants and a tunic, with boots covering his feet.

He was quite the master of disguise. He looked like a peasant now, and not a particularly dangerous one. He could likely make his way on the roads and survive by smiling and looking helpful and proclaiming "long live King Torin."

Her memories of the day were vague and fragmented, but she remembered him. He'd saved her, and then he'd dumped her when she became troublesome.

He walked down the lane as though he hadn't stolen into her home and taken her things. The bastard had taken her knife. She sought her memory. In those last moments when she could still speak, he'd asked about the knife and she'd told him.

"Calm down, wolf." Bron put a hand on her new pet. "We should get answers out of him before you eat him."

The wolf stopped and stared at her for a moment and then began to bounce up and down in apparent glee. Well, at least her new pet was on the same page. The wolf's tail thumped against the hard dirt, and she watched her prey with anticipatory joy.

Bron wished she had a weapon of some kind. Anything, really, but her brand-new husbands hadn't seen fit to arm her. They'd preferred her without her clothes.

The feeling of their skin wrapped around hers assaulted her, and for a moment she could feel them. Their panic. It flared to life in her and she couldn't breathe before she slammed the connection closed. She couldn't afford it. No matter how nice it had been, she wasn't going to allow herself to be used to gift the Unseelie royals with her brothers' throne. Until she saw their dead bodies for herself, she wasn't going to give up. She'd made up her mind to stand and be the princess her people needed her to be.

And that started by having a chat with Niall.

He began to walk toward the road. Bron took a step out, showing herself. At the very least she had the wolf by her side. It might make him think twice. She was going to have to come up with a suitable name for her pet since it seemed like the wolf was the only creature on the plane she could trust.

Niall started and then stopped, staring at her. "Princess Bronwyn."

"Incredible jackass Niall."

The wolf seemed to snort.

Niall's face flushed. "Your Highness, there was nothing I could do. I was surrounded by Micha's men. They would have killed me. I didn't have an army."

She thought about what had happened in the square. It had seemed to be a nightmare at the time, but now she could start to process what she'd seen and heard. "Neither did the man who saved me. He didn't have an army. He only had his brother."

Niall looked around as if expecting someone to show up. "Where is he? Who is he? It doesn't matter, Princess. We need to leave here. It was smart of you to get away and come looking for me. Your father is going to be very proud of you."

He'd had an incredible story concerning her father. "Why should I believe you about my father?"

"Because it's true." He gave her a warm smile and walked far too close to her. "Princess Bronwyn, everything I have told you is true. Your father trained me to find you. He gave me explicit instructions. I've been searching since I became old enough to be a guard."

"If my father is truly a sluagh, then why didn't he search for me himself?" It was impossible to think of her rigidly polite father as an eater of the dead. The sluagh were unshriven dead, dead who refused to move on to the after.

"I believe his essence is tied to his brother's and he cannot be free until his brother is dead." Niall sighed. "I do not expect that you will understand any of this, Princess. Simply know that your father trusts me. Ask me something only he would know. He spoke of you so often. He made me memorize everything about you."

"What did he call me as a child?" It was a secret between the two of them. Or at least her father had told her so.

"He called you his little pixie because your hair was so big he thought it looked like pixie wings when your nanny didn't braid it. He thought your hair was half your body weight when you were a child."

Tears pricked her eyes. *Little pixie.* It was a sweet memory. "All right, let's say I believe you. What does he want me to do?"

He smiled, a self-satisfied look. "He wants you to follow me. He wants you to trust me. I'm going to take care of you. We'll go to Sir Giles's manse. He's been looking for a person to rally behind ever since your cousin died. He's tried several times to get ambassadors off the plane to talk to friendly vampire families. He will give us a safe place and he has a long history with the military." Niall was silent for a moment and then seemed to come to a decision. "And he will see us properly wed."

The wolf put her head down and Bron groaned. "I am not marrying you."

"'Tis the only way, Princess. We shall marry and I will take care of the political part of this. You will need only to be your sweet self and let the people see you. It is all that is required of you."

Her wolf growled and Bron understood the sentiment. "I want my knife back."

Niall stared. "There is no need, Princess. I will handle everything."

"I don't want you to handle everything. I want you to give me my knife back. And I don't need another husband."

"What is that supposed to mean?" His face flushed, his shoulders squaring.

Bron would have sworn her wolf rolled her eyes. "It means that I find myself wed to the princes of the Unseelie. I doubt they would be happy to share their wife, though I find myself in a small disagreement with them."

"You can't be married."

"Oh, yes, I can. I'm bonded to them. Trust me. I feel the connection. I think they both want to murder me right about now." She'd felt their panic, and now even though she had her shields up, she could still feel the fine edge of fear and irritation. She wondered if they could feel her willpower.

Niall huffed. "No one on this plane will recognize the marriage.

They are Unseelie and obviously up to no good. We will wed, and our people will accept it."

"I am not marrying you. And I might not know my husbands very well in this reality, but I know they will take you apart limb from limb, or rather Shim will burn you to a crisp and then Lachlan will play with your corpse."

Not know them? How could she even think the words? She could be as mad as she liked, but she knew how they kissed and how they loved it when she wrapped her arms around them. She knew that Lach tended to take the lead and Shim was the soft touch. Lach had always been more closed off, but once he opened up, he threw himself into everything with an almost wild abandon. The games they had played through their shared dreams when they were children had proven that. Lach would start by watching and standing to the side while Shim held her hand, but by morning Lach would run and play and scream with them. Shim liked stories. Even as they aged. As their dreams turned more physical, Shim still wanted to hear stories from her life and made-up tales.

But that was in her dreams. Dreams, not reality. Reality was Torin killing half the plane. Reality was she was the last of her line still living on the plane, and she couldn't chase after her dreams.

Niall took a long breath. "It doesn't matter. We need to get you to Sir Giles's province. I sent word that I was bringing you."

"Did you? And how were you going to explain my absence?" As far as Niall had known, she was a heap of ashes in the town square.

He flushed. "That's why I needed the knife."

"You were going to find someone to take my place. I'm not sure my father would approve." Of course she also knew how ruthless her father could be. She doubted that becoming a corpse-eating ghost had softened him much. "I suppose it wouldn't be too difficult to find someone with the Finn coloring. And if Father taught you, then you could perhaps teach her how to do a halfway decent impression of me. After all, no one has seen me since I was a child."

He reached out for her hand. "I was doing what it took to secure the throne and get rid of Torin so your father has a chance to be free and your brothers a shot at coming home."

She avoided his touch. It wasn't a horrible plan.

"Well now you don't need to. You have me." Her course was set. Her heart ached at the thought of leaving them. She'd just discovered her Dark Ones, but the only thought that hurt worse than leaving was the idea of staying and discovering all the ways they planned to use her.

Niall settled his pack on his shoulder. "You need to change. We'll have to pose as husband and wife traveling to market or looking for work, but people will ask about that dress. It's too nice to travel in, and it looks as though it got singed. Come on. Let's go inside and get you ready. You can pack up some small items. It should be two days' walk to Sir Giles's."

He turned and strode back up to the tower. Bron followed. She knew she was placing a lot of faith in a man she barely knew, but her father sent him, and she would fare better with a pretend husband than on her own.

"I'll be quick." Bron rushed up the stairs, already pulling at the ties of her dress. The wolf shuffled up behind her, utterly ignoring Bron's command to stay. She opened the door to her small room and let the wolf in. "You only listen when you want to."

She quickly crossed to her dresser and pulled out traveling clothes. Suede pants and a big blousy shirt. Comfortable clothes.

"I suppose you won't let me eat him now. No one ever does." A feminine voice had Bron shrieking.

She turned and there was a naked female on her bed. She was slight, petite, and graceful, with huge blue eyes and a mass of wavy, sun-kissed brown hair. And the wolf was nowhere in sight. A shape-shifter? A hag could shift.

"Don't be afraid. I'm not a hag. Everyone always assumes I'm a hag. Meg says I'm a werewolf, which is much better than what Dante calls me. Shanimal. Silly name and a silly man."

Dante? "Dante Dellacourt? My cousin?"

The woman smiled, a bright thing that lit up the room. "Your cousin, my husband. I think that makes us family, Bronwyn. Or should I call you princess? Your brothers are very informal."

Tears welled. Where there had been terror only a moment ago, a reluctant hope swelled inside. "My brothers?" She was talking to a naked wolf woman who claimed to be her cousin by law. It was all too much. "I find it convenient that you suddenly know my brothers."

The woman's eyes widened. "I do not suddenly know Beck and Cian. I have known them for a while now. At first I think Beck feared that he would have to slay me. It's a good thing he did not try. I would have taken a chunk out of his hide. And Megan would have been very distressed. She likes me. She's my cousin, too. It is good to have family. Although my family is very odd. I like you. You're different. You seem to understand the necessity to be a bit brutal with your enemies. Which brings me back to my original point. I think you should allow me to eat that man. He is going to get you in trouble."

Bron ignored the fact that the slender woman seemed preoccupied with eating creatures. "Who is Megan?"

"Megan is the queen."

"My brothers bonded?" Torin had done everything he could to ensure his brothers couldn't find a proper bondmate. She'd heard rumors that great battles were being fought in the arena when a bondmate could be found. The rumors had it that vampires and refugee Fae would fight to the death in an attempt to possess one.

The woman nodded, a small smile on her face. "A true bond. Your brothers have ascended into their powers. Beckett Finn is a Storm Lord and Cian a Green Man. Though he is not actually green. He is normal looking. I am told the title should not be taken literally."

Beck and Cian had formed a true triumvirate. It was beyond imagining. "I can't believe it."

"They came into their powers a few months ago when they found Megan. As the Unseelie twins ascended into theirs when they bound to their perfect mate."

"Me." She wasn't sure how it had happened, but she knew it was true. It was right there, that invisible thread that she'd always thought of as an inward sign of her own insanity. She'd never seen it for what it truly was—the bond between mates. And not any mates. Symbiotic twins. She bridged them, giving them access to the other half of their soul. And apparently giving them powers. "Shim is a Fire Lord."

The wolf woman nodded. "I think I heard the word pyromancer used. And necromancer for Lachlan."

Lord of the Dead. Heat and Cold. Two halves of a whole, and she'd felt both powers skimming through her system. "Why are you here? Where is Dante? Where are my brothers for that matter?"

Her family. She needed her family. They would help her sort everything out. They would talk to her and make things right. Oh, she longed to see her brothers once more.

"Dante is back in the village. I followed you because I thought you might need some time to think about everything that has happened. I was told you were given the fire drug. I know how it feels. It is terrible and yet there was something wonderful about that first night with my Dante."

Terrible and wonderful. That was a good way to put it. She'd already forgotten the pain, but not the rolling need that had threatened to boil over. She could still remember how it felt to be one with them. To have Lach deep inside and Shim's mind binding to hers as he fed. In those moments, she hadn't been alone. She'd been loved and whole, and it had all been a lie.

"What's your name?" If she was telling the truth, then Bron had been terribly rude.

The woman straightened up, her chin raised in a polite greeting. "Kaja. I am Kaja Dellacourt. I am your cousin, and I would like to be your friend."

Bron couldn't help but flush a bit. Kaja's breasts were thrust out as she made her greeting. "And you are very comfortable being naked."

The woman laughed, a sweet sound. "Megan thinks it is odd, too, but I cannot wear clothes in my wolf state so I have none on when I change. Now, can we talk about all the reasons you should come back to the village with me?"

And back to Shim and Lachlan and Gillian, who wanted her barefoot and pregnant in the Unseelie kingdom? No way. Bron resumed getting dressed, pulling out her most comfortable shoes, a pair of boots Gillian had traded the last of her jewelry for.

Kaja didn't seem to notice her silence. She continued on. "I do not like that man downstairs. He might not be a bad man, but he seems to have plans he intends to see through with you or without you."

"That seems to be the order of the day, doesn't it? Everyone wants a piece of me." Including Torin.

"But your family wants to protect you," Kaja insisted. "I don't think that man down there will do much in the way of protecting you. He will protect his plan, perhaps, but his care for you will only go so far as seeing his plan come to fruition. Of course, you could simply wait until your husbands catch up to you, and then they will kill him." Her eyes lit up. "And they will let me eat him. Yes. I very much like your husbands."

"Then why are you here with me and not off telling them where I am."

Kaja seemed to think about that for a moment. "Because Meg has taught me much. There are many rules on the Fae planes, but the one that is the most important is the Girl Power rule. The queen explained it to me. Girls must stick together because men are all idiots who oftentimes think only with their man parts, and man parts are not smart. Females must show loyalty to one another in the face of man part foolishness. If you are determined to follow this man, who is not your husband or your kin and will likely lead you into something terrible, then I will be forced to follow you because you are my kin, and I cannot leave you to something terrible. And besides, there might be snacks along the way."

Bron stared at her new cousin, unable to keep the smile off her face. Snacks? Dante, it seemed, kept his bride on a short leash. "I don't think I can go back. Do you understand that they want me to go back to their plane and pretend like nothing is happening here in my home? What would you do if the place of your birth was being destroyed?"

"I would warm myself by the fire and pray it took several of the wolves of my pack, but if my new family was being harmed, then nothing could keep me away." She studied Bron for a moment. "And I can understand where a good princess would see her people as her family. You could try talking to Lachlan and Shim."

"I don't think they want to talk," Bron pointed out.

"I have found that my husband will agree to many things when his man parts are in my mouth. You see, Meg is right because many times Dante should not have agreed to such things, but he did agree so I would continue."

Bron stared at her cousin. "I don't think I wanted to know that about Dante."

Kaja sighed. "Megan also told me I must use a thing called tact. I struggle with tact. So we're going to this Sir Giles's home?"

It probably wasn't a good idea to take her new cousin along. "You don't have to come with me."

Kaja got off the bed and shook out her hair. "I do. I cannot break the sacred code of chicks before dicks. Dante will understand. Or he will not and he will spank me. The good news is we are no longer on his plane, and it was so sad that someone forgot to pack the torture device that makes my poor asshole burn."

Bron gasped. "Goddess, Kaja!"

Kaja's brown hair shook. "Yes, see. Tact. I do not have it. But I was smart enough to leave that thing behind."

Bron was about to explain the meaning of the word discretion to Kaja when she heard an odd cracking sound. She went to the window. She could see a huge, dark cloud approaching the village. It moved swiftly and with great purpose.

"What is that? A storm?" Kaja stood beside her, her eyes on the cloud as it stopped over what Bron would bet her life was the town square.

"It's not a storm." A sick feeling hit her gut as the cloud hovered and began to rain down. But it wasn't raindrops cascading to the ground. It was soldiers. "It's an eddy wind. Fae who are skilled at magic can ride them and take others along. It's a way to get large groups of people somewhere very quickly. We need to get to the village."

She turned, satisfied when Kaja changed from woman to wolf in an easy shift that happened so fast Bron barely noticed it. One moment Kaja was a woman and then next a graceful wolf following behind her. The wolf looked up at her with questioning eyes.

"No, Kaja, we're not leaving our family behind." She couldn't leave them now.

Because Torin had found her and she couldn't run anymore.

Chapter Thirteen

Lach had his hand on his sword as he strode out the door. The light hit him, and he realized he'd forgotten his protective glasses. The light on this plane was too damned bright. It had been fine when they traveled at night, but the full glare of afternoon reminded Lach of his vampire DNA.

"And where are you planning on going?" Roan asked.

"Bronwyn is gone."

Roan cursed and pulled out a small box he used to call his men in from their duties. "I don't suppose you know where she's gotten off to?"

Shim stalked through the door. He stopped on his heels as the sunlight hit him. He slapped a hand over his eyes and stepped back into the shade of the house. "Damn me. What is that?"

Roan stood in the sunlight looking infinitely superior in his full military gear. His body was covered with lightweight clothes that protected his skin from the sun's rays. As with many vampires he had implants that protected his eyes. They flowed around his face when in the presence of ultraviolet rays and disappeared when there was no longer a need for them.

Lach had not needed them before, but the sunlight in Tír na nÓg was taking a toll. He could stand outside, but his eyes ached. Shim, it seemed, couldn't even stand to be in the sunlight at all.

"I should have known. Stay inside, Shim. You've had first blood, haven't you? It's why you're stronger. I saw it the minute you walked downstairs. You feel it, don't you?" Roan asked.

Shim put a hand over his eyes, staring out at the vampire. "I've never felt so damn healthy. Well, not since I was a child."

"Consort blood. I've heard there's nothing like it, but almost every royal taking consort blood knows that the ultraviolet effects get worse. Shim, you've had blood, but Lach hasn't yet, has he?"

"No. I didn't think we should both bite her," Lach replied. His brother did look healthier, a fine flush to his skin where he'd been a pale white for years. After that terrible day so long ago when the connection had been cut between them and Bronwyn, and Shim had slipped into his long coma, he'd worried that Shim would never fully recover. He'd gotten healthier, but he'd never regained his full strength until this morning.

And now she was gone.

Dellacourt jogged up. "I can't find Kaja. I'm worried she's out there eating crap she shouldn't be eating."

Roan smiled. "I bet she's run with our princess. Your Kaja is a smart woman, and she has a definite nose for trouble."

Duffy stood beside Shim, his axe at his side. "I checked out the window. It looks like she used the sheets to climb down the side of the house. Why do you think she would do that?"

"Because she's probably scared," Dellacourt said, his irritation obvious. He pulled out his tablet and punched in some numbers. "You should have let me talk to her first. But no, you two had to jump her. I would assume at this point that the marriage has been consummated."

"It wasn't properly witnessed, but she is our wife and I'll kill anyone who tries to take her from us," Lach snarled.

The vampire made a gagging sound. "Who thought it was a good idea for an Unseelie king and a royal vampire to get it on and create symbiotic twins? They should have known damn well it would produce a ridiculously over-the-top asshole. You don't have to kill me, Lachlan. Bronwyn already got away. You might have taken time to talk to her. Introduce yourselves."

"The mating fever did not allow for much talk," Shim admitted.

The vampire's head shook. "Well, naturally. Are you part troll, too? I've heard they sometimes go insane and start eating brains."

Lach felt himself flush. His cousin was a troll.

"I should have known. The Unseelie are not known for their pickiness when it comes to mates," Roan said with a laugh. "Most Unseelie Fae have a bit of everything in their family tree, unlike your Seelie brethren where there is a stigma attached to having mixed blood."

"Do you think she ran because she was disturbed that we're Unseelie?" She would have been raised to think less of the Unseelie and their acceptance of the dark things of the planes.

Dante shook his head. "I think she ran because she woke up and found herself married to two strange men with next to no explanation. Also, her parents always thought she was a little touched in the head. She spoke of boys who played in her dreams. I suppose she meant the two of you."

"Yes." He wasn't sure he wanted to hear more. His father hadn't believed him, but at least he'd had Shim. Bron had no one.

"What would you think if you had spent the majority of your life believing in one thing and you wake up and find out you were completely wrong and what you believed was imaginary is real and has two penises and two sets of hungry fangs? I think Bronwyn can be forgiven for running." He turned as the tablet beeped. "My Kaj, on the other hand, is going to get her sweet ass spanked. She's to the northwest. What's up that way?"

"Our land," Gillian said, her face sober as she stood under the awning. "She's gone back to the tower. She wouldn't leave without her knife."

"She has her father's knife?" Dante asked. "The one that matches his sword?"

Gillian nodded, taking a moment as she looked on the edge of some unnamed emotion. "She does. It was next to her body. I recognized it. I took it with me because I thought it would prove her identity. She's protected it ever since. She would never leave it behind. She intends to kill Torin with that knife."

Lach stared at his sister. "Gillian, why would she have that thought in her head? Bronwyn is a princess. She doesn't know how to fight."

Gillian snorted. "I assure you, she does, and so do I. What was I supposed to do? Was I supposed to hire servants and continue to live as a royal? We were on the run and we had nothing but the jewels I managed to smuggle out. We worked for our food, and I wasn't about to be at the mercy of any man. Before Torin started killing non-*sidhe*, I paid a couple of goblins to train us how to fight. They were the first. Wherever we would go, we would find someone to teach us. She's quite good with a staff and knives and a bow. She needs work with a sword."

"She needs to get to a place where she doesn't have to defend herself." Lach turned back to his brother. "Why didn't we know any of this?"

They'd been in her dreams for years, and she'd never given a hint of the horrors she was facing.

"They were her dreams," Shim pointed out. "She was exactly who she wanted to be in those dreams. You should know that."

In his dreams, he was whole. Bron had never seen the real him until earlier this day. She'd seemed all right with his lack of beauty, but his scars couldn't have helped.

Bron had been on her own with only Gillian to help her survive. And now she didn't even have Gillian with her. How much had she heard of his sister's speech? "Do you think she heard you, Gilly?"

Tears squeezed from her eyes. "I do. I think she'll never trust me again, and it's my own damn fault. If she dies out there, it will be on my head because I'm so bloody arrogant."

"You're a princess, Your Highness. You are everything you need to be, including arrogant. If you didn't believe in yourself and your mission, you and Bronwyn would be dead. You did everything right." Roan stood to the side, but there was no question he was an authority figure. "Now let us do our job and get you all to safety. We need to get to Aoibhneas, and then we can have all the fights and recriminations you like. We can all decide what to do from there."

Gillian stared at him warily. "I thought you're being paid to get Bron and me back to the Dark Palace?"

"I'm being paid to take care of you and to do what's in your best interest," Roan replied. "Your father hired me to find a child. I'm in the presence of a woman with a mind I admire. You and Princess Bronwyn have survived here for a very long time. I'll listen to any plan the two of you have so long as you allow me to listen from a safe location. I don't intend to drag either of you kicking and screaming off the plane. You're smart women. You have a say in your future. That's something Princess Bronwyn's husbands should remember when they're dealing with her."

"You're a dangerous man, Roan." Gillian said the words with a small sniffle, but it was plain to Lach that his sister was taking the vampire seriously.

A single brow rose over the vampire's eyes. "Don't you forget it for a second, Princess."

Gillian stared at him for a moment. "Don't think flattery will work with me."

A smile tugged that vampire's lips up, revealing a hint of fangs. "I wouldn't imagine it. I suspect rope and long days of training will work on you."

"Roan, you go too far." Lach wasn't about to let his sister be abused. Though he was thinking about tanning his mate's ass red. It made him a horrible hypocrite, but it felt odd to listen to the vampire talk about his sister in such a fashion. She was his sister. She wasn't supposed to do things like get tied up. That was sexual, and he couldn't see it happening.

Gillian laughed. "I think I can handle one vampire, though he is overly large. Roan will discover soon enough the depth of my training. And the lengths I've gone to. I assure you, he'll find another consort."

Dellacourt started walking to the north. "Kaja is this way. I put a locator device under her skin a long time ago. That sweet shanimal isn't getting away from me. I recommend you all put locators on your women. They walk off all too often. Now, can we stop the whole sexual tension thing between the princess and the mercenary? Either fuck each other or let it drop. I have a cousin and a wife to find."

Roan's men gathered around, the big lieutenant stopping and staring at Gillian with unabashed interest. Was this the vampire Roan intended to share his sister with?

Was he going to have to kill two vampires? Or should he do exactly what Roan had said and assume that Gillian had a brain and could handle herself? Roan wouldn't force her. He might try to seduce her, but he wouldn't force her.

He was about to follow Dellacourt when there was a popping sound and the sky darkened. He looked overhead and clutched his sword. He couldn't mistake that cloud. It was an eddy cloud.

"Is that what I think it is?" Shim tried to walk out, but his eyes closed. The light was too much for him.

First blood was supposed to give him strength, and it seemed it had. Shim was stronger than he'd been in thirteen years, but it also seemed to have enhanced his vampire half. Shim closed his eyes and tried to step out. Lach shoved him back.

"You're no good if you can't see." Lach could see. It was irritating, but he could keep his eyes open.

Roan had a sonic charger in his hands. It sent pulses of sound waves that incapacitated or killed its victims if the setting was high enough. "Let's see who's come to greet us. They could be friendly."

But Lach was pretty damn sure they wouldn't be. And now he was glad Bron was gone. He would find her. Kaja would protect her, and according to Gillian, she wasn't bad at protecting herself. But whatever was about to drop from that cloud was bad. He could feel it.

"Stay inside." Lach looked back to where Duffy and Shim stood. He could protect them both. "Duffy, you stay here and guard Shim. Gillian, please."

Dark eyes narrowed on him, letting him know she wasn't pleased with being relegated to the house. "I'll stay here. For now."

The air around them cracked and sizzled. Lach looked up. It was hard, but he could see Fae dropping from the cloud. An eddy wind was difficult to locate and harder to catch. He counted ten and then twenty and then thirty soldiers drop from the savage-looking cloud.

Dellacourt cursed as Roan had them stop, signaling the halt with a single fist in the air. Dellacourt leaned over. "Have you ever seen an eddy cloud that size? My uncle showed me one once, but it was tiny. This is at least a hundred yards across."

Lach squinted as he looked up. "I've seen bigger ones back home, but I don't know a single person who could ride one that big. They're hard to maneuver. It takes a lot of magic to make an eddy cloud do your will. And to take that many passengers. Gods. Who is it?"

Roan let them move once more, creeping carefully along the sides of buildings as they approached the town square.

Lach got a glimpse of what was ahead of him. The square was covered with soldiers. Guards wearing the livery of Torin stood in rigid formation. The cloud hung overhead casting a dark, ominous shadow. It was as though the cloud almost made the sky seem like twilight. He could see much more comfortably here. Even the vampires' implants had disappeared in the absence of ultraviolet light. Lach was able to see that the villagers had made their way out of their homes and stood watching the guard, fear on their faces. The last twenty-four hours hadn't been kind to this village. The war had come to them in a brutal fashion, but up until now only Torin's guards had been killed. He could see the villagers now feared for their own lives.

"It looks like they're going to make an announcement. Once we hear what they have to say, we need to get back, pick up the others, and make a break for it. I don't want to be seen." Roan's voice came over the comm system he'd been given this morning. It was a tiny device that fitted to Lach's ear and allowed them to talk to everyone on the team over short distances.

There was a final pop and a woman appeared in the middle of the square. She was a vision in black, her dark hair perfectly coiffed, not a strand out of place. Her black dress had silver threaded through it. She was lovely. And Lach knew immediately that she was a hag.

"Crap me a river. I've seen that face before, though she was a blonde. That's one of Torin's hags." It was Dellacourt whispering now. "Does anyone see a cat? Kill the cat first. I'm serious."

The hag smiled a superior-looking grin as she looked around. She was surrounded by soldiers, but Lach knew who had the real power here.

"Good afternoon. I bring you greetings from your king."

The village was silent. A horrible sense of anticipation hovered in the air. It seemed to have weight, as though a heavy, stifling blanket had been placed over the whole village just waiting to smother everyone.

The hag stopped her pacing. Crimson lips turned down and one eyebrow arched. "You have nothing to say? This village does not respect our glorious king?"

This village was full of peasants. They were up against well-trained soldiers with weapons, and all the peasants had were farming tools. And they were burdened with their children. Lach was happy when someone was smart enough to shout, "Hurray for King Torin."

The rest joined in, though it was a half-hearted shout.

The hag's foot tapped against the dirt. "Where is the mayor of this village?"

Utter silence and then someone was brave enough to step up. Reymon. The shopkeeper left his wife standing with their daughter and son. The daughter looked to be of marriageable age, but the son was still a youngling, his hand clutching his mother's.

Reymon took a deep breath, his hat in hand. "The mayor's gone. It's harvest time. The mayor took the guards to the next province. He's guarding our shipments himself to make sure King Torin gets the percentage he needs."

The hag pursed her lips. "Well, it is harvest time, and I don't really care about the mayor anyway. He's an unctuous prick. So the good news, my soldiers, is we don't have to worry about upsetting the local politicians. The bad news is all for you, Tuathanas's people. The king is in danger. I need all young women past the age of sixteen to be gathered in the square. Any woman between the ages of sixteen and forty must report here immediately."

Lach heard Roan curse in his ear. "It's time to get out of here. Everyone fall back to the shop. We'll locate our two lost packages and hit the road."

"What are they going to do with those women?" He saw Reymon hurry back. Both his daughter and his wife looked to be in danger.

"It doesn't matter," Roan insisted. "It only matters that whatever would happen involves two of our team members, perhaps three if Kaja isn't in her other form when these soldiers catch her. Now fall back."

The soldiers were moving, picking women out of the crowd and pulling them from crying children or angry men. One villager attempted to defend his daughter. Lach watched as a sword sliced through his belly.

It was wrong. There it was. That feeling in his gut. It wasn't merely triggered by Bronwyn. The warrior inside him had had his first blood, and the utter injustice he saw had him begging for more.

"Your Highness, you said it yourself. This is not your fight." Roan had made his way back, placing a hand on Lach's shoulder. "What is your mission?"

"To save my bondmate."

But Rachel Harper's words were ringing in his head. These might be Seelie Fae, but damn if they didn't bleed like he did. And they loved their wives and children. The old and the infirm were struggling alongside the healthy, but they were going to lose.

"Your Highness, I see the light in your eyes. This is a mistake. There are too many soldiers. There's thirty of them and nine of us, and three of us shouldn't be fighting. Shim won't be able to handle the sunlight if the cloud disperses and Gillian and the gnome should stay hidden." Roan shook his head. "I understand the need to stop an injustice, but we have to think about our own women."

A soldier hauled Reymon's daughter to the center of the square. She stood, shaking in front of the hag.

Reymon hadn't been thinking of himself when he'd offered his home. Reymon had opened his own bedroom and thanked the goddess that the Unseelie kings had come.

Was Reymon standing out there wondering where the kings were now, or had he figured out that his own life and that of his whole family would be weighed and judged as meaningless in the wake of Lach's own?

He'd spent years trying to be taken seriously as a prince.

What did it mean to have this power inside him if he never used it? What kind of king was he if he kept walking away from people like Reymon and the Harpers because he was waiting for the right fight?

"Your Highness," Roan began.

Reymon ran for his daughter. Lach could see plainly what would happen. Two soldiers moved to intercept the shopkeeper. It wouldn't matter that he was trying to protect his child or that he was woefully unarmed. They were smiling and hauling swords over their heads.

The right fight was the one in front of him.

"Go on then, Roan. Protect my sister." Lach broke from the group.

Roan hissed in his ear. "And let you have all the fun? Not on your life, you bastard."

Lach heard the sonic boom blast past him. It sent the soldiers scattering.

Chaos ruled around him as everyone started to run.

He hoisted his sword and a fierce joy took hold as he finally gave in to his instincts and began the good fight.

* * * *

"Princess, what are you doing?" Niall jogged beside her, churning up dust as they ran. "We need to go the other way. Is there something you need from town? I don't think we should go back there."

Damn straight they shouldn't go back there, but she couldn't run. Not this time. The village was under attack, and it had something to do with her.

And she wasn't about to let the village go down in flames without her there to help defend it.

"You don't have to come with me. Just give me my knife and we can part ways. My father should have told you. I'm rather stubborn when I want to be."

Niall reached out and grabbed her elbow, hauling her around. His eyes were fixed on hers. "I can be stubborn, too, Princess. I say we're leaving. I cannot allow your soft heart to put the whole kingdom in jeopardy."

He started to pull her close, most likely to haul her over his shoulder, but there was a low growl from her right. Kaja was at her side, staring up a Niall. The brown fur on her back stood straight up, her perfectly white teeth on display.

Niall gasped as he looked down at the wolf.

She rather liked having a wolf for a cousin. "I would back away. Kaja has been looking for someone to eat, and you don't want to be on her menu."

Bron tried pulling herself free, but Niall held fast. His face, previously worried, settled back into the stubborn mask of one who wasn't going to allow himself to be swayed by anything.

"I think I'll take my chances. I'm quite a hunter myself. There's no dumb animal alive who can take me down. Call off your dog. I don't want to hurt her, but I have a mission to complete, and I intend to do so."

She heard a shrill cry and then the unmistakable sound of a sonic weapon being fired in the distance. Vampire tech. Dante really was in that village. "You would sacrifice a whole village to complete your mission? You've been living here for months. Those are your neighbors. They're dying."

If her words moved him, he didn't show it. "And more will die if Torin isn't stopped. This is a small village. People are dying all over the country. So yes, I will sacrifice whoever I must in order to see you safely to Sir Giles and the army he will be able to build around you. You will be a figurehead. That is your true value, not as some crazed woman wielding a sword in the defense of peasants. The nobles will back you. You will be the rallying point. You're far too important to risk."

There would be no reasoning with him. He was a true believer, an absolutist, and he didn't really care about her beyond the fact that she could further his mission. "Then take the damn knife. Find another girl to play my part. You were going to do it earlier. I don't need the knife anymore. My brothers will know who I am."

Niall's eyes widened. He finally dropped her arms. "Beckett and Cian? The kings are still alive? They must have gone mad by now. They're years past the time to bond."

That was exactly what Torin wanted everyone to think. Keeping them from finding a bondmate was one more reason he'd closed off Tír na nÓg. "No, they are alive and well. They've bonded and come into their power. So I'm turning this whole figurehead thing over to them, and I'm going to go and do something right for a change. I'm going to fight for the people around me. Let me go."

He shook his head, grabbing her arm once more. "I can't let you go. You're our best bet. And you could be lying about the kings."

"She is not lying and I am no dumb animal." Kaja had taken her human form. She also proved she could fight on two feet. She reared her fist back and slammed it into Niall's nose, blood splattering in an arc. Niall's head snapped back, and he dropped to the ground with a thud, unconscious. Kaja stood over him. "He is not a smart man."

But he was an armed man. Bron took the knife on his belt. A small guilt assailed her, but it wasn't like she was leaving him unarmed. He seemed to have a blade strapped to every inch of his body. She thought about taking the sword, but she was better with a knife, and the sword was heavy. She held out the sword to Kaja, who stared at it like it was a bug.

"You don't use weapons, do you?"

Kaja shrugged, one shoulder moving up and down as she eased the pack off Niall's back. She rifled through it, coming back with yet another blade.

"I fight with tooth and claw. It's the way of my people. And my main person is about to be in trouble. Dante is fighting. They're all fighting, and there are so many of them. He's telling me to get you someplace safe and then hide with you. He's being quite loud about it. Does he have to scream at me like that? Doesn't he know I can hear him?"

It struck Bronwyn suddenly that Kaja really was her family. She was Dante's true consort if they could speak to each other like this. Her cos was here. He'd come for her. And if he'd come for her then it was because Beckett and Cian had sent him. Her brothers.

Dear goddess, she had a family again.

"Do you know how to use that thing?" Kaja asked, pointing to the knife.

It wasn't her father's knife, but it would do. And she was running out of time. Niall probably had it hidden on his person.

Her husbands or her knife? It was an easy choice to make.

She felt so much better with two knives in her hands. She'd been trained to use two, her body moving in a deadly dance. *Never stop moving*, the goblins had told her. "I can use it. And I'm not hiding."

She didn't want to admit it to herself, but Lach and Shim were there. It had been easy to walk away before, but now she couldn't, not when she wasn't sure they were safe. Niall lay in the dirt, his chest moving but his eyes closed. She couldn't help him. Not if she wanted to help Lach and Shim.

She kept her mental shields in place. It was becoming an easier thing to do. She had to keep them up. If they knew she was coming, they would stop her from fighting and from the sounds ahead, every fighter was needed.

Kaja shifted again. Bron nodded down at her and ran for the village, her heart in her throat.

Chaos reigned. She turned down the street that would lead her to the square. The eddy cloud hung over the square making it a damn fine bet that the worst of the fighting would happen there.

Bron stopped as the door to one of the shops flew open and screams rang through the empty street. She watched as two guards started hauling a young woman out of her home. The woman wasn't going quietly. She screamed her husband's name and tried to fight, but the guards had her firmly in hand.

Bron had been to her wedding. It had been over a year ago, held right in the square. She and Gillian had walked with the bride through the very street where she was now being dragged. Litha was a sweet woman who had recently borne a daughter. She and her husband made candles and sold them at market. She was being hauled down the street, her face streaked with tears and her legs dragging. Her blonde hair hung in her face.

Kaja's tail thumped and her graceful face was turned up as though waiting for the command. Kaja was acknowledging that Bron had more at stake. Bron was so grateful to her cousin. "Go."

Kaja jumped the first guard from behind, her predatory grace and speed on full display. The guard didn't stand a chance. He let loose a strangled scream before Kaja bit into his neck. There was a loud cracking sound.

The second guard turned and hoisted his sword to bring it down on the wolf. Bron reared back and saw her target. Her peripheral vision fled, so the whole world narrowed to one point on the guard's vulnerable neck. The rest of him was covered with thick armor, but he still had to move and there was a nice white patch of skin, the right size for a blade to bury itself in.

She let the knife fly, sending the power of her throw through her whole body as the man in the wine-making district had taught her.

Her aim proved true. Before the guard could start his sword's descent toward Kaja, the knife found purchase. The sword fell from his hands and the guard's body hit the ground.

Litha looked up, her eyes wide with fear. "Isolde?"

It was time to begin to reclaim her true identity. Niall was right about one thing. She could be a figurehead, but that wasn't all she intended to be. "That's the name I gave you, Litha, but it is not my own. I have kept a secret from you."

Litha stared for a moment and then got to one knee. "Princess Bronwyn. You're the one they're looking for. The guards came into my home and beat my husband. They mentioned the Princess Bronwyn and that they're rounding up anyone who could possibly be you. I fear they intend to slaughter us all in the hopes that one of us will be you. Just last night as you were in your cell, Gillian told us the secret. We were ready to attack the guard to free you when the dark man came. The necromancer killed them all. Will he save us now? Where is he?"

Bron took a long breath. At least she wouldn't have to prove who she was to the villagers. It seemed Gillian had convinced them.

"She is right. Those guards intend to kill everyone who could possibly be you." Kaja stood over her victim, heedless to her nude state. "They won't settle for the ones who look like you as you could easily change your appearance."

Litha screamed and ran, hiding behind Bronwyn, though she had four inches and twenty pounds on Bron. Litha was a muscular woman, but the scream that had come from her throat was pure girl. "It was a wolf! Kill it, Your Highness. It must be the hag the guards spoke of."

The hag was here? How many? The rumor was Torin had three in his employ, but one was off plane seeking her brothers. If the hags were here, then they would be the ones in charge. "She isn't a hag. She's my cousin. She's an ally."

Kaja grinned as though the very act of being called family brought her enormous pleasure. "I am Kaja. I am a wolf sometimes and always a woman."

Then Litha's husband staggered out, a frying pan in his hand. The candlemaker had been badly beaten, but it was obvious he wasn't going to stop. He would have fought until the guards killed him. Litha cried and ran to him. He fell into her arms.

"Get your husband inside, Litha. Tell everyone you see to hide. We will take care of this." She would. One way or another. She wouldn't allow the women of her village to be rounded up and slaughtered.

Litha nodded, tears in her eyes as she helped her husband up. "Thank you, Your Highness, but we will fight. You are our hope. Now that we have hope again, we will not give up."

Bron had to take a deep breath. This was what Niall had wanted of her, but he'd wanted a china doll whose face could grace banners, who would be protected. That wasn't who Bronwyn Finn was anymore. Goddess, she wasn't Bronwyn Finn. She was Bronwyn McIver.

A small crowd had gathered, lending aid to Litha and her husband. Bron heard them talking about her. Calling her princess and wishing her luck. Promising to follow her.

"Do not worry," Litha said to the crowd. "Our princess will save us as she has saved me. Gather what weapons you have. We will follow Princess Bronwyn and her shanimal!"

Kaja growled before changing.

Bronwyn got the message. It was time to join this fight for real.

Chapter Fourteen

Shim pounded on the door, cursing the fucking sunlight that was keeping him inside.

What in all the planes had happened? He felt stronger than he could ever remember feeling, and yet something as completely and utterly harmless as beams of light were keeping him out of the fight.

And damn it all, he really wanted to fight.

"Where did Gilly go?" Duffy asked, his small body struggling under the weight of that sword.

"Upstairs, though if she's become like her charge, she's probably tied the sheets together and run." None of the women in his life seemed to want to allow him to protect them. And he couldn't blame them since he was stuck in this damn house.

There was a loud boom, the sound of a sonic weapon being discharged.

Shim could feel his brother's adrenaline. It pumped through his own veins.

"They're fighting. I thought they were doing a recon." Duffy rushed to the door and out into the street. "Can't see anything."

Of course he couldn't. Duffy was barely four feet tall. Shim was six and a half, but he couldn't see a damn thing since he was blinded by sunlight now.

Gillian hurried down the stairs, holding her skirt in one hand. She rushed into the room and toward a small closet.

"You told Roan you would stay here." The thought of his sister out in the battle while he was stuck here rankled.

Gillian looked up, her dark eyes narrowed. "I'll lie to Roan all I like. As it happens, I think I'm likely best served here." Her arm disappeared into the closet and when it came back, Gillian was holding a bow and quiver of arrows. "Reymon likes to hunt. He's quite good, and he's been teaching both me and Bron. The upstairs window has an excellent view. If anyone tries to sneak up the back street, I can take them out." She stopped in front of him. "Don't worry about it, Shim. You're half vampire. It's inevitable you would have some of their weaknesses along with all that strength. I can fight. I'm expendable. I'm not even a true heir."

Gillian was a bastard by all the rules of their society. She couldn't inherit since her mother hadn't been married to King Fergus and had died in childbirth. But Shim's mother hadn't seen things that way. When she'd married Fergus, she'd insisted Gillian be addressed the same way her own children would.

"Our mother loved you."

Tears filled her eyes, and she looked over at Duffy as she nodded. "Queen Constance had a heart big enough for everyone. The Unseelie were blessed with her reign. Do you know how many queens would have thrown me out? How many queens would have taken in Duffy?"

Not many, but then his mother had been an extraordinary woman. "It didn't matter you weren't her blood."

"And it doesn't matter that Bron isn't mine. I know what I said. I meant it. You needed to make sure your claim to Bron was unassailable, but I love that child. Child. She's a woman, but she's also my daughter. Not by blood or birth but by sacrifice. I seek to honor my true mother, Queen Constance, in all ways, and she would never have sat idly by while others suffered. When I spoke of taking over Tír na nÓg, it is because I love these people. I would defend them with my life. Please tell Bron that. Please don't let her hate me."

"No one can hate you, Gilly." Duffy looked awkward standing there, looking up at the woman none of them had seen in thirteen years.

Shim remembered how Duffy would blush every time the princess would say hello to him.

Gillian got to one knee, placing her at eye level with the gnome. "Thank you, sweet Duffy. I did not say it earlier, but it is so good to see you again."

Duffy's face flushed and his eyes turned down. "It is good to be able to place me eyes on you once more, Your Highness."

Gillian laughed. "None of that, brother." She stood, the bow in her hand. "I will watch our backs. Duffy, please shout up if anyone is coming for the front of the store." She winked down at the gnome and fled up the stairs.

"I am not your brother." Duffy said it so quietly Shim almost missed it.

Poor Duffy. So in love with a woman he couldn't have. "Duffy, are you all right?"

"Sure thing. I'll patrol." Duffy cleared his throat and walked outside.

He felt helpless. Gods, he was utterly useless. For the last thirteen years he'd been so weak, and now that he had some modicum of strength back, the sunlight was holding him in.

"Shim!"

He ran to the door. Duffy was pointing off in the distance. "That cloud is covering up the sun."

He was right. Sure enough, there were far more shadows and shade than there had been but minutes before. He stepped out and his eyes burned, but he could walk in this. "I need to find Bron."

Lach would want him to. Lach would want to fight the battles while Shim took care of their wife. He felt his twin's deep satisfaction with that idea. Since they had been on the same plane as their bondmate, he and his twin had been so much more in synch, even without the deepest of bonds.

Lach was fighting. Shim could feel it. He closed his eyes and he could see it in flashes. Lach bringing his sword down and skewering an opponent, strength flowing through his veins like never before. They were outnumbered, but not for long. Every foe they brought down became Lachlan's. The enemy didn't merely lose a fighter. With every death they gained another opponent.

Shim grimaced. Even this low light hurt his eyes. He closed them and searched for some fire. It sparked to his fingertips, but he hesitated to use it. The villagers were running. The scene was far too chaotic. If he started a fire here, how many innocents would he lose?

Bronwyn. He needed to concentrate on Bron.

He opened his mind and sought their connection. Even with her shields up, he knew she was alive. He simply couldn't see through her eyes or feel what she was feeling.

He could, however, tell that she was close.

And she wasn't the only one. Four guards rounded the corner and began walking down the narrow street. Shim pulled Duffy in. He was carrying an axe. No matter how small he was, the guards wouldn't like that. Fire pricked at Shim's fingertips. He could roast them, but the street was so narrow and the roofs around him were all thatched with straw. One errant flame and the village would go up. It had been easier in the town square. There had been room to maneuver.

"You!" The largest of the guards shouted at Shim. "Bring out your women. The king requires all women to report to the town square for inspection."

Shim didn't like the sound of that. Gillian was in the store. He had to hope she was doing what she'd said she would do, manning the rear window. "We don't have any women. It's just me and my brother."

The guards took in Duffy.

"Well, lookee here." The largest of the guard's voice dripped with sarcasm. "The mayor of this town is lax. A fucking gnome. Don't you know your kind aren't welcome here, you piece of shit. No non-*sidhe*. We're going to have some fun tonight. You'll look good on the end of a pike, wee one."

The guard laughed, bringing the others in.

Duffy, not one to shrink back, walked up, his axe in his hand. "Now I'd like to know what you plan to do with those women. I can't think of any good reason to bring forth all the women of a town. What kind of men do you call yourselves?"

The biggest of the guards stiffened, his limbs taking a predatory stance. "I call meself loyal is what I call me. And the king has decreed your kind to be undesirable and all who would aid you to be traitors. Now I think it's about time to take care of this. Glannis didn't tell us to bring non-*sidhe* to her, so we can do whatever we like to these two the way I sees it."

Why the hell didn't he have a sword in his hand? Perhaps because his father had thought him too weak to hold one. Perhaps because until he'd had first blood, he had been too weak to properly wield one.

And Duffy wasn't smart enough to run. He hefted his axe and swaggered out into the street. "I think we'll have to see about that. And I won't let you hurt a bunch of women."

"The wee one thinks he's a warrior." The guards began to circle in a predatory fashion, like jackals looking for an easy meal.

Shim stepped behind his adopted brother. "Duffy, I think we should go back inside."

"That option is gone now," another guard said. "We don't let fucking gnomes talk to us that way. And they're certainly not going to threaten us with axes."

There was another sonic boom. It startled the guards and gave Shim a chance to focus. He let the fire build in his fingers. He couldn't torch the fuckers the way he wanted to, but he could try to take them out one by one. The fire sizzled along his skin. It was so much easier now. The power was right there at his fingertips. He could tap it without losing control. It was his.

One of the guards put a hand on him. Shim let the power fill him.

There was a scream and the guard fell back, holding his hand up. It was already blistering. Shim could feel his power. It wasn't just in his hands or flowing from his gut. He *was* his power.

He sent out a flame from his fingertips, catching the nearest guard's tunic. The guard stepped away from Duffy, trying to put out the flames.

But Duffy was too close to the others. He was wielding his axe, proving that he'd taken his training seriously. He caught one guard squarely in the chest, but he didn't have the strength of a larger man. The axe struck, but it clanged and bounced back off, sending Duffy to his ass in the dirt.

Shim was about to send fire to the guard standing above Duffy when he hissed as a terrible pain caught him on the bicep. Blood flowed down his left arm, soaking his tunic.

Duffy rolled, balling up his small body and narrowly missing the sword that descended toward his neck. He somersaulted his way to Shim and kicked out, catching the guard nearest him in the knees.

But now they were surrounded, and Shim couldn't feel his left hand. His right sparked, a blast of fire, but his control was shot and his eyes were still affected by the sunlight. It peeked through the eddy cloud, causing pockets of blindness.

He could see vague shadows circling them.

"That fucker is using magic. Didn't you know we kill witches here, son?" a hoarse voice asked.

"He burned me. Don't touch him. He has some sort of spell on him."

"Aim for his heart. He might have a spell, but he ain't got no armor."

Shim could feel Duffy at his side, but the gnome had lost his axe. The sun passed again, and Shim's sight came back. He rather wished it hadn't, since now he could see the men who would kill him. Even the ones he'd managed to burn were back on their feet.

"Let's have some fun with them, boys. What do you say?" a muscular guard said.

"Now would be the time for you to start up with the fireballs, Shim," Duffy said. "I think a little flame-roasted guard would do us some good."

Shim held out his only usable arm, and the shot went wild, sending an arc of flame straight to the house across from him. The roof went up like tinder, scorching across the straw and catching both houses beside it.

Fuck all. There were Fae in those houses. He could hear a faint screaming and wondered how many innocents he'd hurt.

The guards looked up and then turned back, settling on their target. Shim.

And then there was a low growl and a wolf pounced. Delicate and graceful and ruthless. The wolf leapt on the guard who had been about to charge and had her teeth around his sword arm. Hoarse shouts filled the air. Shim grabbed Duffy, prepared to run when the guard next to him suddenly groaned and looked down at the long knife in his chest. Whoever had thrown that fucker didn't have Duffy's strength problems.

"Get down!" a feminine voice shouted.

Shim sank to the ground, covering his brother as two arrows sped over him.

When Shim looked up, all four guards were dead and he'd been saved by a bunch of women.

Bronwyn walked through the smoke, her face a mask of willpower. She was a fucking gorgeous warrior goddess, and despite the pain in his arm and the panic in his gut, his cock got hard at the very sight of her.

"Put those fires out, Shim." Gillian walked from the doorstep, bow in hand.

Bronwyn pulled her knife free of the guard's armor, wiping the blood off on her pants. She looked down at Shim, her eyes softening a bit. "Please, Shim. If you can put that fire out, I would be grateful."

The fire winked out as though she had more control over his power than he did.

Bronwyn held out a hand. "Now let's go use that power of yours on someone who deserves it. What do you say? Do you want to help me kill a hag?"

Gillian was at his side, her hand on his arm. "I don't know if he's going to be doing much of anything for a while. That arm is bad. He's lost a lot of blood."

"I'll be fine." Shim struggled to get up. His brother was starting to get into trouble. He could feel it. He couldn't let Lach down or Bron. She'd come back when it would have made more sense for her to run. Perhaps she'd only come back to save her village, but it didn't matter. She was here, and he wasn't about to let a thing like massive blood loss stop him from helping her. He tried to get to his feet.

Kaja shifted, her body forming into her two-legged state. Gillian took a step back.

"She's fine, Gilly," Bron said in a stiff-sounding voice. "She's Dante's consort."

"Damn me, she's naked." Duffy stared. His brother wasn't one to let near death interrupt his deep appreciation of the female form.

Kaja looked down at his arm. "I am Dante's consort so I happen to know that anytime Dante is injured, he feeds. Consort blood heals. Cousin Bronwyn, if you want your husband in this fight, you'll have to sacrifice a little blood."

Bron sighed, but she rolled up her sleeve. "Fine, but don't do that thing where I end up a heap of boneless flesh at the end. I need to fight, too."

He knew Lach would argue that he should do exactly that. Lach would tell him it was the perfect solution. Shim would get his strength back and the act of pulling Bronwyn in would rob her of hers.

And she wouldn't trust him again. She'd saved him. She'd returned when she could have run. Perhaps it was time to start trusting his bondmate.

He let his fangs pop out. Yes, the naked girl was right. He could feel it now. Bronwyn glowed for him, a sweet golden aura around her body. It made her stand out. He looked up, his every vampire sense open now. Kaja glowed, and damn him if Gillian didn't glow, too.

"Roan is right about you, Gilly."

Gillian frowned. "Roan can be right all he likes. It won't help him."

And then Bronwyn's left wrist was right at his mouth. He couldn't help it. He brought it to his mouth and bit down. When the blood hit his tongue, he knew the true sweetness of life.

He sucked and dragged her pure blood into his body, health flowing into him. Power encompassing him. More than simple blood filled him. She invaded his veins, her life, her heart, her spirit. They all soared inside him.

She was shaking by the time he let go, but she straightened up quickly. She rolled her sleeve back down. She'd obviously felt the connection, too.

Shim stood, feeling his strength like the sweetest drug. He grabbed Bronwyn's hand and pulled her to him. Her face fell.

"And now you're going to shove me off to the side, aren't you?"

He shook his head. Gods, but he loved the feel of her so close to him. "I'm going to kiss my wife before we go and save Lach. Just be careful, love. I don't want to lose you."

Finally, he'd managed to say something she didn't have a comeback to. He brushed his lips against her and turned.

Lach was in trouble.

* * * *

The hag wouldn't stop. Lach skewered her soldiers. The minute he felt death descend on the fallen, he used his power to grip them and reanimate their bodies. The dead rose and fought against their former brethren.

But the hag had other plans.

Lach hissed as a searing pain hit his chest. He felt a squeezing sensation, as though someone had reached right through his skin and bone and caught his heart in their hand.

He fell to his knees, Roan sliding down beside him. "Your Highness, we should think about retreating. She's got a heavy shield around her. She's letting the soldiers die, but we can't get to her. I've tried sonics on her three times now and they bounce off. Two of my men are down because the bounce back hit them. One's dead and the other is out cold."

Roan's words hit his ears, but they sounded distant.

You can't win, Death Lord.

The hag's voice seemed to be the only thing he could hear. It filled his ears, crowding out everything else.

Your power is too close to mine, and I've been using mine for far longer. I'll let these sheep die in my place. I'll focus on you. You're the important one here. Tell me where Bronwyn Finn is.

Fuck all. Lach hit his head on the hard dirt. She was inside his mind. He could feel her there, picking through his memories. Cold prickles caught in his mind, the hag plucking from here and there. She caused each one to flash through his head.

Staring down at his brother's body and knowing he was gone. Shim was gone. Bron was gone. Lach's worst nightmare. He was half a man and alone in all the planes. He couldn't stand it. His power flared for the first time.

The memories came fast and furious.

Standing over a woman, her lovely body spread out for his pleasure. He'd tied the knots perfectly, loving the deep concentration it had required. Bondage was a dance between three partners, and he loved the rhythm. But not the woman. He couldn't give her what she wanted because he'd given his soul to one woman when he was just a child. She held his soul, his heart. It was only logical that she owned his cock, too. Lach turned away, knowing his desires would have to burn through him. There was no relief here.

Listening to his father talk to his advisors. Humiliation was a rolling wave as they spoke about the fragile princes. Shim was weak in body and they worried Lach's mind wasn't strong. He didn't try to defend himself. It wouldn't make a difference. They wouldn't listen. If only they would bond, the king bemoaned.

I am bound. I am bound. I am bound.

And yet he was alone.

The hag continued her tour of his brain, seeking knowledge. He felt her satisfaction that he was bound to Bronwyn. It was something she could use, but where was the bitch? The question pounded through him.

Where is Bronwyn?

Each time she asked, his heart squeezed tighter. The hag was everywhere, in every cell of his being, crawling across every inch of his skin. He could smell the rank scent of the hag filling his nose and the clammy touch of her hand on his head.

This was what she wanted to do to Bronwyn. He could see it plainly. The hag wanted Bronwyn for much more than a quick execution. She wanted to take her time with Bronwyn. She was curious. Bronwyn had survived when she shouldn't have. The hag wanted to know why, and when she figured it out she would find a way to make that power her own.

The vision of what the hag wanted made him gag. He felt bile bubbling up. The hag had him in her hand. He didn't know where Bronwyn was. He said it like a mantra. Over and over until he was singing it in his head.

Then you are of no use to me.

That cold hand squeezed, and his heart skittered and froze, an aching agony invading every inch of his limbs. He wasn't Lachlan anymore. He was pain. He was despair. All the loneliness he'd ever felt seemed to have been distilled and poured down his throat like a noxious poison.

This was how he ended. This was what he'd been moving toward all of his life.

And then it stopped. The hand on his heart pulled away. He felt the dirt on his face, but he could only groan.

"Your Highness, we need to move." Roan had a hand on his arm, pulling him up.

"What he means is we're getting our asses kicked. Move yours, McIver." Dellacourt didn't mince words.

He forced himself to focus. The dead lay all around him, but the hag had cut his connection to them when she'd found her way inside his brain. Without the added soldiers, they were woefully outnumbered, and he was still feeling muddled.

He struggled to his feet, reaching for his sword. The villagers had come out in mass. They fought for their daughters and wives and sisters. They fought with pitchforks and frying pans and bows and arrows.

"What made her stop?" Lach asked.

"Bron." Roan pointed to spot a hundred feet to the left where Bronwyn stood staring at the hag.

As though the hag had a direct line to the remaining soldiers' brains, they all turned, abandoning their personal fights and starting toward Bronwyn.

"No." Lach didn't give a shit how unsteady he was. He wasn't letting that hag get close to Bron. He pulled free of Roan.

"Lachlan, don't."

But he wasn't listening. He had to get to Bronwyn before those soldiers did.

Gillian stood to the side and Duffy close to her. Shim was next to Bronwyn, his eyes watching as the soldiers came near.

"I want that bitch alive." The hag's voice echoed through the square.

Of course she wanted Bron alive. She wanted to dissect her and find out what made her tick. The image of what the hag intended to do to his bondmate made Lach run toward her, willing to do anything to keep it from becoming truth.

Bron put a hand out to Shim, who stood there doing absolutely nothing. Nothing at all. His twin simply stood there like he was perfectly happy to let the soldiers take her. Duffy turned, and his small face went white with surprise. He dropped his axe and started running Lachlan's way.

"Lach, no."

Duffy hit his waist with the force of a small but stubbornly powerful train. Lach was knocked back, his ass hitting the dirt, his sword falling from his hand.

Duffy stood, putting a hand on his chest. "Let Shim do his job."

Lach sat up, ready to get to his feet and throw himself in front of his bondmate when he noticed that the fighting had stopped. The villagers had moved back, disappearing into houses or creeping close to walls. And all eyes were on one woman. Bronwyn.

The soldiers began to rush, but Bron nodded Shim's way and there was a whooshing sound that filled the air. Heat smoldered as a ring of fire appeared, surrounding the soldiers and trapping them in a neat cage of flames.

But his brother wasn't satisfied. The flames grew and engulfed the soldiers, their dying cries filling the air.

It was all over in seconds, the flames so hot they disintegrated everything that had stood in the ring.

Shim turned to the hag, a smile on his face. With a flick of his wrist, he sent a long line of white and blue flames toward the hag.

"Damn it. Get down!" Roan roared over the crowd.

Lach hit the deck, taking Duffy with him as Shim's flames hit the shield the witch had in play and bounced back toward them. Scalding heat brushed over Lach, reminding him that he knew what it meant to be caught in his brother's power.

"Sorry!" Shim yelled his way. "I didn't know about the shielding."

Bron stepped forward, not seeming to care there was still a powerful hag who'd been sent to ensure her death. "Did my uncle send you?"

The hag smiled showing perfectly even teeth that seemed a bit too sharp for her face. "The king sends his greetings, Princess Bronwyn, and promises a glorious family reunion."

"I don't think I'll take him up on that just yet." Bron stood, her shoulders back. "You aren't welcome in my village, hag."

The hag sighed, her elegant gown moving with the sound. "I know when to take my toys and go home. By the way, I spent some time in that one's head. A dark thing he is. Be careful that he doesn't eat you up with his ambition. He wants the crown. He'll say he loves you to get it, but you don't think the Unseelie will truly accept a Seelie queen now, do you? Good luck, dear. Even if you get a crown, it won't mean much when your head is separated from your body. And, Death Lord, I have a parting gift for you."

The air around the hag shimmered, and then her hands flew out, a visible cloud racing his way.

Just before it engulfed him, Duffy leapt, tossing himself into the cloud. Horror overcame Lach as darkness covered the gnome, enveloping his body until there was nothing of him that wasn't black smoke.

Duffy screamed. Lach started to reach for him, but Roan and Dellacourt pulled him back.

"Don't you dare. You can't help him now." Roan had a strong grip.

Shim tried to get to Duffy, too, but Bronwyn got in his way. "Please."

The eddy cloud shifted as the hag disappeared once more into its depths. The sky cleared and brilliant sunlight rained down.

Shim dropped to his knees, covering his eyes. Lach squinted, trying to see his little brother, the truly fierce one of their clan.

The cloud was gone and Duffy remained. His body was still, so still. Lach pushed past the vampires whose implants were safely guarding them from the sun's bright rays. He struggled himself, but Gillian and Bronwyn had sheltered Shim. They hauled him off, trying to get him under the cover of the buildings.

Lach put a hand on Duffy's chest, praying for the beat of his heart.

One eye opened. "Damn me, Lach, but that was something." Duffy sat up, flexing his muscles. "I don't think I like that hag. I'd rather fight soldiers. A sword has got to hurt less than that damn cloud."

He stared at his younger brother, letting his hand find Duff's shoulder. For a moment they sat, acknowledging what could have been lost.

"Come along, Your Highness. You and Shim must both be fitted with the proper devices to protect you from the sun. It won't take long. One pinch and it's over. Well, one long, horrifyingly painful pinch and it's over, but we won't have to worry about ultraviolet light again." Roan helped him stand. "Hurry. The hag will be back and she'll bring reenforcements. We have to move and quickly. We need to make the forest by dark or they'll find us for sure."

Lach stumbled toward the shade where Bron sat with Shim. Her chin came up, a stubborn look on her pretty face.

She'd run. She hadn't stayed and discussed the situation with them. If she had, they could have fled the minute the eddy cloud had shown up.

He and his bride were due for a very long talk. And perhaps it was time he put the relationship on the proper footing, starting with the wayward princess feeling her husband's hand on her ass.

In the background, he could hear Dellacourt yelling at his wife and threatening all manner of punishment.

Yes, it was time his bride learned the meaning of discipline.

Chapter Fifteen

"Stay close to me, Duffy," her husband said to the gnome. "But not too close."

Duffy sat on a rock near the river, his face turned up toward the moon. The gnome had been quiet all afternoon. He'd simply shuffled along behind them as they had fled the village. The villagers had all agreed that the hag would be back and she would bring another army with her. They had decided to scatter, forming three large parties moving to the south, west, and north. And their small group was moving toward the east, to the mountains.

But they had to move carefully and not in a straight line. And that, she'd been told over and over again, was all her fault. Despite her brilliant plan to save them, apparently the fact that they had needed to be saved at all was, again, her fault.

"I'm going to set up our bed for the night. We've got a big bed, but we're away from the rest." Lach's voice was deep and dark and she practically shivered listening to it.

"You and Shim can sleep wherever you like." She knew she was being stubborn, but he'd acted like an ass the whole long walk here. And her feet hurt. And she wasn't about to apologize to him.

Lach's handsome face was half hidden by moonlight. "I'll tie you up if I have to, wife."

"Don't call me that." Again, she knew she was being stubborn. Even she was thinking of him as her husband.

"It's true and your moping isn't going to change the fact." Lach stared down at her like an impossibly gorgeous, intensely difficult hunk of granite. He was so big. She knew Shim was just as big as Lach, but there was something about Lach's presence that overwhelmed her. "Would you like to know why we're not sleeping close to the others?"

She could guess what they had in mind. Four hands on her body. Two mouths kissing her. Even thinking about it made her heart race. After the events of the day, she wanted to do nothing more than close her eyes and find them in her dreams and sink into that magnificent safe place that had been hers for all of her life. But they were real now and nothing was safe about any of this.

Lach's mouth turned up in an arrogant grin, letting her know she was doing that broadcasting thing again. "We'll get to that, love. But first we're going to talk and then we're going to bond. The full bond. So I always know where you are."

"Like Dante did with Kaja?" She couldn't help her smirk. Dante had been righteously angry with his wolf wife. It had taken him a good ten minutes after the hag had disappeared to remember to greet his cousin. He'd been far too busy yelling at his wife.

Lach stood staring down at her, those muscular legs of his in a wide, arrogant stance. "I think Dante knows exactly how to deal with his wife. Do you hear them? He doesn't seem to care who does. Come here."

The minute Roan had declared this would be camp for the rest of the too-short night, Dante had taken Kaja toward a small cave above the lake that fed the river. He'd grabbed their supplies and their food. He'd nodded to Roan and kissed Bron on the forehead and then stated plainly that no one was to interrupt him.

"Not even you, brat." He'd winked down at her and then hauled his consort away.

Lach took her hand, and she was half dragged toward the cave that housed Dante and Kaja.

There was the loud slap of flesh hitting flesh. "You want to shield against this, Kaja?"

Kaja's voice was a breathy moan. "I would never shield against this, my love."

Dante growled. "Only because you know every time I spank this pretty ass, I feel it on my own. You're seriously underestimating how much I fucking love my hand on your ass. I'll take a little pain so you remember this lesson. And, Kaja, I know you left that plug behind. What you don't know is that gingerroot is plentiful here on the Seelie plane, and I'm going to get damn good at carving so I still have things to shove up your backside."

Bron took a step back. Could that really be her sweet cos? He sounded so…dirty. She remembered him as a teenager, chasing after pretty girls, but never had he talked to one like that.

"Don't judge him. He's with his consort. Whatever play they enjoy is what is right for him. Listen to Kaja. Does she sound upset?"

There was a smack and then a long moan. "Dante, please. You can't hold out on me forever."

"You know I can't, baby. But after the stunt you pulled today, I'm going to try."

There was another loud smack, and Kaja moaned. Bron turned away, completely confused.

"He's hitting her." But Kaja didn't sound like it upset her. Kaja sounded like a woman who was having a good time. Bron didn't understand. Her father had been so gentle with her mother. "Shouldn't he be kinder? She's his mate, but he says impolite things to her and he hits her."

And Bron was becoming a bit aroused listening to it. What did that make her?

"No, he's spanking her, and she likes it. Vampires have a relationship with their consorts they call Dominance and submission. Your cousin is the Dominant in the relationship, especially when it comes to the sexual part of the marriage. Kaja submits, and she's happy to do so. As for the impolite things he's saying, there's nothing polite about a marriage. Formality and politeness aren't going to happen in our bedroom. What you're hearing is intimacy. That's the real man, the one who was terrified he might lose his woman. There's nothing polite about that." Lach stared down at her. "We're going to have that relationship. You have to know that's what we've been headed toward.

Even in our dreams."

In their dreams, Lach and Shim had dominated her in the most delicious ways. She had wondered about the tone of her dreams. Now she knew she'd been playing out Lach and Shim's fantasies.

But she'd been right there with them. What did that say about her?

She turned and walked back toward the campsite. It was a warm evening. The vampires had eaten meal pills, and the Fae had dined on bread and cheese and meat the villagers had packed. They had also packed wine which Gillian sat drinking straight from the bottle. She stared at the river, pointedly not looking Roan's or the lieutenant's way. The vampires didn't have the same problem. Their eyes never left Bron's mentor. They didn't look polite. They looked hungry.

"You're going to fight this until the end, aren't you?" Lach asked. "Do you deny our claim on you? I know you feel the connection. So it has to be something else. Did you honestly believe what the hag said?"

The hag had looked straight at her and said that all her husbands wanted out of her was a crown. She'd said they wouldn't have a problem getting rid of her once they had secured her kingdom.

She wasn't at all sure they didn't want the crown. Certainly Gillian wanted them to have it. But she was fairly sure of one thing. They didn't want her dead. The hag didn't understand what it meant to be a bondmate. Lach and Shim might not believe in her abilities, but they would want her alive. They would need her.

"I'm not an idiot. I know you don't want me dead."

"And I don't want your brothers' crown. I'll prove that to you when we go back to the Unseelie plane and stay the hell out of this war. Your brothers can have this plane. We have our own kingdom."

And that was just one of her problems. This was her plane. "You can't expect me to walk out on this war."

"I can and you will. This isn't your war anymore. You're the princess of the Unseelie, and you will rule over that plane. Your children will be in line for the Unseelie throne. I won't allow you to stay here and be slaughtered for a crown that isn't your own."

She felt her fists clench in frustration. This was exactly what she'd worried about the whole long trek to the river. And she couldn't even think about children. Except she might have to. Her marriage had been consummated. She'd awakened with the evidence of it all over her thighs, mingled with her virgin's blood. And still, her children would be half-Seelie. And no matter what Lach said, until her brothers had produced a child, she was still in line for the throne and her children would be, too. In line for the throne and in Torin's line of fire. "I am not leaving until Torin is dead."

"You'll do as your husbands request. And your brothers. They want you safe as well. They don't want you in this fight." He reached for her hand, catching it before she could move away. "Come along. Shim is waiting for us. It's time we had that talk."

She hurried to keep up with him. "Talking requires one person to listen. I doubt that's going to be you."

A single shoulder moved up and down. "Shim was always the better listener."

He was frustrating. "Lach, would you abandon your plane if it was at risk?"

"Never really thought about it, and it's not the same. This was never your kingdom. It belonged to your brothers."

"By your definition the villagers shouldn't have fought either, but they did. Not because this is their kingdom, but because it's their home. It's where they raise their children. It's where their parents gave them birth. Damn it, you can't expect me to leave."

Lach stopped, taking a deep breath. "I understand. I truly do, but you're too important. I can't allow it and neither will Shim."

She turned away from him. She wasn't exactly sure what to do. She wasn't stupid enough to go off on her own again. That had been a spectacular failure, but she couldn't let them haul her off the plane. She'd be barefoot and pregnant in no time at all. She'd be pregnant with babies who would probably be incredibly oversized and grow into ridiculously arrogant and handsome young men.

Her brothers. Her brothers would be more reasonable. Well, perhaps Cian would be more reasonable. He would see her worth.

"I'll stay with you for the time being." Until she could see her brothers and make them understand.

Lach's voice rumbled out of his chest. "This marriage is for life and you know it. You're caught and there's no way out. Why are you acting like this, love? I don't understand. You're acting like you don't know a thing about us, like you never kissed me, never held me. We've been together since we were children. All of my life, I've known you."

She shook her head. "You might have been ready for this all your life, but I haven't. I didn't think it was real, and honestly, it wasn't. It was a fantasy. I was a lonely child and an even lonelier young woman, and what do you truly know about me? I didn't even know your names until recently."

"Because you're the broadcaster," Lach explained. "Your psychic power is far stronger than either of ours. You broadcast your thoughts and emotions, but you didn't listen very well."

The thought made her stop. "I didn't know I was supposed to listen."

"Well, Shim and I have spent all of our lives listening to you."

"I know you love the feel of sunlight on your face." Shim stood behind his brother, his eyes illuminated by the firelight. "I know that when you're alone and all you can hear is the wind rushing through the wheat you planted and the sun is high in the sky, you feel powerful."

Tears pricked at her eyes because he'd so beautifully explained the sensation. "It's because I planted it. I knew people would be able to eat because I worked."

Lach took a step in so he was shoulder to shoulder with his brother. "I know your laugh. It hasn't really changed since you were a child. When you laugh, it isn't some polite thing. You laugh from your gut and it fills my every sense with joy. You light up the room when you walk into it, even if it's only a dream."

"I am no beauty, Lach. Haven't you figured that out by now? I know I projected myself that way in our dreams, but I'm not beautiful. I don't even look noble anymore. My hands are callused, and my skin is tanned from the sun."

"And I'm scarred. Shim is the only one here who didn't try to look perfect," Lach pointed out.

Shim shrugged. "It's because I am perfect."

"I don't mind the scars, Lachlan," she admitted. "But I know that the world isn't going to view me as a beautiful princess."

"We do. Gods, Bronwyn, you're the loveliest woman in all the planes. Do you really need the world to think so, too?" Lach crossed his hands over his massive chest, the stance so arrogant, but she could hear the boy he'd been.

He'd been the protector, even in their dreams, even when he'd been a child, he'd been the one to go first. Not because he had to lead, but because whatever happened, he wanted it to happen to him instead of her or Shim.

And Shim had been sweet, so sweet. He'd been the one to sit for hours holding her hand as she looked out over imaginary lakes and ponds. When she would cry, Shim had been the one to hold her while Lach looked on, his fists tight, angry that anything could make her sad.

They had been dreams, but she did know these men.

The situation was far more complex than they were making it out to be.

"I could make it easy on you, Bron." The look on Lach's face let her know she wasn't shielding at all.

And neither was he. He sent her an image, or Shim did. It didn't matter. She was blasted with the mental image of her tied up and waiting for their pleasure. But only after she'd earned it. She'd terrified them, and they wanted a piece of her hide.

Like Dante was disciplining Kaja. They could show her. They could initiate her into those dark pleasures. They had trained for it, studied the art of giving pleasure, but they had taken none themselves.

Shim smiled. "I wouldn't say none, love. Just none from other women. There was an enormous amount of yanking our own dicks. I swear, Lach there damn near wore out his wrist when we were teenagers."

Lach slapped his brother on the chest. "Like you were better. I was the one who had to listen to it. Bronwyn. Bronwyn. Oh, you feel so good, Bronwyn. The only consolation was that he never lasted very long."

Shim frowned. "I did so."

Despite her precarious position, she felt joy at seeing them act like obnoxious brothers. This was one thing she definitely remembered. They had always bickered.

She was so damn confused. She wanted them, but she wanted her freedom, too. She wasn't sure she could ever go back to being that perfect princess she'd been raised to be. She'd lived too much, seen too many things.

She turned her back on them. If she gave in, she'd be exactly what they wanted. Sweet and submissive and more than likely pregnant in a month. She would be relegated to the sidelines. It couldn't happen. "You two go. I'm going to stay by the fire. We'll talk again when we see my brothers, and we'll sort out this whole marriage thing."

"Marriage thing?" Lach parroted her, pure astonishment in his voice.

"We have our answer, Lach. It's time to go," Shim said.

She was surprised at the disappointment she felt with Shim's utter reasonableness. It was wrong, but she'd wanted a bit of a fight. Her stomach was in knots. She was in a corner, and she had no idea how to get out. She wanted to sleep with them, wanted the comfort of their big bodies surrounding her, but she didn't want the responsibility of making the choice. It wasn't fair. She was being exactly what Dante called her. She was a brat, but she couldn't make herself turn around and ask for what she wanted.

"You're right," Lach said, his voice a grave finality.

She wasn't going to cry. Damn it all. She wasn't. This was what she'd wanted. She'd wanted time to sort everything out without the distraction of lips and tongues and hands and cocks.

She gave a shout as Lach hauled her up and tossed her over his shoulder. "What?"

"You gave us your answer, Princess. We'll do this the hard way."

She gasped as Lach's hand came down on her ass. "How dare you!"

"Oh, I dare, Princess. You're going to find out how much I dare. And don't you even start saying this isn't exactly what you want. You broadcast so loud I'm surprised the damn squirrels can't hear you. You want us to take you. You want to be able to wake up in the morning and go right back to believing you can get out of this. Well, I'm going to tell you that you're getting what you want. We will take you, but you're going to know you're ours by morning, love."

The fact that his words were so very true did nothing to assuage how angry he made her. "Put me down now, you overgrown idiot."

Another smack. "Every time you curse me, I'm adding five to your punishment. You're at thirty right now. Thirty smacks to that sweet ass of yours. Do you want more?"

She wasn't getting any reason from an overly possessive vampire.

She looked toward the fire, hoping to find a vampire more amenable to her cause. "Roan. Roan, my brothers are paying you, right?"

Roan never even looked up from the fire. "Not at all, Princess. Your brothers don't have a single piece of gold between them. Your father-in-law is paying me. And he's paying me quite handsomely. I would advise you to take your well-earned spanking with dignity and then attempt to please your husbands. I think you'll find you have an enormous amount of power over them should you choose to use it wisely."

Damn mercenary. "You aren't going to be any help at all."

Now the mercenary looked up, and there was a grin on his face. "On the contrary, Your Highness. I think you'll find I've been very helpful. After all, I'm the one who gave them the kit I think they're about to use on you. It has all sorts of helpful items in it."

Gillian stood up, her eyes flickering between her brothers and Bronwyn. "Can't we talk about this?"

"Sit down, Princess," Roan said in a deep voice that he more than likely used on soldiers to keep them in line. "You are not going to come between husbands and their rightfully bonded mate. They won't hurt her. They're bonded. They feel what she's feeling. Do you think your brothers would enjoy her pain?"

"Gillian won't help me." She'd made that plain.

Gillian sat back down, wiping at her eyes. "It seems I'm the villain at every turn with you, Bron. I know you won't believe it, but I do love you. And so do my brothers."

Lach strode past Shim, his long legs eating up the forest floor.

"Is this really what you want, Bron?" Shim asked. "Because we can be gentle."

"She doesn't want gentle." Lach kept right on walking.

Bron held her head up. It was either that or watch Lach's perfectly formed backside move. "Fuck you, Lach. And you can fuck yourself, Shim."

Lach stopped. He set her on her feet, but she didn't stay there long. He got to one knee and flipped her neatly over. She found herself facing the grass, her ass in the air. Oh, goddess, she'd pushed him. She'd known what she was doing and she'd done it anyway because she wanted this. She wanted to see what made Kaja moan, but she

249

didn't want to ask for it.

"You know exactly what you're doing, don't you?" Shim sounded tortured. "This doesn't mean anything to you. This is physical for you."

"There's no use talking to her. She knows what she wants, and she's figured out how to get it." Lach's big hand steadied her. "One last chance, Princess. We can play this the way we would prefer. We would prefer to simply love you tonight. There will be time enough for games later. We want to bond. We want to know you inside and out."

And then they would know how to handle her every single time. She was already at a disadvantage since they seemed to be able to read her thoughts. No. She couldn't let them in. This was all she could give them. For now. Maybe forever. "Fuck off, Lach."

His hand hit her ass with a loud crack, and tears sparked from her eyes. The pain was sharp and cut through her. Lach barely gave her time to process the first one before he struck again. Ten times his hand rained down. Bron couldn't breathe. She couldn't move. She couldn't think past the feel of Lach's hand on her ass.

And the feel of his cock hardening. She could feel it rising against her side, but more than that, she could feel it as Lach felt it, jutting out from his core, his cock filling with blood. There was a primal anticipation taking him over. This was a good place for him. This was a place he loved, and it was so much sweeter because she was here with him.

His hand came down again, but he'd eased up. Not on the strength but on the pace. This time the pain jarred her, making her jump, but Lach's hand stayed on her ass as though keeping the heat in, allowing it to sink into her skin.

"Not so bad." Lach rubbed the spot he'd hit.

Damn him. He could feel her, too. How was she supposed to stay distant? "You're not the one who's going to have a red ass tomorrow."

"I'm not the one who ran away and put everyone in danger. I'm not the one cursing you at every turn. I'm not the one being stubborn about a marriage that's been in place for most of our lives."

Every accusation was punctuated with a smack and a long caress.

"And even if you did, what would I do about it?" She forced herself to concentrate on the unfairness of it all. But it was hard because she really, really wanted to focus on how soft and wet her pussy was and how long and thick and hard Lach was getting.

"If I do any of that, I promise to present my ass to you. I'll take whatever punishment you see fit, love." He cracked his hand once more. "Now, I know you can feel what this is doing to me, but maybe I should put it in words so you can't mistake what's happening. I love having you over my knee. I love having your ass in the air waiting for my discipline. It makes me feel ten feet tall. I love how the sight of you gets me hard and ready to fuck. You're my mate. You're the reason we both waited thirty years. No other women, Bron."

"None for me." Shim got to one knee, his hand on her back. "I'm a virgin because I belong to you. Does that make me less of a man? Many in our kingdom think so. Women have been thrown at us for years because we're not a delicate people. We fuck and we fight and our people admire kings and princes who do so as well. Do you know how many times we've had our manhoods called into question? But we wouldn't be swayed because we belong to you. Tell me that means something. Tell me I didn't wait thirty years for a woman who doesn't really want me."

"Let me up." She had to get up. She couldn't lie here. Damn him. They were coming at her from all sides. Lach with his dominance and Shim with his soft heart. "Damn it, Lachlan. Let me up."

Two more smacks, but then she was on her knees. "You're going to be the death of me."

She was pretty damn sure they would be the death of her. Shim sat on his heels, looking at her. She'd grown up with symbiotic twin brothers. Two bodies, one soul. She could call them by different names, but they made up one whole man. Whatever Shim was saying, Lach felt it, too.

Thirty years of longing. She reached up and cupped his gorgeous face. How many women could say their husbands had waited thirty years for them? And in all that time, years had gone by when they weren't even sure she'd been alive. "How long would you have waited?"

She asked the question, but she knew the answer.

"Forever, Bron."

Goddess, what was she supposed to do with that? But she'd waited, too. She hadn't even thought of other men, wouldn't have wanted their attentions. These men had dominated her life and her dreams since she was old enough to remember them.

"Was Gillian really coming to negotiate a marriage?"

Lach sighed. "Yes. She was the only one who believed we could see you. She was the only one who believed in the bond. If Torin hadn't fucked everything up, we would have been promised to you when you turned sixteen and married at eighteen. We would have had a whole damn life, Bron."

"We would have younglings. And you would have known how much we loved you every day," Shim said.

Sweet words, and they settled deep in her heart, nursing some ache that had always been there. But Torin had come between them. He had ripped them and everything around him apart. They didn't have younglings and she hadn't known she was loved. They wanted to pick up as though none of it had ever happened and simply resume the life they should have had.

"Don't," Shim practically pleaded. "Don't. Not tonight. Please just one night. Earlier didn't count. You weren't fully with us. We can deal with all that stands between us in the morning, but tonight give over."

It was what she wanted, too. Though she could say all the stubborn words she liked, she wanted them. She wouldn't have other lovers. She would have Lach and Shim for however long she could and then no other. They had been bound by invisible threads likely from the moment she'd been born, and she would never love another.

"I want it all." She said the words quietly. "I want your sweetness and Lach's…whatever you would call what Lach does. If I use my own words, he'll spank me again."

"Oh, poor princess," Lach said, his hands on her waist. "She was terribly treated." His fingers crept under the top of her pants.

"Lach?" She tried to push him away. They were in the middle of the woods, and Duffy wasn't far away. The gnome could likely hear everything.

"Hush or I'll have you naked right here. I have a theory. I want to test it." His hand delved under her pants, traveling down.

She tried to pull away, but he held her fast. Damn him, even that seemed to make her hot.

"How wet is she?" Shim leaned over, and she could see white

fangs and those deep eyes. In the dark it looked like his whole eye was as black as the night around them. Sweet Shim looked like a predator ready to eat her up, and she would let him because she knew what it felt like when he fed.

Lach's hand made its way to its destination, and she had to sigh. His fingers slipped over her clitoris. She'd touched herself a thousand times while thinking of her Dark Ones. Why did his hand feel so different? His fingers on her flesh made her spread her legs wider to give him better access.

"The poor princess was so traumatized by her spanking that she's soaking wet." His fingers slid all over, delving between her labia and parting her.

She knew she should probably feel some shame, but it was near impossible. They had waited. She had waited. Why should anything between them be wrong? She could hear her father talk about ladylike behavior and how important it was she never behave as less than a lady, but she'd died and then lived in terrible circumstances, and somewhere along the way she'd left the lady behind and become a woman. No perfect lady could have survived. But a woman, a real woman, was strong, and she didn't shrink from loving pleasure.

"That's what I want, *a chumann*. That's my woman." Lach kissed her ear and played in her pussy, the intimacy causing her to nestle close to him. This was what had made Kaja moan. The fact that there didn't have to be boundaries between a wife and her husbands. There was a beautiful freedom that came with love, that opened all doors.

"Do I really just send my thoughts out?" She leaned back into him, not fighting now. She wanted what he could give her.

Shim's hands were on the bottom of her pants. He tugged and she didn't protest. She was with her husbands. It wasn't wrong. "You are so loud, love. And you don't only send thoughts out. You pull power from us when you want to."

She sat straight up as Shim gave her pants a firm pull. "That's how I called fire. It was because of you."

He tugged and managed to get the trousers to her knees. "Yes, love. You pulled it from me and made things go quite haywire on my end."

Lach's tongue licked along the shell of her ear. "Everyone thought

253

he would burn the palace down. Luckily it's mostly stone."

Shim gave her pants a final pull and then tossed them to the side. He held her ankles in his hands. "Every time you felt truly threatened, you pulled it from me, though it's become stronger as we've gotten older. This last time was hard to control."

"When the guards were trying to kill Ove?" It was the last time she'd felt the fire. She remembered that she'd wanted a way to defend the brownie, and she had known she could call on fire.

Shim sat back, staring at the juncture of her thighs where Lach's fingers played in her pussy. "Yesterday. You pulled power from me and it almost destroyed the farm we were staying at. Gods, you have a beautiful pussy."

"Shim, we need to figure this out. I don't want to destroy a farm the next time I feel threatened." But it was hard to think. Her pussy was swelling under Lach's hands. He seemed to know just how to touch her.

"No, we don't. Not tonight." Shim stood. "Tonight is for us. Let's get her back to our camp. I didn't set all of that stuff up so we could fuck her in the grass."

She gasped as Lach pulled his hands away.

Shim reached down and hauled her up. She was still wearing her shirt.

"Take it off. I want to see your breasts." Shim proved he could be demanding, too.

Lach moved to stand beside his brother. He was licking his fingers, sucking them into his mouth. He was tasting the juice from her pussy. She had to watch him. He licked his fingers clean.

"I said take your shirt off. I won't let you take me less seriously than Lach. You have two seconds to get that shirt off or I'll be the one spanking you."

She pulled her shirt over her head as fast as she could. Not because she was worried about the spanking, but she understood what Shim represented. The emotional half of the man. The sweet part. The intellectual half. She never wanted him to think she didn't respect him, didn't want his passion.

She tossed the shirt away. They would find it and make sure she had it to wear tomorrow because their whole lives were about her.

Shim growled, his hands coming up to cup her breasts. "That's what I want."

She stood naked in front of them, completely aware that she was standing in the forest without a stitch on. Cool air made her nipples peak.

Shim reached out. "This is my night. Lach can spank you all he likes, but my cock is going to be inside you tonight."

"It's my first blood." Lach put his hands on her shoulder, his fingers tracing the line of her neck. "But don't think I won't get inside you, too."

Her whole body softened at the thought of having them both. She wasn't a simpleton. She knew what it meant. One cock would find her pussy and the other would be in her mouth or her ass. And she wanted to try it all.

Lach's hands traced her curves from behind while Shim crowded her front. She was trapped between them, her every cell aware of how little stood between her and two cocks. Shim's long, dark hair brushed her nipples, a soft cloud nestling against her.

"Touch me, love." He reached down and brought her hands up to his hair where it was pulled together in a long queue, held by a leather tie. "Take my hair down."

It was a *sidhe* ritual, the taking down of a warrior's hair before going to bed. A fine tremble went through her as emotion swelled. They hadn't done this the first time due to necessity and the fever pitch of it all. This time was more deliberate. This time felt real. She pulled the tie at Shim's neck and his hair fell free, spilling across his shoulders and halfway down his chest. Shim's hair was an ebony waterfall. Bron let her hands wander through the silky stuff. The beauty of his hair did nothing to take away from his masculinity, rather it sharpened and defined it.

Shim stared down at her, his face now framed by his hair. It was something only his wife would see. Everywhere else the glory of that hair would be hidden in his formal queue. This was for her. Hers to see, to touch, to wash and dress.

A wild wave of possessiveness clutched at her. They were hers. No one else's. No other woman would touch them or know their beauty inside and out.

"Yes." Shim pressed his pelvis to hers, holding their hips together. "That's how we feel. Ours. But Bron, it wouldn't have mattered if a thousand men had touched you. You would still be ours. We would still want you."

She laughed, thinking of the few times she'd come close to some man taking advantage of her. That was when she'd felt the fire first spark in her hands. "You were there to protect me."

"Always." His mouth hovered right over hers, lips brushing in a butterfly kiss. "I was always there. Sometimes I was with you more than I was in my own life."

"I worried he was fading a few times." Lach kissed her neck. "He would just lie there. He was trying to feel you."

They had reached out across the planes. She tilted her head up to take Shim's kiss. She went on her tiptoes. "I can't imagine I was doing anything interesting. Everything good that happened to me, happened at night in my dreams. I couldn't wait for the day to be done so I could close my eyes and live my real life."

Shim finally pressed his lips to hers and kissed her mouth. Where Lach dominated, Shim cajoled, his lips playing against hers, tongue peeking out in a dance of seduction. He held her head in his hands and thrust his tongue deep, caressing hers in a silky glide.

Over and over he took her mouth, teaching her how he liked to kiss. Learning it himself. She could feel his wonder at tasting her. She was his great adventure. And he wanted his hands on her.

She pulled at his tunic, tugging it free of his belt, and finally found what she wanted, soft skin over hard muscle. Shim was a work of art. She felt the ridges of his stomach and the deep notches at his hips. She explored the way his chest tapered to a lean waist.

"That's it, love. Gods, Shim, with her here I can feel what she's doing to you. Open yourself. Send it all out." Lach pressed his cock against the seam of her ass.

Longing swamped her. Desire. Want. Need. It came at her from all sides, filling her brain with images of what they wanted.

Her in between them, taking everything they had. They would fill her pussy and ass with cock and ride her until they'd spent every ounce they had. They wanted to fill her. They wanted her desperate for them, as desperate as they were for her.

Shim pulled back and reached for her hand. "Come along. Unlike my brother, I want my comforts. Lach would shove you to the ground, but I have something else in mind."

"I would," Lach admitted. "Or I saw a very nice tree I could toss her up against if she didn't like the ground. He's a bit prissy. He needs a bed."

Though the thought of Lach's passion did things to her insides, she was going with Shim on this one.

He led her a short way through the forest, the silvery moon lighting the path. She saw the glow of candles before they entered the small clearing.

There was a bed, one of several Roan had brought in small packs. Vampire technology sometimes seemed a bit like magic. The bed had been a small cube no bigger than the palm of her hand, but when the right command was given, it turned into a comfortable place to sleep. Shim had set up several torches to approximate candlelight. Her eyes misted when she saw the shamrocks and marigolds and Saint-John's-wort strewn on the bed. A proper bedding to ensure a long marriage.

Yes, Lach might shove her against a tree because he couldn't stand to not be inside her, but Shim wanted all the trappings. Even on the run, he'd tried to make things beautiful for her.

It was right there on the tip of her tongue to say "I love you," but she held back. She couldn't. Not with so much left unresolved between them. "Thank you."

His eyes closed and she was sure he'd heard her thoughts, felt her hesitation. But he smiled down at her. "You're welcome, love. Now undress your husbands."

She wouldn't fight him on that. Shim was her husband. Lach was her husband. She didn't remember the moment she'd bonded with them, but it had happened all the same. The connection was undeniable.

She pulled Shim's shirt off and laid it to the side, then did the same for Lach.

"On your knees," Lach commanded. "We both need some attention before we take care of you. I watched females in my cousin's club kiss their lovers' cocks and pleasure them with their mouths. I want to do this. I want to fuck your mouth, Bronwyn."

His face was tight as though he was worried she would reject the idea, but she got to her knees. She remembered how he'd tongued her pussy and licked her until she'd come. She wanted to give him the same pleasure.

She undid the tie of his pants. Lach and Shim stood side by side. She undressed them, handling trousers and boots and putting them away until both her men stood in their full glory. Two magnificent bodies. She felt small on her knees, her men staring down at her. Small and protected and desired.

"Touch me." Shim had a hand on his cock. "Touch me here while you suck on Lach."

She placed her hand on Shim's cock. It was long and thick, so thick she could barely grasp it in one hand.

"Tighter. I won't break. Rub me." Shim's hips pumped.

She pulled on his cock, surprised at how soft the skin was. She ran her hand up and down, satisfied with the way he sighed. His pleasure hummed in her brain.

And Lach's impatience was a palpable thing.

"Now, Bronwyn."

She leaned forward, licked at his cock. She started at the base and ran her tongue along the stalk all the way to the bulbous head. Warm, pearly liquid seeped from his cockhead. She tasted it. Salty and so masculine, if a taste could have a gender. She worried the tiny slit with her tongue, wanting more.

"You're a dangerous woman." Lach put a hand on her head. "Now suck me inside. I want to fill your mouth."

She pulled the head of his cock into her mouth, running her tongue all over it, glorying in the shape. Her pussy began to pulse in time to Lach's pleasure. He was focusing it on her, giving it to her. She followed her instincts, sucking hard and drawing him in. She felt his low moan of pleasure in her gut.

She sucked on Lachlan's cock, whirling her tongue around and around. The pressure was building. His breath sawed in and out of his chest. She was doing this to him. This dominant warrior was responding to her caresses. She pulled him deeper, relaxing her jaw. It was easy because she could feel what brought him pleasure. He wanted her to eat his dick up and swallow him whole.

Leaning forward, she took him to the back of her throat and

swallowed.

Lach stiffened and his hands held her to him. He came, jetting into her mouth, coating her tongue. It felt so good. Her pussy softened as though she was the one having the orgasm. She shook as she swallowed.

Lazy satisfaction rolled off him as he let go of her hair and his cock came out of her mouth. "So sweet, Bronwyn. That was so sweet."

She didn't have more than a second to enjoy the feeling of power before Shim was on her. He pulled her up and brought her to the bed with him. "No more waiting, wife."

No. She didn't want to wait one second longer.

Chapter Sixteen

Shim felt like he would explode if he didn't get inside her. Watching her suck his brother off while her hand played along his cock had been agony. She'd been so beautiful on her knees in front of Lachlan. He wasn't as dominant as Lach, but he loved the sight of her submitting. She would be beautiful in bondage, her arms and legs tied down and spread wide for them. She would be at their mercy, forced to take what they gave her, pleasure and erotic pain. They would spank her with their hands and crops and canes and then pleasure her wet pussy with tongues and fingers and cocks.

He wanted weeks, months, years of nothing but bonding time, nothing to think about but where he would put his cock into his wife's soft body. He could lose himself in the sex.

But he might only have one night. Her stubbornness still brimmed at the surface no matter how submissive she seemed. She would fight going back to their home plane. He could lose her.

He took her ankles in his hands and spread her legs wide. Moonlight caressed her skin, making her shine. His vampire senses were in full force and Bronwyn was like a torch lighting up the night, drawing him to her. Her dark hair lay on her breasts, the nipples peeking out like jewels hidden in silk. And her pussy. He could see how wet she was, smell it. Her arousal scented the air like perfume of a nightblooming flower. Glistening and wet. Her pussy pouted, the lips puffy and succulent and the nubbin of her clit nestled in between.

His treasure.

"Taste her. She's like honey on your tongue." Lach watched the scene, standing at the edge of the bed. His brother was already hard again. It had taken every shield he had to keep his brother's orgasm from starting his own. But he wanted to come inside her. He wanted to feel her pussy all around him right before he gave her everything he had.

His cock pulsed, but he wanted a taste. Her blood had been his strength, but her pussy was a meal, too.

She wiggled restlessly as he kissed up her leg.

"Be still. This is his time." Lach had moved onto the bed. He scooted in behind Bron, cradling her as Shim had when they'd first made love. His hands found her nipples and twisted. "You behave or I'll spank you again and you'll suck us both down. And we'll shield. You won't get anything. Be a good wife."

She didn't want that. She didn't want to go without. It was obvious to Shim because she went utterly still under him. Shim could feel her need. She was already addicted to this sharing, to the deep intimacy that came from the bond. And it wasn't even full yet. When they fully bonded, fully opened their minds and souls, the connection would go even deeper.

He got to his belly and slid up the bed. His mouth hovered over her pussy. She smelled too good. It was the smell of a lifetime's lust finally satisfied.

Shim drew his tongue along the seam of her pussy, gathering up her juice.

Bron moaned and shook.

"You like that, love. You like having a tongue shoved deep inside. You like your men treating you like a feast. We'll eat that pussy every day. You'll wake in the sweetest way, with a tongue lapping at you, making you hot." Lach's words echoed Shim's thoughts.

He wanted to feast every day. He rubbed his nose through her labia, trying to imprint her scent on him. She was a juicy piece of fruit. He speared her with his tongue, going deep in an imitation of what he wanted to do with his cock. He fucked her with his tongue and then suckled her clit, her mewling cries making him feel powerful.

"Every day, love. We'll pleasure you every day because you're our whole world."

He looked up her body. Lach's fangs were scraping her neck. He and his brother were in perfect accord. A double-pronged assault on her senses. Cock and fangs penetrating in perfect time.

He got to his knees. Bron stared up at him, her dark eyes glistening. He could feel her longing for more than simple sex. She wanted the intimacy, the joining, the connection.

He lined his cock up and finally pressed home.

Tightness and warmth, heat surrounded him, squeezed at him. Bron's legs wrapped around his waist, hugging him close. He had to fight his way in. She was ready, but still so tight. Every inch gained was pure pleasure. He fucked in and out in short bursts, further and further until his cock was encased and his balls caressed the cheeks of her ass. He was inside her. He was a part of her. This was what he'd dreamed of.

He pressed in and opened his senses, sharing the feeling with Bron. He wanted her to know how sweet she was, how good it felt to be deep inside her so she would understand that he would protect her with his life, his soul, his very being.

Bronwyn's eyes widened and her cunt tightened around him. "Goddess, it feels so good."

He pulled out and fucked his way back in, every inch a revelation of pure pleasure.

Lach's eyes were full and dark in his head. His fangs gleamed in the moonlight. Their eyes met, the warrior half and the intellectual, both with one thought. This woman was their world.

He dove deep, listening to Bron's cries, finding that one sweet spot in her body that sent her flying. Her womb tightened. Gods, he could feel her come and it made his cock explode. He pounded into her, over and over. He never wanted to stop. Her pussy spasmed around him, her whole body shaking.

Lach groaned and struck, his fangs penetrating her neck. His brother's first blood triggered another rush of pleasure—Lach's from that life-giving blood flowing into his body and Bron's from the delicious feeling of fangs sliding deep and drawing on her vein.

Shim gave up. He let the wave take him, riding it with his other half and his woman.

When Lach released the vein, Shim let himself drop onto Bronwyn's soft body. Her heat enveloped him. Her softness called to him.

He fell asleep to the steady beat of her heart.

* * * *

Bronwyn crept out of bed after she was sure Lachlan and Shim were fast asleep. Sleep. It was a state she would appreciate, but it would not come for her. She'd lain there for what felt like hours, her body perfectly sated, but her mind raced.

It had been right there, the need to fully bond. She understood the process. It was a bit like a marriage of convenience versus one of true, pure love. She could do what she needed to do without the deepest of bonds. She would still be able to bridge the twins, giving them access to both halves of their soul. She would still be able to feel them both and share sensations, but she wouldn't know them, not in the deepest, most intimate sense.

She picked up Lach's shirt and drew it overhead. It hung past her knees, covering her efficiently. She stared down at them. Shim's arm was still outstretched as though reaching for her. Lach was on his back, his head to one side as though he needed to hide his scars even as he slept.

What had caused those scars? The scarring had gone far beyond the physical. Those scars went down to his soul. He would tell her if she asked, but if they bonded, she would feel his pain, perhaps know how to heal it.

She stepped away. Did she even want that? Goddess, she didn't know anything. Her whole world had been turned upside down again as surely as it had thirteen years before. Torin had killed her parents, but finding out Lach and Shim were real had as big an effect. Her world was changed, and she was forced to decide the way her life was going to go.

She walked out to the river, cool grass beneath her feet. The night air held a slight chill, but she welcomed it after the heat of their bed. Bron stopped at the river's edge, not daring to go much further. She wouldn't run again, but she intended to take a stand. She couldn't run away and hide from this war.

The river ran past her feet, a bubbling swell of water that kept going until it reached the sea. The river was in constant motion, but Bron felt caught. She could jump in and bond and allow Lach and Shim to carry her off or she could stay stubbornly in place like a log that had gotten caught in the middle of the river. It didn't move, simply allowed the water to strip off the bark and pulp until nothing was left.

"Bron?"

She closed her eyes briefly, immediately recognizing the voice. It was the same voice she'd heard every day for the last thirteen years. It was a voice that had cajoled and softened the world around her, but now all she heard that voice saying was how she was to be used.

"What do you need, Gillian?"

There was a huff. It was a laugh completely devoid of humor. "I need to take back about three minutes of my life."

"Only three?"

Gillian moved to stand next to her. "I wouldn't take back a second of our time together. I wish we'd been able to flee the plane. I truly do, but I wouldn't have left without you. Never."

That was brutally obvious. "Yes, well, you did seek me out with a plan in mind, didn't you?"

"Don't we all have plans? We all have hopes and ambitions. It doesn't make us terrible. I wanted to find the woman who belonged to my brothers. I wanted to unite our tribes," Gillian explained.

That wasn't all she'd wanted. "You wanted power."

Gillian's jaw tightened, a sure sign she was frustrated. "Of course I wanted power. I still do. You know what it means to be a woman. Without power we have to rely on our men or our king, and Torin proves that this is not a good idea. Goddess, even my own father uses me as a bargaining tool, and I know for sure he loves me."

Bron had seen the way the vampire mercenary and his lieutenant had stared at Gillian all the long trek through the woods. "It's not so different, is it? You did the same to me. You walked into my father's palace with the intention of either purchasing me or selling yourself."

"Damn it, Bronwyn," Gillian cursed. "Why do you have to put it that way? It's not the same. Not at all. I went to negotiate a marriage between the crowns. You knew you wouldn't be allowed to marry as you liked, didn't you? And my current situation is not at all like yours."

"I don't see how." They'd both basically been sold.

"Because you've known them all of your life and they all of yours. I did not consider it buying or selling you. I thought I was bringing you home." Gillian reached out for a moment and then seemed to think better of it. She pulled back into herself. "Since my brothers could speak, they talked about their princess. I felt as though I knew you as a sister before I ever set foot in the White Palace."

"Then why didn't you tell me?"

Gillian shook her head, staring into the river. "Because you were so lost after what had happened and then you said something about the connection being broken. You cried out at night that you couldn't feel them, that your Dark Ones were gone. I thought my brothers were dead."

Gillian had thought Lach and Shim were dead? Those first few months after Torin's coup had been a desperate time. She'd been dead inside. She'd searched for the connection but nothing had come, as though a black space had opened in the center of her being and something that had always been filled was now empty. She'd walked around, simply a body moving without any more purpose than to be alive.

What had Gillian gone through? Cut off from her family and everything she knew, she'd been the one who had forced Bron to survive, finding tutors so they could both learn the skills they needed. It would have been so much easier to escape the plane alone.

"Why did you stay?" Bron asked.

"Because I wasn't sure at first," Gillian replied after a long pause. "I thought perhaps that the magic I used to bring you back cut the connection. I used a white spell that drew energy from someone who cared about you. I gave you a bit of my own life force. I'll be honest, I was surprised it worked. I was desperate. I didn't know what else to do. After a while, when the connection didn't return, I had to assume they were gone or something terrible had happened. Then I decided I would honor my brothers. They would have wanted you taken care of. And then somewhere between years two and three, I simply loved you as a sister and would have done anything to protect you."

She wanted to believe, but she could still hear those words she'd said as Shim had held her. "You certainly reverted to form the minute you realized your brothers were alive."

"I'm not proud of that. I was so happy and I felt powerful for the first time in years. I'd succeeded. Bron, I had done the impossible. I had survived and all I wanted was to celebrate that fact. You belong with them. You have to know it." Gillian spoke with the fervor of a true believer.

She shook her head. "I don't know them. You don't understand what it's been like. You seem to think that I went into these dreams and Lach and Shim and I exchanged all sorts of information. We didn't. They were dreams. I didn't even know their names. I didn't even understand they were real."

"No, I don't understand the connection. I don't know how it works. The way they explained it to me, they could hear and feel you clearly, but they didn't think you always could hear them. That's why you need the full bond. You're strong, Bron. You're a strong bondmate. Roan says you glow more brightly than any consort he's ever seen. Maybe that means your powers to bridge them are stronger, too. So strong that they could feel you, be pulled to you even across the planes. I don't know. It doesn't matter. What matters is that they know you. They love you. You're married. Accept it."

Bitterness welled despite the fact that she was already deeply involved with them. "Yes, you should take your own advice. Accept it. You're practically married, too."

Gillian frowned and a weariness came over her. "It's not even close to the same. They don't know me. They simply want a consort to strengthen them and elongate their life. I mean nothing to them. And I doubt I shall be able to get away. I thought about trying to run."

"Why don't you?" If she was truly miserable at the thought, then Gillian could run. She surely knew how to survive. She knew the plane and had lived here for a long time.

Gillian looked back at the tree line. "I will never get the chance."

Bron followed the line of her sight and there he was. Tall and dark, with broad shoulders and a brooding stare. He was larger than his partner, though he was the subordinate soldier. Harry Riley stood watch over his treasure. No. Gillian wasn't getting away. Not if Harry had anything to do with it.

"I heard them talking." Gillian's voice sounded hollow. "They intend to take shifts, and the other vampires have their orders. I am not to be allowed privacy. They must keep their eyes on me at all times. Roan told me he won't touch me until my father blesses the union, but he insists that it will happen. I am going to ask my father to find them another consort. Surely there will be more once the plane is open. If your brothers do their jobs, I can be free. Unseelies who can bond are rare. They would be happier with a Seelie mate."

But the look on Harry's face told Bron he was already invested in the one he had.

"Well, then, sister, if you manage to talk your father out of selling your body for his convenience, then you'll be better off than me. I have no father to look out for me, and I doubt your father made a deal with my brothers that didn't include my marriage."

"Gillian. It's time to go back." Roan came out of the woods, a frown on his face. "We have a long day tomorrow. Come back to bed."

"Bastard," Gillian muttered under his breath. "We'll see who has the upper hand when we return to my kingdom." She turned. "I wish you would forgive me, but I know you won't. Please don't take it out on my brothers. They've waited all their lives for you. They don't know anything else."

Gillian shuffled back, seeming determined to take her time, and Roan seemed equally determined to be patient. The vampire followed her when she walked past him, giving his lieutenant a nod. The lieutenant nodded back and then his eyes were on someone different—Bron.

"He won't leave."

Bron was startled by the voice, but then noticed what she hadn't before. The gnome sat a few feet away, his back against a huge tree, his bare feet in the water. Duffy. His name was Duffy and she'd been told that he was Lach and Shim's brother. Not by blood, but by their mother's kindness. It had been easy to see that both men loved the gnome during their long walk. Lach, in particular, had taken care to see that the gnome remained close to him, picking him up when he fell behind.

"He'll stay there and make sure you don't run," the gnome continued. "I heard them talking about it earlier. Their main job in life right now is making sure you and Gilly make it back to the Dark Palace. You because you're the future queen and Gillian because she's their prize."

Bron thought about saying good-bye and trying to find some solitude, but with Harry's eyes on her, she doubted she could be alone. She stepped over to Duffy and sank to the ground beside him. The water gave off a definite chill. "Aren't you cold?"

"No. Ain't that funny? All me life I've complained about the cold and now I can't feel it. I know I should be cold, but I just can't feel it. Must be the spell." The gnome spoke in a monotone, shaking his head a bit.

"Are you all right?" That spell had been filled with dark magic. She couldn't imagine what it had felt like. Duffy's screams were still ringing in her ears.

"I'm not good. I know that. I just gotta find a way to be all right again. I think I have some things to do before I can be right." He sighed, a long breath that seemed to hold a world of regret.

"It was brave what you did." That bolt of power had been coming for Lach. It had been meant for him, and the gnome had taken it full blast.

"No, it weren't. It was me duty. I know Lach's not me brother. There's not a drop of blood between us, but it's me job to protect him. He's going to be the king, and he'll be a good one if you would take the time to teach him."

"I hardly doubt he needs to learn anything from me. He was raised to be king."

"Yes and no," Duffy explained. "The king was raising them, teaching them, and then one day along about the time they were seventeen, something happened. I wasn't there, but I know that Shim's power flared for the first time. Shim was in the stables, getting ready for a riding lesson. I was with Lach. Lach suddenly got pale as a wraith and he fell to his knees, holding his chest. He got up and started running and I ran after him. I could see that the barn was on fire from a long ways away. Flames were shooting out of it like someone was firing a cannon, but it didn't stop Lach. He ran inside and when he came out, he was on fire, too. It had shot up his face and all around his body. He was engulfed."

"How did he survive?" The thought made her heart clench, but she understood why Lach had risked everything. It hadn't simply been his brother he'd saved. It was half of his soul. If Shim had died and Lach managed to survive, he wouldn't have been able to ever access his intellectual and romantic sides. He would have been the warrior and nothing more. Lach valued what Shim represented.

"No idea, but Shim didn't have a mark on him. We didn't know it then, but fire can't touch him. He can walk through it and it don't burn him. It sure burned Lach. He was a mess. It took five healers to save him and even then, they weren't able to fix the scars on his face or hands or chest. Anywhere Shim actually touched him. I remember him saying he'd lost his handsomeness and there was a part of him that was relieved you were gone since you wouldn't accept him like that."

"That's not true." There was nothing wrong with Lach's face. Shim's was more traditionally beautiful, but Lach's had character. He was devastatingly handsome. "But I don't see what this has to do with making him a king. Did his father value looks so much?"

Duffy laughed. "Nah, in the Dark Palace, those scars were actually a good thing. It made him look tough. Battle is supposed to harden a man. No. The scars didn't bother his father, but Shim being in a coma did."

She gasped at the thought. "Goddess, did the healers not do their job?"

"The healers tried everything on both him and Lach. Lach's body was healed, but he was weak, so weak. He just sat at his brother's side for almost a year. Eventually he regained his strength. The healers kept Shim fed, but finally he awoke. We thought he would recover like Lach had, but he didn't. Not until today. Not until first blood."

"I don't understand the whole blood thing," she admitted. "By the time someone would have explained it to me, I no longer had any contact with my vampire relatives."

Duffy's eyes were flat stones in the moonlight. "Your blood, consort blood, has something inside it that makes a royal stronger and faster and healthier than a normal vampire. They tried to force consort blood on both Lach and Shim but they refused."

Because they belonged to her. "So their father thought they were weak."

"Didn't think," Duffy corrected. "They were weak for a long time. The king wouldn't let them train or teach them anything. He was simply obsessed with keeping them alive."

She understood how that kind of attention could affect someone. "Rather like Lach and Shim with me."

"But Lach and Shim didn't have the power you have."

"I don't have any power at all."

"Yes, you do. The bond, the true bond, will show your husbands who you are deep down inside. Lach couldn't show his father what he wanted, needed. He could only tell him. He couldn't make him feel it the way you can. I know my brothers. They want to please you. When they realize how important this is, they will back off. They'll stay with you on this plane, and they will fight for your people."

It would be a gamble. She could get caught in that web, too, but she didn't like her other options. And it was such a temptation. To meld with them, mixing their souls, never to be alone again. It was everything she'd wanted.

Could she be brave? Could she afford not to?

Duffy seemed to know he'd swayed her. "Do it, Your Highness. Go back to bed and bond with your husbands. The answers you want are right there. And it could answer a few of their questions, too. If it doesn't work, you'll know to run."

She stood and stared back at the campsite. If it didn't work, she would have to, but she feared they would be able to find her. Always.

It was win or lose, but perhaps it was better to find out one way or the other. She would have to think about it.

"Why don't you go back to the camp?" She hated the thought that he was out here all alone. "Roan has devices to warm you."

Duffy simply turned away. "No. I think I'll sit here a while and watch the stars. Like I said. I don't feel the cold no more."

Bron nodded and walked off. She wasn't afraid of the cold, but the heat was another matter. She was worried the heat of their true bond would burn her, singeing away all that was Bronwyn Finn and leaving only a consort in her place.

* * * *

Torin looked from one hag to the other. "What do you mean she got away?"

It had been a simple fucking plan. Go to the district where the hags themselves had promised him Bronwyn resided. Go to the district and kill every woman who could possibly be Bronwyn. Simple. Easy. All fucked up.

"The Unseelie princes were there." Glannis didn't look up from her perch. She stared down at the bones she'd just thrown. She'd rattled them in an open skull, chanting and spitting and offering up blood. Now she studied them. It looked like a nasty mess that some forest creature had crapped out, but Glannis apparently saw something in it.

"Why the hell are they here? They've stayed out of things. Why do they give a shit?" The last thing he needed was trouble with the Unseelie until he was ready to deal with them. The Unseelie king had his own trouble. He had idiot sons, the dumbass versions of the Seelie princes. He'd heard something had gone desperately wrong with the princes. They'd been injured in a fire, and that meant his line of succession was in question. The Unseelie didn't believe in weak monarchs. Fergus was trying to deal with his own kingdom. He didn't have time to fight with the Seelie. And Torin liked it that way.

Una cocked a hand on her ridiculously gaunt hip. "Glannis thinks they might be bound to the princess."

Torin threw his head back and laughed. The defective princes had snuck onto the plane to retrieve Bronwyn? "So why didn't you kill them?"

Glannis finally looked up, her rheumy eyes serious. "I tried. I failed. And they are not defective. Not in the least. The warrior king has already come into his power. He's a Death Lord."

A shiver went up Torin's spine. He'd always wondered about that damn divination the hags had given him before his ascension. They had told him he would win the day. He would be the king. Only one person could harm him in the end. He'd leaned over and been prepared to hear the name Beckett Finn.

Bronwyn had been a surprise. But if Bronwyn had somehow bonded with a fucking Death Lord, he might be in trouble. Perhaps that damn prophecy had been about his niece's husband and not his niece.

"Why didn't you kill him?" Surely his hags could do something about it now that they knew what the real problem was.

"I tried, Your Majesty. It would have worked but some filthy gnome got in my way," she admitted. "I couldn't hex him again. The first one took too much energy and now he'll be ready for it so all I got to do was kill a damn gnome. But I've come up with something else. His necromancy only works on creatures, Fae and animals and other somewhat sentient beings. So I intend to attack him with something he can't take control of. I just need to find him. I believe he's in the forests. He's going to move toward Aoibhneas. It's how he got in."

Yes. He didn't understand that, either. "How the fuck did he get in? I have guards on the entryway."

The two hags shared a long look before Una answered. "There are always small rips and tears. A smart Fae would be able to get through."

"I don't want anyone to be able to get through."

Una took a long breath. "Your Majesty, it is impossible to tell where these weak spots are unless you happen across one. And that village wouldn't have told us. It keeps its secrets."

Yes. Aoibhneas was the perfect fuck storm. High in the mountains with both natural and magical defenses. And the Fae who lived there were rebels by nature. He'd kept them contained with heavy guards on the roads and a long history of leaving them be, but he would come for them eventually and they had to know it. Aoibhneas would be the logical place to launch a rebellion. But it was small and so isolated.

What if the Unseelie decided to invade?

"You have to kill the necromancer."

Glannis threw her hands up. "That is my plan. Now I just need to find them. I stole back to the village and found what I believe is her hair and his blood. The intellectual half was there. I don't have anything from him, but if those two do anything magical, I can find them."

Torin stared down at the shit on his desk. It better do what was expected. It better lead him to his niece and her husband.

One way or another someone was going to die. And he was going to wipe that fucking mountain town off the map.

Chapter Seventeen

Two days later, Lach wondered if he was ever going to get home.

Roan finally called a halt to the march. Since they'd left the village, they'd spent long hours trudging through forests with little rest.

And he'd never felt better.

"I'll go set up." Shim gave him a smile. He was eager to get the night started, but Shim was thinking about the sex and not the forlorn look that Lach kept seeing on Bron's face.

She was exhausted. She was confused. And there was a core sadness that was killing his soul. The last two nights she hadn't even fought them. She'd come to the bed they made and offered herself up. She'd made love with them, shared her blood and her body. She'd submitted in the loveliest of ways.

And it wasn't enough because every time he'd offered her the true bond, she'd retreated. He looked over and she stood by a huge tree, her back leaning against it. She held herself apart from the group. She hadn't simply retreated from the true bond. She'd retreated from everyone. Bronwyn answered all questions in two or three words. She didn't even look at Gillian, a fact that seemed to add to his sister's misery.

If he didn't need Roan, he might kill him. Except he'd overheard

Roan and his lieutenant talking the night before and he'd really watched them all day. Their every move was about Gillian's safety and comfort. Their talk the night before had been a long, slow dialogue about how to tempt Gillian into giving them a chance.

He understood Roan and Harry. *Damn it.*

"You're hungry?" She wouldn't let him carry her through the forests. She wouldn't let him shield her. At least she accepted that he could feed her.

She gave him a wan smile. "I am."

He nodded and moved away, walking up to Roan. They were running out of supplies. They were running out of time. And every village they stopped in, his wife insisted on riling up the villagers.

And it had been fairly easy since the villages were empty of guards. They were all patrolling around Aoibhneas now, a phalanx Lach wasn't sure they could break through without some loss of life.

Roan looked up from his tablet. "Can I help you, Your Highness?"

"You can tell me when we'll be able to get my wife home. The Seelie princes are due here any day now. You know that they're just waiting for a big enough hole in the wall to come through with an army."

"I'm doing my best."

It was said with Roan's clipped efficiency, but something about the way he said it made Lach suspicious. "Tell me why we're moving the way we're moving. Aoibhneas is in the opposite direction."

Roan's eyebrow raised and his mouth turned down. "Every time we attempt to move to Aoibhneas, we get cut off by the guard. We talked about this last night. We've moved from village to village in an unorthodox path in order to deceive the guard as to where we are going."

There was a major flaw in the mercenary's logic. "We're not deceiving anyone since you allow my wife to be put on display. She's giving speeches. She's making herself a target."

"She's building her brothers an army." Roan looked over to where Bron stood. "She needs to feel like she's a part of this. Can you not understand that?"

"He's right. You can't understand." Duffy stood at his side. "You don't know what it means to want to fight and not be able to. I know

I've played around, but we all know I wouldn't be able to do anything at all on the battlefield except let warriors trip over me."

His brother's sorrow made Lach's heart clench. He'd never meant to make Duffy feel that way. And he'd certainly never meant for… He wasn't going to think about that moment in anything but the broadest of terms. "You saved me, Duff."

"By throwing my body in front of a cloud."

Gillian got to her knees in front of Duffy. "You saved Lach with more than your body."

Gillian's words were a bit shaky. Lach was rather glad to see it. She'd been as shut down as Bronwyn for days.

Duffy flushed and looked toward the ground. "It pretty much felt like me body."

"It wasn't your body that made you leap in front of that cloud. It was your strong, brave heart," his sister insisted.

Duffy shook his head. "I ain't brave, Gilly. Not for a second."

She put her hand out, lifting his face up to hers. "How can you say that?"

"Because I ain't never said the thing I wanted to say," Duffy admitted. "I won't say them. I'm small and insignificant. I know how Bron feels. She wants to fight but no one will let her. They'll pat her on the head and tell her she's doing fine. They might let someone train her so's she doesn't complain too much, but when it comes down to it, she's not going to be allowed to fight."

The words made his gut clench. "Damn it, Duffy. It's not the same. And I was trying to protect you. Can't you understand that? I didn't want you to die."

Duffy sighed as though he'd heard the excuse a thousand times, and he likely had. "But, Lach, there are some things that are worth dying over. Haven't you figured that out yet? You would die for Bronwyn. Do you think she's less a woman than you are a man? Do you think she doesn't want her life to matter?"

What the hell was Duffy talking about? Didn't he understand that everything he'd been doing was about how precious Bronwyn was? How precious he himself was?

He was about to answer when a trilling alarm went off and Roan's whole body shifted to full alert. He had a sonic blade in his hand in an instant, and he and Harry pulled Gillian behind them.

"I have alarms set up all over," Roan explained. "I placed them before we settled into camp. It could be a deer or it could be Torin's guard. The last village said their guards had been pulled out just the day before to hunt for the princess."

Lach was relieved to see Shim hauling ass back to camp. He grabbed Bron and forced her behind them.

Dante walked in, his hands in the air. Kaja was at his side, in her wolf form, her delicate nose in the air.

A large man walked behind Dante. He was at least Lach's height at six foot five. He had an Unseelie look about him, and Lach would bet he wasn't a pure *sidhe*. Emerald-green eyes and pitch-black hair made a stark contrast to Dante's reddish blond.

"Dude, I told you we're not Torin's guard," Dante was saying. "I showed you my fucking fangs, man. I'm a desperate vampire looking for a consort. Do you know any? Because I will pay."

Kaja growled.

"I've learned not to believe everything a person says. People lie, even when they have knives to their backs." The dark man looked around. "You have women here. Why the hell do you have women here?"

Dante gave him a careless grin. "I'm ridiculously wealthy. I keep an entourage with me, even in faery forests. The men are here to ensure my safety and the women are here to do what women do."

Gillian huffed. "As if I would touch you, Dellacourt."

The dark man stiffened. "Dellacourt? Are you one of the vampires who's related to our kings?"

A little laugh came from the trees above. "Yes, he is, Master Zane. He's the billionaire playboy turned fairly ruthless political advisor. And the wolf beside you is his wife." The phooka. Of course. It was chaos. Naturally the phooka showed up. It was in its tree form, hanging upside down from one of the low branches. "I believe I mentioned we could call them allies."

Dante breathed a deep sigh as the man named Zane let him go. "Sorry, guys. I was giving into Kaja's need to hunt when this asshole jumped me. When did the lemur thing start talking? You know we're in a faery forest. It's really best to shoot anything that talks and ask questions never."

Lach felt Bron trying to get a good view, but he wasn't certain anything had been settled yet. He blocked her, unwilling to expose her at all.

Zane sheathed his incredibly large knife and looked at Dellacourt. "So all that talk was bullshit. You don't need a consort. You have a wolf."

Kaja changed, her transformation so quick if he blinked he would miss it. "He has a consort, though after calling my friends cheap women, he might not get his meal tonight."

Dellacourt shrugged out of his jacket and wrapped it around his wife's shoulders. "I am sorry, lover. They are very expensive prostitutes. Is that better?"

"Much," Kaja agreed. "One would always rather be expensive. Queen Meg taught me that."

Dante sent his consort a pointed look. "Too bad she didn't teach you to bite the people who pull a knife on me."

Kaja shook her head. "He wasn't going to use it. He's protecting his son. And someone else. There are still two more out there. I could smell them. They're afraid. And on the run. Fear is easy to smell."

Zane turned back to the forest. "Nathan, you can bring Charlie out now."

A second man, this one slightly shorter but just as fit, his brown hair curling over the edges of his tunic collar, walked out of the woods carrying a young man in his arms.

"I told you I would bring you to safety," the phooka said.

Nathan struggled with the body in his arms, but he seemed resolute. "You told us you would take us back to Aoibhneas."

Shim moved forward. "You're the Harpers' friends. The one whose boy was taken by Torin."

Bron moved, sidestepping Lach and slipping toward the newcomers. Gillian moved, too, though Roan and Harry did nothing to stop her.

"She's very good with white magic," Roan said. "Why don't you bring the child over here to the bed?"

Roan tossed the cube to the ground and in an instant it was a full-size air bed. Nathan gently laid his son on the top. The boy looked to be more of a young man, roughly fifteen or sixteen. He was malnourished, his body a mass of gangly arms and legs.

Nate put a hand on his son's head, smoothing his hair back. "He was taken when we brought our wine to the marketplace. We're isolated. We hadn't heard that Torin was laying claim to all bondmates. Honestly, we didn't know Charlie could bond."

"The mayor told us he could." Zane stood over them both, his eyes worried.

Nathan's lips turned up in a smile. "The mayor is insane and he told us Charlie could bond because of that device Caleb made for him to track Planeswalker demons. Please excuse us. Mayor Mel is a brilliant warrior, but he's preoccupied with what he calls the coming Demon Invasion. Anyway. Zane and I were haggling and then Charlie was gone. He's been missing for two years. If Torin is selling bondmates to vampires, why wouldn't he feed our son? Wouldn't a vampire want a healthy mate?"

Roan stared down at the boy, his mouth a harsh line. "Your son is certainly a consort, or what you would call a bondmate. I see his glow as clearly as the female consorts here."

"And any vampire would be horrified at his condition," Dellacourt assured them.

Lach felt a building rage. Torin hadn't meant to sell this boy. No vampire would accept that his consort had been treated in such a way. "I'm not a full vampire, but I know for a fact that the one way to have gotten the Council to enter this war was for word to leak that consorts were being abused. The vampires would have invaded."

Gillian kneeled by the bed, laying her hands on the young man. She closed her eyes and seemed to be calling on that part of herself that worked magic. "He's been fed upon, but not in any way I understand."

Lach's stomach turned. He remembered the vision the hag had sent him. "The hag. She's been eating at his soul."

Nate made a low moan of pain and clutched his son's hand. Zane turned a stark white.

"What does it mean?" Zane asked.

Thank gods his smarter half liked to study. Shim folded his arms across his chest. "It's not as bad as it sounds. Hags, even some non-corporeal dead, can feast on the living. What I believe she's trying to do is absorb his psychic power."

"She wants to be able to bond?" Bronwyn asked. "Why?"

Shim shrugged. "I don't know, love, but it would explain the ritual of soul eating. It would take a long time. She would have to drain him over a couple of days or weeks. She would take his blood, withhold food and water. She would torture him. Anything to break down his resistance. The body needs a soul. It would rather die than go without one, so she has to be careful. If she simply killed him, the soul would go wherever souls go."

"Through the door," Duffy said. Lach felt his heart twist as his brother, his little champion, spoke. His small hands clenched together. "There's a door and light. It calls to a soul, tells you to go through, that more adventures are waiting, just waiting past that door." He shook his head and a deep breath filled his lungs. "Or that's what I've heard."

Shim looked at Duffy, suspicion clear in his eyes, but he continued anyway. "She has to bring him to the brink of death, bit by bit so the soul hovers, unsure whether it's time to go or not. And she catches it and consumes it in a ritual. I've only read about it, of course, but technically it should give the hag any powers the soul contained. Consorts and bondmates have measurable psychic energy. I'm sure that makes her spells more powerful."

"She's making up for the lack of three." Charlie's eyes opened, his voice strained.

"Don't, son," Zane said. "Rest. We'll have you home to your mother soon."

Charlie's head shook. "Already feel a little stronger. How did you get into the dungeon?"

"Believe it or not, a sluagh guided us. He knew how to sneak in." Nate gripped his son's hand. "I know this sounds crazy, but he looked just like the old king."

Bronwyn sniffled. "My father. I was told he fought to stay even after he died. He's still fighting for his kingdom."

A kernel of guilt opened inside Lach. Duffy's words echoed in his ears, but he wasn't going to let them sway him. Bronwyn needed to be safe. Duffy needed to be safe. Safety was better than any cause.

Charlie's head turned at the sound of Bronwyn's voice. "It's you."

She smiled, a little sadly. "I am Princess Bronwyn. I am so sorry I haven't done anything to help."

"No," the young man said, a smile turning his lips up. "Not the princess. You're the voice. You're the voice in our heads. Goddess, I can't believe you're real. Can't you all hear it? Do you hear the hum?"

Kaja walked to the bed. "I have heard it for days, but Dante thought it was all the vampire technology."

Gillian's eyes turned down. "I've heard it since the day I met her as a girl. But it was faint. Just a hum in the back of my mind until the last few days."

Lach closed his eyes, the enormity of what his wife was hitting him squarely in the chest. He didn't want to be sure, but he had to. "Bronwyn, think something."

She glanced at him, confusion on her face. "I am almost always thinking something."

Shim seemed to understand immediately. "Think something at Gillian. Specifically. Try to get her to hear you."

Bron turned toward Gillian and her brow set in a serious line.

Gillian, Kaja, and Charlie all winced, each holding their heads. "You don't have to shout."

"Sorry," Bron said.

"And I don't think I'm old enough to hear those words," Charlie said, his face looking boyish for a moment.

Kaja gave her a smile. "You should use a sharp knife, Bronwyn. A rusty one will cut off your husbands' manly parts very slowly."

"I think she was hoping to cause some pain, baby," Dante said.

"Well, I don't see why they would stand there and allow their little men to be sawed off with something dull," Kaja argued.

Shim looked at Lach as the others seemed to laugh and find Bron's power curious, but Shim had a grave look in his eyes. "You don't think she could do other things, do you?"

"I hope not, brother, otherwise she would be a powerful weapon. I also think I know why the hag is trying to steal power from consorts." The thought had occurred to him almost immediately.

But Shim was right there with him. "They intend to kill Torin and take over the plane."

Charlie held out a hand, and his father helped him to sit up. "Yes. What the big guy said."

The phooka laughed and fell to the bed Charlie lay on. "The big guy is the Unseelie prince, Charles."

Bronwyn stared at the phooka. "Why are you here? You're the same creature who convinced me to run."

"Then he is the same creature who I am about to throttle." The fucking phooka seemed to have his hand in everything. Lach was ready to put the little shit out of his misery.

"I am simply more adept at this game than any of you," the phooka replied, his midnight-black tail twitching. "I am certainly smarter than the Unseelies. Princess Bronwyn is the most important piece to this game we're playing. If you take her off the board, this plane falls to Torin and Torin to the hags. The only reason the hags haven't taken over yet is the fact that they lost a sister. Everyone knows they're stronger in threes, but they found a way around it."

"To become soul eaters," Gillian said hollowly. "I don't understand what any of this has to do with Bronwyn. Is she going to hum the hags to death?"

Bron looked up at Shim. "How do you send power to me?"

Shim frowned. "I don't think I do. I feel you pull it from me. The first few times I fought it and it went wild. When I realized what was happening and let it flow, I could control it a bit more."

Bron took Charlie's hand. "Don't be afraid."

The young Fae had a wisp of a smile. "I know what fear is. I've moved long past it. Fear is something you get through or you die. So feel free to experiment, Your Highness."

Bron took a deep breath and closed her eyes.

"Damn it, Bron." Shim gritted his teeth. "Fine, but this is a mistake."

Even Lach could feel it. Bron reached and held the connection. She drew on it, passing up his cold power for Shim's hot one. Lach was fascinated. Now that he knew what was happening, he realized it had happened before. His power was buried deep, deep down inside, but Shim's simmered at the surface. It was easy to reach and hold. It was easy to share.

Charlie gasped and looked down at his hand. "Bugger me. I'm on fire and it doesn't hurt."

He wiggled his fingers, flames at the tips. His fathers both stared.

Dellacourt cursed. "She's a conduit. Gods, she isn't a broadcaster. She's a bloody conduit."

Bron's whole face lit up. "I can help us win. I can win this war."

Lach shook his head. "Absolutely not. You're going home and there you will stay. Roan, if you don't have us in Aoibhneas by dark tomorrow, I will find my own way. If any of you thinks for one bloody second that I intend to let you use my mate as a fucking psychic cannon, you're insane. She is not going to any battlefield."

Lach turned before Bronwyn could curse him.

Curse him or not. She would be alive at the end of the day.

* * * *

Bron approached Lach with no small amount of trepidation. Shim walked behind her, his boots shuffling along the ground. Shim hadn't argued, hadn't said much at all. He'd simply watched Lach walk away after ordering Duffy to not walk past the river.

The gnome had looked up with a sad expression on his face until Gillian had taken his hand and asked him to sit with her while she healed Charlie.

A curious excitement flowed through her, but it was tempered with sadness. She had one more play to make and then it would be over.

She would lose her kingdom or her men.

"Please don't be angry with him." Shim reached out and grasped her hand.

Funny. His hand felt right tangling with hers, as though all these years it had been waiting to be entwined with his. She'd only been physically with them for a few days and already she knew she wanted them forever. She was happy just being around them, but happiness wasn't the only thing important in life.

She respected the fact that they would one day rule a kingdom. They owed their people. Couldn't they understand that she owed hers, too?

"I'm not angry. I'm sad."

His eyes turned down, watching the place where their fingers met. "I can feel it. It's worse than mad. Please, Bron. Can't you understand?"

"I can't. Don't you love your people? Wouldn't you do anything to keep them safe? You will rule over them one day." She remembered her father's words. "A king is only good to his people if he is useful."

It was a lesson her uncle hadn't learned.

"After Lach was burned and I was weak, I think my father decided we would never be fit to rule. Bron, we weren't brought up to lead. We were hidden away because my father feared we would either be killed or judged as too weak to rule. So we concentrated on the one thing we had."

"Me." She understood that much. They loved her. She accepted it. Over the last days, they had treated her with an affection that went far beyond courtesy. They seemed to anticipate her needs. When they had stopped in a village, they would bring her favorite cheese and bread and fruit. When her feet hurt from walking, Lach had dropped down, removed her boots, and rubbed the soles of her aching feet until she was purring.

She'd never felt so loved and taken care of. They held her at night, passing her between them. Lach would hold her with a possessive strength that made her feel safe, and Shim with such delicacy that she felt adored.

Why couldn't they see to her soul? She could answer that question. Because she'd been too afraid to show them.

That ended tonight and she would either have them on her side or she would have a decision to make—one she feared she'd already made.

"Shim, I am sorry for how your father handled your illness and Lach's injury, but you have to see that I can win this war."

He used his free hand to touch her face. "I see that you can die. Gods, Bron, a handful of days wasn't enough."

She was going to have to show him. She couldn't tell him what she was going to do. They would shut down. But she knew them. She knew what they longed for. She would make love with them and when they reached out for the true bond, she would take it, give them her soul.

And she would have her answer.

There was no more point in talking. She went to her tiptoes. Shim was so tall. He made her feel small and delicate though years of hard work had proven to her how sturdy she was. She brushed her lips to his.

It was good to feel feminine. They reminded her of all that should have been hers.

She should have been a fragile thing, a sweet princess who waved at her people from the palace walls as her husbands made the decisions. She should have laughed with her maids as her mother had. Her whole world would have been wrapped up in children and love and making things beautiful.

But she knew too much. She couldn't go back. She wasn't that dainty girl.

She was a warrior. She had to fight.

And, in this case, the battle would be a sweet one.

"Bron, you're killing me." Shim kissed her again, his tongue playing along the seam of her lips. "We need to talk."

"There's nothing to talk about." She ran her hands up his chest, reveling in the feel of his ripped stomach. For all his previous weakness, he was a muscular man. Every inch of him was lean and hard. She let her hands drift to his tight waist and pulled his hips to hers. It wasn't something she could get away with when making love with Lach. He would turn her over his knee and smack her ass if she thought about taking over, but Shim liked it when she got aggressive. She could feel how much it made him feel wanted.

She let her tongue forage deep as she rubbed against him.

She adored the differences in them. Because they were split, she could really know every aspect of the man. His dominant half and his softer heart. She was welcomed to both sides of his souls. He was right there, a whole man laid out in two parts ready for her to love, to adore, to worship. She couldn't think of anything better.

Yet she had something she had to do. She had a plan in her brain and it was a horrible thing. But it just might work.

She felt Shim's hands skim her breasts as he came up for air.

"Please tell me this isn't good-bye."

It wasn't. She hoped it wasn't. "Can't we just make love?"

He sighed and she felt the moment he gave in. He leaned over and picked her up, his strong arms lifting her high on his chest. He walked toward their base.

Lach sat on the bed Shim had made, his head in his hands. He looked up as they approached. For a single second, she could see his naked pain before a mask of cold will settled over him.

"It won't work, Bron. I won't accept good-bye." He straightened his shoulders. "You should go to bed because we have a long trek in the morning. I'll find a way into Aoibhneas. I will find us a way home. I understand what Roan's been doing. He's using the fact that the guards are patrolling to start building an army for Beck and Cian Finn. I won't allow you to be used."

He wouldn't allow her to be in a moment's danger no matter how important it was to her soul. He needed his arrogance, but it got to her sometimes. She wrapped her arms around Shim's neck and kissed him, knowing exactly how to get to Lachlan McIver. She let her tongue play against Shim's, allowing it to show as they kissed. She could feel Lach's interest rise.

"It won't work, Bron. You can't fuck your way out of this." Lach's voice was hoarse.

She didn't intend to fuck her way out of it. She intended to show them the truth of her.

Shim lowered her to the bed, his weight coming down on top of her. She opened her mind to him. His had been open from the moment she'd kissed him. His cock was hard, pressed against the leather of his trousers. He loved the feel of his own arousal. He loved the fact that it wouldn't be long before he would be inside her. He craved it.

Shim broke off the kiss long enough to pull the shirt over his head. "Take it off."

He wasn't normally dominant. She felt her eyes narrow. "Why?"

His face went hard and he reached down and flipped her over. A loud smack filled the air. Bron gasped. Shim had never spanked her. Never even hinted at it. But he knew how to do it. He slapped her ass in three quick successions and then he flipped her back over. "I said take off your shirt."

Bron felt Lach's eyes on her. He watched her with a heated stare. Sweet and slow didn't do it for Lach. He liked it hard. He liked it rough. He might be able to ignore them, to hold on to his righteousness if Shim kissed her and petted her and treated her delicately. Shim was trying to draw his other half in with his show of dominance.

And Bron could help him by being difficult. "I don't want to."

He ripped her shirt off, holding it between his hands and tugging it

285

into two pieces. He bared her breasts and then caught her nipples in between his thumbs and forefingers, twisting with force. Her eyes watered and her pussy got soft and moist.

"This is my time, Bron. We agreed to it. You obey in our bed because you won't obey anywhere else."

She bristled at the accusation. "I'm not given much of a chance to disobey."

Her nipples were tweaked again, pain making them throb with awareness.

"No back talk." Shim drew his hand away. He got off the bed and lifted the bottom of her skirt. He tugged it over her hips, dragging and tossing it aside. "Turn over and put your ass in the air."

"What do you think you're doing, brother?" Lach asked. He was standing over them, his arms crossed over his massive chest and a frown on his face. "You don't believe in discipline."

Shim didn't. Bron had figured that much out. He believed in play and fun and studying. He was an odd combination of sweet, playful, and intensely smart. He reminded her so much of Cian, though he held a wealth of soul-deep guilt her brother didn't have. There was a river that ran between Lach and Shim. They loved each other, held on to each other, but she wasn't sure they trusted each other.

Bron wanted to know why.

"If you're not going to make sure she behaves, then I have to." Shim looked at his brother, an arrogant expression on his face. "Feel free to leave. I can handle her just fine. When she doesn't behave, I'll simply torture her for a while."

Shim picked up her ankles in both hands and flipped her over, forcing her to her stomach. Her ass was naked and cool air caressed her skin, but only for a moment before Shim smacked her fleshy cheeks again, the sound cracking the air around her.

"Damn it," she complained. "That hurt."

It had, but now there was a sweet heat in the place of the pain. She wriggled her hips.

Lach seemed to decide to be the voice of reason. "Can't you see what she's doing? She thinks she can manipulate us with sex."

Shim's hands were on her ass, tracing the curves and making her shiver. "She can try. It doesn't mean it will work. More than likely she'll play the siren and call me to her and get a cock up her ass for her troubles."

He parted her cheeks. Bron tensed. "I don't know about this."

Three smacks made her howl. He was serious.

"Where did you think this was going, *a chumann*?" Shim spread her legs wide. "Did you think I would be satisfied with your pussy? Never. I want to fuck every part of you. I want your mouth and your pussy, and I definitely want that tight ass around my cock. I've watched it. I watched it one night in my cousin's club. A pretty sub was being initiated. Her dominant partner tied her down. Legs and arms. She couldn't move. She was draped over an ottoman. He was a vampire, of course, as was she. A little blonde thing and I wondered how she would take it. His cock was so big, but she allowed him to tie her down."

"I remember." Lach's voice was a low roll of thunder. Shim's plan was working. Bron could see Lach's erection tenting his pants. "Her ass was in the air, like it was the center of her whole being. He spanked her first. He used his hand and then a paddle. He got her nice and pink. I thought he was hurting her, but then he held his fingers up and they were coated in her cream. That spanking had made her pussy all juicy."

She gasped as Shim smacked her ass. He struck again and again, never giving her a moment to take it in. He slapped her ass, the fleshy parts and then right at her center, along the crack. Heat bubbled up from within, making her heart race. The pain each time was brief like the cusp of hurt that quickly turned to something erotic before flaring again. Wave after wave of pain and heat and sparks of pleasure hit her as Shim continued his torture.

Goddess, she wouldn't have expected it from him, but she was the reason for this dominant show. She bridged them and they could access each other, understand each other, so much more now that they were all on the same plane. Shim could understand Lach's need to dominate and temper it with his need to worship.

That's what this was for them. It was a revelation. This play, as they called it, was another form of deep affection, a way to show her their love.

She lost count at fifteen. She simply gave over to all of it and felt the pain melt away. Everything melted. The past and the future. The war. Their own problems. All that mattered was the smack of Shim's hand on her ass. A dreamy feeling took over. She didn't have to be a princess here or on the run. She could exist fully in this one moment, forever held in their love and admiration. She only needed to serve them and be served by them.

This was a safe place.

Shim stopped, but it didn't matter. She was exactly where she wanted to be.

"Show me," Lach commanded.

She sighed as she felt Shim's hand on the folds of her pussy, pressing in and around. He moved easily because like the woman in the fantasy, she was juicy and ripe.

"She enjoys discipline," Shim said. Then she could hear as he softly sucked the juice off his fingers.

Lach chuckled and she felt the bed dip. "It's a good thing since she obviously will require so much of it. But you remember the rest, don't you, brother?"

"I do." She felt Shim's hands on her hips. "Higher, love. And spread your knees."

He forced her knees wider until she was in a position that left her utterly vulnerable. She was bent over with her ass high in the air and her legs spread wide so her cheeks split and exposed her asshole to the cool night air. She might have protested, might have felt a deep shame, but the spanking had taken her past that. It had placed her somewhere it no longer mattered. Silly things like shame and embarrassment held no sway here. There was only sweet submission.

"I remember the way the other dominant men admired the sub's pretty hole." Shim was talking around his fangs now.

Bron shivered at the thought. Those fangs were delicious. They carried her somewhere else as much as their cocks did. When her men fed, she was pierced by sweetness and a deep, bonding intimacy.

"It is beautiful," Lach said. "But she's so small. Do you think she can take a cock?"

"I've played around. I've stretched her, but Julian told us the discomfort can be replaced by our pleasure."

They would share it with her, the feel of breaching her tight asshole. They would send out just how good it felt.

"Yes, love," Shim said, obviously picking up on her thoughts. She would have to learn how to not think so loud around her husbands. "We'll share the feeling."

Lach growled as his fingertips traced the line of her spine. "We'll let you know how hot your ass is and how tightly your muscles clench down on our cocks. Gods, Bron. It's so intimate. I remember the consort's face as she first took a cock."

"She whimpered and cried a bit as her lover forced his dick in. He had to be careful, so careful. He had to seduce her ass, an inch here and a little more there until finally it opened to its master and swallowed him whole." Shim's fingers rimmed her hole, and sure enough a whimper was forced from her throat.

She wanted to protest. She wasn't sure this was a thing that could work. She was small and their cocks were so large. She'd only taken Shim's fingers, and only for a night or two. She wasn't even sure she liked the sensation, but their desire was overwhelming.

"Did the consort like it?" Bron asked, her voice coming out on a squeak as she felt Shim dribble oil on her asshole. She'd been told the vampires always carried a small bottle of what they called lubricant. Vampires, it seemed to Bron, were a deeply perverted people if part of their preparations for daily life were to always be ready should the chance to fuck an asshole arise.

Shim worked the oil in, over and around, massaging her most intimate place. She felt her asshole quiver as though it meant to fight and keep the invader out.

Lach's hand traced up her spine and settled on her neck, a possessive gesture. "The consort submitted and took her master's cock. She was beautiful and she was rewarded with a long orgasm and a deeper bond. But I worry that isn't what you want."

"I do want to be closer." It wasn't a lie. And she definitely wanted them to know her better.

He stroked her hair as Shim worked her ass. "I'm not stupid. I might be the warrior half, but my brain functions, too. You're going to bond. You're going to show us what you need and then you expect that we will be so overwhelmed by love for you that we'll let you fight, but I think it will work the opposite way. We'll be so madly in love we'll protect you more and that will make you hate us."

A simple truth came to her. She wasn't ready to say the words yet.

She wasn't there. She'd loved in her dreams, but reality had smacked her straight in the gut. Reality was so much harder, and they'd had a lifetime to come to terms. But she knew one thing for absolute certain. "I could never hate you."

"I pray to Danu that is true." He leaned over and kissed her, a soft brushing of lips against lips. "Because it would kill my soul, and I don't have any power over that."

Shim's fingers foraged deep and she groaned.

A sexy smile came over Lach's lips. "What's he doing to you?"

"He's tearing me up." But it also felt good. She wasn't sure how many fingers Shim had deep in her backside, but they burned and stretched and made her nerves come alive.

"It only feels like that, love," Shim said, his fingers slipping out of her. "She's doing beautifully. She's stretched wide and waiting for a cock. But don't let her come until I get inside." He walked down toward the river.

Bron felt her eyes widen. Both? Now? But she didn't have time to protest. Lach lifted her up. She wasn't sure when he'd shed his clothes, but his body was bare, his cock standing straight up against his washboard belly. He lifted her as though she weighed nothing at all and placed her over his cock.

"Take it, Bron. Take my cock. Fuck it, Princess. Ride me."

Bron reached down and held him in her hand, pulling him into position and lining him up to her ripe pussy. She was so wet, but she still felt impaled as she began to slide onto Lach's monster cock. He filled her up. She had to control it, slipping down inch by glorious inch.

Lach gripped her hips. "Damn, woman. You're killing me. So fucking tight. So good."

She finally seated herself fully, his cock invading every inch of her pussy. She could feel him practically touching her womb. He would come inside her, filling her with his essence. She could already be carrying his child—a future king. Should she do as they asked? Should she hide herself away and bear children and let the men run the kingdom?

But didn't she owe her children a strong mother? So many obligations. She owed her future children, her dead parents, her hopeful brothers, her husbands, her people.

What did she owe herself?

"Not now, Bron. Please." Lach looked up at her with troubled eyes pleading.

He was right. It wasn't the time to worry or let future cares cloud her. This was their time, a shelter from everything else. Tomorrow might fall like a hammer on all of them, but tonight was a beautiful thing. Bonding.

Lach sighed as she drew up a bit and moved back down, his cock moving inside her. A wave of pure pleasure hit her and it was from Lachlan. He loved this, loved being inside her. This was his home.

"Lean over, love. Put your chest against Lach's." Shim had returned from the river where she was sure he'd dumped his clothes and cleaned himself. He pressed down on her back, forcing her forward.

"What's he doing?" Bron asked. Her nipples brushed against Lach's hard chest.

"Getting ready. He's oiling up his cock so he can fuck your ass, love. This is what we've always wanted. You in between us. You completing us. We weren't whole without you. We would be shells if you went away." Lach held her, opening her for his brother's invasion.

She gasped as she felt his cockhead press against her asshole.

"Feel me, love. Listen to what I'm feeling. Know me." Shim sent out a wave that slammed against her.

Every nerve in his body was focused on her. Every muscle was ready, every cell in his being awake and alive. He'd waited his whole life for this moment, and it went beyond the sex. He'd waited to bond, the true bond. He'd waited to know her. Shim didn't want sex. He wanted to make love to the woman who bridged his soul. He wanted to share with her. Even though he'd had Lach, he'd been so alone without her.

Shim didn't know how or why they had connected at so early an age, but he never questioned it. He'd known she was his and he was hers. No other women had even been a vague thought. He'd wanted Bronwyn. Needed Bronwyn.

She felt his heart pounding in his chest as he fucked in short strokes, opening her a bit more each time.

"Feel me," Lach said, his eyes steady on hers.

He loved being in her pussy, loved the feel of her all around him. He loved the heat of her body because he thought there was a cold, dead place inside him that only she could fill. He was lonely, too. Shim was light and heat, but he had only a chill. He had worried all his life that she would reject him because he was made of the cold, dead things of the planes.

She shook her head, tears filling her eyes. "No. You're not cold."

He didn't answer, but the look on his face told her he didn't believe.

She kissed him, feeling Shim as he finally breached her ass. "You're not cold, my Lachlan. You aren't cold to me."

"Never to you, love."

Shim overwhelmed her with the feel of her asshole clenching around him as he finally slid deep. If there was discomfort, she couldn't feel it. She could only feel his pleasure as he pressed in, the tightness making his balls draw up, curling in ecstasy.

It was so tight. Tighter than ever since she was packed with their cocks.

Shim pulled out almost to the rim while Lach pressed up until she could feel his balls against her flesh.

This was what she'd dreamed of. Both her men. Her Dark Ones. They filled her, surrounded her, protected and held her. For so long they had been the dream she'd retreated to, and then they were a reality she might have to flee from, but here and now they were everything.

She rode them, pumping back and forth, accepting everything they had to give. She sank into them, their pleasure, their emotion and gave them back her own.

Pleasure singed her spine, heated her skin.

She felt the moment Shim's orgasm started. It blasted through her system. She heard herself shout and the men move. Lach pulled her down, grinding into her. His pelvis rubbed across her clit, sending shivers of pleasure, opening her up, enfolding her senses.

Lach shouted beneath her, and she felt the hot wash of his orgasm filling her pussy.

They fell into a heap and Bron felt it. Both men reached out to her, opening themselves to the bond.

"*Is tú mo ghrá*," they said in one voice.

She gave them back the traditional words. *You are my love.* It's what they would have said had their marriage been properly witnessed. "*Is tú mo ghrá.*"

Bron reached out and grabbed the bond and fell headlong into chaos.

Chapter Eighteen

Bron watched her brother walk away. Was she Lach or Shim? She couldn't tell. They were mingled together inside her.

Lach. She was Lachlan. He worried about his brother, even at an early age. He was five, perhaps. And Shim seemed so much younger to Lach. And Duffy. Duffy was so small, far smaller than the brownies who kept the palace gleaming. How would they survive?

The world seemed cruel, but even now he knew his place. A troll had struck him hours before, laughing and asking if the little prince could handle a crowning. He'd whipped his tail around and smacked Lach in the head. Lach had heard Shim's cry. Lach had managed to stifle his pain, but it had been shared with his brother.

We aren't allowed to cry. Never allowed.

He'd picked up a chair, and only his mother's presence had stopped him from killing the troll.

So much rage in such a small body. Rage and anger and worry for his other half. Shim was his better half. He had to be protected at all costs. Shim was the one who contained their power to love, and Lach wanted to feel that.

He needed Shim far more than Shim needed him. And Duffy needed them both. He had to protect his brothers. Always.

The scene shifted and she felt Shim. She could tell the difference now. Shim's soul wasn't as restless as Lach's was, though now it was heavy. So heavy. He looked down at the woman on the bed and his heart ached.

Why didn't she wake up? She looked pale, but nothing else seemed wrong with her. She needed a bit of blood. His mother was a vampire. Blood. That was all. She needed to eat and then she would wake up and he could climb into her lap. He was getting too big, but mother didn't seem to mind. Mother still cuddled him close and sang songs and told him stories. Even Lach liked her stories about her home plane. And Duffy loved the songs. He was still small enough for her to carry. Sometimes Shim envied his brother. He loved being close to his mother.

Why wouldn't she wake up? Surely she hadn't meant to go swimming in the river. Everyone knew it was dangerous. She hadn't fallen in. She hadn't drowned.

She was the queen. Queens didn't drown. Mothers didn't drown. Mothers woke up and took care of their sons.

Shim looked back at the place where his father sat. He'd aged overnight, his hair going white the minute they'd brought mother in, her heavy dress dripping with water.

Who would take care of them?

He reached for his mother's hand and prayed she would wake up.

Bron's brain hurt. They bombarded her, as though both speaking at once. Lach loved his brothers and the palace. He loved running wild and knowing it would all be his one day. Shim loved the library and the books his mother had bought from all over the planes she'd traveled to. He didn't want to be king. He wanted to be a traveler, but most of all he wanted the princess. His princess. His playmate. He searched for her during the daytime and then one morning when he was just past sixteen, he read a magazine article. A DL from the vampire tablet his cousin had sent him. He would be seeing his cousin Julian soon. Oh, he was so much more worldly and wise, and he'd thought Shim should study the plane his mother had come from.

And there she was. A picture of a girl named Bronwyn Finn. His heart stopped, staring down at the photo in vivid color. The girl was wearing white and smiling, a daisy in her hair. She stood next to two strong, dark-haired lads and two vampires, a young man and a slightly older girl. Bronwyn Finn, princess of the Seelie, was visiting her cousins the Dellacourts.

Shim picked up the tablet and ran to find his brother.

And then everything seemed to slow down.

Bron stood in a barn, her hands brushing her favorite horse. Shim. This was his memory. Shim was satisfied. Satisfied with life. He missed his mother, but things were finally going well again.

And he'd found her. He'd found the girl from their dreams. Shim smiled and patted his horse, thinking of Bronwyn all the while. It had been fun at first. She'd been a playmate who knew all sorts of games. And over the years, he'd known he was in love with her. Since the moment he'd realized what love was.

And now he was going to marry her. Gillian had gone to arrange a marriage. She was the only one who believed the princess in his dreams was real. He and Lach had tried to tell Father, but he didn't want to listen to them and he'd forbade them to talk about it to anyone else, but Gillian believed.

He was going to marry his Bron. She was real and his heart was so full.

And then it hurt.

Shim hit his knees. His whole body ached, and he could have sworn there was a hole in his gut. What was happening to him? Fear took over, but then he heard the hum. He heard it each night in his dreams, and when he concentrated very hard, he could sometimes hear it during the day. It was a soft noise, usually, but now it was a roar in his head that drowned out everything else.

Except his brother. He could feel his brother's panic. How could he hear his brother? Lach was on the other side of the palace, but Shim knew he was running.

And he knew something else, too. Bron was in trouble.

Bonded. Somehow, she'd reached across the planes and made that connection that tied them to each other outside of their dreams. She'd grasped some invisible thread and she was pulling him to her.

And it hurt. The agony. As though his being was yanked somewhere it shouldn't go.

He felt the fire building in his belly. He heard her panic. Despite the horrible pain, he forced himself to listen—to himself and his body. The fire was his power, given to him by the bond, pulled from him by an intensely strong bondmate.

She was in danger, and he had the power to save her.

Get me close, love. Get me close. Can you feel me? I am with you always. Always, love.

She had to listen. He could do this. He could control it. It was right there on the surface. Fire would save her, save them all.

And then his power died.

Too weak. She was too weak. Gods. Shim screamed. He could feel her fading, dying. Not now. Not when they hadn't kissed, hadn't loved, hadn't melded into one another's souls.

Rage threatened to take over. He'd been promised. He and Lachlan. She'd been promised to them. More than any crown or kingdom, she was their birthright and he wouldn't be denied.

He heard his brother shout as he did the only thing he could. He reached across the cord that connected them and sent his life to her.

As he felt her breath, he took his final gasp, and the world became fire.

Feet pounding. Panic was flooding his system. Shim. Something was wrong with Shim. Something had changed, in his head, in his soul, in the whole fucking world. He'd been standing there talking to Duffy and suddenly he'd known where Shim was, been able to feel what he felt, sense what he was thinking. He'd always been able to feel his other half, but not like this. This was overpowering, overwhelming.

And then it was over. Lach felt the connection cut and silence reigned. Nothingness. He couldn't feel Shim at all, as though he didn't exist.

Lach ran. He knew where his brother had been. The stables. And now he saw something that terrified him.

Fire blazed, engulfing every wall of the small stables where the best horses were kept. The family's private stock. And it looked like nothing would be saved.

But Shim was in there and if he couldn't be saved, then Lach had nothing left at all.

Shim was the smart one. Shim was the one who could love. Shim was the beautiful part of his soul. Without Shim, there was only Lach, and Lach was violence and dominance and cold power.

Lach didn't wish to live without the best part of his soul.

He heard Duffy screaming at him to stop, but he couldn't. If Shim was gone, then the fire could take him, too.

Heat assailed him so strong that for a moment he couldn't move, couldn't breathe. The smoke was so thick he almost couldn't focus. His eyes watered and his lungs burned. Something large knocked him down, and he watched in horror as Shim's horse fled, its entire body on fire.

But there he was. Shim lay on the floor, his body still as the flames leapt around. Some seemed to shoot from his body, but he didn't seem to be burned. His clothes were a mess, but his skin was pristine.

"Shim!" Lach screamed over the cracking of the fire. He looked overhead. The beams would come down any minute. He didn't have a second to lose. He had to get his brother out of there. He leapt across the flames, his skin scorching, and picked up his brother.

And dropped him. His flesh was on fire. Horrible burns erupted on his flesh where he'd touched his brother. The skin bubbled and boiled.

And he couldn't give up.

Lach gritted his teeth against the agony and lifted his brother again.

He screamed, the pain filling his every sense, but somehow his feet moved toward the door. Somehow he made it outside where the grass was cool.

He fell to his knees and knew beyond a shadow of a doubt that his brother was dead.

There was nothing inside Shim. Nothing at all. His body was a shell and a molten one at that. Lach's body was burned, his skin torched, every inch an agony, but something cool and calm came over him.

Power flowed for the first time. It started in his center and reached out. He could feel them. The dead. There was power in them, an unspoken essence that they each retained, whether bone or ash. Power remained and Lach called on it.

And his brother took a deep breath.

Lach fell back, his vision fading, the pain taking over. His brother was...alive? He wasn't sure. But Lach could feel his soul once more.

* * * *

Shim came out of the bond, his whole body shaking. He clenched his fists and looked down at his skin. It looked normal, but he knew now it wasn't.

He was a corpse. He had been since the day he'd given his life to save Bron's.

He was a walking, talking corpse.

"You aren't dead," Lach said harshly. His voice was strained, as though he really had been screaming, and not just in the dream. "You aren't dead. Maybe you were, but you aren't now."

Tears streamed down Bron's face. "I killed him. I killed Shim."

Gods, he didn't want her to take it that way. "No. I gave my life to you, *a chumann*. I didn't want to live without you."

She sat up, her breasts exposed in the moonlight. "Gillian didn't bring me back. Shim did."

"Yes, and somehow I brought Shim back," Lach insisted. "He isn't dead. I know when I'm reanimating someone. I can feel it."

Shim felt his eyes narrow. "And how many corpses have you reanimated over a long period of time, brother?"

Lach's face was pale, except for the scars which appeared as red as the day he'd gotten them. "More than you know. More than I want anyone to know. Shim, you're alive. I didn't remember much, but I remember now. I called on my power and it flared, like your fire. It flared in a big way and it brought you back to life. Damn it, Shim, use that brain of yours. You eat and sleep and you can feel your body. A corpse can't do that."

"You don't know. You don't know that." The thought horrified Shim. He was dead. He'd been dead. Was he still dead?

"I killed you."

Bron. He had to hold on to Bron. His head was swimming. His body felt like a foreign thing, but he moved to hold her. "You didn't kill me. You didn't."

"I felt it. I was you in that dream," she explained. "I felt my hand reach out and pull at your soul. I reached out and took your life to save mine. How could I do that? You're dead because I killed you."

"He isn't dead," Lach insisted. He got off the bed and shoved his legs into a pair of trousers. "Will either of you bloody listen to me?"

"You should have left me, Lach," Shim spat back, his anger bubbling to the surface. How could he go on knowing what he was? How could he make love to his wife when he was a dead thing animated only by his brother's power? He'd given his life for her, but Lach had brought him back and turned him into a monstrous thing.

Lach's fists clenched. "You would rather be dead than dependent on me? Is that how much I mean to you?"

Shim felt Bron stiffen in his arms. "He didn't mean that. He values you."

"What are you talking about?" Shim asked.

Bron turned her face up to him. "You said I didn't listen, but I think you're the one who missed something here. Didn't you see what he did for you? Didn't you feel why he did it?"

Shim shook his head as though he could sharpen his memory by getting rid of the cobwebs polluting his brain. They were all there now. His and Lach's and Bron's memories were shuffling through his head like a wild mixed-up stew that had been stirred and now bubbled. Lach had run into the burning building. Lach had been horribly burned—by his body—and yet he'd picked Shim up again.

And Shim was dead. Dead. Dead.

"He won't listen." Lach turned away. "And it's not about this bullshit. He felt what it's like to really be me for the first time and he doesn't want anything to do with it. Well, guess what, brother, get used to it. We're bonded, fully, and now you have a piece of my darkness inside you."

Shim didn't know what exactly was fueling him. He knew deep down he needed to take a moment, but that word kept riding him. Dead. Dead. Dead. He wouldn't have children. They would all be Lachlan's. Bron would turn away because she couldn't want a dead body in her bed. Lach had set himself up to win everything. "And you have what you always wanted, brother. You have a tiny piece of light to illuminate that wasteland you call a soul."

There was a sharp crack and a flare of pain. It took him a moment to realize where it had come from. Bron. Bron had hauled off and smacked him right across the face. Smacked him hard enough that his flesh ached.

"Don't you dare talk about him like that, you idiot. How could you? After everything he did for you, you could say that to him?" Her eyes were bright with tears as she looked up at him.

Shim felt sick. What was he doing?

Lach, his brother, his other half, his protector, turned away.

Shim held his hand to his cheek, a horrible wave of guilt crashing over him. "Lach."

"Don't," Lach insisted. "There's nothing to say. I always knew it would be this way. Don't you think I knew you were the better part of us? It's why I couldn't let you go. But you aren't dead. I gave you some of my life or my soul. I don't know how it worked. I just know I pulled every ounce of power I could and I focused it on you. Maybe you weren't dead. Your power was still flaring. I only know that I focused everything I had on saving you. And I've done worse things, brother. Things you don't know about. Things you and Duffy won't ever forgive me for. But I did it because I love you both. I don't know how to live without you. But I'll figure it out. I'll see Bronwyn home, and then I'm going to leave. There's no place for me here."

Lach stalked off. Shim felt a roiling shame. Now all the memories were surfacing. How sick he'd been. How long he'd lain in an odd fugue state, somewhere between living and dead, and how his brother had never left his side.

How could he have said that to him?

Bron got out of bed, her every movement a brisk and angry testament to her emotional state. "I don't know that I will ever forgive you for that."

"Bron, I'm sorry." The words sounded stupid. Idiotic. Futile.

"You know how he feels and you still say such things to him? He was trying to save you because he thought he was worthless without you. He thought he was a dumb animal without your half of his soul." She pulled Shim's shirt over her head. "I have to find him."

Shim got to his feet. So much had gone wrong. It should have been a beautiful thing, their true bond. It should have been followed with more lovemaking and the taking of her sweet blood. But it felt as if everything was ashes and he was the reason.

And he'd forgotten what he'd learned of Bron.

He'd seen her. He'd seen what a sweet child she'd been. Loved and coddled and slightly marginalized because her brothers were so much more important. He'd felt her overwhelming will to live, and not simply because it was an animal instinct, but because she hadn't been finished. She hadn't done what she'd needed to do.

She needed to make a difference. She needed to matter in some tangible way, in some way past her soft body and sweet looks.

Bronwyn Finn McIver needed to fight.

Shim sat down on the bed, his head in his hands and his heart aching in his chest. He'd messed everything up because he'd refused to listen to the two people who mattered most in his world.

Lachlan needed to protect his heart, and he wrongly thought it resided in Shim's soul. Bronwyn needed to matter and Shim had locked her away so she could never be what she needed to be.

He'd fucked up.

And there was only one way to make it right. He had to talk to his brother, and he had to convince him that Bron's fight was their fight.

If she wanted a battle, then they would be right by her side. He wouldn't lock her away. The things he loved most about her were her fierce heart and the love she was capable of. If he locked her away, some beautiful piece of her would die, and he couldn't be the one who did that to her.

There was a loud crack. Shim froze in place because he'd heard it before. The sound of an eddy wind charging in.

Shim took off running because it looked like the battle had found them.

Chapter Nineteen

Lach felt the moment the eddy wind covered the air above him. He had a split second before there were soldiers on the ground.

And his sword was back at camp. Gods, he'd walked off without his sword.

Immediately Lach reached out to try to find the dead and call them to aid, but his power was so much weaker now.

Why couldn't he call it?

"Lach?" Bron's voice called through the trees as the soldiers surrounded him.

How many? Too many. And he wasn't sure where Bron was. He struck out, his fists his only weapon. There were dead around, but only animals, and small ones at that. He was in a forest, far from the cemeteries and crypts that would have brought him an army.

He felt a burning sensation at his side.

He threw his elbow behind him and caught a soldier in the face. Where was Bron?

And then a shout came up and the sound of metal on metal. There was a clanging and a roar.

Duffy wielded his axe, cutting soldiers off at the legs. They fell to their knees, large hacking wounds making it impossible for them to walk. A soldier brought his sword down on Duffy's head, but Duffy simply kept fighting.

"Get Bronwyn!" Duffy shouted. "Get her and my Gilly out of here.

This is my job, brother. This is my fight."

Lach looked down at his little brother, so much pain in his heart, but Duffy was right. It was his time, no matter what Lach wanted.

Lach fought his way out of the throng as the first sonic boom hit. Roan had found his way to them and he and his vampires were battling the soldiers. So were the men from Aoibhneas. Nate and Zane were fighting, knives in their hands.

Bron. He had to find Bron.

And then he saw her. She stood at the clearing, facing the river. She was dressed in nothing but Shim's battered shirt, her sweetly curved legs bare and her naked feet in the grass. She looked so young and fragile.

And the hag held her by the neck.

The hag, with her midnight-black hair and even darker eyes, smiled and held up her hand, and in a wink of an eye was gone, her body pulled up by the eddy wind she'd ridden.

His sweet Bron vanished.

Shim came running, but the battle was done. He looked up into the air, lifting his hands. Lach could sense what he was going to do and ran to tackle him. He hit Shim full force and held his hands down.

"You can't use your power. You don't know what that will do."

"My power can't hurt Bron," Shim insisted. "Fire can't hurt her. She was in the middle of that fire for minutes when we found her the first time. It knows who its master is."

"And air? How about that, Shim? If you burn away the eddy cloud and she falls a hundred or two hundred feet, how will you save her this time?" Lach felt sick.

And then he felt her. A calm presence. Bronwyn's voice filled his head.

Bring the war to me. Bring them all to me. She won't kill me. You have time and I have power. I love you. I love you both. Trust in me. Believe in me.

Lach sat back, her words hitting him like a hammer. He knew what she intended to do.

"We have to go after her," Shim said, standing up. "They'll take her to the palace."

It would be the sensible thing to do. He could rally whatever troops were left and he could search for her. He could save her and carry her away and give the fight back to her brothers. He could still have what he wanted.

But it wasn't what Bron wanted. What Bron wanted was a chance to end the war. She didn't want the crown and she no longer wanted revenge. He'd felt that deep in her soul. She wanted to end the war, to bring back the kingdom of her youth and to give her people their freedom.

His wife was a hero and he'd been a coward.

He shook his head. "No. We go to Aoibhneas. We gather her brothers and whatever troops we have and then we march."

Shim stared at him for a moment. "But that leaves her in danger."

"It leaves her in a place where she can turn the tide." He didn't want it. Every cell of his body revolted at the thought, but Bronwyn mattered more.

"And if she dies?" Shim asked.

His heart would be a gaping hole. His life would be over. "Then we'll find her through that door Duffy talked about. We found her once. We'll find her again. But if we don't let her try this, she won't be the same woman we love."

Shim took a long breath and held his hand out, gripping Lach's. "Then we are in agreement. And Lach, I am so sorry. I didn't mean it. Alive or dead, I am your brother and I love you. I am grateful to be walking and loving our wife."

Lach stood. The forest around them was quiet now, the soldiers disappearing with their hag. They'd found their prize and once it was in hand, none of the rest of them mattered.

"Where is Her Highness?" Roan asked.

"Gone." The word sounded hollow.

Dante's clothes were torn, covered in blood, though he bore no mark of his own. It was easy to see how he'd healed so quickly. Kaja bore two holes in her neck. She'd obviously forced her husband to feed and heal after the battle. She looked up with tears in her eyes.

"Gone? How?" Kaja asked.

Shim came to his side. "The hag took her, but Bron wanted to go."

Dellacourt snarled their direction. "She wanted to be taken? She wanted a hag to cart her back to the very man who had her killed in the first place?"

Charlie, the boy from Aoibhneas, walked with an arm around each of his fathers. "I can hear her."

Shim stepped forward. "What do you mean?"

Nate looked down at his son. "He's stronger now, but maybe his time there is still affecting him."

Lach wasn't about to put up with that. He'd been marginalized for far too long. "No. Listen to him. Let him speak. If he says he hears Bronwyn, then I want to know what she's saying."

Charlie looked him in the eye. "She's not really saying anything, but she's feeling. She's feeling strong and she wants the rest of us to feel strong, too. She's ready." Charlie stood up, pushing his fathers away a bit so he could stand on his own. "I'm ready. We're all going to be ready."

Lach nodded, his mission clear. To bring the battle to Bronwyn. Like it or not, he was her soldier now.

"Lach, you have to come quick." Gillian was suddenly at his side. Tears streaked down her face. Harry stood behind her, a deep frown creasing his brow.

Gillian grasped his hand. He allowed himself to be pulled as he looked back at Roan.

"Prepare to move. We're heading into Aoibhneas. Someone find that damn phooka. He'll know a way. He's herded us to this point. The least he can do is get us where we need to be." He followed after Gillian and then his heart nearly broke.

Duffy.

It was time. Time to say good-bye.

"He saved me." Gillian wept. "He fought so hard, but they kept attacking him. Lach, do something. I should be able to heal that wound. I've laid hands on him. I've sent him everything I have. Why won't he heal?"

Tears welled in Lach's eyes. "Because the dead don't heal."

Shim gasped behind him. "Oh, gods. He died days ago. That's how you knew I was alive. Because Duffy died and you've kept him with us."

Duffy's eyes came open.

"I'm so sorry, brother." Lach looked down at the wee gnome who had been his heart friend for as long as he'd known what a heart was. Duffy had been their companion, their playmate.

"I knew it. I always knew it, brother." Duffy sat up, looking down at the wound on his chest. It wasn't bleeding. "I was mad at first, but now I know why I got to stay. I did it, Lach. I fought and I won. I got me battle and I saved me girl. Even though she never was me girl. It don't matter. I get that now. It don't matter that she couldn't love me back. It only matters that I loved her and I got to be a better man because I loved her."

Gillian. All those long years, Duffy had still loved Gillian, his childhood crush on her forming the core of his being. Lach had known Duffy had a thing for Gillian. Even from a young age he'd refused to call her sister. He'd loved her from afar and now he'd sacrificed for her.

Bronwyn loved them back. She didn't deserve any less. Love was something Lach had worried about all of his life. He'd called what he felt for Bronwyn love, but he'd always worried it was more about possession and obsession, that his dark heart couldn't hold a softer emotion.

He'd been wrong. He loved his brothers. Loved his father and mother. Loved his sister.

Gods, he loved Bronwyn Finn and there was nothing dark about it. She was his light, not Shim. However their soul had split, it was in him to love. His heart wasn't a cold, dead thing. It was huge and it could only get larger. He loved Bronwyn and that meant loving every piece of her, including the part of her soul that demanded she fight.

He'd adored the girl who ran through his dreams. He'd lusted after the lover, but he worshipped the woman she'd become. Not simply a princess, but a queen. A woman was always a queen. She was the queen of her home and her family. Bron's family was simply bigger than most, and like every woman with a family, she would sacrifice. She would make the world right for them, giving her body and soul to those she nurtured and loved.

He would be strong. His woman had taught him what his father never had—how to truly be a king.

He looked at his sister and whispered. "He's loved you for always. Give him something."

She nodded and sank to her knees, tears falling like raindrops. She leaned over and kissed him. "You are my hero, Duffy."

A brilliant smile lit Duffy's face. "That's all I ever wanted to be." He gripped her hand, his small compared to hers. He looked up at Lach. "You have to let me go now, brother."

Lach knew the moment had been coming from the instant he'd reached out and pulled Duffy from death. He'd felt Duffy die in that black cloud that had been meant for him and he'd reacted. He'd called on his power and brought him back. "I didn't want to let you go. Not alone, Duffy. I don't know what's out there. I didn't want you to die."

Duffy smiled up at him. "Dying ain't nothing to be afraid of. Be afraid of not living. I got me battle. I got what I always wanted. I got to be a hero. Now, it's time for me to find another adventure. There's a door, Lach. It was right there and it was calling to me. And I weren't alone. I saw me mothers. Both of them. The one what raised me and the one what gave me birth. Death is a doorway. I want to know where it leads. I want the adventure that waits for me and whatever happens, I'll see you again. I'll conquer whatever is out there and make a place for us."

His tears fell now. For Duffy, for Bron, for himself, for Shim.

"I love you, brother." Shim got to his knees and put a hand on Lach and reached for Duffy.

"Love you, too." Duffy's voice had gone hoarse. "You were the best brothers I could have hoped for."

Lach reached out and completed the circle. He and Duffy and Shim. His childhood in a circle of hands grasping. "I love you both. My brothers. I will keep you in my heart, Duffy."

"That is a good place to be."

Lach released his hold.

Duffy smiled, closed his eyes, and walked into eternity.

Lach rose to his feet a completely different man. He looked to Roan. "Gather what we need. We make for Aoibhneas tonight after I bury my brother."

He expected an argument but Roan bowed. "Yes, Your Highness. I am at your service."

"As am I." The phooka leapt from the trees and, in an instant, switched to his horse form. "I will get us to Aoibhneas. I know a secret way in."

"Dad, isn't that Uncle Max's horse?" Charlie asked.

Zane shook his head. "We're just going to go with it, son. And I know exactly what you're talking about. The mayor has a series of caves he keeps hidden. We know how to get home."

"Then we leave in an hour," he commanded.

Shim picked up Duffy, holding his small body close. "Lach, I…"

Lach shook his head. "I love you, brother. No more fighting. All that matters is winning this war and getting our wife back."

Shim nodded and followed. Lach prayed the morning would find him closer to his goal—getting Bronwyn back in his arms.

* * * *

Bronwyn awakened to the smell of home. She could smell the bread the bakers in the White Palace made for each and every meal. It was a smell that had haunted her dreams since she'd fled. She'd tried to recreate the bread, snowy white and buttery soft with the smallest hint of honeyed sweetness, but never got it right.

She opened her eyes because no matter how lovely the smell was, this place was no longer home. She groaned, her head aching. How long had she been here? A day at least, though it already seemed like a lifetime. A day away from her husbands. Would she ever see them again?

"The hags certainly worked you over."

Bron turned her head and then wished she hadn't. Her every muscle ached. She was so, so weary. All through the long night the hags had tortured her with spell after strength-sucking spell. Pain had wracked her system and then a horrible weakness had overtaken her.

"They're sleeping now. They don't sleep often and no one knows where they go to do it, but it seems the only time they don't listen in."

A blonde woman came into view. She was regally perfect, with her thin crown and slender figure. Cold blue eyes and a narrow chin completed the usurper queen's appearance.

"Maris. To what do I owe this honor?" Bron wished she had the saliva in her mouth to spit at the bitch.

Maris chuckled a bit. "Goddess, you're loud. I actually heard that."

Bron's whole heart sagged. She'd forgotten. Maris was a bondmate. It was exactly why she'd been engaged to Bron's brothers. How could she pull this off if the queen herself knew what she was planning?

A smile curled Maris's thin lips. "You've been an annoying hum in my head for years."

She'd been so stupid. So very dumb. She should have listened to her husbands. She wasn't cut out for this. She was just a girl. She was still a dumb girl.

"Stop scaring her, Maris," a deep voice said.

The queen rolled her eyes. "It's the only fun I have anymore."

Niall stepped out, dressed in the livery of the Queen's Guard. "Your Highness, I see you finally made it. Though I might point out that if we'd done this my way, you wouldn't have been horribly tortured last night, and most likely for a few nights to come."

"A little torture never hurt a girl," Maris said. "And she looks strong. If she's anything like her brutish brother, then she should know a thing or two about torture."

Niall frowned her way. "You know he doesn't like it when you talk about Beck. He explained that."

Maris nodded and a bit of her bile seemed to flee. "I know. I hold on to it though because my fear of Beck's proclivities is what got us here in the first place. Where is he?"

"Making certain the hags aren't around," Niall explained. "And why are you here? If your husband catches you, he'll find us all out."

A slender shoulder shrugged. "Torin is scared of the girl. He was angry the hags brought her to the palace in the first place. I had to think fast on my feet or he would have had her throat slit. Torin's guard would have done it in a heartbeat. We don't own them, Niall. I saved her. I should think he would be pleased with me."

"Who are you talking about? Goddess, am I in some strange dream?" Bron asked. She was so confused.

"Drink this." Maris held a cup to her mouth and forced her head back. It was slipping down her throat before she could cough it back up. "Give it a minute."

She stepped back and Bron tried to gag, but her arms were bound tight to the chair she sat in. The hags—she'd discovered there were two of them—had cackled as they'd cinched her in tight and began the ritual that would loosen her soul from her body. Now Maris had used her bindings to force some poison on her.

Maris grinned at Niall. "She thinks I killed her."

Niall sighed and got to one knee. "Bron, Maris is on our side."

Bron shook her head. If there was one thing she knew, it was that Maris was an evil bitch. "No. She's the one who let Torin in."

Maris shrugged. "Can't a girl make a few mistakes? Ooops. I made the wrong move and got your parents killed. Your father has forgiven me."

"My father?" What Niall had said before came back to her. Her father had become a sluagh and chained himself to this place. At the time she'd barely believed it. Could it be true? "My father is here?"

A cool wind seemed to pass through Bron and a phantom coalesced in front of her. Her father floated, an insubstantial but welcome presence. "Hello, my little pixie. It's been a long while."

A sob threatened to escape her throat. "Father."

He smiled down at her. A ghostly hand reached out to touch her face. "We have so little time. The hags are waking. You've figured out what you are? And what you can do?"

She nodded. "I'm a conduit. That's what they called me."

"Your mind works on a frequency that every bondmate can hear, and you can access your brothers' powers." His voice, not quite above a whisper, tightened. "If you've tapped into power, I have to assume your brothers are here. Beck and Cian have come into their powers, then? They've formed a true triad?"

Bron stared at her father. "No. I mean yes. They have bonded and have power, but they aren't here yet."

The ghostly figure in front of her frowned. "Then whose power have you accessed? It should only work with a true triad."

"My husbands," she replied. "Lachlan and Shim McIver, princes of the Unseelie Fae. My Dark Ones."

Her father's image shimmered for a moment and then became a bit more solid. "They were real."

So real. "Yes. And they're here. They're going to Aoibhneas to gather the troops."

Her father was silent for a moment. "So many things to have

gotten wrong. It doesn't matter anymore. All that matters is they will come. If they came for you each night in your dreams, they will come for you now. You have to be brave, my daughter. You have to be the princess I never taught you to be. I am so sorry to require this of you, but you can't do what you need to do until the battlefield is set."

Niall stepped in when her father became quiet. He pulled a knife from his belt. Her knife. "I didn't do what I should have done. I didn't find another to take your place. I came back here to wait for you. There is only one Princess Bronwyn, and I knew she would come here. This is for you when we win the day. We have to kill Torin and the hags, too. We get one shot at this. They've become very powerful."

"They control the guards for Torin," Maris explained. "If you don't kill the guards as well, even with the hags gone, they will continue to fight and continue with their mission to kill you and your brothers and everyone who is against them. Even now Torin is pulling them back from Aoibhneas since you're here. They will guard the palace now and they will be in place when the kings arrive. Goddess, tell me they're bringing an army with them."

Bron hoped so, too. "I know the Unseelie are sending a force. And from what Lachlan told me the village will come."

Maris groaned. "I hate that village. They're all insane. Aoibhneas is where the crazies go. The mountains do something to their brains. And I heard some of them prefer to walk about naked. I pray they bring weapons."

Bron wanted a few answers. "Why are you doing this?"

Maris's cornflower-blue eyes turned down. "I was a foolish girl."

"You hated my brothers."

She shook her head. "I hated the fact that my father sold me to them. I was chattel and nothing more, and Cian couldn't stand the sight of me. And quite frankly, Beckett Finn scared me. I'd heard rumors that he liked to hurt his partners."

"I explained that, Maris." Her father's voice was a tortured groan.

"I know, but I didn't understand at the time. I wanted a way out. I was in love, you see. I loved my maid. We grew up together and somewhere along the way, I realized she was everything to me. We kissed when we were sixteen. The day before I was sold to your brothers. I was scared I would lose her. I thought Torin would be easier. He would reward me for helping him and send me on my way and Anna and I could be happy." She took a deep breath. "I did it all because I loved a girl. A girl who Torin killed because she wasn't pure. Your father found me. He forgave me. I don't know why."

"Because death clarifies all things in life, Maris," her father said, his voice warm. "And I know that forgiveness is the greatest gift we have to give and a thing we should pray to receive. Hating you wouldn't have solved anything, but reaching out and offering absolution did. It brought us here. It will bring us victory." His gaze turned back to Bron. "Do not misunderstand me, daughter. I have not given up the after with your mother because I want vengeance. I gave it up because I want my children to know peace."

Maris frowned. "Well, I want the bastard dead, and I don't care how it happens. I would have done it myself but killing Torin doesn't take care of the hags, and they're worse. Your father figured out what you are long ago and set Niall out to find you. I've done my duty and kept that bastard busy, but I'm ready to be finished. I'm ready to face Beck and Cian and whoever they've married and accept their judgment."

Maris wanted to die.

Her father cocked a head sideways as though he heard something the rest of them couldn't. "They're coming. All of you out. Bron has to face this alone. Bronwyn, they won't kill you. Stay strong. They think that by eating bondmates' souls they can take the psychic power into themselves, but they can't hear you. When they're through, reach out and find strength in your brothers and sisters. They wait for you."

Niall and Maris were already out the door and her father faded.

Bron reached out, but to a different mind. She reached out to Lach and Shim. She felt their love before the door opened and the hags filled her world.

She shut it down because her husbands didn't need to know what was happening to her.

* * * *

Deep in the night, when the agony was done, Bron wondered how much more she could take. They'd bombarded her again and again with spells. Some took her strength, some her will. The worst was the one that robbed her of all her joy.

Call to them. Her father had told her to. Apparently she'd been calling all of her life so it made sense to do so again. She couldn't call to Lach and Shim. They would be terrified. She had to find strength another way.

Hello.

A simple thing. A greeting, but it was all her mind could handle.

Hello, I am Erin. The voice was quiet, but she heard it all the same. And she felt a tiny spark of energy.

I am Wes. Again, a voice and a bit of strength shared among prisoners.

I am Mina.

They came when she called. A hundred voices with sparks of strength that alone would have been nothing at all, but together, they bound her in will and power, re-forming her soul. They gave what they could and connected together through Bronwyn's brain and heart.

I am Maris. That voice was quiet, tentative, but the energy she sent was not.

They continued through the night. By morning, Bron was smiling when the hags entered and she opened her mind to her loves.

Come for me. My time is now.

Chapter Twenty

Shim looked around the village and wished Bron was with him. She would love Aoibhneas. It was beautiful and the inhabitants were all slightly insane.

But Bron was miles away and he couldn't get to her.

And his brother was gone as well.

Shim took a deep breath and hoped the mayor had one sane bone in his body. "I promise not to make any deals with demons. Now can we sign this treaty and begin preparations?"

Mayor Mel leaned forward. "You have passed the truth tests."

The truth tests had involved drinking an enormous amount of some liquor the mayor made himself and then answering a bunch of questions because the mayor believed no one could lie when drunk. The mayor had asked him and Lach a multitude of questions about their feelings on demons and parallel planes. He seemed to think that somewhere out there was another him and this other version of the mayor had it all wrong and shouldn't be worried about creatures from the skies, but rather about demons. Shim and Lach, for their parts, had mostly talked about how much they missed Bronwyn and her breasts. Getting drunk made Shim think about all of his wife's soft parts, and he'd been sick with worry over her. Well, and with the liquor.

Finally this morning Roan had found the tear in the wall and gotten Lachlan through to bring the Seelies back.

Shim wished they would hurry. He'd been left to negotiate with what Dante had called a whack job.

The vampire had proven to be rather good at negotiations himself. He smiled at the mayor. "Excellent. I assure you the prince has no intentions of allowing demons to take over his kingdom."

Shim shook his head. "Not at all. It's written down somewhere."

And if it wasn't, Shim would make it a law.

A woman with steel-gray hair stared the mayor down. "Sign the documents. You know we're going in."

"Fine, woman. You don't have to harp on me." He winked at his wife. "But you better tell the women because if I know their husbands, they'll start trying to lock them up and keep them out of this."

The mayor's wife grinned. "I made sure they all have keys to the lockups, and each has a sonic sword and one of those cannon things." She looked over at the vampire. "One of our daughters bonded with a royal vampire by the name of Stefan. He makes sure we have all the weapons we need."

Dante piped up. "And all the sex toys, too, I bet. Sorry. Talbot Industries makes billions off the toy market. And now I find out he's an arms dealer, too. Kaj, when we get back to our plane, remind me to buy up Talbot stock. I like him. He's smart."

Kaja smiled at her husband indulgently and shook her head. Shim didn't believe Kaja and her husband were ever going back to the Vampire plane. Not for more than a visit. She seemed happy here in Aoibhneas.

The mayor signed his name with a flourish and stood. The town square was filled with villagers, all anxiously waiting. Shim could see the Harper clan standing near the boy named Charlie. Paige had her hand clasped firmly in his. They were young, far too young to wed, but it was plain to see the love in their eyes.

The whole village seemed to quiet as the mayor stepped up. "We go to war."

A huge shout seemed to shake the ground. There were hugs and slaps on the back and celebratory cheers.

All for a war that might take his wife's life.

"Your Highness? You seem sad." Rachel Harper placed a hand on his arm.

"I'm frightened." He probably shouldn't admit it, but it was true.

She sighed. "So am I. We all are but we're more afraid of living like this than we are of dying."

Shim's eyes threatened to water again. Damn it. It was always there, that fine edge of grief at his brother's passing. He kept expecting to look down and see Duffy at his side, making a wisecrack and hauling his axe with him.

Shim hadn't been able to leave the axe behind. Perhaps he should have, but something deep inside wouldn't let him, as though he had to keep a piece of his brother with him.

He kind of wished he had something of Lach's now. And Bron's.

"I was so sorry to hear of your brother's passing." Rachel Harper looked up at him with kind eyes.

She was going to fight. Shim knew it. She would fight and her older children would, too. Her husbands would fight. She was probably terrified, but she would do it because it was the right thing. Rachel understood what Bron knew, what Shim was only starting to discover. "He would have been honored to fight at your side."

A ghost of a smile curved up her lips. "I thought this wasn't your fight, Your Highness."

"It's everyone's fight. That's why they call it the good fight, isn't it?"

She curtseyed, the first formal gesture he'd seen from anyone on the plane. "You will do your kingdom proud, Your Highness."

Shim stood in the middle of the square and breathed in as Bron brushed against him with her mind.

Come for me. My time is now.

She was so serene, so perfectly powerful. She was ready.

And Lach wasn't here.

"Mrs. Harper, thank you, but I need to find Harry." Roan had gone with Lach.

Dellacourt was suddenly at his side. "What's wrong?"

"Bron's ready. We have to go." He took a long breath. She was ready and he was miles and miles away.

"Uhm, we're two days march from the palace. She better stay

ready for a while." Dellacourt looked around. "Or we can hope Roan brings back an army of bikes. Do you understand how much easier warfare is on my plane? We all sit in our rooms and fire at each other remotely. Seriously, I have snacks and drinks during wars. I always get my face fucked up on Faery planes. It's barbaric."

Shim had begun to notice the vampire talked really fast when he was getting emotional. It had annoyed him greatly at first until he'd realized that for all Dellacourt's complaints, he'd walked away from his whole world.

Dante Dellacourt fought the good fight.

"I shall try to preserve your beauty," Shim replied.

Dellacourt flushed a bit. "Sorry. It's just I've been waiting for this fight for what seems like most of my life and now that it's here, I worry about the cost. I won't back down, you understand. I will pay it, but I worry."

He looked back at his wife. Kaja wouldn't stand in the background. She wouldn't allow herself to be locked away. She would fight beside her husband because that was what husbands and wives did.

But Shim needed to consider other things now. He had a war to stage and the most important piece was in place. "How do we get everyone to the palace and quickly?"

"We ride the winds." Beckett Finn strode up the road, his voice ringing out.

Shim sighed because he could feel his brother again. Lach walked slightly behind the kings of the Seelie Fae.

Beckett and Cian Finn strode into the square with their wife between them. Not a one wore a crown on their head, but everyone in the village dropped to one knee.

Shim was happy to see the kings, but happier to see his brother. He rushed to Lach. "Did you hear her?"

Lach nodded, his whole face beaming, looking more vibrant than he could ever remember his brother looking. "I did. And we were hurrying." His smile grew vibrant. "Father worked hard while we were gone. He found a witch. She tore open a huge fucking hole in the door. Torin is going to know we're here now. Take a look at what I brought, brother."

Shim looked behind Lach and felt his mouth drop open. An army marched behind Lach. Shim couldn't count them. They seemed endless. He saw Maon, his father's chief advisor, and the whole council dressed for war. And then he saw Gillian, flying past him, her feet working so hard they barely touched the ground. His sister ran and flung herself at their father.

His father caught her, holding his daughter to him with everything he had.

"When I got home, they were all waiting," Lach said, emotion in his voice. "Vampires. Our people. Beck and Cian's people. They wouldn't be left behind. Our father most of all."

"Dad?" Dellacourt shouted out and ran toward a big man in boots and a hat.

But Shim was concentrating on his father.

King Fergus of the Unseelie Fae kept his arm around his daughter as he strode over. "Shim, I'm so proud of you, son."

He felt his heart clench. How long had he waited to hear those words? Lach stood beside him, his big brother, lending him strength. "Thank you, Father."

His father looked him in the eye, as though trying to send his will into his son. "I mean it, Shim. You were steadfast. You knew the truth and you and Lach held fast and despite everything I threw at you, you brought back your sister and you...you honored your brother." Fergus stopped, emotion choking him. "When this is all done, we're finding Duffy and bringing him home. He belongs in the family crypt with his mother and his ancestors. He did us all proud."

Roan walked up behind their father. "Your Highnesses, we stand ready to fight. We are a small force compared to what we're up against, but we're strong. Mr. Taggart has brought a force of fifty well-trained ex-soldiers. Julian Lodge and his business partner, Stefan Talbot, paid to have everyone outfitted with the finest in weaponry, and they've come along."

The group of vampires were dressed in black and armed to the teeth. They looked deadly.

Cousin Julian gave him a broad smile. "You know I never miss the chance to shed some blood."

They were here. His whole family. His whole kingdom. The ones who'd thought he was defective now stood behind him. Something opened wide in Shim and was full for the first time in his life—pride.

That feeling was quickly replaced with panic. "It's good to have an army, but we need to get them moving. Bron is ready."

Beckett and Cian stood in the middle of the square, speaking to the villagers. Meg was hugging Kaja and Dante.

Beckett looked to Shim. "I told you, we'll ride the winds. This war will be won today, thanks to my sister. I hear she is well."

Shim moved closer. "She was. She's been shielding. I worry she's hiding from us."

"I know she's hiding. I saw what the hag wanted from her." Lach shuddered. "She won't kill Bron for a day or two, but she'll torture her. I can't imagine what Bron's been through. We've waited. She's ready. I'm not willing to leave her there one moment more. I'll sprint all the way if I have to."

Cian put a hand on Lach's shoulder. "You won't have to sprint. We have a plan. Beck's been practicing. But you have to listen. He's been working on his speech."

Beck slapped at his brother's shoulder. "It's not a speech."

Cian smirked back at him. "It's a speech."

Beck hopped onto the fountain and looked over the crowd. A great cheer went up as Cian joined him and reached out to help his wife up. Queen Meg stood in between her husbands, her face beaming out at the crowd. She was ready just like Bron was ready.

Shim was ready. He'd only just realized it. He was ready to fight and to win because he wasn't about to lose at this point.

Beck held a hand up and all talking ceased. His voice rang out over the courtyard and beyond. "I want to thank you all for being with us on this day. 'Tis a long time coming. You, my people, have suffered much since my uncle stole my father's crown, but I am here to tell you, you are not alone. There are others waiting to join us. Today we march on the palace and we take back what belongs to me, to my brother, and my wife, and most importantly we take back what belongs to you. Your kingdom, your rights, your lives, and if blood spills, then it will be righteous. We will be outnumbered and we will win."

A long shout went up, threatening to shake the ground.

"That was a speech," Lach said with a shake of his head as though he couldn't think of anything worse for a king to do.

It appeared Shim would have the speechmaking duties in their future kingdom. But for that kingdom to work, they needed their queen. "We're a day's march from her. What if the hags kill her?"

Beck leapt down and walked to Shim. "We aren't more than an hour from our sweet sister. I told you. We will ride the winds."

An eddy wind would be the fastest way to travel, but first Beck would have to find one and catch it, and finding one big enough would be a huge challenge. This army was at least a thousand men and women. They would need more than one eddy cloud. "King Beckett, shouldn't we begin the march and try to find eddy clouds along the way?"

Beck grinned broadly. "I don't have to find an eddy cloud, my brother. I will simply make one. I am the master of storms and I can bring a cloud to carry us all."

Beck opened his arms and the sky clouded over, the largest eddy cloud Shim had ever seen coalescing right above them.

"Show-off," Queen Meg said. She grimaced. "I've only tried this once before and it was worse than anything Six Flags had to offer."

Kaja was brimming with excitement. "I enjoy it. Except that my mate tends to get a bit ill."

Dellacourt held up a small bag. "I have barf bags for everyone!"

Beck looked at his brother, a long moment passing between them. "Let us go and see our sister once more."

Cian nodded, his hand on his heart.

Cian and Meg disappeared, pulled up by the eddy cloud, and all around him the warriors of their ragtag army were pulled up by the cloud and the will of the Storm Lord.

"Let's go and claim our wife," Shim said, reaching a hand to his brother.

Lach took it, their wills as one now.

The cloud scooped them up and they were ready for battle.

* * * *

Torin watched out over the balcony, a sinking feeling in his gut. His kingdom. When Seamus was king and their father before them, Tír na nÓg was a place of stunning beauty, a calm, pastoral paradise.

He could see the fires from far-off villages and masses of peasants coming for his head.

One single day. 'Twas all it had taken. A day and a meeting on the road with vagrant monsters. That gang of trolls and goblins had taught him everything he needed to know about the world. It didn't matter whether a man was a prince or a pauper, death and violence and brokenness came for everyone unless a man took power.

Why couldn't his people see he was trying to save them? He was smarter than them all. It was why he was king. He hadn't simply been born to the part. He was ruthless enough to fight and kill for the crown.

"And it's mine. It will remain mine." He said the words out loud even as his guard formed a phalanx around the palace.

"My children will win this day."

Damn him. The last thing he wanted was to see his brother. His sluagh brother. When this day was over and he remained king, he would force the hags to rid him of all sluagh, all monsters. He would slaughter them all, every last one. Their blood would make the Seelie fields fertile, and then he would dispose of the vampires and the Unseelie and he would rule over all the planes.

Seamus shook his non-corporeal head. "You always were ambitious. It's too bad I didn't see how far you would go."

"You suddenly read minds, brother?" Torin forced his attention to the battlefield. It was a waiting game now. He wasn't sure if they would march in today or the day after, but he had word that his nephews were on the plane, and that meant they would attack.

"It's almost a sure thing what you were thinking." Seamus floated around the room, the act almost a mirror image of the pacing his brother used to do while thinking through a problem. "Why don't you let Bronwyn go? Can't you see the hags lied about her?"

The fact that Bronwyn Finn was here in his palace and still breathing made him sick to death. She was here, the one woman who could kill him. Her throat should have been slit the moment the hags found her, but his wife had pleaded their case. "The hags think they can pull power from the girl's soul. Enough power to defeat the true triad."

"Which one?" Seamus asked, his voice nonchalant as though he was politely asking about the weather.

Torin turned to his brother. "What do you mean? It's only a rumor that those idiot boys of yours managed to find a bondmate and create a true triad. I think it's just a story the villagers tell to give them hope."

Seamus sighed. "Do you even hear yourself speak? The fact that your own people would even be forced to make up tales to bring themselves hope that one day your reign will end should tell you everything you need to know."

"They are stupid. I'm protecting them."

"You are a fool, Torin. You're justifying your own immorality, but it doesn't matter, because it isn't a story. Beck and Cian have come into their powers, but they aren't the only true triad. My Bron has formed one with the Unseelie princes. So I ask again, which true triad do they seek to kill, and why didn't your own hags tell you of this news? I assure you, they knew."

And yet they had only mentioned that the idiot Unseelies had some small magic. They had not mentioned the triad. Why had they not mentioned the triad?

"Who are you talking to?" Maris asked, walking into the room. If she was upset about the battle about to take place, she didn't show it, but then his wife was a block of ice that nothing seemed to penetrate.

But he didn't need anyone to know he saw his brother's ghost. "I was musing about why my hags might keep something from me."

He felt his eyes narrow on his lovely bride. So beautiful. So fucking vapid. Could she be in league with the hags? Was it possible?

She huffed and crossed to the mirror, smoothing back her already perfect hair. "Well, they are hags, darling. You have to think that at some point in time they'll turn on you. I thought you had a plan to take them out when we no longer need those nasty bitches. If you like, you can start it now."

He was mollified a bit. Seamus huddled in the corner, exactly where he should be, hidden and unseen. "I thought you wanted to keep the Finn girl alive because the hags needed her."

She sighed, a long-suffering sound. "Well, there's a reason you're the king. I don't know anything about this. I have no idea why I would say such a thing. Why would I sincerely wish to keep your niece alive? I hate that whole family." She put a hand to her head. "I actually don't remember very much about the last few days. Ever since that Finn girl was brought here, my mind has been a bit cloudy. Do you think it's something I ate? I shall have a long talk with cook just before I have him strung up. So sad to have to find another cook. Good help is so hard to find these days, but there's nothing for it. I should probably execute the entire kitchen staff."

She really was an empty, dull vessel, her only contents being pure malice. And she was stupid. "It wasn't the food. It was the hags."

Maris's face twisted a bit. "Why ever should the hags be preparing food? I thought they spent all their time with the Finn girl. One of my maids walked by the room they had her in. She thought she heard some ritual of pulling power."

"Yes, they said they needed to pull the power in case my nephews have formed a true triad." The power would be necessary to block whatever they had ascended into.

"See, this is why you're smarter. I heard that and wondered if we should allow it. After all, when they're more powerful than all of our armies, what is to stop them from taking the crown?" Maris smiled brightly. "But, of course, it's surely the very helpful thing you were talking about. You're never wrong."

Oh, he wanted to slap the bitch, but she was right. He hadn't seen. He'd been too arrogant, believing he had power over them. Long ago they had made a deal, bonded and signed by a Planeswalker demon. They would help him ascend and he would hold them at his right hand. The deal was only struck down by death, and neither party could kill the other, but if the hags simply allowed him to die, they could take over his kingdom. If the hags used his niece and her power, they could rule with no retribution.

He had to kill his niece and take the power back from the hags.

A loud crack took him out of his thoughts. The sky outside turned black as night, the sun sinking behind an enormous cloud.

"What is that?" Maris asked.

He had only to look at the smirk on his dead brother's face to know the truth. "It's an eddy cloud. The rebels are here."

They began descending from the clouds, their numbers far more than he'd expected. Immediately there were the sounds of metal against metal and a sonic boom as the vampires proved themselves to be terrible allies.

Still, he glanced down. His guard had more numbers, and they weren't without their own weapons.

And none of it would matter if the hags took all the power.

Torin ran for the dungeon with only one thought on his mind. Bronwyn's time had come.

Chapter Twenty-One

Lach hit the ground, bodies falling all around him, and realized he hadn't known the true meaning of the word chaos. The sounds and smells of battle assaulted him.

Clanging from swords striking swords rang out across the field. In the distance he could see the White Palace, a gleaming pearl amidst the gloom of afternoon. The cloud they'd ridden made it seem more like twilight, but they had hours to go before night. His new implants weren't even necessary to shield his eyes from the sun.

Dellacourt brushed past him, Kaja in her wolf form at his side and the queen's hand clutched in his. "Good luck to you, Your Highness. Kaja and I are on Meg duty. We're getting clear of the field, but I can talk to you through the implants. I'll look for a way past the guard and into the palace so you can get to Bron."

Lach clutched his sword and with his instincts guiding him, brought it down on a guard trying to cut through the queen's torso. First blood and the first corpse of the day. The soldier fell and then almost immediately got back up and bowed to his new master.

Queen Meg's eyes went wide as the moon. "Holy crap. That is so freaking cool."

Dellacourt shook his head and hurried her along. "No time for cool shit, Meg. Time for hiding and keeping your head on your body."

As she was hustled away, Lach could still hear her. "But that was awesome."

"You have a fan," Shim said with a grin.

He looked at his brother who held Duffy's axe in his hand. He'd been so weak for so long.

Shim proved his weakness was gone by hefting his axe and neatly decapitating a guard. He grinned at his brother. "I thought the head was the best way to go since you can use arms and legs without the head."

That was his brother. Always a giver. Lach pulled at his new soldier and sent him into battle.

Lach heard a long scream and was shocked to see the guards who had been foolish enough to get near the tree line were being pulled up into them. The trees themselves seemed to bend, their branches working like arms and claiming the guards. The guard Lach watched screamed and attempted to hack at the branches that held him, but a vine wound around his neck and his scream was cut short. The guard disappeared into the foliage, sucked up in clawing green arms.

A short distance away, Cian Finn held his hands up, controlling the trees. The Green Man had his own army.

Lach gave himself over to the fight. He saw the Seelie warrior king in the midst of battle. He obviously preferred to fight over using his power, but Lach knew he would call on it if he had to. In such close quarters any weather the Storm Lord brought down on the enemy would come down on their own heads, too. Shim was the same. He would start a fire, but it could engulf their own troops. Shim's power would be used for another purpose.

As long as the hags lived, no one would be safe. Torin could fall, but if the hags somehow got away, there would be no peace for any of them.

His body moving like a well-oiled machine, Lach tore through the guards. He allowed the fierce joy of battle to push him like a wave toward the palace.

Lach sent a corpse to protect his brother and then another. He would feel infinitely better if he knew Shim had someone to watch his back even if his new guard no longer had a head on his body.

Lach saw a familiar face holding a small body in his arms. Max

Harper was covered in blood, but he stared down at the phooka.

"I don't understand," Max said, glancing up at Lach. "He leapt in front of me. Why would this creature do that?"

The phooka's eyes were half closed, his blood draining quickly. Lach could sense the creature, who should have lived for centuries, was close to death. His tail twitched slightly, an unconscious move. "Imprinted on you early, you bastard. I've been with you most of your life. I was your pet and the hawk who followed you and the horse you complained about but always fed so well. I know you, Max Harper. Hard on the outside and such a soul! It was an honor to share a piece of you."

Max stared down. "I didn't even know."

"You didn't have to." The phooka looked up at Lach. "And don't use me, Death Lord. My time is come. Did you know there's peace in the after? The Summerlands are real. I feel it."

The phooka let go, his soul flying wherever souls flew. Lach wasn't sure, but he'd learned that death wasn't something to fear. It was simply a power that resided in him and once the war was done, he would learn to use it in a gentler way.

But now he used it to save Harper. He commanded one of his soldiers to leap in front of the horse trainer and take the blow meant for him.

Harper got to his feet, the sword in his hand. "Thanks."

"Don't waste his sacrifice." The phooka had been an odd creature, a thing that could cause great chaos, but love had sent him on a different path.

A million thoughts raced through him. Love. Ambition. Protection. Possession. They could all be used for good or bad. Love had nearly cost him his wife, his need to protect her so great he discounted her own soul.

Love was merely a tool, and how a soul chose to use it became the measure of the man. The phooka had chosen wisely, and Lach was determined to learn the lesson.

He called his army of dead as he ran to his brother. It was a gamble, but she would need everything they had.

I am ready. Pull them back. Her voice was a sweet whisper through his soul.

Lach opened himself, giving her everything, heart and soul and life and power. It welled up and surged across the distance between them.

Shim shook and, in an instant, his brother fell, a limp body on the ground.

Lach got to his knees and prayed he could save him once more.

* * * *

The hags were upset.

"How is she so strong? She should be hanging like a carcass by now." They stood back as though assessing whether or not she was a threat.

She was the least threatening thing in the damn room. As far as she could tell, she was in the dungeon. This seemed to be the hag's special room. She'd woken up here, bound to the wall. She'd tried to see what was around her. To her left it looked like there were shelves and shelves of herbs and various scary items that they probably used to do bad things. And there was a pot in the center that was already bubbling, already preparing to stew.

"There's something very wrong with her."

Bron had to cover a smile because the hags were confused. All through the long night they had tortured her, leaving her a limp, sad thing. And then the bondmates had answered her call. Over and over they had sent small bursts of energy to her. But more than any amount of life force, what they had truly sent to her was hope.

Bron held herself up. She could feel her men. They were a soft hum in her soul, buoying her. They were out there now. She'd sensed them the moment they had dropped from the eddy cloud and the battle had begun.

Yet the hags still focused on her.

Could they not hear the battle? They didn't seem to care even if they knew it had begun. They were deep in the dungeon, but Bron could hear it broadcast from another bondmate or perhaps several. Now that she'd learned to listen, she could hear them. She recognized Kaja's voice, but there was another. A very strong voice sending out love and hope and prayers for something she called kicking serious ass.

Bron wasn't sure what that meant, but she was grateful to the bondmate who was sharing her thoughts even if she didn't know she was doing it. Hers was the strongest of the voices and she was so hopeful. This woman, and Bron could tell she was female, was ready for the fight. She was ready for something she called her happily ever after.

Bron liked the idea. Happy forever. She just had to grasp it.

During the hours when she'd reached out to the bondmates in the palace, her mind seemed to have formed some sort of network, pulling them each in and connecting them all. She'd learned some were close to death, others simply waiting for that time, and many were being held for high-ranking vampires. They knew something was wrong with them, something had been done to them, but they didn't know what. They were all afraid.

And they all wanted to fight.

He's coming.

Maris's voice was the oddest of all, but she seemed to be playing her part. Her part was to ship the king to her. Bron needed to know where Torin was. She needed to make sure he was close when she brought her power down.

The hags stared at her, and then the slender one brought her hands up, slamming them toward her, a gray mist rising.

A jolt of hot pain struck through her system. She shielded, keeping it utterly inside her own body. She didn't want to frighten the others or cause them pain. Her body was caught in the mist the hags sent out. This mist was gray, unlike the pure black that had engulfed Duffy. Her heart clenched. She knew he was gone. Now that she'd felt the mist, she knew Duffy had died in it and Lach had carried him. There was no other explanation.

It proved Shim was alive, no matter what he said. Shim still felt and ate and complained about the cold.

She shook and her insides felt like they would burst, and she held on to those simple thoughts. She heard the hags argue and then another wave hit, the mist filling her whole being. Her limbs shook and her bones ached. She tried to remember every inch of their faces and how they liked to hold her. Shim would snuggle, his body cuddling hers, his legs moving between hers as though he was trying to make them one. And Lach. Lach would surround her, pushing the world out until it was only the two of them. Nothing compared to being between them. When she was cuddled between them, everything was right.

The fog lifted, and she was left shaken.

"That's better." The hags hadn't bothered to introduce themselves. There was a wretchedly thin one and the other resembled a glob of rancid pudding with eyes. Bron couldn't stand to be around either. She'd preferred it when they had hidden their true faces.

The thin one looked at her critically. "I don't know. She still looks pretty healthy to me. And we'd better hurry, dear one. Did you feel that eddy cloud?"

The puddle of goo with eyes replied. "I did, sister. The triad is here along with her husbands. We knew this would happen. We counted on it. They should breach the palace walls, and then Torin will be slaughtered and we'll have her power. Do you understand what that means? The idiot doesn't know how to use it, but I will be able to."

Bron kept her face perfectly still. She didn't need them to know that she was well aware of how to use her power. She intended to use it on them.

"Are you sure? You thought you would be able to hear them by now." The emaciated one tapped her foot against the floor, her cold eyes darting around.

Her sister sneered Bron's way. A long, taloned hand pointed toward her. "I just need one more soul. Hers. She's the key, but then we figured that out long ago. Our mistake was in trusting Torin. He was supposed to have caught her and brought her for execution."

"Instead the dumb bastard just killed her. I wonder how she came back. I'm sure she was dead."

The big hag with cold, dead eyes stalked toward her. She put a hand on her chest, right above Bron's heart. "All things will be learned when we pry that damn soul out of her body. And then I'll be the one who binds her husbands, and I'll be the one with the power."

The idea of this odious woman having access to her husbands' power made Bron sick.

The slender one frowned. "I don't see why it has to be you."

The hags continued to argue as they raced to get the ingredients for another spell. This one, Bron was sure, would nearly kill her, and she didn't dare open herself. Not yet.

She would have to be strong. When she opened wide, she would pull their power, and there would be no going back.

The hags began to walk toward her when the cell door opened and Torin raged in.

He stopped in front of her, giving her a once-over, his eyes narrowing and his lips thin. A spark of recognition hit him, but he turned from her as though she didn't deserve a moment's notice.

Her uncle was older, his hair gone to silver. He looked nothing like the man who would sit at her father's side and talk at night. He was wrinkled now, care and guilt obviously taking their toll. But he was still strong. He hauled two guards with him.

"Take the hags into custody," Torin announced, his voice ringing out.

The hags laughed. They stood their ground, staring down the guards. "I don't think they want to do that, Your Majesty. They might discover they prefer their man parts on the outside of their bodies."

The guards hesitated. They were all here.

I'm ready. She sent the message out to everyone, but especially to her loves.

And then Maris entered the room. Bron couldn't believe it. She should have run the minute she'd convinced Torin to find her. Maris should have fled the castle or joined the bondmates. It had been her and Niall's job to ensure their safety.

The hags began their threats and Torin his screams for vengeance. He didn't even look Bron's way. But Maris did. She moved in close. She still wore her thin, diamond-and-gold crown.

"Do it," Maris whispered.

Bron shook her head. Despite all the chaos Maris had caused, she couldn't kill her. She'd repented in her way. "I can't. You know I can't. Maris, you know what's going to happen."

Maris whispered. "I've protected the others with a spell and Niall is with them. Fire won't touch them. And I always knew this was how I would end. I don't want to live, Bronwyn. I want to go home, and my home is no longer here. Do it or I will tell them what's happening. You will lose your chance. You will lose everything."

Bron was weak again. So weak. She felt sick, her stomach rolling. She could barely move her fingers. How would she do what she needed to do? Misery swamped her. She'd been so close, but she was going to fail. She was going to let them all down. Her people. Her brothers. Her loves. Herself.

Her vision was starting to fade.

A cool wind buoyed her and a familiar voice filled her head. "Then take my strength, daughter. It was always meant for you and Beck and Cian. My children."

Her father floated in front of her, the hags and Torin ignoring him as they continued their argument. Her father kept his eyes on her. "Tell them I did love them. My sons. They will make great kings, and you are already a queen. You didn't need a crown, Bron. You only needed your own strong heart."

He moved forward, his essence merging with hers.

The whispers died, but she was shot through with life. Her father had given her everything. He'd waited, given up his after, to give her one last gift. One last chance at life. She was suffused with energy. She brimmed with it. She could do this.

"What just happened?" the skinny one asked, looking around the room as though searching for a threat.

The hag took a step back, Bron's will a palpable thing. In that moment, she felt like a queen.

The hags cackled and Torin yelled. The guards began to tap their swords looking for something to kill. Bron could hear her compatriots waiting for the time and the time was now.

Bronwyn did what she'd been born to do. She opened her soul and connected them all. A hundred bondmates, their power soaring and reaching out. The hag who had eaten all those souls gasped, and Bron realized the hag's mistake. The hag was Bronwyn's, caught in a net of her own making. Those souls that lived inside her wanted to be free, and Bronwyn gave them a way, a path to the after.

The large hag shook and her head fell back, all the souls rushing out through her mouth and eyes and ears, killing her in an instant.

Torin turned and tried to flee, but Maris caught him. She fell to the floor, trapped in the power. Her mouth opened and a scream rent the air, but she held on to Torin, dragging him down, keeping him close. Bron felt her will. This was for her. This was for her love and the girl she'd been. Maris believed in vengeance and she was at peace with death.

But Bron believed in love. Vengeance had burned away in the face of love. Love for her family and her husbands. Love for her people. Love for what was right in the world.

She was the vessel and it was right.

Bron felt the fire. It sizzled through her soul. She pulled it from Shim, dragging his power into her hands, and with a great yell she sent it out. It raced from her skin. Heat, white and hot, flashed through her, a great wave of purity. She sent it to engulf the hags and Torin and Maris, sent it out further to every soul on the hags' leash. There was no way to free those they had corrupted except to send them to the after.

Fire reigned, pouring from her every cell, a cascade of purifying blaze that wiped clean Torin's evil.

Bron let it rage and rage, the heat crackling around her and then, when she was sure it was enough, she let it go.

She slumped down, her body held up only by the chains that bound her. Her clothes had gone in the crisp of the flames, the fire burning so hot that there was nothing but stone and metal left in the room. Even the bones were ashes.

Weariness settled over her, but she needed to hear them. Feel them.

Nothing. The connection had burned out as it had before.

Or was it something worse? Minutes passed and she struggled against the bonds. She needed to get to them. What if it had all been for nothing and they were dead and gone and she'd been left alone?

She loved them. Unabashedly, unashamedly, and now that she'd served her purpose she wanted nothing more than the life they had promised her. Their own kingdom and children to love, a lifetime to know her soul's mates.

She needed that lifetime. She needed her forever.

Boot steps hurried along the floor, echoing through the hallways. "Bronwyn?"

"Lach!" Her voice was hoarse, but she called out anyway. She knew his voice. She opened herself and there it was. The connection was tenuous, but it was there. It would grow again. They would nurture the bond between them, and they would have it again.

His face came into view, his gorgeous, imperfectly perfect face, and then Shim was beside him, his eyes tired, but his lips smiling.

They held her, their arms encasing her and lifting her up.

"It was a close thing, love," Shim said.

"Shim passed out again. You have to remind me that Shim passes out every time you reach into his head and pull his power out. He damn near killed me." Lach kissed her.

Joy welled inside Bronwyn. It had worked. She was alive and whole and ready to live past this. "Get me out of here."

Lach shook his head. "Not a chance. We like you just the way you are, love. Bound and safe."

"We've decided locking you up will keep you out of trouble." But he was smiling and winking as he said it.

She grinned. They thought she was trouble now. Wait until they met their children. She was sure there was lots of glorious, amazing trouble to come.

Chapter Twenty-Two

Lach sat back and watched as Bronwyn bonded with her new sister-in-law. After a joyous reunion with her brothers, the two walked arm in arm, aiding all those who had survived. The vampires had brought tools and Donald Dellacourt was already arguing with his son over how this current political state would affect the stock market back on the Vampire plane. The group from Aoibhneas had put up tents and had begun tending to the wounded under the direction of a red-haired Fae healer with the worst disposition Lach had ever seen. Queen Meg was doing her best to make everyone feel comfortable, but it would take a while to get the palace back in order. After all, his bride had torched a good portion of it.

And Gillian. Gillian was gone again. She'd kissed him on the cheek and disappeared.

Roan and Harry were hot on her trail.

Bron laughed at something the queen said, the throaty sound making Lach's cock jump.

"We should never have found her new clothes," Shim said with a sigh.

Lach laughed. "She's going to be a queen when our father heads off to the after. She can't walk around the Dark Palace without clothes on."

"It's a terrible shame and a waste of such beautiful flesh." Shim sighed as Bron looked over and waved.

"I'm going to absolutely forget everything I just heard you say about my sweet sister," Cian Finn said, looking very much the king. Everyone was busy cleaning up and burying the dead, but there was a general buzz that swept up every worker. Though there was mourning, there was also hope. Cian smiled as he watched his sister with his wife. "I can't thank you enough for finding her or for loving her. She tells me she's very happy and intends to put the Dark Palace to rights."

She'd certainly charmed his father. King Fergus had taken to his daughter-in-law immediately, declaring his sons not good enough for her, but he'd said it with a smile and wink. "I think you'll find everyone in our kingdom will be eager to accommodate her."

Cian raised a brow. "And if they're not?"

Shim showed off a hint of fangs. "We're Unseelie, Your Majesty. We know how to deal with difficult subjects."

Well, they would certainly know how to deal with anyone who fucked with their wife.

The warrior king joined his brother. "Lachlan, we were wondering about something."

Wondering about how well he'd pleased their sister the night before? Wondering how many times he and Shim had made her come?

"I hardly think they're wondering about that, Lach," Shim said, laughing under his breath.

A horrified expression crossed Beck's face. "Stop. I can guess. I don't even want to know you think that. Goddess, she's still fourteen in my head."

She wasn't fourteen anymore. She'd been a sweet girl, but what a woman she'd become. "Sorry, Your Majesty."

Beck shook his head. "We're family. None of that. We could end up calling each other by titles all day. So, did Bron tell you about our father?"

Bron had told him everything. About her father becoming a sluagh and her brothers' ex-fiancée trapping Torin. He wanted to kill the one named Niall, but apparently he was some sort of hero in the Seelies' eyes. "She told me her father had sacrificed himself to give her the energy to go on."

Beck's arms crossed over his chest, his eyes settling into a worried stare. "Does that mean he's gone for good?"

Lach sat up straight. He hadn't even thought about it. He'd been too busy holding Bronwyn and reveling in the feel of her against his heart. "He was a sluagh. He might have faded, but he's still here. It will take him a long time to gather enough energy to appear before us again. But he'll stay here most likely. He tied himself to this place. Becoming a sluagh was a choice for him."

Cian's voice grew tight. "Can he choose again?"

Lach stopped, his brain wrapping around the idea. What had Duffy said? Death was a doorway. Death was nothing to be afraid of. What if Lach's power was more than pulling corpses from the ground and playing the puppetmaster? What if his power could have meaning and true purpose?

Death was a doorway, and Lachlan McIver intended to open it.

Bronwyn was suddenly at his side, Queen Meg with her. "What's going on? I felt Lach's power stir."

Shim took her hand. "He's going to try something. Help us. He needs a bit of my power, too."

Beck Finn put a hand on his shoulder. "Bron, take some of mine."

"Mine, too," Cian said, laying his hand on Lach. "Funnel it to Lachlan."

Fire and earth and the storms above. And a doorway.

Lach let the power flow and reached out. Nothing was ever truly lost and Seamus Finn, King of Seelie Fae, was no exception.

Ashes and dust. That's what his body was, but Lach found them and drew them to him, forming a pile of what had made the man. Lach breathed his own unique power into it.

Seamus Finn stood, a ghostly apparition, but quite solid for a shade. He looked startled to be seen. "Beck? Ci?"

They moved away from Lach toward their long-dead father.

"Father, Torin is gone." Beck seemed solemn, as though reporting to a superior, not a son to his father. Cian simply stared.

Seamus shook his head. "He doesn't matter, son. You do. You and Cian and your sister. Oh, Death Lord, I cannot thank you enough for this chance. I feared I had given it up to spare my daughter. Beckett, I was a fool. You are a good man with a good soul and those needs of yours aren't wrong. I had them, too, and my father beat them out of me. I pray I'm not too late to change that for you. There was a piece of me that was empty because I didn't follow my heart."

Meg smiled broadly. "I fixed him, Your Majesty. Trust me. He's perfectly fine with all those needs now."

Seamus smiled at her, reaching out a hand that couldn't touch her. "Sweet Queen. Take care of my boys. Cian, I am so sorry. I didn't understand you. I loved you, but I didn't know how to handle you. Can you forgive me?"

Cian clutched his wife's hand. "Yes, Father."

"I love you, Ci. My time is short. I feel the pull. I love you, my children. This kingdom is yours. Rule with wisdom and love and grace." He stopped and looked at Lachlan, surprise plain on his face. "What is that, Death Lord? I see a light."

A deep sense of peace swept over Lachlan. This. This was his power. This was his calling. All of his life he'd hated the cold, dead power, but he'd been wrong. His power was about life. His power was a service to his people, and all living creatures were his people. Death was merely another part of existence. "It's the after. Some Fae and witches call it the Summerlands. It's your time."

"But I chose. I became a sluagh." The words were a staccato protestation, but hope was dawning on his face.

This was his gift. "Choose again, Your Majesty."

Seamus turned, looking at something only he could see. "My wife. She's here. She waited. I didn't deserve any of this, but I will take it with a grateful heart. Good-bye, my loves."

Seamus shimmered for a second and was gone, his choice made.

Shim gave him a broad smile. "You did good, brother."

Bron did one better. She threw herself into his arms. "Thank you. Thank you, husband."

Lach wrapped her in his arms, his other half clinging to her back. He was a man with half a soul, but she'd completed him.

Death was nothing to be afraid of. Not when he was so loved.

Epilogue

Once upon a time, in a land closer than you would think...

Megan Finn, the queen of the Seelie Fae, loved to watch her children play along the river. There were three, each a gorgeous handful, and though she'd bemoaned the lack of drugs that had been her birthright on the Earth plane, she wouldn't have had them anywhere else.

Tír na nÓg was her heaven.

Meg waved from the balcony to her husbands, who were teaching their children to fish. Their daughter, it turned out, was by far the best fisherman of the day. She hauled in her trout, beaming up at her fathers and sticking that bratty tongue out at her brothers.

Soon they would travel to the Dark Palace for their annual celebrations—a renewal of their close ties to the Unseelie. She looked forward to seeing her sweet sister-in-law and their two boys. She hoped Dante and Kaja would come home from their travels long enough to join in the festivities.

Meg waved again and then turned to look over her kingdom.

She'd been born so far away, and yet she seldom thought of that place anymore. This was home. She'd fought for it and grown for it.

She'd become a woman here. This was where she'd loved and lost and found herself anew.

Meg turned her face up, letting the sun shine down.

This was where she found those three elusive words.

Happily Ever After.

Author's Note

I'm often asked by generous readers how they can help get the word out about a book they enjoyed. There are so many ways to help an author you like. Leave a review. If your e-reader allows you to lend a book to a friend, please share it. Go to Goodreads and connect with others. Recommend the books you love because stories are meant to be shared. Thank you so much for reading this book and for supporting all the authors you love!

Sirens in Bliss

Nights in Bliss, Colorado, Book 10
By Lexi Blake writing as Sophie Oak
Now available.

Re-released in a second edition with new content.

What happens after happily ever after?

It's the event of the year. The wedding of Leo and Wolf to their beautiful sub, Shelley McNamara, has all of Bliss up in arms—and makes everyone think about love and marriage and family.

Wolf and Leo have to deal with the sudden reappearance of their father. Rafe Kincaid is handed an opportunity that might take him and his family away from Bliss. Aidan, Lexi, and Lucas O'Malley find themselves at a crossroads in their marriage. And Stefan Talbot must face his biggest fear—possibly losing his wife in childbirth.

So come to the Feed Store Church, pick a seat, and enjoy the chaos as all your favorite characters from Texas Sirens and Nights in Bliss, Colorado, come together for one eventful weekend.

And some of them may never be the same again.

Note: This is a reunion book, which shares an overall story arc and many crossover characters with the Texas Sirens and Nights in Bliss series. This is not a stand-alone.

About Lexi Blake

Lexi Blake is the author of contemporary and urban fantasy romance. She started publishing in 2011 and has gone on to sell over two million copies of her books. Her books have appeared thirty-three times on the *USA Today*, *New York Times*, and *Wall Street Journal* bestseller lists. She lives in North Texas with her husband, kids, and two rescue dogs.

Connect with Lexi online:

Facebook: Lexi Blake
Twitter: authorlexiblake
Website: www.LexiBlake.net
Instagram: www.instagram.com/lexiblakeauthor